THE SAINTED TRILOGY

EVIL AWAITS

BOOK ONE

by

MICHAEL MEDICO

© 2018 Harbour Point Publishing
Harbour Point Publishing, LLC
Northport, New York 1168
thesaintedtrilogy@gmail.net
www.thesaintedtrilogy.net

Printed in the United States by Harbour Point Publishers, Northport, NY

The Sainted Trilogy, Harbour Point Publishers.

Library of Congress Cataloging-in-Publication Data
Evil Awaits, Book One of The Sainted Trilogy
(Formerly titled The Sainted)
Medico, Michael p. cm.

Fiction—General 2. Fiction—Thriller 3. Fiction—Horror Fiction, I. Title.

Paperback ISBN: 978-1-0879-1149-6
Ebook ISBN: 978-1-0879-1177-9

Second Edition Printing

DEDICATION

To my wife, family and friends,
the joys in my life

*"In this holy flirtation with the world,
God occasionally drops a handkerchief.
These handkerchiefs are called saints."*
—Frederick Buechner

*"They say there's a heaven for those who will wait.
Some say its better, but I say it ain't
I'd rather laugh with the sinners than cry with the saints.
The sinners are much more fun..."*
—Billy Joel

"Oh, no they're not."
—Chris Pella

PREFACE

Gracciano-Vecchio, Italy, 1268…The midwife finds her way through the dark streets on her mission is to greet the newest citizen of her small town. It is late at night and Donisa sees there are no lights coming from the houses and the small shops that line the stone and dirt paths. Even though it is dark, she knows the streets better than most; after all, she grew up in Gracciano-Vecchio.

As Donisa hurries to her help deliver the newborn, she can't help but think how she loves this town and the beautiful regions of Toscana. Gracciano-Vecchio is a small, sleepy hamlet compared to Montepulciano with its monastery and brothels. She makes the sign of the cross at the mention of those houses of shame, but these regions have been home her entire life, and she is happiest here. Her family, the Zacci's, has been farmers and shopkeepers for more than six generations, and for this Donisa has the roots that she is thankful to the Lord for. How they treasure her and how they make sure she is cared for and blessed with an abiding love of the Lord, family, the land and of life itself.

She continues to hurry along the muddy paths as these thoughts of her past and her family makes her smile. Donisa turns the corner and the de Segni Mansion comes into view. It is by far the grandest home in all of Gracciano-Vecchio with its ornate balconies and beautiful gardens. The de Segni family is very well known in the region as devout and benevolent. Senor de Segni's wealth is great, but so is his faith and charity, and he is held in high regard by the entire town. When Donisa arrives at her destination, she knocks on *the door. As late as it is, she knows the whole household will be up, eagerly awaiting her arrival.*

Donisa knocks on the door. The footsteps of a young maid servant can be heard running to the door. The young maid opens the door and Donisa enters, hurriedly removes her shawl and hands it to the girl as she asks, "How is Senora de Segni doing? Is she almost ready?"

The young girl is concerned for her mistress saying, "The senora is in labor, and she is asking for you…", but before the servant girl finishes, Donisa is rushing down the long corridor to the senora's room.

Donisa is greeted in the hallway, by Senor de Segni; a tall, ruggedly handsome man whose nobility is apparent as he commands great respect from all who know him. He is pacing the floor in anxious anticipation. He looks very worried, and his concern for his wife is evident in how he greets the midwife.

"Where have you been? Do you know how much pain my wife is in?"

Donisa thinks to herself, of course she knows how much pain the Senora is in. Hadn't she delivered more than thirty beautiful children into God's world alone and an equal number that are surely in Heaven into the arms of the Blessed Mother? What of her own six children, the miracles in her life?

"Senor de Segni, please do not worry. Your wife will be fine, and your baby will light up your home as none other could! Now leave me to my work, and let me get her ready."

It is the custom of the time that the men would wait outside the bedchamber which has now become the birth room. But Senor de Segni is not one to be ordered to remain outside the chamber, especially at a time like this. He insists, "I will not leave! I will be here at her side, and I will welcome my child into the world."

Donisa knows there is no arguing with this man, so she sets about the business of bringing new life into this house. As she opens the door to the bedroom, the midwife sees that Senora de Segni is lying on the bed waiting for the moment of her child's birth. Donisa observes that Senora de Segni is in early labor but the pain has not detracted from her beauty. The Senora was born to wealth and comes from a family that owns many tracts of land surrounding Siena. She was betrothed to her husband, Senor di Segni, in what seemed a marriage of wealth to wealth. As it turns out, however, there seemed to be a bond between the two that was as immediate as it was unexpected, and for these past eight years, the couple lived in happiness with an enduring love that grew stronger each day.

The room that the Senora rests in is as warm and inviting as one could hope for and, given the family's means, not unexpected. A fire is lit in the fireplace, and the warmth it generates comes in waves and seems to defeat the chill that is part of Toscana weather in early spring.

Donisa enters the room, and she quickly comes to the bedside of Senora de Segni. The senora's eyes are closed so Donisa reaches out to the woman and holds her hand. When the Senora, in obvious pain, turns to sees that it is the midwife she grips her hand tightly. The Senora tries to smile as she says "I am so happy to see you, Donisa."

Donisa tries to comfort the woman in her care. The midwife has a sixth sense when it comes to all things related to childbirth and she carefully examines the senora saying, "I feel that the child will be coming very soon, within the hour."

Donisa has asked that a blanket, cloth and warm water to clean the baby be made ready and that the Senora is made as comfortable as can be expected, given her situation. A stillness settles over the house and all who reside there as her husband, the Senor, takes his place by his wife's bedside and the entire household prays with the family as all prepare for the blessed event.

The peace of the moment is then broken by the first painful screams of labor, which comes in spasms, one after the other. The Senora holds tightly to Donisa's hand, as the midwife gives orders to the Senora as she tries to free her body of the child in her womb. The sweat on her brow is wiped away by the midwife, and Donisa's comforting words and exhortations seem to ease the apprehension that the senora is surely feeling.

Senor de Segni, who has been quiet until now, seems to turn frantic. He has been kneeling next to his wife and implores Donisa, "Is there any comfort I can give? Will she be well?" Donisa can only guess what dread and anxiety he must be feeling for his wife. She turns to face the distraught husband and she tries to assure him by telling him, "All is well and going as God planned. We must be calm and have faith."

Another cry comes from his wife that tears at her husband's soul and he is helpless to do anything to relieve his wife's agony. The senora continues to scream as extreme pain of childbirth engulf her until, in a rush of relief, her screams are soon overtaken by a fountain of tears and a joyous cry that signals the birth of a child…a beautiful baby girl.

Donisa smiles through her tears as she cleans the newborn and wraps the beautiful baby girl in a blanket made of the finest Italian lace. The midwife gently hands the baby into the arms of her waiting mother. Both Senor and Senora de Segni look lovingly at the infant who appears awake and gazing up at them. So much has changed, so much is new to them; they are now complete… they are now a family.

It is at this moment of absolute joy for the new parents that a heavenly sound fills the air. It is unlike any sound that anyone in the household has ever heard. With that sound, there appears a bright light that pours through every window like liquid gold, and it soon fills the bedroom and totally surrounds all who are there.

The light seems to come from above and below—from all sides as it slowly encircles the house, illuminating each room, making the surroundings brighter than any glorious summer day. The light radiates warmth, but no heat; one can look into the light and not be blinded. Senora and Senor de Segni are terrified for their child and for themselves. All in the household want to flee, but suspecting it is a sign from the Lord, the entire household kneels on the floor and continues to pray.

At that instant, bright burning torches appear and surround the bed where the mother and child lay. To all it is a sign, a sacred sign. Donisa knows, the parents know, that they have brought into the world a blessed child, welcomed by divine lights…a child of God, and her name

CHAPTER 1

Huntington, NY. They, whoever they are, call it the "Gold Coast." All along the North Shore of Long Island, financiers, industrialists, entertainers and your run-of-the-mill rich folks built large estates, and they have called this beautiful setting home for decades. But even the wealthy have their problems, and over the years the large estates have given way to smaller, but stately homes and later subdivisions of multimillion-dollar "McMansions" with all the trimmings and taxes that go along with status these days.

My name is Chris Pella. I live in the town of Huntington and while not the toniest place among the moneyed, the town does have its charm and a fair share of people with enough wealth to live life on their own terms. Huntington, sometimes called "The Little Apple", is located on the Long Island Sound with beautiful vistas of the surrounding communities all the way to Connecticut. The area also encompasses affluent towns of Lloyd Neck and Lloyd Harbor, Huntington Bay, Cold Spring Harbor, Dix Hills and many other communities rich and humble, large and small.

Huntington Harbor and the areas around it are a combination of New England tradition, Hampton's chic and North Shore style. There is easy access to some of the best sailing around, and this is where I live. Power crafts and sail boats alike cruise the waters of the bays and harbors hat comb the area. These waterways provide easy access to 'the Sound', as locals call the Long Island Sound where you will always find all types of boats there to moor, swim, fish, water-ski or just party. You can also take your boat right up to Prime, a popular restaurant, and have the privilege of paying a premium for a drink while enjoying a spectacular view of the harbor.

The downtown Huntington itself has become somewhat of a magnet for upscale restaurants like Honu if you have the urge for tropical, exotic tastes or perhaps Mac's for great steaks or Buenos Aires for food with a South American flair. If you're feeling a bit more casual there's always the Finnegan's or Mundays or many of the other casual dining places located in the town. I enjoy eating out, and while my metabolism helps keep my weight down, my wallet tells me how often I can indulge.

Huntington has some wonderful and amazing venues for music, entertainment and the arts. The Paramount, one of the top venues for music in the whole country, hosts a variety of contemporary music, comic talent. The Cinema Arts Center is a mecca for the independent and international film crowd, the Heckscher Museum for fine art lovers and so much more. The town has become sort of a mecca for entertainment and dining, and if you don't believe me, try and find a parking spot on any weekend night.

There are many parks, beaches, ice-skating rinks, country clubs, health clubs, public golf courses and even parades…well, you get the point. It seems there are more great things to do per capita than any town that I've ever been to, and it will always be my home. I love where I live, I like the people, and given that I started out as a 'nice Italian boy from the Bronx', I feel pretty lucky to have landed here.

I am an only child and I am named in honor of St. Christopher. As the story goes, St. Christopher was crossing a wide river when a small child asks to be carried across. St. Christopher lifts the child, but when he put the young boy on his shoulders, he finds the child to be astonishingly heavy. According to the legend, the child being held by St. Christopher was a young Christ carrying the weight of the whole world. I know his sainthood, even existence, has been called into question by some historians in the church, but my folks loved the name and the legend of St. Christopher and so do I.

I'm single, 35 years old and while I not being braggadocios, I'm generally considered good-looking by the women I date. I also like to think of myself as a "good guy" …certainly no Saint Christopher, just a good guy—maybe that could be my epitaph. I live in a two-bedroom condo that I've furnished in a traditional way, as I consider myself a traditional kind of guy. I dress in what I believe is referred to as "preppy chic," and I love those shirts with the horses and alligators and the red, white and blue logos. So, you don't get the wrong impression, I make sure I only buy stuff on sale, and I really know how to get great deals on clothes. Lord and Taylor, Macy's and Bloomingdales at the mall seem to know what I am looking for because just as I think I need some new clothes, I get mailings with little cards that give me an "extra 20%" off the sale price… not too shabby.

I have two holdovers from my childhood and Catholic upbringing; I attend Mass every Sunday, and I say a prayer every night before going to bed. It seems old-fashioned in this secular world, but it affords me a kind of peace that I can't imagine getting from the latest edition of "Dancing with the Stars" or "The Bachelor."

I was born in the Bronx, and I never completely lost the accent so I lay it on thick when I get the opportunity to work it to my advantage. There was this one time I met a woman, Emily, who hails from England. We seemed to hit it off right away and after some small talk, I asked her out. On our first date she tells me she loves the way I speak and that most of the people in London love New York accents better than, say, a Texan accent. Emily also told me that she thought my Bronx accent was especially sexy. I never really gave any thought of my accent as anything more than what it is…and that is anything but sexy. Still, I took the compliment in the spirit that it was made and, later that night, had the best sex I'd had in a long time. I guess it pays to have a sexy voice.

Both sets of grandparents came from Italy and they had a number of paisans, friends and acquaintances who settled in the Bronx, so they followed them there. The section of the Bronx I grew up in became an enclave for these immigrants, and while they all wanted to became Americans, they enjoyed the fact that they were able to hold onto some connection with Italy and the towns they came from.

As I'm of Italian descent, you should know growing up Italian definitely has its perks. From the food, to the holidays, to the sense of family, I take pride in Italian culture and my heritage. I guess I owe that to my parents, grandparents and other close family and friends whom I often think about in the warmest of terms.

My parents are both gone now, but my memories of mom and dad are vivid and full of the experiences, large and small, that shape the way I act, think and live my life. My parents, Anthony and Gilda, were born here in America, but both sets of my grandparents are from Italy and settled in America when they were very young. My mother's father became a tailor and my mom's mother stayed home to take care of her family. Neither of them spoke English when they arrived in the US, but they learned to speak the language well enough. Over the years they studied about America and the important aspects of what they needed to know to become citizens. So, when they took the oath of citizenship, they told me it was one of the proudest days of their lives.

My mother and father grew up in the Bronx where they attended the local public schools. It was important to my grandparents that their children be brought up as proud Americans and learning English was something essential. Both my mother's and father's parents always considered living in this country to be very special and instilled in their children and grandchildren that they should be grateful to be in this country, the United States of America. Both sets of grandparents also made sure that my mother and father learned to speak Italian and to take pride in that tradition. Speaking Italian came in very handy when my parents and grandparents wanted to chat about private matters without me understanding what they were saying. Once I learned to speak Italian however, mom, dad and I were able to have some wonderful conversations over the years.

Every culture has their jokes and for my family, they seem to be funnier in Italian – I remember a porcelain ashtray in our home with a an old saying imprinted on it that said, "Il espire che punta la mia suocera morì di avvelenamento", which I'll translate, as I assume that many of you may not know or speak Italian. The joke on the ashtray says, "The snake that bit my mother-in-law died of poisoning." Anyway, the joke could lose something in the translation, and although I never thought it was funny, the saying always got a laugh from the old folks in my family.

As I've told you, I grew up in an Italian section of the Bronx, and in my mind's eye, ears and nose I can still hear the merchants, and see the old women shopping and smell the cheeses, meats and breads from the stores along Arthur Avenue. Each Sunday my father and I would make our way along the avenue to buy food for the feast our family would enjoy after Mass at the Immaculate Conception Church. My dad, Anthony (who never liked being called Tony), would buy a large chunk of the special Grana Padano, a cheese that would fill the air of Ferrari's Italian Deli. The aroma alone would make our mouths water along with the cured meats, spicy Italian sausages, crusty semolina bread, large ripe tomatoes, sweet roasted peppers and black and green olives and so much more. It all came together as the antipasti that is served and eaten before the family sits down to the 'real' dinner.

For Sunday dinner what else but pasta, covered with a thick, rich to-mato sauce that is so good you took bread and lapped up all that was left. It was made from an honored family recipe that my mother learned from her mother who learned it from her mother and back for many genera-tions. I remember that my mom would start cooking at 7 a.m. on Sunday because the sauce or "gravy," as some like to call it, would need to cook and simmer for at least four hours. After coming home from mass, she would add the meatballs, beef braciola and sausages, then cook the sauce for an-other two hours so the flavors of the sauce with the meat would intensify. I enjoy cooking to this day and I still use my mom's recipe for her sauce, and I never rush the process. I take just as much time as my mom did and the sauce called for. I like to alternate the different pastas I like to eat, so when I finally sit down, the memories of Sunday dinner with my family comes flooding back. I think that mom would approve of my cooking and the fact that I kept the tradition going and the thought makes me smile.

After my dad and I would leave Ferrari's my father and I would go to the bakery next door and buy cannoli or éclairs or sfogliatelle for dessert. Our Sunday meals became a welcomed custom, one that gave us time to catch up as a family. Much of the time was also spent along with our extended family, and we would speak of all that is happening in our lives. The Sunday meals help me to understand my folks, their lives and dreams, what they expect of me, and what they expect of themselves. It was at these dinners that I learned about our family history, how my parents met, how grateful they are to have one another and how much love they feel for each other even after the passion subsides. Sunday meals have always been the time to slow down, eat to our hearts' content and count our blessings. The Pella's aren't rich by a long shot, but you couldn't tell by the food on the table and the happiness and comfort we feel in each other's company.

As a young boy, I'd watch the old men playing bocce in the park and the women sitting on the stoops of their buildings talking, laughing and all the while never realizing there is anything more to life than what they enjoy every day. I guess this way of thinking and the genuineness of these people help me form a positive attitude about life even when reality hits me like a brick. For me, though, the greatest influences on my way of thinking were my parents. I really loved my mom and dad when they were alive as I still love them now. Anthony and Gilda were great parents and, as corny as it may seem coming from a guy my age, I always try to make them proud. My parents were generous, tough and funny and filled with so much love for me that it was kind of special and embarrassing at the same time.

My dad never graduated high school because his family was poor and he needed to go to work. At first, he was hired to do menial jobs and he worked as a laborer on a number of sites. Over the years, as he became more skilled, he was given more responsibilities and ultimately became a foreman on a number of construction projects during his lifetime. I'll always remember that his hands were like sandpaper, his knees wracked with arthritis and the lines on his face were the road map of a tough, hard-working life. While he could have complained, and he had every right to, he never did. It was what he needed to do to provide for his family and to make a better life for me. It is America's immigrant credo that their children would have a better life than they have, and he worked hard to make sure of that for us.

For Gilda it was different. Her parents recognized that she was a bright child and, although it would require great sacrifice, they made sure she would graduate high school and go onto college. When the time came, she enrolled in City College, received her degree in biology and embarked on a career as a laboratory technician. My mom had a keen mind and a structured, analytical way of thinking that made her the perfect person for her vocation. She loved working in the labs, running tests and analyzing the results, but always questioning those results until she was satisfied that they were valid and proper. For her it became a way to help doctors help patients, and she was very good at her job. Even when she met Dad, fell in love and they got married, she continued to work as a laboratory technician up until the time I was born. Once I was born, they both decided that my mother would quit her job and become a full-time mom. Gilda and Anthony did this at great personal sacrifice, and I believe it made all the difference in my life.

My dad never went further than the tenth grade before he had to quit school so he could work to help support his family. This was a lifelong regret for him, and it was for this reason that he worshipped at the altar of education. Unfortunately for me and because of his passion for education, it was preordained that I would have to go to college. I say unfortunately because I hated going to school. I was a decent student, but the thought of going to four more years of college after graduating high school gave me nightmares.

I hated everything about college, I hated the classes, I hated the professors, I hated the books, I even hated the cafeteria – but I loved my parents more, so after four years I graduated from the State University in Buffalo with a liberal arts degree, a business minor and a 3.1 GPA. Okay, maybe "hated" is too strong a word, but I was dragged kicking and screaming through college, and when I got my degree, I swore I would never step into a classroom again!

The State University at Buffalo is a very large institution and my graduating class had more than a thousand students. At my graduation ceremony, I made sure that my mom and dad got front row seats to the ceremony and, when I received my diploma, I saw my father sitting there smiling and beaming with pride. Anthony and Gilda are gone, but those memories of them are like an elixir to me. My recollections of our life together are filled with love and they bring me great comfort. These memories even help to relive the loneliness I sometimes feel now that my folks are in the Lord's hands.

Once I graduated college, I set about doing what every 21-year-old does: look for a job, have as much fun as I can and I try to find my place in the world. But life has a way of throwing you curveballs, and much of what I would experience seems to be preordained.

CHAPTER 2

The reason I am telling you all this about my upbringing is because you may want to know a little about me and some of what shaped my life and my personality. I also think you should know that I can communicate with The Sainted.

What I am trying to tell you is that the saints speak to me, and I talk back to them. The Sainted appear to me through weird and puzzling visions that I will tell you about a little later. In these visions the men and women, who are revered by the faithful as saints, reveal incidents and experiences from their lives to provide me with guidance, inspiration and even warnings of evil things to come. Even though I can speak with the Sainted, I am far more eager to listen and learn what they have to tell me. Much more often than not, I am permitted to witness the many miracles they perform and through what I witness, I find myself staring and gaping in total amazement.

I know that you think all this Sainted talk sounds crazy, but you've got to believe that it's the truth and it's been this way most of my life. I was eight years old when my entire family, grandparents, uncles, aunts, cousins and all, moved to Huntington, Long Island from the Bronx. My relationship with the saints, however, didn't start until I was about fourteen and it has been like that ever since. I don't think it has anything to do with Long Island being the epicenter of some heavenly repository of saints, I think it's just me. Some may call this special talent a curse or burden, but for me, it's definitely a gift; my own personal miracle.

Imagine having St. Peter let you know whether you're making it through the pearly gates or having St. Joseph show you how to build an armoire.

Just kidding, it's not like that at all.

My interaction with The Sainted happens like this. I can be doing just about anything; I can be having a cup of coffee, walking down the street or looking at beautiful pleasure crafts from my condo overlooking the Huntington Harbor, and the visions will come to me without warning. I am still in the present, but everything seems to freeze in time. My surroundings change, and I am transported to whenever or wherever my saints want to take me.

As a fourteen-year-old kid, I guess I could have been out playing ball or trying to imagine what it would be like to kiss Joanie behind the backstop at the Mill Dam ballfield, but that's not what was in the plan. So, what was in the plan? Well, the plan is to show me visions that reveal lessons in learning from their past experiences take me on amazing adventures in time and disclose mysteries that speak of the eternal battle between good and evil! Some of the visions are wonderful, some are terror filled, but no matter how strange the visions are, for me they became life altering. Later on in my story you will come to see what I mean about all that I've experience that has changed my life, but in spite of it all, I would not have given up the journey for all the treasure on earth.

My times with The Sainted began like this.

Winters can be tough on Long Island, and one year and, as the weather turned very cold, I got really sick. I lay in bed with the most horrible fever, chills, cough and sore throat that you can ever imagine. Because I was so sick my mother decided to keep me home from school. I guess I could have overplayed my condition, especially since I never liked going to school, but I didn't need to pretend to be sick because this time I was really sick. I'm sure you know the kind of sick I'm talking about; light-headed, chills and sweats, the whole ball of wax, and I had it in spades.

My mother became very concerned about my condition and she kept taking my temperature and changing my sweaty pillow case. She called our doctor who prescribed some medicine but she had to go to the drugstore to pick up the prescription. Since I was fourteen at the time, I guess she felt that it will be okay to run out for a little while, so reluctantly, she left me alone, but with strict instructions that I stay in bed. Mom had a lot of rules, but this one was easy to obey given that every time I tried to get up, I'd collapse back into bed, and that's where I would stay.

When mom left, I was alone in the house but as I lay there in bed, the entire room began to spin and I'm overcome by feelings of dizziness and nausea. I began to think that it is the sickness that is making me so disoriented, but that wasn't it at all and while I am in this state, I receive my very first vision.

In the vision, my room is transformed into an ancient expanse in what appears to be a desert country. I am in the center of a small town that is surrounded by a flat, sandy vastness with outcroppings of rocky hills in the distance. In the midst of this expanse, I find myself standing outside a large mud and stone building near the center of this small town. The large building is one of a number of smaller and larger dwellings and shops where the people are going about their business.

I have never seen anything like this place—well anything like this place outside of books or movies about ancient times. My eyes go wide as I gape at all that I am seeing of the surrounding area. At first, I was completely still, not wanting to move but, something compels me to walk inside the building behind me.

As I walk cautiously inside, I enter a very large room. The room is sparsely furnished, with little in the way of decorations; it is more like a place where people work and not live. In the room, there are a number of cots set up along the long walls on both sides. I observe that on each of the cots people are being treated for what appears to be all kinds of different kinds of conditions from sicknesses or diseases or wounds.

While I'm standing near to the wall, I look outside through a window, and I see a group of soldiers dressed in what looks like uniforms. They are the type ancient Roman soldiers wore, but I know I am not in Rome, or at least not the Rome I've seen in the movies or on television. I observe that the soldiers are patrolling the marketplace near the building and all seems peaceful enough. The people of the town appear to be shopping for cloth, spices, food and other basic items available there. I also notice that the shoppers in the market take great pains to avoid the building I am in. They would walk by, looking away and covering their mouths. It is obvious to me that I am in a hospital, and I could tell the people outside are consumed by fear of catching any of the diseases being treated there.

I continue to observe two other things that become obvious to me; first, nobody inside the building or outside in the market seems to notice I am among there. Second, I no longer feel sick and the dizziness and nausea are gone.

When I first became aware that this was a hospital, I observed that among those inside are two physician brothers, twins actually, treating the patients. The men hurry from one patient to the other shouting instructions at the nurses and aides and giving comfort to the sick and dying in whatever way they can.

"Quick, bring water for this man; he is burning with fever!" shouts the one doctor, as he wipes the brow of a man who is vomiting. The other doctor and a woman who appears to be a nurse are busy cleaning another patient as best they can. The meticulously thorough cleaning of the patient's body looks to be more of a remedial treatment than simple bathing, and both the doctor and nurse keep at it.

"Bring me the mint! Bring me the mint!" shouts one of the twin doctors. He is now comforting a woman holding her head in agony. He takes leafs of the mint, places them into a bowl and begins to make a solution of some sort. He crushes leaves with a pestle and mortar and then persuades the woman breathe in the aroma of the solution containing the crushed mint leaves. In a few moments I could see that her pain subsides as it seems to bring her some measure of relief from the headache.

My initial wonder turns to confusion and I ask myself, where is this place? Why am I here? Who are these men?

All the nurses and helpers in the hospital are focusing on their tasks and taking direction from both of the doctors. This frenzied activity goes on until one of the nurses suddenly screams, "He's dead! He's dead!" At the sound, the twin physicians come running to the bedside of a dead black man. All activities stop and a hush comes over the room. In death, the look on the man's careworn face seems to diminish enough to convey that he is at peace now; that he is free of pain. The doctors say a prayer over his body wishing him eternal life and his heavenly rewards. All of those present in the room, doctors, nurses, aides and patients alike stop and join in prayer for this man. The doctors then do something that literally shocks as I become aware of what is about to happen.

The doctors begin to cut off the left leg of the dead man.

With a long, sharp metal instrument, the doctors begin their work. They take great pains to assure that the leg is cleanly severed and done with minimal damage to the bone and the skin surrounding the hip. Working tirelessly and with great concentration, the doctors amputate the leg taking great care so as not to do any further damage. They place the severed leg on another table, where it is washed and covered with a clean white cloth.

The dead man is then carefully wrapped in a shroud and when the nurses' finish, one of the doctors say, "Prepare him for burial."

The doctors now turn their attention away from the dead man to their next patient. Lying in a bed next to the dead man is another man writhing in agony as his screams echo through the entire hospital chamber. The man's leg is infested with sores and pustules that have become ulcerated and the infection covers most of his skin. Immediately, the twin physicians begin to prepare this man for another procedure of some sort. Ancient medical tools are laid out on the table in advance of the procedure that is still a mystery to most in the room, especially me. The doctors begin preparing an herbal compound, mixing it with what they call a 'spathumele'. The mixture smells horrible, but that doesn't stop the doctors from their work. The mixture is placed into a bowl with mint and hot water, creating a steamy herbal liquid, but for what purpose I can't imagine. With the bowl containing the herbal mixture in hand, the nurse begins to wipe the man's head as she allows the steam to be inhaled. In a very short time, his screams lessen, and he seems to fall into a semiconscious state.

"Cosmas, have you cleaned the body and leg well?" said one doctor.

"I have, and I am ready to begin," Cosmas said to his brother.

Damian commands the nurse, "Continue to wipe the man's brow while we are preparing him for what is to come." As the nurse continues to wipe the sick man's forehead, his cries stop, and he seems to drift into a stupor. Once the man falls into this semi-conscious state, the doctors start to pray.

"Oh Lord, we beseech you to grant us the wisdom and skill to save this man. We pray for Your intersession and strength to guide our hands so that we may help in this, his time of greatest need. We ask this in the name of Your son, Jesus Christ."

At the end of the prayer there is a collective "Amen" from the doctors, nurses and some of the patients.

The doctor called Cosmas picks up the first tool, a long gleaming knife or scalpel of sorts, and he begins to cut off the man's ulcerated leg. The patient let out a muted cry, but the nurse continues wiping the forehead, administering the herbal mixture and soon the man falls further into a restless state of unconsciousness. The nurses are holding the man down as his movements are making the operation all the more difficult. With all due speed, Cosmas finishes cutting off the ruined, infected left leg from the man's body.

Although it is a cool day, Cosmas, Damian and the nurses assisting them are covered in sweat. The twin doctors worry about the bleeding, knowing that the danger to their patient is greatest now. Cosmas whispers to Damian, "I need to stem the flow of blood or he will die, but I do not want to alarm the nurses." With that being said, Damian picks up a clean linen cloth that has been laid out on the table with the other surgical instruments and he sprinkles some dried, crushed herbs onto the cloth bandage.

"I have the cloth with yarrow, and I will hold it in place."

As Damian places the cloth onto the hole where there once was a man's leg and the bleeding slows dramatically. During the time that he administers to the man, Damian frequently changes the cloth, but after removing the fourth bandage, the bleeding has practically stopped and the initial crisis has passed.

When Cosmas and Damian are done and with great care, they dispose of the amputated leg in a sack made of some type of brown woven material. The nurses then lift the man off the cot, quickly change the bloody bedding and place him back onto the cot. He is now completely unconscious, but he is having trouble breathing. With the man being unconscious, the need to continually wipe his brow is over, at least for the moment. Cosmas then carefully lifts the amputated leg they had taken from the dead black man and he places it onto the clean cot next to the opening on the unconscious white man's hip.

Cosmas declares, "We are ready, let us start."

Damian and Cosmas begin to remove the protective white cloth from the severed leg and position it next to the unconscious man. Once that is done, both doctors begin to graft the black man's leg onto the white man.

"Take pains to assure the leg bone is in place and prepare for the stitches" declares Cosmas. For many hours, both doctors work tirelessly as they sew the healthy leg onto their patient, taking time to be sure that all is going as can be expected. The nurses are busy going about all their duties to help the doctors, but you could feel that they are in awe of all that is going on. The gathered assemblage knows that, on some level, something miraculous is taking place. During the entire procedure, both doctors continue to pray, which seems to calm and reassure all who are taking part in this surreal scene.

As the doctors continue to stitch the new, healthy leg onto the still unconscious man, Damian and Cosmas turn toward me and step out of their bodies. The hospital room fades and becomes no more than a haze with the doctors still taking care of the man, but their spirits are now standing apart and in front of me. A halo appears around the heads and bodies of the men, not only the type of halo you see in paintings or books, there is also a glow that encircles their entire body.

Damian looks straight into my eyes and asks, "What is it that you see in this place you are in?"

At first, I didn't know, or maybe didn't want to know, who he is speaking to. I turn behind me to see if anyone else is there.

Damian continues to stare straight at me. "You, I am speaking to you."

With that, I point at myself and say, "Who, me?"

"Yes you, we have known you were here from the start. You have been summoned here, so that we may tell you of what is required of you."

Once the realization that I am speaking to spirits become apparent, I immediately start rattling off everything that is on my mind. "Who are you guys? Where am I? How did you do that? Is the guy going to be alright? Why do you have the bright light around you?" The questions are coming out as fast as I can think of them.

"I am Damian, and this is my brother Cosmas. You are in Cilicia, and it is nearly 300 years after the death and resurrection of our Lord and savior, Jesus Christ. We have been given an honor of which neither of us is worthy; we are called saints, saints of the Holy Church. In life we looked to do the Lord's work as doctors, serving those sick and in need of help, and now we continue to do service to the Lord from His heavenly kingdom."

Cosmas then says, "The man whom we have saved has been given a miracle. He will live and walk again, and it is only through the blessings of Christ that it has come to pass. We still need to know, what is it you see in this place?"

I am dumbfounded. I am talking to someone who lived more than 1,700 years ago, and he is asking me questions. "Uh, I don't know. A hospital, I guess."

With that answer, the brothers look at each other and smile. Damian says, "It is far more than that. It is a place for hope, for renewed faith, for charity, for love of your fellow man and for life and yes, even for death. It is where we have found what is required of us." Cosmas also explains, "We are all here in this life with a purpose. Our purpose was to help the sick, to comfort the dying and to serve the Lord. Do you know your purpose, Christopher?"

I didn't know what to say, so all I say is, "No." Then I start to think, wait, Christopher... he knows my name, I can't believe that he knows my name.

It's as if Damian can read my mind, "Yes, Christopher, I know your name, and I know why you are here."

"Why? Why am I here?" I'm anxious to know.

Damian then says, "You were brought to this place to see the power of the Lord, so that we may let you know what is required of you, your purpose."

He continues, "You are here for the same reasons the hospital is here. Throughout your life, you will be called on to serve the Lord by helping people to ease their pain, to find hope where there is only despair, to find comfort where there is only pain and to renew their faith so that they may find the peace of the Lord through His Son, Jesus Christ."

"How am I supposed to do all this? I'm just a kid."

Damian ignores my question and continues, "You will also be asked to deliver justice and to face those who have brought evil into the world. The danger you will face will be great and it is through faith and blessing of the Lord that you will prevail."

I look at Sts. Cosmas and Damian and I can't comprehend how I'll be able to do the things that they tell me I need to do. I try to explain, "But I'm just fourteen, a kid, what do I know? Who will listen to me?" I stammer and become anxious at what I am being told and I am overwhelmed by the spirits of the brothers. I know now that they were truly great and holy men, but back then, they sounded like my high school principal.

Cosmas and Damian look at each other and in an instant, the room disappears. I am transported to a place that seems to be floating on a cloud of light. Everything is bright white and for the first and one of only very few times, I become frightened. The twin brothers stand before me and, as they raise their hands in prayer, there appears all around them hundreds, maybe thousands of apparitions.

Damian seems to know that I am scared and says, "There is no need to fear what you do not understand. What you see are our sisters and brothers, those who have gone before you and have been given their reward in heaven, the gift of God's peace and eternal love."

Cosmas continues, "These saints in Christ all have a bond, they all have had their faith tested, they have given themselves to the Lord and they all understood their purpose…why they lived and what was expected of them."

Damian and Cosmas then each move aside and I see the spirit of St. Francis of Assisi standing before me. A halo and bright light encompass him as he smiles as he speaks to me. "You will go into the world and experience happiness and trouble, and you will witness life and death and, in your search for goodness, you will also be forced to confront the evil in some of those you meet. And when it is required, you will be expected to help in any way you can. There will be times you will confront the true nature of evil, but know that you will not be alone. We, the Sainted, will be there with you." Sts. Francis, Cosmas and Damian and the multitude of the saints at the gathering all smile at me. They fold their hand like they are praying and the vision of The Sainted dissolves into a bright glow and, with that, my first experience with the saints come to an end.

I am now back in my room, staring at the ceiling, sick as ever. My first vision is over and, for the first time, I feel completely overcome with the emotions related to all that had just happened. I try, but I can't fathom the meaning of it all, and I reckon that it will not be my last visitation.

As I lay in bed, I think to myself, "Me, Chris Pella, a fourteen-year-old kid, experiencing visions of ancient times, witnessing an operation that is impossible for the time, miraculous even, speaking to Sts. Cosmas and Damian, being transported to a gathering of saints and told of my purpose in life…imagine that."

CHAPTER 3

In the intervening years, I have communicated with 176 saints so far. The Sainted from the earliest Christian times, some more contemporary saints, some female saints, some male saints and they are all very real to me.

The Sainted appear to me in all types of visions and in these visions, they speak to me. Some of the visions I am shown are simply reflections of the past to help me understand who I am and my place in the scheme of things, but others are exceedingly more profound. Each of the saints I have met generally have three things in common; their holiness, their abiding faith in God's plan and His Son, Jesus and that they have suffered or persevered to one degree or another for their faith. Some of the saints had been martyred in the vilest and cruel ways, while others passed in relative quiet—all the while offering up their lives or suffering as penance for some real or imagined sin.

Consider St. Fabius. He was a Roman soldier that lived in the third century. St. Fabius refused to carry a Roman banner because it used pagan symbols. He was given a chance to "get his mind right" so to speak, but he refused. He was reprimanded by his commanding officer and was given no alternative, but to submit to this idolatry or face death. When St. Fabius refused this command, he is promptly marched out in front of the troops, tortured and put to death. In those days, the Romans specialized in particularly nasty and painful forms of death, and as a result he was martyred because of his faith.

You've got to admit, that took some set of balls, but when I asked him why he chose death over life, St. Fabius told me that he didn't have a choice. He said that his belief in his Lord is absolute. What mattered in the end was that this is the only option left for him. Choosing death over denying your faith—that's a saint for you.

You also need to understand that Christians, especially Catholics, are big on saints and even have designated "patron" saints for just about everything. There are patron saints for many countries, cities, town and provinces as well as patron saints to protect us from all types of illnesses and handicaps. There are patron saints for all occupations like "marble workers", "waiters and waitresses", even protection against plagues caused by "rats."

For the uninitiated, Patron Saints are selected by the hierarchy of the church and by virtue of their example and accomplishments and miracle performed during and after their lifetime. These saints are chosen as the protectors or guardians over many different aspects of life and are revered for the blessings they may endow.

So now, let me introduce you to St. Barbara. St. Barbara is the patron saint of the US Field Artillery…that's right, US Field Artillery. St. Barbara lived in the fourth century and was brought up as a heathen by her tyrannical father, Dioscorus. Her father was so despotic in the way that he treated his daughter that her father built a tower where he forced St. Barbara into total seclusion. While in this state of loneliness and desolation, St. Barbara gives herself to prayer and study and she was converted to Christianity in secret.

When Dioscorus finds out about St. Barbara's conversion, this totally sends him off the deep end; my words not hers, and he decides to take revenge. Dioscorus was so infuriated over his daughter's conversion to Christianity that he denounces her in full public view. She then is forced to suffer many indignities and is brutally tortured and, in the end, St. Barbara was beheaded by her own father, who acted as her executioner. Now, this is where it gets really miraculous. As she lays dead, St. Barbara's soul is released and carried to heaven by the angels. Furthermore, God becomes so angered by what The Saint's father, has done, He brings His wrath down, on Dioscorus; swift and devastating. The skies open and Dioscorus is struck down by bolts of lightning and relegated to eternal damnation as punishment for what he had done.

Now I guess you can see why St. Barbara has become the patron saint of the US Field Artillery.

St. Barbara is a wonderfully gentle soul who seems to be embarrassed by all the attention she's received since her passing. When she tells me her story, my mouth must have dropped open because she starts to laugh at me.

"What's so funny?"

"You cannot yet know what it is that God has planned for you," St. Barbara says. "He may have trials and torments far worse than I was ever made to suffer, so you will need to be strong in your faith even as you face your own death."

St. Barbara wants me to know that what matters most is her faith… her love…even her forgiveness of what was done to her by her father. That quality seems to be a characteristic of many of the saints that I've met … they are happy, at peace and just can't see what all the fuss is about.

No matter where or when these visions come, even when they occur in the middle of the night, I am very seldom frightened, except for the one time which I've told you about. This may be hard to you imagine coming from a kid of fourteen, but it's the truth. Part of the gift that was given to me is that all the saints I've met and interacted with never make me feel I have anything to fear from them. When I have a saintly vision, I may be overcome by a sense of puzzlement or unease, but as I delve further into the visions, my thinking becomes clearer, and I experience an awe-inspiring sense of awareness and wonder. It is only after these visions are gone that I am weighed down by what I'm told or what I am required to do and the significance of it all.

What is also weird is that I seem to have some sort of understanding, a grasp of what these saints are trying to say. It is not always clear at first, but I am able to apply these lessons no matter what language the saints spoke when they were alive. They try to make it simple for me to understand no matter how abstract or involved their message is. Even if I don't get the meaning of the visions at first, I am made to comprehend that it is all part of the gift. To be able to think and to comprehend are all part of God's plan, so to speak, and I still marvel at each and every experience. I guess I could have told my parents about the visions and The Sainted, but for some reason, I feel that this gift had to be kept a secret.

After my first vision I find myself eager to learn so I began to read all I can find about the saints; about their lives, their works and their miracles. I frequently go to the library in town and spend time looking through the information available. While other kids would be checking out books on sports or cars or dinosaurs or science fiction, I'd be checking out copies of 'The Encyclopedia of Saints' and 'Butlers Lives of the Saints.'

After I find the books, I want to take home, I go to the front desk to check out them out., The librarian, Mrs. Stemple, always looks at me in a strange way and one day her curiosity must have overcome her so she says to me, "What a wonderful young man you are, reading all these books about saints. I'm sure your parents are very proud." My face is turning bright red and I start to think to myself, "Shit, why does this always happen to me?", then I say, "Thank you, Mrs. Stemple, these books are for a report I'm doing for school and my parents are proud of me." What else could I say?

Mrs. Stemple then walks around the counter of the library and pinches my cheek and gives me a motherly hug and smile. I start to look for a rock I can crawl under when I see my best friends Danny and Dennis watching this happening and cracking up in the corner. Then, as luck would have it, my nightmare continues as Joanie, the girl I have a big crush on, walks by and smiles at me at the same time Mrs. Stemple pinches my cheek. Now Joanie starts to crack up, and I can't wait to get out of there. I exit the library with all due haste and I take my books, my bike and my pride home and I stay in my bedroom most of the next day.

Over the next four years, I keep reading as much as I can about the saints and their lives. As it happens though, over the next four years, I would have other visions that will help me understand my gift. Some of these visions, though, can come at very inopportune moments, and I'd like to share one that happened on the night of my Senior Prom.

CHAPTER 4

I attend St. Anthony's High School in Huntington. Joanie is now my steady girlfriend and I invite her as my date to the Senior Prom. The day comes when I finally get to take her out way past midnight. Joanie and I are both nearly eighteen, and we are very excited. At the time, I had a car that was a real classic; a 1975 Buick Skylark convertible. Very hot! The Buick had a 350 cubic inch 5.7-liter V8 and it is painted in beautiful royal blue with a white convertible top and a white interior. I installed a used pair chrome mag wheels that cost me $200 and I think they look great. The day before the prom, I wash and wax the car and put one of those pine things on my rearview mirror to get rid of my gym shorts smell. I stand back to admire my handy work; the Buick looks great and smells great and I am ready for the big night!

I pick Joanie up at her parent's house about a mile from where I live. John and Josephine are wonderful people and, because they are Italian, I always feel right at home. While Joanie is getting ready, John takes me aside for "the talk" that I'm expecting. He tells me about not drinking, how to respect his daughter and that he trusts me. Translated to English, this means that if I did anything other than kiss her, I am a dead man. I look respectfully at him, nod in the appropriate way and assure him that I have nothing but the best of intentions regarding his daughter. Although, I ponder, we may have different definitions of the word "intentions."

When Joanie finally comes down the stairs, my jaw drops in amazement; she looks beautiful and I can't believe that I'm taking her to the prom. I brought flowers that she wears on her wrist and it matches the color of her dress perfectly. In truth, it was my mom who called her mom and got the color, and she went out and bought the flowers for me to give. Anyway, who cares, we are ready and that's what matters!

Joanie and I drive to the Huntington Town House for the prom to meet our friends for the dinner dance. We talk non-stop, laugh at everything and get really close when we dance. However, we are constantly told by the priests, teachers and parents who are chaperoning, we have 'to leave room for the Holy Ghost.' Of course, all the guys all mumble the age-old retort to each other, 'Let him find his own girl!' After the prom ends, the entire group agrees that we all had a great time and we drive to meet a group of friends and continue to party for hours. We meet at a club out in the Hamptons and try to get them to serve us beer, but that doesn't work, so we settle for soft drinks, fried clams, pizza, burgers, loud music and a lot of fun.

Just before dawn, Joanie and I decide to go alone to Fleets Cove beach in Huntington to see the sunrise over the waters on Huntington Harbor. We are listening to the waves as they crash onshore and find ourselves gazing into each other's eyes. I reach for her across the front seat and we begin to make out. As it becomes more intense, I reach down for her breasts and I begin to think to myself, "Oh boy, this is it! I'm gone get laid!" It's kind of like the old Meatloaf teen anthem, *Paradise by the Dashboard Lights, "I remember every little thing as if it happened only yesterday!"* Joanie and I are now in various stages of undress, and we settle into a comfortable position in the back seat. I'm fumbling to find the hooks on Joanie's bra that will finally reveal what I had only touched through eight layers of clothing up to now. It was then, at this exact moment, that I heard a voice…

"Must you shame yourself in such a manner?"

I jump off Joanie and scramble to find out who is there, outside in the parking lot at Fleets Cove beach.

Joanie jumps up too and asks, "What's wrong? What's the matter?"

I then hear the voice say, "Are you so weak that you must reject the virtue that should guide your life?"

"Oh my God, who are you?" I say to no one.

"I'm your girlfriend, remember?"

"Not you, uh, I mean, who's out there?"

"Did you hear something? Is there someone out there?" While Joanie looks up and down the beach, a vision of St. Bernardine of Siena overwhelms my senses.

"I am Bernardine of Siena, and I have come to save you from yourself and help you reflect on what you are about to do."

Joanie is anxious as she says, "I looked all around and I don't see anyone up or down the beach. What did you see?" Joanie is getting nervous, so she locks the door of the car and turns to me.

I'm now is deep conversation with St. Bernardine. "Suppose I don't want to be saved from myself?"

Joanie, now clearly concerned says, "What the hell are you talking about?"

I had done some research over the years since my first vision and I tried to become familiar with as many saints as I could. I'm getting very peeved so I ask, "Aren't you the patron saint of advertising?"

"Patron saint? Advertising? What the hell are you talking about? Are you okay?" Joanie says and she appears to be clearly freaking out by now.

Now I'm fumbling with my shirt and trying to zip up my pants, while Joanie appears to be on the verge of a full-fledged panic attack, thinking that there is someone outside the car door. I try to calm her down, but hysteria is now taking hold.

"Take it easy. I thought that I heard the police outside speaking to me, and I got a little panicked."

"Police! Where? Where are the police? Oh! My God! My mother! Oh no, MY FATHER!"

St. Bernardine ignores Joanie's obvious hysteria and responds, "I am humbled to have been chosen as a patron of iconographers; those who have as their chosen vocation in advertising as it is now referred to."

All time stands still and The Sainted then allows another vision to come to me. It is the fourteenth century, and I am in a medieval hospital.

A young St. Bernardine comes to the door of the hospital and rushes inside. He seems to know that the plague raging throughout his beloved Siena is creating a desperate situation for all. In the city's hospitals, many of the townspeople are dying each day, and St. Bernardine and his coworkers are trying to help relieve their suffering. No one is immune to the dreaded disease and many of the workers in the hospital are also falling ill and dying. The conditions are wretched and, as more and more people are falling ill, and there are fewer people able to help them.

The situation among the sick is dire and St. Bernardine and other are doing what they can to comfort those afflicted, but there is little that can be done. Sadness overcomes St. Bernardine and he prays for God's love and healing while continuing to work with the sick and dying.

I and both frustrated and confounded and I am getting angry when I ask, "Why are you showing me the hospital?"

Joanie jumps up, "WHAT HOSPITAL? AM I GOING TO GET SICK? WHAT DISEASE DO YOU HAVE?"

By then I don't know if I am talking to Joanie or St. Bernardine. It's a stupid question to ask, but I ask it anyway, "Why aren't I speaking to the patron saint of virginity?" It is then that I thought that Joanie would punch me out.

"I am a VIRGIN you idiot! I thought that this was our night. I didn't realize that I would have to deal with a total nut job!"

I know there is no way out of this, and I want to tell her about my vision, but reality got in the way as I try to explain, "I am not a nut job, Joanie. I know this sounds crazy, but you have to believe…"

St. Bernardine then interrupts me and says, "St. Catherine of Siena was not chosen for this vision. It is I who was asked to intercede in this your hour of need."

"Need?! Need?! Are you kidding? What I need is…"

Joanie then screams at me, "What you need is a shrink and a cold shower! I'm outta here", and with that she zips up her dress and slams the car door. I try to call her back, but she is so sure I have become totally insane that she won't even turn around. Joanie walks to her home, which is conveniently just across the street and down the block from the beach.

So here we are…the Buick, St. Bernardine and me all together. I try to summon the strength to deal with this, but all I can say is, "Look what the fuck you've done!" Immediately I know I've made a mistake because you don't talk to St. Bernardine, or any saint for that matter, in this way.

"I will not listen to blasphemy and indecency from you. Do you not realize what might have happened? How could you, in a moment of weakness, commit an act that may have caused that young girl to bear your child? What of your lives, your plans, your hopes and dreams? Are you both to be so encumbered at such a young age?"

I feel my anger, along with my libido, fall sharply and when I am able calm myself, I ask, "Is this what I can expect throughout my life?"

"Did you not see the hospital and all who were sick and dying? What do you think those people expected…what was their fate? They all had dreams, they all had desires and they had family they loved. All those people had hopes for happiness, and what they received was not what they expected. What you can expect is that God's will be done. With that, the vision of St Bernardine disappears, but his words still linger. I take my shirt, pants, what little is left of my dignity, start the Buick and leave Fleets Cove Beach.

What became of Joanie? Well, we are still very good friends. She married a guy who works in, of all things, advertising. They have two sons, really good kids, and they live about a mile from where I do. I see Joanie from time to time in town and every now and then she will smile at me, shake her head and laugh…a little.

CHAPTER 5

As you've gathered, I can see the saints, I can hear them, I can touch them and I can even speak with them. I ask them questions as I try to understand the meaning of the visions and messages given to me. They speak to me directly or in parables, quote the scriptures and they even make me privy to their lives and miracles. Though I can attempt to describe what I have seen and heard, words will never be adequate.

The constant in all these visions is that they are meant to teach, inform, inspire and to warn me of what is to come. The saints themselves can't always intercede; they leave that intercession mostly up to me. The Sainted are like coaches who can give me pointers but, when it's my turn at bat, I'm alone at the plate. What sometimes makes it very hard is that I can't discuss this with anyone because if I did, I'd probably be locked up in some asylum. I can almost envision myself, strapped to a chair, blubbering about Michael the Archangel coming to release me from the torment. In reality I know this won't work, so I keep my secret to myself. There is this one person, however, who I can go to, and I'll introduce him to you a little later.

Looking back here I am, a kid of fourteen, heading into puberty at breakneck speed, and that's when I got to speak with my first saints, Cosmas and Damian. Believe me; you don't forget your first saints.

It was the time that I met with St Augustine of Hippo, however that I had one of my most disturbing and life changing visions. It is impossible to describe the man and his life without writing a book by itself, so I'll give you the much-condensed Wikipedia version:

"He was a Latin-speaking philosopher and theologian who lived in the Roman Africa Province. His writings were very influential in the development of Western Christianity.

According to his contemporary, Jerome, Augustine "established anew the ancient Faith." In his early years, he was heavily influenced by Manichaeism and afterward by the Neo-Platonism of Plotinus. After his conversion to Christianity and baptism in AD 387, Augustine developed his own approach to philosophy and theology, accommodating a variety of methods and different perspectives. He believed that the grace of Christ was indispensable to human freedom, and he framed the concepts of original sin and a just war.

When the Western Roman Empire was starting to disintegrate, Augustine developed the concept of the Catholic Church as a spiritual 'City of God' (in a book of the same name), distinct from the material Earthly City. His thoughts profoundly influenced the medieval worldview. Augustine's 'City of God' was closely identified with the Church, the community that worshipped God."

He is revered by Catholics, Anglicans, various Protestant denominations especially Calvinists as well as the Eastern Orthodox Church.

Not bad for a guy who is the patron saint of brewers. Oh yeah, I should also mention that his mother is a saint, St. Monica. Imagine the pressure!

St. Augustine doesn't like talking about the early part of his life because in his younger days, he liked to live life in the fast lane, so to speak. He and his friends spent a lot of time drinking and partying until he realized the futility of it all. After that, he managed to completely turn his life around. People who struggle with addictions also turn to St. Augustine for inspiration.

Remember when I told you that many of The Sainted visions left me in a state of calm and clarity? Well, this is not one of those times. Even though he died in 430AD, it is St. Augustine who introduced me to Satan back in 1995 by quoting from the prophet Isaiah, complete with a vision of the fallen angel and of hell itself:

> *"How art thou fallen from heaven, O Lucifer, who didst rise in the morning? How art thou fallen to the earth that didst wound the nations? And thou saidst in thy heart: I will ascend into heaven, I will exalt my throne above the stars of God and I will sit in the mountain of the covenant, in the sides of the North. I will ascend above the height of the clouds; I will be like the most High. But yet thou shall be brought down to hell, into the depth of the pit."*

To say that this particular vision was so shocking is to vastly understate how distressed I became. The horror of the vision, the finality of hell, the purest evil embodied in Satan should have driven me to madness, but that is not the purpose of the vision. St. Augustine helps me understand the meaning of this journey of the mind and soul.

After what seems like hours, I feel the need to tell St. Augustine, "I think Satan is the biggest fool of all time. He had it made, God's love, and he blew it."

I was shown this vision for a purpose that St. Augustine is quick to point out. It is a warning of the possibilities of pride, temptation and how it removes you from the grace of God. "It is pride that turned Satan against God, it is pride that condemned him to the fiery depths and it is this pride that makes him seek the souls of mankind."

I can tell you one thing for certain—hell is "hell." I guess it would be hard for anyone to grasp the reality of the situation, but here I am in the middle of a vision so overwhelming and profound that it changes my life forever. No matter how you look at it, this pretty heavy stuff for anyone, at any age, to understand and I am blessed to have The Sainted show me the truth of it all.

I've come to know St. Augustine pretty well through these and other visits and visions. I've even learned that he likes to stroke his beard and he could use a lot more time in the sun. When he's counseling me though, all I can say is that he's about the smartest saint you could ever want to know. On the flip side, he can be a little pedantic, you know, boring at times—and too academic for my tastes, but he's a saint, and I guess he earned the right to live eternity on his terms.

I am a sinner, and I know it. I have always been haunted by what St. Augustine had shown me in the first of his visions. It seems to me that this comes close to the biblical vision of hell, and I am sure that this is what is waiting for me when I buy the ranch. I imagine myself in the fiery pit, devils dancing while impaling me on long, pointed spears, surrounded by all the other sinners getting what we deserve. Again, my words fall far short of what I am trying to describe. Somehow the vision both *is* and *isn't* like that Hieronymus Bosch painting, but I still imagine that I am the centerpiece of it all and that always gives me pause to reflect on St. Augustine's warning.

In subsequent visions, St. Augustine does give me some reason for hope, knowing that I might not make it to Heaven on the first try. There is a place called Purgatory, and he quotes from his own book, *The City of God*:

> *"Temporal punishments are suffered by some in this life only, by some after death, by some both here and hereafter, but all of them before that last and strictest judgment. But not all who suffer temporal punishments after death will come to eternal punishments, which are to follow after that judgment."*

I am not prepared for this vision of purgatory. It is not a place, but more of an unimaginable state of despondency. I am engulfed in all-consuming despair. What I am consumed by is a vast nothingness; a surrounding darkness that settles over me. This state I find myself in weighs down my soul with a sense of total self-loathing, combined with a sense of hopelessness and helplessness. It is only at that point of complete and utter desolation that I perceive a small tear in the fabric of my despair. I am able to see a light, radiance more than mere brightness. In an instance, momentary joy lifts my hopelessness, and my spirit gives rise to the anticipation and promise of what could be.

I guess I can try to say something funny now, but this is the hope that I've held onto for the last seventeen years.

CHAPTER 6

As the saints are not in a position to support me, I need to support myself. I own and operate a collector coin business in my hometown, Huntington. I've expanded my operation to include an online coin collecting site, social media sites like Facebook and ecommerce sites like eBay. I also travel to coin collector exhibits and shows where I sell and trade in these treasures. My father loved to collect coins, and I inherited his passion for collecting so for me, owning my store combines a hobby and a way to make enough to support myself. It is the perfect occupation for someone who never really cared for accumulating wealth. Even though I'll never get rich unless I find a hoard of gold coins, or somehow, I get a hold of a 1933 The Saint-Gaudens Gold Double Eagle, I love being my own boss and collecting, trading, buying and selling old coins are all that I ever want to do.

I operate the St. Aloysius Gonzaga Coins and Currency. I know it sounds weird; after all, what does a saint have to do with old coins? Well, it seems St. Aloysius was born into wealth and gave it all up. He is the Patron of Christian Youth and is a model of selflessness to a very materialistic generation. So here I am, a guy selling money and not caring if I make much of it…weird but true.

St. Aloysius Gonzaga Coins and Currency is a small shop on Main Street in Huntington Village filled with mostly US coins, collectible tokens, medallions, paper currency, books about coins, coin holders and various supplies for collectors. It's about what you would expect to find in any coin shop just about anywhere. As I hold some of these treasures, I often wonder how many other hands also held them, what did their owners buy, did the money do some good or did it corrupt?

Over the years, the store has become a kind of gathering place, usually for the older guys that like to collect coins and trade stories. I always have coffee out for them and I enjoy listening to them tell of their collections, their amazing finds, their families and their lives. Some of the men even take their kids and their grandkids here to pass on the love of coin collecting. Sometimes it sticks and sometimes it doesn't but all in all, St. Al's is a happy place, and I enjoy the time I spend here.

Owning the store also gives me freedom, freedom to delve into the meanings behind my Sainted visions and the mysteries that often seem to come along for the ride. Over the years, my saints have become my friends—yes, even St. Bernardine is a friend.

Throughout my life, I take these signs and visions and attempt to interpret them in order to get a sense of their true meaning. The saints—I guess you could call them heavenly advisors—allow me to see what they want, prodding me to find the inspiration to heed their message or do their bidding even bolster my faith. Oh, I really don't mind, but it's sometimes difficult to know what to do, or how to act when you are told of things in verse, parables, disturbing visions or obscure metaphors.

My experiences with the saints, the puzzling visions and messages have turned me into an amateur detective of sorts. I attempt to work on clues given to me by the saints, along with their expectations that I use these communications to help others for their good and the good of all. These visions also help me learn and understand how to solve problems, unravel crimes and even intercede in affairs of the heart. I must tell you though, this exercise is at once frustrating but it can be immensely satisfying.

Take St. Jude, for example—yes, that St. Jude, one of the twelve Apostles. He visited me while I was in the Aunt Chilada's Mexican restaurant having lunch one Saturday. Now St. Jude lived at the time of Christ, and talk about anxiety, one of the original Apostles wanting to communicate with me. In between bites of soft tacos with grilled chicken and guacamole, St. Jude appeared to me in what is considered to be one of the holiest of visions in all of Christianity.

The room is long and narrow. The men seated at the table all await the word that is their last hope. There is wonder and reverence, but there is also fear. What will become of these men? Who among us will have the courage to follow the man from Galilee? What would Jesus ask of them?

My eyes are wide, my mouth is open and I am totally immobile. I am there, at the Last Supper, and I am at a loss to know why I am privileged to see this and what it all means. I try to ask these questions, but St Jude holds out his hand to lets me know there is another vision to come.

For Jesus has been telling the unclean spirit to come out of the man. The demon has seized on him a great many times. Those who are witness the man's torment try to secure him with chains and fetters, but he would always break the fastenings, and the devil would drive him out into the wilds. Jesus confronts this man and asks him, "What is your name?"

He says, "Legion"—because many devils had gone into him.

I ask St. Jude to help me understand the vision because I can't fathom what this all means. St. Jude seems to know what I am thinking as he tells me, "There is evil in this world, and you can never know from where it comes, even from those you know. It may sometimes be found in the hearts of men, but always in Lucifer. You will be needed to seek out the most heinous malevolence, battle it for the innocent and restore faith in the Father."

"I know there is evil, but how can I fight something so evil?"

St Jude replies, "You are much stronger than you can ever know. Your strength comes from God through the Son, His heavenly angels and all the saints. You will never be alone." The sacred vision suddenly vanishes, but after all these years of signs, sermons and visions, I know my work is just beginning.

CHAPTER 7

Why did this four-year-old girl feel such terror…why could she not enjoy this beautiful day God had given her? She loves to walk with her Momma through the beautiful fields on their way to the market like they do every week. The women of the household always follow, as is their custom and it gives Senora de Sengi a quiet moment with her beautiful Agnes.

They will buy food for their table—vine ripened tomatoes, the vegetables of the season, a cask of wine and more. On the way home, they will pick the flowers that Agnes will give to her father that night. Flowers are something Senor de Segni loves, and he always makes his little Agnes feel like she is the most precious thing in his life. It is a truly wonderful day.

So why should today be any different?

The women pass the hill overlooking the casa de putana near Montepulciano. The sun is high in the sky, but it gives no warmth, and little Agnes becomes more and more frightened. Her momma sees the fear in her child, and she becomes frightened herself. The sun's light slowly begins to disappear as darkness moves across the sky. It appears like an impending storm, only this is no signal of rain to come. All among the small group see the growing darkness that ungulates with movement and with it their terror grows.

Agnes' mother grabs her in her arms and looks up and immediate sees hundreds and hundreds of huge black crows gathering like an ominous sign of approaching evil. The crows seem to form a giant gapping mouth that looks to swallow both of them. The shrieks from the crows are painful to hear; it is like the shrill screams of many demons seeking to terrorize all who are there.

With Agnes in the Senora arms, she and the women all start to run, but there is no shelter to be found. As Agnes' mother runs, she falls and the child tumbles out of her arms. The crows sweep down, and Agnes is helpless to defend herself against the vile blackness that swarms about her head. The Senora and the women scream and beat their hands trying to save the child. The crows are relentless and none can stop the onslaught.

The crows cut and claw at Agnes with their talons and beaks and keep attacking the child who is helpless to defend herself. It is only until the women are able to beat back the crows with sticks and rocks that Agnes is free of the violence that would surely have killed her.

Agnes' mother and the women run to comfort the child and clean her of the wounds to her small face and body. What they find, however, is a little girl without one scratch or wound on her body.

How can this be?

Why is this little girl free from any harm?

What miracle is this?

While tears flow, the women try to purge the image of what could have happened to the poor child. Agnes looks past her mother, past the women who she knows love her, past it all and she whispers to no one, "il Diavolo."

CHAPTER 8

I guess this is as good a time as any to introduce you to my Uncle Al.

Chief Spartaco "Al" Barese is a veteran police officer with 34 years on the job, 20 years in the Suffolk PD. He is my mother's younger brother and he was named Spartaco (aka Spartacus) by his father, my grandpa, Agostino, who loved to read Greek and Roman history. As family history tells, each time grandpa would read some classic when my grandmother was going to have a baby, their child would get the name of some god, goddess or one of the legendary heroes, heroines or ancient characters he was reading about.

I have Aunts Inez, Aurora, Flora and Uncles Orpheus and Spartaco. Our family history also tells that, Grandpa had a change of heart when my mother was born, and she was named Gilda after the character in the opera Rigoletto. As far as Uncle Al is concerned however, he never goes by his birth name—and be warned, you take your life in your own hands by calling him Spartacus or Spartaco, so everyone just calls him Al.

Chief Al Barese has been the lead investigator on a number of violent crimes during his career, including murder. You may remember the "Parkway Murders" back in 1997. Uncle Al was a detective at the time, and it seems that there was a serial killer that would find his victims and their broken cars on the side of the road off random exits on the Northern State Parkway here on Long Island. As time went by, the murders became more and more violent and the local politicians are putting extreme pressure on the police as the general public becomes increasingly frightened.

Detective Al Barese who is working on the investigation becomes part of the team of decoys who act as stranded motorists in need of help. Those on the team believe that this is the way to trap the killer and, as a stranded motorist volunteer, Al needs to be out at night to help with the effort. Well, it's is all planned, Uncle Al and other officers would pretend to breakdown near different exits to see if they have any luck. The officers are well trained and the back-up teams and the units are prepared for anything. Uncle Al, using a different car each night, would appear stuck along the side of the parkway with his emergency flashers on. Night after night for nearly one month, he and the other decoys have no luck at all and the horrific murders continue happening.

The media is relentless in questioning the competence of the police department and reporters take every opportunity to slam their lack of progress in the case. The constant negative drumbeat on TV and in the papers is very frustrating, and it is beginning to affect the morale of all the men on the force.

It so happened that on a Thursday in late April, Uncle Al is on his way to the next stakeout when his car really does breakdown. He curses and yells at the crumby piece of crap he is driving and calls his commander. He tells him what's happened and that the team should use another officer as the decoy. Al then makes a call to the tow truck company that has a contract with local municipalities and he waits to be towed into the repair shop. After waiting for about an hour, the tow truck shows up, but Uncle Al is still so pissed off about the car that he can't take any solace in being rescued. He drives back to the repair shop with the tow-truck operator all the while fuming about what's happened. The truck driver backs into the garage and unloads the car in one of the empty bays. The driver, who is also the mechanic, comes back a few minutes later and tells him that it will only take about 30 minutes to fix the problem, so Al can sit and wait if he wants to. Uncle Al takes a seat in the waiting room and pours himself a cup of coffee under a sign that says, "For our Sleepy Customers." As Al opens a two-year-old copy of Hot Rod Magazine he begins to feel tired, and his eyes become heavy and he lies back in the chair and closes his eyes.

The next thing Al remembers is waking up in a dizzying state and being dragged down a hallway by his coat collar to the back of the garage. When he tries to resist, he realizes that he has been drugged and can no longer summon the strength to fight back. The driver, who is dragging my uncle, drops him at the end of the hallway. As Al looks up, he sees the tow truck driver walk over to a toolbox in the corner of the garage where he picks up a tire iron.

What happened next is still unclear, but it seems that the tow truck driver didn't realize that Uncle Al was a cop. My uncle, knowing what was about to happen, manages to reach for a gun he always carries in his ankle holster when he is on the job and undercover. In a half-conscious state, he raises the gun to confront the tow truck driver who looking down at him. Uncle Al yells at the tow truck operator, "Police, stop now! Put down the tire iron, and get on your knees with your hands behind your head."

The driver becomes enraged and rushes toward my uncle. He has the tire iron raised and is about to bring it down across Al's skull when my uncle fires a shot that blows a huge hole right through the driver's chest. The tow truck driver stands for a moment, looks down at the gaping hole in his chest and drops to the floor, dead. The killer had already murdered ten people and I thank God, Uncle Al wasn't number eleven. The heroics of Detective Al Barese became a sensation for about a week in the press and on TV. He became a celebrity of sorts, and all his buddies on the force took pride in him bringing the killer to justice and honor back to the work they do. This incident is what put Uncle Al on track to become Chief Detective. Although you would think these kinds of violent and perverted acts would become business as usual for him, he really never got used to it.

Throughout his career, Uncle Al became known as a stickler for details and his "by- the book" style was instrumental in getting convictions in some very high-profile cases. He is steady, knows the facts inside and out and no defense attorney can shake his confidence, although many defense attorneys had tried. Chief Barese gained a reputation as a skillful, expert witness and his truthfulness was never questioned. All in all, Uncle Al is a prosecutor's best friend and a genuine asset to the police department where he commands and gets the respect of everyone in his unit.

After my father died, Uncle Al became a second father. He is always there for me, helping me when I need advice, helping me move into my condo, spending the holidays with me and just being there for the everyday problems we all have. Some days Uncle Al would come by the shop, or I would meet him near police headquarters in Yaphank. We'd get lunch, talk, laugh and sometimes cry. All in all, he is a great man and I love him.

When my mother died, I tried to keep it together. After the wake was over and all the people were gone, I looked at Mom's sweet face, lying in the casket and I became overwhelmed. She lay there in her favorite red dress, but there was no joy on her face, only silence in death. A lifetime of love is placed in a casket, and I have to say goodbye.

I try to hold back the tears, but it is Uncle Al who breaks down first. Here is a man, fifty-six years old, 6' 1", 210 pounds, tough as they come, with a personality big enough to match his mouth and he wept like a baby. He loved and cherished my mother and when she died, part of him went with her. I remember trying to understand what he was going through and comfort him, but we just hugged and cried together because it seemed like the right thing to do in honor of her memory and lament our loss.

Uncle Al always makes sure that he continues to be an important part of my life. He's a bachelor and because of his job and the risks that go along with it, he never thought he should get married. He's a good-looking guy, very funny and has plenty of girls to date and I'm sure that the thought of marriage has crossed his mind, but he never took the plunge. Anyway, I suspect he feels closer to my mother's memory when we are together, and I always feel safer when he is around.

By the way, Uncle Al is the only person in the world that knows I communicate with the saints. He can't see or hear what I see and hear, but he believes everything I say because of what we've experienced together.

The first time that Al and I worked together was merely by accident. The granddaughter of my friend Fred, one of the older guys who always come to my shop, goes missing. Tina is his only granddaughter and she is the light of his life. When she was little, he would bring Tina into the shop and all the guys would make a big fuss over this pretty, little girl as her grandfather beamed with pride. Through the years, we saw less of Tina, but Fred kept us updated and it seems that all is well.

It was only recently; we became aware that Tina is going through a difficult time. Her parents divorced a year earlier and, at 14 years old, she took the news very hard. Her grades dropped, and she began to cut classes so she could hang out. Tina had gotten into trouble with the police on a few occasions, but the transgressions were minor and she was able to evade any real punishment.

Tina is nearly 16 years old, and when she goes missing overnight, her parents assume that it is another effort at rebellion. In the past when this happened that it was discovered that Tina was just sleeping over at a friend's house. Tina had gone missing before but never more than overnight and now she is nowhere to be found. Her parents called all her friends and the school office, but no one seems to know where she is. More than 24 hours have gone by and Tina's parents became frantic and they report the missing girl to the police. The police meet with the parents; they were given a photo of Tina and they took down all the information needed to complete their reports. Given her past issues with cutting school and staying out all night, the police are skeptical that she is in any real danger. They make the assumption that this is just another attention getting trick on her part and that believe Tina will show up soon. The Suffolk Police did issue a missing person's bulletin; however, they knew that there is little that will be done to find Tina in the next 24 hours.

Fred comes into the shop but I can see the transformation in him. He looks as if he's aged ten years in two days. My heart goes out to Fred, who I consider a good man and good friend. I try to keep his spirits up, but his heart is broken and there is nothing for me to do. I can see the fear in his eyes and hear the panic in his voice as he speaks of Tina and what trouble she may be in.

Fred is sitting in one of the chairs and looks up at me with as sorrowful look as I have ever seen on a face. He asks me, no, he begs me to talk to my Uncle Al to see if anything more can be done to find Tina.

"Please Chris; you've got to ask your uncle to help. My Tina could be in real danger. I hate to even think where she could be or who she might have gotten involved with."

I know that Fred is frantic but I know Uncle Al is overloaded with work and that this is not the type of case his department usually takes on.

I promise Fred I will ask my uncle to see what he can do and that seems to give him a small measure of hope. When Fred leaves the shop, I figure I'd get my pleading with Uncle Al over with, so I pick up the phone and dial the headquarters for the Suffolk County Police Department.

The operator at the main desk picks up the phone and says, "Suffolk Country Police Department, how may I direct your call?"

"Hi, can I speak to Chief Detective Barese please."

"One moment please," she says.

Uncle Al extension rings and he picks up his phone, "Chief Detective Barese here."

"Hey, Uncle Al, remember me? It's your favorite and most handsome nephew in the whole world." I always say this to get him to smile.

"Favorite nephew? You don't sound like my favorite nephew. Leo is my favorite nephew. He calls his uncle all the time, makes me special meals and he even spends an evening with me from time to time. HA! Favorite nephew, indeed!"

"Hey Unc, get real. Leo never calls you; he never would even think of cooking you a meal and he never tries to see you because, God forbid, he should spend an evening away from that skank of a girlfriend."

"Wait, hold it." Uncle Al seems puzzled, "You say Leo never did any of those things for me?"

"Yeah!"

"Then who am I speaking to?" Al asks.

"It's me, your loving nephew Christopher!"

"...And you did all those things for me?"

"You bet I did, and I even let you pay for dinner when we go out."

"Ah, then you can't be Chris, you must be my favorite nephew, Tommy!"

"Cut it out, Uncle Al."

"Okay, Okay. How are you, Chris?"

"I'm good. How are you?"

"Well, aside from a few unsolved murders, a $685 car repair bill, no vacation in three and a half years and local asshole politicians that should stick to taking bribes and not interfere in my business, I'm doing great!"

I try to sound pleased at his good fortune, "Glad to hear things are going so well, but I have a problem."

"Shit, I knew it! I just knew it! I knew I shouldn't have picked up the phone. What now, you want me to fix a speeding ticket or something? No way. You do the crime; you do the time. That's the rules, and that's what I say."

"Seriously, I need your help." I must sound really concerned because Uncle Al becomes worried, "Sorry Chris, what happened, what's wrong?"

I explain what Fred told me about Tina has disappearing, and her family is frantic with worry. I tell my uncle that he is the only one I can turn to, and I hear a heavy sigh over the phone.

"Chris, you say this kid has done this before and you know that it's almost certain she's done it again."

"Listen, I know that you are probably right, but she has been missing far longer than any time before and she usually comes back home or at least calls. This time, nothing and with all the crazies out there, well I don't want to imagine what could happen to her."

"But Chris, that's not my department. We have a whole unit that works on cases like this, and they will be happy to…"

I interrupt, "Uncle Al, the family has called and all they get is lip service from the guys on the other end of the line. I know they mean well, and I know they are very busy, too, but Tina could be in real trouble."

I hear another sigh from Uncle Al on the other end of the line, "Alright, let me see what I can do, but I am not sure how much I can get done."

Appealing to his vanity, I say, "Are you kidding? My Uncle Al, the man who single handedly solved the Parkway Murders and used the killer for target practice can do anything! That's my Uncle Al!"

Now he's getting aggravated at the bullshit I am throwing at him and he answers, "There's one murder I won't want to solve…it's called the 'Coin

Shop Owner Murder,' and I personally know the killer and the 'killee'. Now get off the line, so I can do some work."

"I love you."

"I love you, too."

CHAPTER 9

More than four days have passed and we've heard nothing about Tina. Fred has stopped coming to the shop and he just stays at home depressed and despondent about his missing granddaughter. I try to call him, but he doesn't have the energy to speak and he merely acknowledges my call and hangs up.

Of course, I check with Uncle Al, and he has to acknowledge that the more time that goes by, the more chance that the worst could happen. He has seen it before, kids that go missing and wind up as victims of child prostitution or become drug addicts or both. Their lives are ruined even before they have a chance to live. Al has seen it too many times, and he is afraid it could have happened again with Tina. As Chief, Al Barese has a lot of sway over the officers in all the various departments, and he feels sure that whatever can be done is being done, but he likes to check with each person in his department working on the case.

"Hi Dan, this is Chief Barese."

"Hi Chief, I know why you're calling and no news on the Tina Staley case. I hear from her parents every day and I have to deliver the same message. It's like she's disappeared and there isn't a clue to be found." Now Dan Orello is very good at his job. He's a 24-year veteran of the force, and he is about as thorough an investigator as you can get. As a matter of fact, Uncle Al depends on Dan to help make sure that everything is done right when they are working together on crimes being investigated. They both assure that all the "i's" are dotted and "t's" crossed before a criminal is brought to trial and either he or Dan have to takes the stand to present the evidence.

"I know you're doing everything possible, but this case has me worried. I keep thinking what it would be like if this was my daughter. I guess it's good that I never got married." Al says this to Dan, but it seems like he's talking to himself.

"Hey Chief, everyone knows you are personally involved with this case, and they want to get it resolved. Everything that can be done is being done. Take my word for it."

"You know I trust you with my life. Thank everyone for me."

"Will do," and with that, Dan hangs up.

The next time I speak to my uncle, he gives me the usual update. I give him the usual "I love you," and we both hang up. It has been a slow day at the shop as it is nearly 5 p.m. I close up. The weather this evening is warm and being outside feels good, so I decide to walk around the village before I go home. The people walking around town seem to be in no rush and as it is very pleasant, I take my time. I pass the usual shops and find myself in front of my favorite bookshop, Book Revue. They have a huge selection of new books, but they also carry used, rare and autographed editions; it's the kind of place I can get lost in. I don't mean that it's so cavernous you can't find your way out, but it's just so wonderful that you find yourself lost in the pages of the books you pick up.

I always wander over to the remainder table where I can get great bargains on books. It may take you a few visits, but eventually, I will find books that suit my taste, mood or inclination. I like reading fiction and, on this visit, I find a slightly used hardcover copy of The Girl Who Kicked the Hornet's Nest for only $3.95…wow, this is a deal. I read the first two novels in the trilogy and enjoyed them immensely and grab the last one as my own.

Book Revue has a coffee and pastry bar and little reading areas and alcoves where a customer can sit down in a comfortable chair and read to their heart's content. It is while I am sitting there that my next vision comes.

My comfy reading nook is transformed into a small dark room where there is a bed—no, more like a cot and kneeling on the floor is a woman. She is alone and has her head bowed in prayer.

"Jesus Christ, Lord of all, You see my heart and You know my desires. Possess all that I am. I am Your most devoted servant: make me worthy to overcome the evil of this place."

The Sainted never acknowledge my presence when the vision I am seeing is taking place at a time when they were alive. While I am observing her moment in prayer, I hear the laughter of men and women and what sounds like the moaning of people having sex. Because I am, in fact, a spirit while experiencing these visions, I am able to walk through walls and doors or any other solid surface. I walk through the wall out into the hallway. In truth, I've never been to a brothel, house of prostitution or whatever you want to call it, but take my word for it, this is a brothel. A number of men and women are walking around half-naked, chasing each other from room to room.

While standing outside the door where I'd seen the woman pray, I watch all this going on. It is then a drunken Roman soldier comes staggering up to the room and he flings open the door. He immediately grabs the praying woman and tears at her clothes. I forget for a moment that I am a spirit and I jump at the soldier in hopes of saving the women from being raped. As I jump, however, the room disappears and I find myself falling. When I land, I look up and, smiling down at me is the woman who was praying. It is St. Agatha and she is surrounded by the same glow I have seen surrounding all the saints that have come before her. I get up off the floor and stand before her. She is holding something in her hands, she was holding a tray and on the tray are two human breasts…hers.

In life, St. Agatha experienced many torments and tortures, but she always remained steadfast in her faith. In this vision, St. Agatha allows me to see her suffering at the hands of Quintianus, a Roman Prefect at that time. He wants to possess this woman, but she had pledged her virginity, her life and her soul to the Lord and refuses all his advances. Quintianus is furious and subjects St. Agatha to further suffering and she is sent to prison after being raped in the brothel.

In prison, one of the tortures she must suffer is to have her breasts cut off; I am dumbfounded at the horror of it all. If you could have seen this cruelty, you would be as grief stricken as I am for this beautiful person.

> *The vision continues as St. Agatha speaks to Quintianus: "My courage and my thoughts be so firmly founded upon the firm stone of Jesus Christ, that for no pain may they be changed. Your words be but wind, your promises be but rain, and your menaces be as rivers that pass, and how well that all these things hurtle at the fundament of my courage, yet for that, it shall not move."*

I don't know what to say, but I didn't have to say anything as it is St. Agatha who steps out of the vision and speaks to me first.

"My suffering is of no consequence now because I live for eternity with the blessing of the Lord and He is all anyone needs. I know it is you who are troubled and I know what it is that troubles you."

As I look at her, I am grateful that St. Agatha knows what I have to say, but I say it anyway,

"I am troubled, but not for myself. My friend's granddaughter is missing. She's so young and I just know that she is in danger. Can you please help me find my friend's granddaughter?" I stop speaking since I am trying to suppress a tidal wave of emotion.

St. Agatha says, "To find the way to her salvation, you must look for her in the darkest of corners where light refuses to go." I didn't know what St. Agatha meant by these words. I've often had moments with the saints where the messages are so cryptic that I need to take time to just think. As I am contemplating what is meant by all this, St. Agatha holds out her hand, and I touch it.

My breath is taken away and I gasp as I immediately I see Tina in another vision. She appears to be strapped to a bed unconscious, but somehow, I know she is alive. She is in a dark, filthy room with half-eaten food laying all over the floor and cockroaches climbing all over the furniture, the bed…and Tina. There is something else I see; there are small glass vials and plastic syringes and needles scattered all over the floor.

St. Agatha allows me to be brought into Tina's horror, but she holds out hope. "In the depths of despair, there is always hope. The child clings to the hope of deliverance from the evil that has her under his control. It is in the Lord that you must place your faith and trust and it is in the Lord that you will find salvation for her."

The connections between Tina and St. Agatha's words aren't initially apparent to me. The enigma of the message, the vision and the ghastliness of Tina's situation make me pause and then I finally make the connection. Prison…brothel…torture…St. Agatha's vision was meant to show me how she was subjected to evil and how the same thing is happening to Tina. The Sainted Agatha turns away from me and her body becomes like beams of light and she disappears.

In the next instance, I find myself seated in a brown leather chair with the book on my lap. As I realize that I am back in the present, I jump off the chair, drop the book and run to the sidewalk outside Book Revue. I know I have found an essential clue to help find Tina, and I know that I need to call Uncle Al.

I immediately dial his number on my cell and his phone rings and he answers, "Chief Barese here."

"Uncle Al, I know where she is. I mean, I know where I think she is. I mean, I know where she could be. The place…" I am rambling on and on, speaking faster than my mind can process the words.

"Whoa…take it easy, Chris. What are you talking about?"

"Tina, I'm talking about Tina. I think I know where she is."

"How the hell do you know where Tina is?" Now Uncle Al is getting nervous. He knows I'm not one to make up stories and I never lie to him, well almost never.

"I just know—not the exact place, but I know where she is."

"Okay, calm down, where is she?"

"She's being held captive in some kind of a drug house, drug den, brothel or whatever the hell you call it."

"A drug den or brothel? Is this some kind of joke? A drug den or brothel!" I could almost see Uncle Al leaning back in his chair rubbing his eyes and thinking he should have become a tailor like his father.

"Chris, how could you possibly know that she is in a brothel or, what did you say, a drug den?"

"I just do Uncle Al; I know she is there."

"Listen I need to have a little more to go on than coin shop intuition. Which is it, a drug den or brothel? Where is this drug den or brothel: and the question of the day…how the hell do you know?" Uncle Al's a cop, and he won't give up. I know he wants to hear something from me that would make sense to him. I can't tell him the truth, so I lie to him one of the very few times and, what I hope is the last time in my life.

"I got an anonymous phone call, and the person told me that Tina is being held against her will by some real bad guys and that if we don't get to her soon, something very bad will happen." I am speaking very fast because I know that Uncle Al would know I am lying if I slow down.

"First, why did the person call you and not her mother or father or even the police? Who did you speak to, was it a man or a woman? Why didn't this person tell you where this supposed drug den or brothel is located? How do you know if this person has some ulterior motive? Chris, we can't just mobilize the Suffolk County PD and send them on a wild goose chase over an anonymous call from an anonymous source."

"Unc, this isn't a wild good chase. The call is from a woman and she didn't say where the place is, but she told me Tina is in grave danger. I guess Tina might have mentioned my name to this woman. Maybe Tina told her that her grandfather is my friend or maybe Fred gave her a card from the coin shop. I really don't know why all I know is that I am the one she called." I think to myself that I can't believe how convoluted things are getting because of the lie I'm telling, and I know Uncle Al is suspicious.

"Listen Chris, you can try, but you can't bullshit a bullshit artist. What's going on here? I need to know, and I need to know now." When Uncle Al says now, he means now.

"Do you trust me?" I say in the most sincere, straightforward way I know how to.

"Of course, I trust you, Chris. You know that."

"You have to trust me this time without knowing how I know. Please, Uncle Al, Tina is in trouble, she is being held against her will in some really nasty place, and I know she is in great danger."

I don't know what other way to say this, but I end I just tell him, "I'm sorry I lied to you. I never will again."

"Okay Chris, I believe you, but now I need to make the department believe me, and I need to have proof. Let me get back to you. I love you."

He hung up before I could say, "I love you, too."

CHAPTER 10

First thing in the morning, a meeting of all the detectives working on the case is called in Chief Barese's office. There are four detectives in all; two work out of the missing persons unit and two out of homicide. Among the assembled squad are two women and two men, they all sit down, coffee in hand, listening to what the chief has to say.

"I want to thank both Detective Christian Oliver and Detective Avery Michaels for coming over to homicide to help out with this case, I appreciate it. Detectives Dan Orello and Christina Shannon know that I have a personal stake in helping to get this solved and here is what I know as of now."

All team members are focused on the chief as he tells them what he has learned. "Last night, I received an anonymous phone call. It was from a woman who says she knows where Tina Staley is." This information is passed along to his team in the most serious voice that the Chief could muster. As he looks around the room, he observes each of the detectives looking at each other and the chief guesses they have many questions.

Sitting next to Dan Orello is Detective Christina Shannon, the second most senior member of the team. She is in her late 30's, very pretty, small in stature, but you wouldn't want to mess with her because she is tough as they come and she doesn't take crap from anyone.

Det. Shannon is the first to speak, "How do we know this is real and not some phony lead by a deranged pervert?"

Chief Barese doesn't like it but has no other choice but to lie. He tells the team, "When we spoke, the woman was able to provide information that only someone who saw Tina would know." Up to this point, the police have treated Tina's case as just another missing person. There was no formal police announcement asking for help finding her, nothing in the press or TV reports asking for the public's assistance, no photos on milk cartons or anything like that. Al tells all those assembled in his office "The caller had information that no one else would know other than the family and us. She told me about the small scar on Tina's chin, her age, what she was wearing; an onyx ring her dad bought her, her high school ID card, the works."

"Where did this anonymous caller say she is?" Detective Christian Oliver asks. Now, Detective Oliver isn't what you'd call a "by the book" cop. He has great instincts that have been honed over a stellar career and he is the one person who is most like the Chief.

Al responds, "She says that Tina is being held captive in some kind of drug house or brothel. She wouldn't say where it is, but she did say that Tina had been there about a day. I know this might sound highly suspect, but I believe her. Those drug gangs have been known to kidnap these kids that run away and I think it's worth following up."

Detective Oliver tries to find a reason for this sudden finding, "Do you think she might have been one of the other hookers or addicts that called? Maybe she got religion?"

"Could be, I don't know." Al admits.

Detective Avery Michaels, the other woman on the team, says what everyone wants to avoid saying, "You know Chief, Tina may be drugged up, hooking or even dead by now. These people play pretty rough, and a 16 year old kid is no match against these gangs of depraved scumbags. They'll kill her and think nothing of it."

"I know that's possible, but until we know for sure, we have to follow this lead. Does anyone have any other thoughts or questions?" Al is looking at his group for any angle that could be helpful in this case.

"Have you considered that she might be there of her own free will? She could have been taking drugs all along and now she's being pimped to support her habit." It is a possibility that no one wants to contemplate, but someone has to.

Chief Barese reluctantly admits, "You're right, it is a possibility, but Tina has no history of taking drugs and her parents have had her tested. From what I've been told by the parents, she has been rebellious since there divorce and her behavior is being seen as lashing out at them. Besides she is still a little kid in my eyes and we have to see if we can find her. In the end, we'll know one way or the other." This is a sad and sobering possibility to everyone, and above all, Al is a realist.

Detective Dan Orello offers an action plan: "I'll get working with vice to develop a list of known drug dens and houses of prostitution in this area and beyond. I'll also get a list of known pimps and hustlers and put some pressure on them. We'll also circulate photos of Tina to some of the beat cops and they can start to question these lowlifes when their paths cross."

"Good idea, and let's keep this low profile, but I want a report every day with an update on the status of the investigation. Are we all clear?"

"Yep," responds the team and they all leave.

After everyone left the meeting, Chief Al Barese sits back and starts to think about his conversation with Chris last night. He is always a thoughtful man and his instincts are kept sharp after so many years on the job. He picks up Tina's file and reads it again. She is a problem kid and she got into trouble, but she didn't appear to have anything that would point to her living on the edge. Lots of kids have problems, but they don't all turn into addicts or prostitutes, someone usually turns them. Who could be trying to turn Tina?

Uncle Al continues to wonder about all that I've told him. Something comes to mind and he picks up the phone and dials the coin shop.

I answer the shop phone in the usual way, "Good afternoon, St. Aloysius Gonzaga Coins and Currency."

No 'hello' or anything, as Al just speaks, "When you got the information on Tina, did this person mention any other name or hint at someone or something else?"

"I really don't remember her saying anything I thought was important other than what I told you. We only talked a minute or two and I…" Then I thought of Quintianus, the Roman Prefect who brutalized St. Agatha.

Uncle Al is prodding me to try and remember something, no matter how small I may think it is that could be of help to him and his team. "Listen Chris; try to think, it's very important. Is there anything else that could help us get to Tina?"

How could I tell Uncle Al what I know or how I know it? I know what I know because of my vision, but I can't tell him that.

Uncle Al is getting impatient, "Chris, come on, speak to me. There has to be something else."

I am looking to find a way to tell my uncle something that seems unconnected, but could be helpful. "Well, there is something, but it doesn't make sense to me, and I thought that it was just gibberish."

"Listen, anything that was said, even gibberish, can be a clue. What did this mystery woman say?"

"Well, she told me something that sounded about like 'Quintianus' or 'Kintianus' or something like that." At least I have gotten that much out and I hope that Uncle Al could make something of it, what, I don't know.

Now I hear Uncle Al talking to himself and mumbling on the other end of the line. "Kintianus or Quintianus…? What the hell is that supposed to mean?"

I know Al's mind is working at breakneck speed so I tell him, "I don't know, it sounds so weird that I didn't think it meant anything. I'm sorry I didn't mention it to you sooner, but I hope this helps."

"Okay, let me think about it, but if you come up with anything else, and I do mean anything, call me right away."

"I will, and I love you."

But Uncle Al had already hung up.

I sit back in my chair behind the counter and I don't know what to do about all this. I can't let him know what my life has become…about the saints…the visions. I feel helpless, but I know that my uncle is in charge and that always makes me feel better. Just then the phone rings, but before

I have a chance to say St. Aloysius Gonzaga Coins and Currency, I hear a voice say, "I love you too," and he hangs up.

CHAPTER 11

It has been more than five days since Tina's disappearance and I'm very concerned because I haven't had another update from Uncle Al. I know it' been just a short while since I spoke to my uncle, but I need to have something to hold onto that would help calm my nerves. I also haven't been able to speak with Fred and I'm getting very concerned.

I try and call him again and when he answers the call I immediately say, "Don't hang up Fred; it's me, Chris."

"What do you want?" It is a vacant greeting from a man who is in the depths of depression.

"I won't even ask how you're doing, but is there anything you need? Can I get you something to eat; can I help in any way?"

Fred just says, "No."

I was calling him, hoping that if I can update Fred on the status of the investigation, it might give him a small measure of hope. Even though I hadn't heard from my uncle, I try to put as positive a spin on the situation as I could. "I wanted to call and let you know that Al and his team are still working hard on Tina's case. They've got four detectives looking into all possibilities. I know they will find her; I know she will be safe…I just know it."

"How can you know she's safe? How can you be so sure? She is my angel; my princess and she's gone. I can't imagine where she is or what might have happened to her. I don't know what I'd do if anything happens to her." I could tell that he is on the verge of a total breakdown. Tina is his pride and joy and she loves him equally.

I remember a story he told me and his friends at the shop one day. It was the first time he took Tina out on his own. Just Grandpa and Tina, and they had the whole day together. She was nearly three at the time and a wonderfully happy, playful little toddler. Her mother was concerned about all the things that moms are usually concerned about, but Fred assured her that Tina was in the best of hands and he will make sure she is safe and happy. So, Tina's mom agrees and packs up a diaper bag with, of all things, diapers and diaper wipes, a change of clothes, sippy cup of apple juice, bag of Cheerios, a sweater in case it gets cold, another bag of healthy snacks and a toy for when she is in the car. So, with Tina in one arm and the diaper bag in the other, off she and Fred set out on their adventure.

Bright sunshine, a delightful summer breeze and giggles galore—the whole day is wonderful. Grandpa and Tina go to Heckscher Park to feed the ducks and swans stale bread. Sure, it's against the rules, but it makes Tina so happy. Fred always laughed as he told us of how Tina would giggle every time the ducks put their heads in the water and grab at the bread with their beaks. Well, Fred rationalized the violation; it wasn't that much bread and, if they ever got caught, he would gladly pay the fine.

After feeding the ducks, they walk over to the playground and Fred puts Tina on the swing. He tells us how he pushes Tina higher and higher and, with each movement of the swing, Tina would laugh louder and louder. At that moment Fred thought that he had never been happier in his whole life then at that moment.

Their next stop was lunch. Fred took Tina for chicken nuggets and French fries and for dessert they went to a make your own yogurt place where he buys Tina a vanilla cup with rainbow sprinkles. Spoiling Tina became Fred's hobby and every time they went out together, he would buy her a toy. They stop at Toys Galore and Tina finds a mermaid doll that she loves so Fred buys it for her. Tina hugs the doll and names her "Annabelle," which Fred smiles when he tells us that it's actually the name of her neighbor's dog.

The day goes by in a flash for Fred and when he takes Tina home that evening, he tells her that they had made a memory. Then Fred tells us she gave her grandpa "the biggest, tightest hug he ever got," and it became a day that Fred would never forget. All the regulars that come into my coin shop love to hear Fred tell the story, to see his face light up and hear him laugh. He is truly a great guy and now he is in such pain that all of us want to help, but we feel helpless ourselves.

I try to speak to Fred in as calm a voice as I can muster. I am very concerned that he is not eating so I ask, "Can I bring you over some chicken cutlets? How about some pasta? I made sauce the other day, and I think you'll like it. What do you say, Fred?"

"I'm not hungry," he says in a voice so low that I don't know what he said.

"What did you say, Fred?"

"I'M NOT HUNGRY!" He yells, dropping the phone and I hear him burst into tears.

When I hear this, I say, "I'm coming over now."

I close the shop, jump into my car and drive over to Fred's home. He lives in a small house in a cul-de-sac about fifteen minutes outside of town. Fred's wife, Carol had passed away a few years earlier after a short, but painful, battle with pancreatic cancer. After Carol died, Fred sold their home and he moved into a smaller place on a smaller plot of land. He always likes to tell everyone he did it because he's lazy and doesn't want all the yard work around the house, but we all know it's because of the lifetime of memories he had with Carol and the loneliness he feels each day he walks through the door.

I park my car in his driveway and run up the front stairs. I ring the bell, but there's no answer, then I try knocking on the door, but there is still no answer. Finally, I try turning the doorknob and find the front door is open so I go in.

I'm standing in the hallway and I call out, "Fred? Fred, it's me Chris."

There's no answer so I call out again, "Fred, where are you, are you okay? Fred, please answer me."

There is no immediate response and I become worried. "Come on, Fred, speak to me." I need to find my friend, but even if I did find him, what would to I say? How can I help make him feel better?

"In here," I hear Fred's voice, mournfully hollow, coming from the small sunroom that faces his back yard. I rush to the rear of the house and I am shocked by what I find. Fred, who was always a healthy, robust figure of a man, seems to have withered away in less than five days. Fred likes to wear stylish clothes and he always looks well-groomed. All his friends think of him as kind of a fashion plate and he likes to dress the part, but this is not the Fred I am now looking at. He appears gaunt and unkempt, his hair is a mess, he hasn't shaved in days and the clothes he is wearing are worn and wrinkled. I'm sure that Fred has been sleeping in them, what little sleep he gets.

Out of fear for his health and sanity, I say, "Fred, I am so sorry for what's happened, but you have to try to keep it together for Tina's sake. She would not want you to do this to yourself." I try to reason with him, but he doesn't want to listen to me or anyone else. "Just leave me alone." It is a pathetic cry from a man who has lost all hope.

"Fred, there is always hope. You have to believe that, and I know that the police will have some news for you and your family very soon. You need to just have faith." I don't know what else to say.

After hearing what I said, Fred tries to struggle to his feet. He holds onto the edge of the couch and turns toward me. There is menace in his eyes and a vacant stare on his face and I sadly am aware that this is not the Fred I know. This is a totally distraught man. In his weakened condition, he rises to his feet and takes one feeble step toward me.

"Faith? You say I have to have faiiiiiiii …" with that, Fred falls into a heap on the cold, hard tile floor.

I panic, "Fred? Fred? Oh my God, Fred! Are you okay?" But he isn't okay; he is unconscious, bleeding from a deep cut after hitting his head on the tile floor. I immediately run to the phone and called 911.

The operator answers: "911, do you need police, fire or ambulance?"

I am very upset and I try to tell the operator what has happened, "Please, I have an emergency; my friend is passed out on the floor. He cut his forehead when he fell and he's bleeding badly. Please hurry; he needs help right away, please help him."

The operator asks for Fred's address and I give it to her. She also asks, "Does your friend have any other injuries?"

"Not that I can tell."

"Does he take any medications?" She continued.

I try to think, "No, not that I know of, but I can go to his medicine cabinet to check if you want me to. I know that he is a patient of the Huntington Doctor's Group, I think they would know."

"Okay, we'll call them. Do you know if he's been drinking alcohol?"

"No, I don't think so. Please hurry, he could be really hurt."

The 911 operator says, "The ambulance is on its way and they should be there in the next three minutes." She tells me to hold on the line until the ambulance arrives and, within thirty-seconds, I hear the sound of sirens.

As a small business in the town of Huntington, I am a strong supporter of our local EMS unit. These men and women are amazing as are all the other EMS workers around the country. Many of the members are volunteers who work all shifts, they give up personal time and they take courses to sharpen their skills. Their expertise and knowledge have saved countless lives and every time you see an EMS worker you should go up and shake their hand and thank them for all they do. I have never had to use their services until now and I am forever grateful for their compassion.

The ambulance pulls up to Fred's house, and two people get out. They maneuver the stretcher up the steps and into the sunroom where Fred lay on the floor. After they do a cursory examination and take his blood pressure, they temporarily put a bandage to stem the flow of blood. The two EMS workers carefully lift Fred onto the stretcher, buckle him in and wheel him through the house and out to the ambulance. Fred is diagnosed as being severely dehydrated, so the crew administers a saline drip and hooks him onto a portable monitor in the ambulance this way they can closely observe his vital signs on their way to the ER. The EMS crew then asks me pretty much the same questions that the operator had asked while they secure the gurney in the rear compartment of the ambulance. Once they are sure the patient is safe, they turn on the siren and rush him off to Huntington Hospital.

I wasn't allowed to ride in the back of the ambulance with Fred, so I hurry into my car and follow the ambulance to the Emergency Room. I park and run to the admission window where a nurse is stationed, "My friend Fred Klein was taken here to the ER, and I want to know when you will have any news of his condition."

The nurse that is stationed in the emergency room looks at her computer and tells me, "Mr. Klein was just admitted, and he will need to be examined by the emergency room physician. I won't have any news for a least an hour, so please take a seat and I will let you know as soon as we hear anything." She is obviously use to dealing with people who are anxious family members and friends, so I hunker down for the long wait.

While I am waiting at the hospital, I decide to let Uncle Al know about Fred so I go outside to make the call.

When I get him on the line, Al becomes very concerned about Fred's condition. "How's he doing, Chris?"

"I won't know for a while, but he was in pretty bad shape when I found him. He's in the hospital's Emergency Room and they're examining him now."

"I hope he'll be okay. Give him my best, even though he probably doesn't want to hear from me."

I know how my uncle must be feeling about the investigation but I also know he is doing everything he can to find Tina. "Uncle Al, Fred is so down right now he doesn't want to hear from anyone. I know, in his heart, he appreciates everything you're doing."

Uncle Al suddenly changes his tone, "Hey Chris, by the way, I'm glad you called. I thought that I would let you know that your gibberish, you know that 'Quintianus' thing you told me about, well it may turn into something and we are checking it out." My uncle, being circumspect also says, "It might be nothing, but my team will follow up and I'll keep you posted."

I am stunned to hear this, "Are you kidding me? Uncle Al, you can't leave me hanging like this. What happened? What's the lead? Please tell me, I promise I won't tell anyone else; I swear!" I hope that I can appeal to his sympathetic side, especially since I'm the one who talked him into taking this on.

"Chris, you know I can't reveal any confidential information about an ongoing

investigation."

"Come on Unc, I've been worried about this from the start. Look at what's happening to my friend. I promise, cross my heart and hope to die, that I won't tell a soul. I'll even pay for our next dinner, unless I can't afford it, then you can pay." I say this all in my best impersonation of an Eagle Scout.

As he heaves a sigh, Uncle Al says, "Chris…"

"Please, you've got to tell me."

"Shit, okay, but if you say a word about this, I'll cut off your penis and there'll be no more British women for you…ever. Got it?" I know it might sound like a joke to you, but I know he means it.

In as serious a voice I can muster up, "My solemn word."

"That word, 'Quintianus' is not a word, it's a name or the root of a name and it comes close to a name that belongs to a scumbag named Heriberto Quintana. My team took that name 'Quintianus" and ran it through the criminal database and up pops 'Heriberto Quintana'. I must admit, it's like finding a golden egg."

"Heriberto Quintana? Who is he? Where is he?"

"Quintana's a real lowlife drug dealer. He gets young girls and boys hooked on heroin or crack and pimps them out to whichever pedophile has the money. He chooses young kids, runaways mostly, kidnaps them and forces them to take drugs. By the time they're hooked, there's no way out for them. He literally turns them into sex slaves, turning tricks and making him and his gang a lot of money in the process; oh, he's a prince alright. Heriberto Quintana operates here on Long Island, where he's the head of a particularly vicious branch of a gang from El Salvador, MS- 13."

I remember reading about this gang in news reports. "MS-13, I've heard about them. Is that who you think has Tina?"

"Well, we can't be sure, but a lot of the pieces seem to fit, so we're going to follow up. By the way Chris, good going on that lead, you may have given us important info in this case and other cases of missing kids, let's hope."

"Hope", that's the word I used with Fred, but now there is really room for hope and I start to have some myself. "Thank you, St. Agatha," I say to myself, but Uncle Al is still on the phone.

Al reacts, "St. Agatha? Who the heck are you talking to?"

"Sorry, Unc, it's a little prayer I say when I want to give thanks."

"Well, don't thank St. Agatha yet because we still need to find Tina and we still need to get the scumbag, excuse me, alleged scumbag, who may be holding her captive. I'll keep you posted, and remember, call me with anything else you can think of and don't say a word to anyone. Okay?"

"Okay and Uncle Al, thanks. I love you."

"I love you, too."

I return to the waiting room which seems to have gotten a lot more crowed since I left to call my uncle. All I can think about is what Uncle Al told just me. Could it be true; is Tina actually be held captive by MS-13? A half hour later, a doctor comes into the waiting room and looks around. He must have seen me jump up from my seat, so he approaches me, "Goo afternoon, I'm Doctor Raymond Thaler, the Emergency Room physician on duty, are you the man who found Mr. Klein?"

"Yes, I'm Chris Pella, doctor." I put out my hand and we shake.

The doctor says, "Pleased to meet you Mr. Pella. How did you come to find Mr. Klein in this condition?"

"Please call me Chris. Well, I've known Fred, I mean Mr. Klein, for years. He's been in a terrible state of depression and I was very concerned about him. I went to his house to see if he was okay, but he would respond to me when I called out. I finally found him in a back room of his home and he became very agitated when we talked. When he tried to get up, he fell down on the tile floor and cracked his skull."

I tell him about the events surrounding Tina's disappearance and how devoted Fred is to her. When I finished my story I ask him, "How is he, Doctor?"

"Are you a relative?" the doctor asks me.

"No, but I'm a close friend. All of his friends and family are very concerned and I think family members are on the way here now."

"Well, I can only give the family the complete details on his condition, but I can tell you that he is lucky you found him in time to get him to the hospital. We are treating him for severe dehydration, hunger and a serious concussion from the fall."

I am very concerned, "Will he be alright?"

The doctor seems to choose his words carefully: "It'll be touch and go for a while, but I believe he will recover. My fear, though, is that if he continues in this depressed condition, he may just fall back into the same state and the next time he may not be as fortunate."

"What can I do to help, Doctor?"

"There is really nothing anybody can do. We have him sedated and I'll know more in the next 24 hours."

"Thanks for all your help, Doc. Please, let me know if there is anything I can do." With that, I leave the hospital and head home.

CHAPTER 12

I continue to be worried about Fred, but I'm excited at the same time. Maybe it's nothing, but I don't think so, and St. Agatha has shown us the way. Her suffering at the hands of Quintianus and Tina's suffering at the hands of Heriberto Quintana are too coincidental to be circumstantial. At 2 a.m. I am sitting up in bed thinking about all that's happened; about Tina, about Fred, about Uncle Al and I can't sleep.

I get out of bed and go down to the kitchen for something to drink. I pour a glass of orange juice, and I sit down at the kitchen table. With the vision of St. Agatha fresh in my mind, I can't help but think about Tina's personal horror, Fred's mental and physical condition and my call with Uncle Al. All these thoughts are jumbled together and they keep going round and round in my mind.

If I can't go to sleep and I need to think, maybe I should get out of the house and just drive around while I get my mind straight? This seems like a good idea at the time because its 2 A.M. on a weekday and very few people would be on the road at this hour. I get in my Mustang, start the car and take off going south on Route 110, a main North/South thoroughfare here on Long Island. I have the radio turned to my favorite classic rock station and they are playing the 70's Asia classic "Heat of the Moment" and I begin to sing along. I'm sure you know what it's like when you get behind the wheel with no particular purpose and no particular place to go…you just drive, and that's what I did.

I am deep in thought, accompanied by more classic rock, when I finally look around to try and determine where I am. It seems that I have been in the car for more than 45 minutes and I'm now on the South Shore of Long Island, in a squalid and run-down part of town. Looking around, I notice that most of the storefronts are dark and some are boarded up. I look to the side of the street at an entryway to one of empty storefront and I spot a woman who is standing in the shadows. She looks up and down the street, and before long, a car pulls up to the curb. The driver opens the window and after a short conversation takes place, she opens the door and they both drive off.

It is pretty easy to guess what has taken place. I think it would be wise to make a hasty retreat, so I make an illegal U turn and start back going back north on Rt. 110 toward Huntington. As I stop at a red light, I see a small group gathered on the corner, two girls and a man. They are arguing, but about what, I didn't know. I assume that the girls are hookers and the man is a customer. I open my window to try and hear what they are talking about. I'm jolted out of my concentration by the last of a horn. The light has turned green, and there is a Dairy Barn truck behind me. I assume the driver is in a hurry trying to make his deliveries. I immediately put my foot on the gas pedal and move to the side. The driver gives me a dirty look as he passes and I'm sure he thinks that I'm a "john".

When I pull over, I park and shut off the engine and the headlights. I don't think the group notices because they continue to argue. All I can make out is "…no fuckin' way" and "I'll cut you bitch…" and other expletives that seem to be a natural part of their vocabulary. Then, in a flash, the guy hauls back and throws a punch at one of the young girls and she falls to the sidewalk. I am about to get out of the car when I see the man pull out a knife and threaten the other woman. He reaches down and grabs the dazed and bleeding girl by the hair and begins dragging her down a narrow alley. The other girl follows both of them, and I can hear her sobbing and pleading with the guy, not to hit her friend anymore.

Now it becomes apparent that the guy is their pimp. I don't know what to do and I am about to call the police when I think of Uncle Al. Now, you already have some idea of how much I bother the man, but this time it's after 3 A.M., and I'm sure he's sleeping. He will probably promise to strangle me when I wake him up. I say to myself, "What the heck!" and I call his number.

A groggy voice answers, "Ugh…what the hell time is it? This better be important."

"Hi Uncle Al, it's me Chris!"

"I'm gonna strangle you, you worthless piece of shit…"

I innocently say, "Did I wake you up? What time is it?"

"It's 3 a.m., and yes, you did wake me up."

"Sorry about that, but listen, Uncle Al, just hear me out." I tell him that I couldn't sleep and that I had driven down to the South Shore. I then tell him about the hookers and the pimp and all about what I've seen.

Uncle Al now seems awake and says, "I'll call the vice crime unit and get them down there to check it out." Uncle Al then stops for a moment and sighs, "By the way, Chris, I know what you're up to so you better get out of there right now. These people are dangerous and they will kill you no sooner than look at you."

I am a bit puzzled by what Uncle Al just said and I ask him, "What do you mean; 'you know what I'm up to'?"

"You know what I mean, Chris. Out at 3 A.M…druggies…prostitutes…pimps…Tina! You're out looking for Tina. Let me tell you something, son …" Uncle Al only calls me "son" when he's serious, "…You don't want to be there even if Tina is with these scumbags. The minute they think she's a threat to their business; they'll kill her and leave her body parts throughout Jones Beach parking lot just to make a point."

"But I wasn't even thinking that this might be where Tina is. I swear I was just driving in my car."

"Well, that's good, now turn on the ignition, put it into drive and get the hell out of there. You hear me?"

I understand the wisdom of my uncle's advice, "Yeah, I hear you. Thanks, Unc, I love you."

"I have no idea why…God only knows…but I love you, too."

CHAPTER 13

I'm still sitting in the car, the keys are in the ignition, my hand is on the keys, but I don't start the engine. I guess, subconsciously, I could have been thinking about Tina and the possibility that she is in this area. It never actually crosses my mind until speaking with Uncle Al that I keep thinking about whether I should follow the two hookers and the pimp to their place of business. To say nothing of what should I do when I get there?

The police are coming, and I decide that if God and the saints are on my side, how can I lose…after all this is what I'm told is my purpose in life? So, I get out of the car, lock the doors, after all it is a bad neighborhood, and walk towards the alley. The alley is a long, dark walkway with holes in the blacktop and garbage all over. I stay close to the wall on the right side of the alley as I make my way down. I can see no light from within the doorways that line the alley and all the windows, covered with iron bars are dark, too.

I am about to turn back, thinking the group had gone through the building and out another exit. As I start to walk away, I hear the squeak of rusted hinges from a metal door that leads to the alley and two men exit.

I look around for a place to hide and I find a small dumpster. It stinks of spoiled food and rancid grease. I nearly gag because the smell is so sickening, but it seems preferable to getting my throat slashed, so I crouch down and try to hear what they're saying. One of the two men at the door lights a cigarette and begins talking in Spanish to the other man standing alongside him. I speak Italian and took high school Spanish, so I'm able to get some of the meaning in the conversation,

> Man 1: "Why (unintelligible) hit (unintelligible). She's a top earner and when (unintelligible) about this he'll slit (unintelligible) throat."

> Man 2: "How can I get (unintelligible) shit all over me. She (unintelligible) big problem for a (unintelligible) her out."

> Man 1: "(Unintelligible) my friend, it is you (unintelligible) the problem."

The conversation continues for a few minutes with both men saying much of the same thing. One recurring part of their talk is a reference to someone who must be the leader of their gang. It seems they both are afraid of the man and of what might happen. After the one guy is finishes his cigarette, he drops it on the ground, crushes it with his shoe and they both go back inside.

I get up from my hiding place behind the dumpster and sneak over to the door where the two men had been talking. I try the doorknob while whispering to myself, "You must be the biggest asshole in the world to try to go inside and see what's going on. Are you some kind of idiot? Uncle Al is going to kill you if those guys don't kill you first". I say all this to myself believing that the door is locked, but as luck would have it, the door is opened. I remember the sound of made by the squeaking rusty metal hinges, so I slowly turn the knob and carefully open the door. The last thing I want is to make any loud noise that could possibly bring these dirt bags out of their hole.

With to door open enough for me to squeeze through, I see that the door opens into a small space lit by only by a single 30-watt bulb. It's still too dark and I am unable to see who's in the rooms beyond the entryway.

I slowly close the outer door, but leave it slightly ajar so I can make a quick run for it if I have to. As I make my way down a short hallway, I hear murmurs of people talking in one of the rooms ahead and I slowly make my way towards where a conversation is taking place. I find a walkway between the rooms where there is a large pile of cartons on one side of the entrance. I hide behind them and peak out of a space between the boxes so that I can see what's going on in the next room.

I can clearly make out the voices of one of the two men from the alley and one of the girls. The girl is sitting on a half-broken chair speaking to one of the men that from the alley. The girl who looks like she couldn't be more than 15 years old and apparently a hooker, starts screaming, "Look what you did to my face! My jaw is swollen! My lip is cut! Who's going to want me now? You're a piece of shit; you know that, a piece of shit!"

The man answers in a calm voice, "Listen baby, the only reason I hurt you is because you don't respect me. How can I do my job without the respect of you all?"

The girl curses the man and then she begins to cry uncontrollably. I sit watching this and getting angry at the way this girl has been savaged by violence and drugs.

The pimp is showing no signs of pity as he continues to speak in a calm voice. "You see baby, you call me a piece of shit and then I can't get no respect from the other girls. I tell you it ain't right. You got to know who is in charge here. Now baby, let me make it up to you, I got something you want."

He reaches into his pocket and pulls out a dirty syringe. The pimp takes a spoon and a vial of something, pouring the contents of the vial into the spoon and starts to heat it up with a cigarette lighter. The contents go from solid to liquid in just about a minute, and he fills the filthy syringe with the fluid. The young girl, who has been sobbing, now is just whimpering as she stares at the needle.

"Please, I need it. I need it."

"No problem, you'll get it, but I gotta know."

The poor girl is now becoming frantic, "Please, I need it now. Please, Ernesto!"

Ernesto is taking perverted pleasure out of baiting the young girl, "You get what you need when I get what I want."

"Please…please…" she is pleading and on the verge of hysteria.

"Come on baby, what do you say to me? Come on, say it."

She says, "I'm sorry."

"Now baby, it don't sound to me like you mean it."

She tries to sound sincere, "I mean it Ernesto, I'm very sorry."

Ernesto holds up the syringe and the young girl look longingly at the needle and says to her, "Baby, this is really good stuff and I know that you need it, but I'm not hearing that you're really sorry."

Now the girl is close to groveling, "Please, I'm really sorry that I didn't respect you, Ernesto. I mean it, I'm really very, very sorry for causing you trouble."

"Well, that is much better baby. See it don't take much to please me. Now come here baby and let me make you happy."

With that, the girl gets up from her chair and unsteadily begins walking towards Ernesto. He has a big smile on his face as he holds out the syringe. Just as she reaches out, he pulls the needle back and starts to laugh. He holds it out to her again, and again she reaches out, but at the last second, he pulls it back. Ernesto keeps doing this, laughing every time she tries to grab the needle. The poor girl starts to cry as she slumps onto the floor while Ernesto keeps laughing at the poor young hooker's sorry state.

While I'm deciding what I should do, the decision is made for me. I feel the tip of a knife press against my throat and, as I slowly turn, I am facing a short Hispanic man whose arms and neck are covered in tattoos.

He yells out, anger filling his voice, "Ernesto!"

Upon hearing the voice, Ernesto looks up from the girl on the floor and he goes pale. The syringe falls out of his hand, and it's immediately picked up by the girl. She takes the needle, plunges it into her arm and crawls over to the couch where she crumples into a ball of human misery.

You can hear the fear in Ernesto's voice as he asks, "Heriberto, what are you doing here? I thought you were at the warehouse. What's going on?"

Heriberto presses the knife a little harder on my throat. He is close to drawing blood as says to me, "Get up now."

I'm on my knees, but I get up into a standing position and Heriberto pushes me out from behind the boxes into the room.

Ernesto is as shocked as I am scared. "What…who the hell is this?"

Heriberto looks at Ernesto with contempt in his eyes, "He's the cabrón who snuck in here while you were fucking off."

"Heriberto, I swear that I was…" Ernesto stops because he knows that he's in trouble and lying will only make it worse.

Heriberto pushes me into the room, and I trip on the legs of a chair falling onto a stained rug that covers the floor. This is possibly the worst situation that could have happened. What have I done? Uncle Al was right; somehow my desire to find Tina clouded my judgment and now I'm staring up at a man named Heriberto that could be the same guy Uncle Al told me about. I figure that there's a good chance he could have Tina and she could be somewhere nearby maybe even in this same place.

Heriberto looks over to the couch and asks Ernesto, "What have you done to my property?"

"Heriberto, she was giving me a hard time. She stole money from me and I needed to get her straight and…" but Heriberto cut him off.

"You needed to get her straight? My property—and you needed to get her straight?"

"But she gave me no respect; I can't let her get away with that shit."

Heriberto's face changes to something bordering on ager like I have never seen before. He walks over to Ernesto and within six inches of his face, he says, in the most menacing tone I have ever heard,

"You have to earn respect." And in an instant, Heriberto flings open his knife and plunges it twice into Ernesto. Ernesto stares at the knife and the blood coming out of his chest and stomach and he falls to the floor, dead. My mind is spinning because I've witnessed a murder and I am now in the middle of a situation that I am sure I can never get out of.

"Manulo! Do you hear me, Manulo? Get the fuck in here now!" A few seconds later, the other man that was in the alley with Ernesto comes running in and he, looks down at the dead man and stops in his tracks.

"Heriberto, what happened?"

"Ernesto and I had a little difference about the meaning of respect. I won the argument. Now I want you and Julio to get rid of him. Do you understand? NOW!"

"Sure…sure. I get Julio and we'll…" Manulo's voice trails off and he hurries out of the room.

Heriberto turns towards the unconscious hooker lying on the couch. He shakes her hard, then harder, then violently, but the girl won't or can't wake up. "Puta!" he shouts at her, but he gets no answer and he turns to me. Heriberto still has the knife in his hand as he takes three steps to where I lay on the floor.

He is standing over me and says, "Get up."

I don't have much of a choice, and even though I am a good six inches taller, Heriberto looks like a giant with a switch blade in his hand. I boost myself off the floor and stand in front of this man, the man who committed murder right in from of me.

Heriberto is staring down at Ernesto's body and says, "Ernesto was a good friend of mine. Did you know that?"

Like a jerk I answer, "No, I didn't."

"What the fuck! Who asked you?"

He turns to me and continues his intense, penetrating stare, so now I think it will be better just to keep quiet. My mind is racing, trying to think of what I should do next. I guess I could try to jump Heriberto, but he is so fast with the knife that I know I wouldn't have a chance; just ask Ernesto. I'm beginning to panic, but just when I think I have no chance left to live, Manulo and Julio enter the room.

Still staring at the dead body of Ernest, Manulo says, "We are here to take him out to the van."

"Well, get him the fuck out of here. What do you want, my permission? And you better not get any blood on the floor of the van, do you understand?"

"Sure, Heriberto, sure we understand. We'll wrap him in an old blanket." Julio and Manulo throw and old blanket over Ernesto and drag his body out to the hall toward the door to the alley.

There is total silence in the room when Heriberto finally speaks, "I think I'll introduce you to Juliano, eh? I think you will like him. Well, do you want to meet Juliano?"

I don't know what to say for fear of making him angry again, so I only say, "Yes." I figure that it would buy me some time in hopes that Uncle Al calls the police and they are on their way.

"Oh yes, I am sure you will like Juliano and he will like you." A big smile comes over Heriberto's face and he chuckles. "He will ask you many questions about things like life, death, food, perhaps even why you are here."

Heriberto asks with mock puzzlement, "Why are you here?"

I don't know what to say, but I know I have to come up with something. "I hear that you have young girls here, and I want to…" with that, he takes his fist and slams it across my face. The punch is so powerful that it knocks me off my feet.

"You want young girls! You've got some cojones. How do I know you're not a cop or someone's big brother looking for their sweet little cono?"

My face is badly bruised and it begins to throb. I think that he may have given me a black eye because that begins to hurt, too.

An insane look comes over Heriberto and he screams, "Do you know who I am? I AM HERIBERTO QUINTANA and I will bring down all the forces of hell on you. DO YOU KNOW WHO I AM?"

He could be screaming at me, or just at the world, but I remain down on the floor waiting for things to calm down. Manulo and Julio come back in the room and look at me on the floor and then back to Heriberto. Both men have blood all over their hands and shirts from dragging Ernesto to the van.

"We got him into the van, and we're going to dump him in the canal."

"Wait, I want you to take this ojete upstairs. Put him in the room at the end of the hallway. We are going to have a party later and Juliano is coming with some gifts. What do you think ojete, do you want to party with Juliano? Answer me, you piece of shit."

All I can say is "Yes."

"Oh, I'm so glad because the last thing you want to do is make Juliano sad that you will not party with him."

Manulo and Julio smile at this as they empty my pockets of car keys, wallet, pocket change and all. They both grab me by the arms and start to drag me up a flight of stairs. The building is a real dung heap and I hear the crunch of vials and other garbage that crush under my feet. The men take me down a dark hallway with doors on both sides, a few are open and some closed. I try to look inside the doors that are open to the rooms and I see some unfortunate young girls and boys; kids really. They're just lying on filthy beds, fast asleep probably due to their drug induced states.

We reach the end of the hallway when Manulo lets go of my arm to open the door to the room Heriberto told them to take me. As he reaches for the knob, I look over to my right shoulder and I see Tina. She's in the exact same room that St. Agatha had shown me in her vision. Tina appears unconscious, but I know that she is probably drugged and is in no position to help herself, so I can forget about her helping me.

Manulo opens the door and they both throw me into a dark space that is no cleaner than any of the other rooms that I've seen. They lock the door and leave. As I lay on the floor, a rat passes over my legs. I jump up and run to a corner of the room where I hope there are no other rats, roaches or any other vermin. I'm in some pain from the punch and in confusion over the circumstance that I find myself in when I receive a vision.

The world stops and my rat and roach infested prison is transformed to a large house that is located in a small town in the province of northern Galilee. I am in the home of someone who appears to be very wealthy and all those present in the room are looking at the woman supplicating to Christ.

She is very beautiful and very proud, this young woman kneeling at the feet of Christ. In life she's a sinner and her sorrow for what she has done knows no bounds. It is like a ponderous weight on her soul and as she kneels at the feet of Christ, her tears flow. She wishes, she pleads for His forgiveness and anoints His feet with oil.

Christ is filled with such compassion for the woman that He lays hands on her head. In an instant, the seven demons that have tortured her poor mind and body are exorcised. The vision evaporates and with it, the form of St. Mary Magdalene steps out of the place and speaks to me, "You must look to save this girl. Like the Lord struck the demons from me, He will strike the sickness from her and you will be His resource."

I have no idea how can I save Tina? I am a prisoner myself, and even if I did get to her room, how would I get her out of the building? I am also thinking of Juliano; who is this man and what will he do to me?

I know I don't have much time, so I ask St. Mary Magdalene, "What can I do? I am a prisoner myself. Tina is unconscious, she could be drugged and she may have been raped. How can I do this by myself? I need your help. Please, help me, show me the way." The vision continues,

Christ stands before all. Mary and the assembled look at the man from Galilee in solemn reverence and Christ speaks, "Many sins are forgiven her because she has loved very much." Then he turns to Mary and He says kindly, "Your faith has made you safe; go in peace."

St. Mary Magdalene speaks to me, "Can you understand that if the Lord could forgive the worst of sinners, He can forgive us all?" The Sainted looks over to Tina lying in bed and says, "She is loved and you will find a way so she can be saved. It is our Lord's will and His will be done."

I am overwhelmed by the vision of Jesus Christ Himself. I am trying to fathom what I have seen, what the words meant and why I am so privileged. I am deep in thought when the vision of St. Mary Magdalene vanishes and the door to the room crashes open. I am startled by the noise and look up. Heriberto walks into the room first and then followed by a well-dressed and very handsome looking man that I assume is Juliano.

Heriberto is the first to speak: "Ah, we hope you are enjoying your stay with us. Juliano is here as I promised, and we want to be sure you are comfortable." As he says this, the gang leader looks down and smashes his foot down onto the head of a rat that is crossing the floor.

The rat explodes into a mass of guts, brain and blood and Heriberto yells, "Mire lo que le hizo a mi pantalón!"

Juliano speaks for the first time, "Now, Heriberto, don't worry about your pants. It seems that you are making our friend nervous."

With an exaggerated bow, Heriberto says, "Oh, please excuse me. I didn't realize I make you so nervous. I wouldn't want you to feel unwelcome." His voice makes my skin crawl. I need to try and make some kind of effort, so that they won't harm me so I plead with them both, "Please listen I didn't mean to sneak in like I did, I'm very sorry! I only wanted to find some action. Please, you've got to believe me, I didn't see anything and I promise I won't tell anyone. Just let me go, please let me go!"

Juliano smiles, "Of course we'll let you go, but I understand our friend Heriberto promised you a party. I love parties, don't you?"

I continue to plead to Juliano, "All I wanted was some action. I promise I won't say a word to anyone, please, just let me go."

"I wouldn't dream of letting you go before we have our party and I will be sure you get all the…what did he call it Heriberto?"

Heriberto smiles, "Action."

"Action, that's it, action! I will be sure you get all the action you want."

The horror of my situation is growing, and it is apparent that Juliano and Heriberto have no intentions of letting me go; in fact, I believe they have great torments in mind before they kill me.

Juliano continues to smile at me as he asks Heriberto, "Heriberto, what do you say, I think it's about time we introduce our guest to some of our protégés, don't you?"

"Yes, that's a good idea; after all, that is what he came for." He turns to me and says, "Come my friend, I want to introduce you to a new arrival."

With that, Juliano motions to Manulo and Julio as they enter the room. Manulo ties my hands behind my back and both men grab me by the arms and lead me out of the room. I don't have far to walk when they push me into Tina's room. I am surrounded by the four men and, as commanded, they stand me at the edge of her bed.

Heriberto begins to taunt me. "The little puta is just waiting for you. I hope your cock gets good and hard because she likes it up the ass."

Juliano mockingly scolds Heriberto, "Now, don't be so crude Heriberto, our friend, what is his name? Oh, yes, it's here on his license, Christopher Pella, says he wants some action and, yes, we did promise him a party, didn't we? Oh, and Christopher, today is your lucky day as it is within our power to accommodate your desires, is it not Heriberto?

Heriberto smiles, "Si, we can give him what he wants."

Juliano then turns to Manulo and Julio and says, "Boys, if you would please leave the room, I am sure our guest would like some privacy." Both men turn and leave the room and I am alone with Juliano and Heriberto.

Juliano's look turns serious as he tells me, "Oh Christopher, there is one thing I failed to mention. After this is over, we will need to have a real heart to heart talk. It isn't at all good of you to sneak into our home and disturb our tranquility. Heriberto was so upset that he had to kill poor Ernesto. I feel that in all good conscience, someone will need to take responsibility. In the meantime, consider this our gift to you."

Tina is lying there, still unconscious as Heriberto pushes me onto her bed. He begins to unbuckle my pants. I kick and yell at him to stop. He just laughs at the position I am in as continues to try to take down my pants. It is then we all hear a commotion coming from the room on the floor below.

It is a muffled sound that I can just barely hear, but I try to concentrate. It seems I can make out the words, "Police, drop your weapons and put your hands on your head!"

I hear gun shots and screaming and a scuffle of some sort. I recognize the loud voices of Manulo and Julio who must be in the midst of all this. Juliano looks unconcerned as he turns to Heriberto. "Would you please go downstairs and see what the fuss is all about. I'll wait here with our guest until you return." Heriberto pulls a gun from under his shirt, checks to see if it is loaded and leaves the room.

Now Juliano and I are alone, except for the unconscious Tina. Juliano looks at me with a cold, hard smile and he starts to pace along the front of the room. "I do believe that the authorities have found our little home away from home, don't you think? It's seeming a real shame, I just love what they've done to the place, oh well, c'est la vie."

I struggle on the bed, trying to get free of the restraints that have my hands tied behind my back. As I struggle, I spit out my reply to Juliano, "I think you're a fucking lunatic, and in about two minutes, you're going to find out what the word 'payback 'means. Look what you've done to Tina, just look at her." For the first time since I was caught by Heriberto, I am thinking that I just might get out of this.

Juliano's voice drips with sarcasm as he says, "Oh my word, such anger and all I did is give you what you want. You are most ungrateful, Christopher. I am sure Tina would have loved you to be her first, shall we say, experience."

I begin to yell out to the police downstairs, "Hey! Come upstairs! I'm here with a lunatic who kidnaps kids and gets them hooked on drugs!" I kind of sound like a poster child for Americans against Perverts, or some such group, but I scream it out anyway.

I then hear the more gunshots and screams of pain coming from some of the people downstairs. Some of the screams seem to be in Spanish, so I assume that the police have the upper hand and Manulo and Julio are out of commission. Juliano is just standing there, looking at me and smiling as I try to get myself up and off the bed.

Juliano continues staring at me, "I know who you are."

"What … well, bully for you asshole, you've got my license."

The smile leaves Juliano's face, "I know who you are, what you are and what you do. I know you came for this pitiful creature."

At first, I don't understand what Juliano is talking about, but I immediately become startled when I realize what he could be talking about. I think that he can't possibly know about my coming for Tina. How can he know about my secrets? No one knows about my gift, my visions and my saints.

Juliano explains as he continues pacing the floor of Tina's room. "You think you can stop me with your pathetic, little visions? You do not know the real power, the real power of genuine evil."

I look Juliano straight in the eye and say, "I may not know the real power of evil, but I do know the real power of goodness."

Juliano sneers and chuckles, "Very clever Christopher, you may want to tweet that out if you ever get out of here alive." Juliano' face and demeanor abruptly change to reveal a dark and frightening countenance, "But you have never had to face ultimate evil, and I will delight in helping you understand its true meaning."

I have no response to this madness except for the next vision.

Tina's room now becomes transformed and Juliano and I are transported to the holiest of places. We are in a cave; a crypt and St. Mary Magdalene is on the floor and she is weeping. Once Juliano sees where he has been taken, stops pacing and becomes visibly frightened, "What have you done to bring me to such a place?" He seems to ask the question to no one in particular.

St. Mary Magdalene's spirit rises out of her prostrate self and stands before Juliano, speaking directly to him, "The Lord is risen and it is an abomination that you are even able to see His empty tomb."

Juliano looks at her and then turns to me and says, "Beware, for I am the Beast." He then totally transforms himself into a demon so hideous that I immediately recoil from the horror.

St. Mary stares him straight in the eye as she begins to pray: "Our Father who art in heaven, hallowed by Thy name. Thy kingdom come, Thy will be done …" and before The Lord's Prayer is finished, Juliano shrieks in rage and vanishes.

St. Mary looks at me and says, "The young girl is troubled, but let her know that she is loved. As Christ loves us all, He loves her and she will find peace. Her family loves her and she will know happiness in their care." St. Mary Magdalene smiles at me and disappears.

CHAPTER 14

I am back in the room on the bed, lying next to Tina. Juliano is nowhere to be seen and I am sure he has returned to the hell he came from. I start to scream hoping that the police will hear me. "Help us…Help us…we're upstairs! There's a young kid, and she's hurt, help us!" I scream at the top of my lungs. A team of police officers run into the room, guns in hand, ready for the worst. As they see me lying on the bed, they don't realize that my hands are tied because they look at me with utter revulsion.

"Stay where you are, you piece of shit! Keep your hands behind your back, and don't move." It seems that I have been called a piece of shit more times in one day than ever before.

As my hands are still tied, I have little choice, but I try to get up anyway. I try to explain, "Please, help me. Tina needs help and my hands are tied."

One of the cops say, "I said stay where you are, and don't speak."

Another one of the officers come to the side of the bed where I'm lying down and says, "What are you doing here? Are you one of the pieces of shit that prey on these young kids?" Again, I 'm called a piece of shit but I know he's angry, but I need to try and explain why I am in this place.

I speak in rapid-fire, "My name is Chris Pella and this is Tina Staley. She is the granddaughter of one of my friends, Fred Klein. I was trying to find her and I got caught by the scumbags that run this place. You can ask my uncle, Al Barese, he's the chief…"

The cop cuts me off: "You know Chief Barese?"

I tell the police, "I do! He's my uncle, my mom's younger brother, and he can vouch for me. I swear it's all the truth, just ask him."

The cop goes silent: "He's here now."

"That's great; you can go and ask him right now. He'll let you know that I'm telling the

truth."

The cop just looks at me and says, "He was part of the fire fight and he's been shot. It looks pretty serious and there's an ambulance on its way."

I feel like I'm in shock, "Uncle Al, shot?" What had I done?"

The man, who is like a father to me, is lying on a filthy floor in some drug-infested slum and I am responsible. I start to choke up. The police officer sees that I am so upset that he comes over and unties my hands.

"Can I see him? I need to see him."

The policeman says, "He's downstairs with the medic, just follow me and I'll take you to your uncle."

As he unties my hands and helps me to stand, I ask, "Can someone please help Tina and the other kids here? They've been beaten, drugged and molested, please can someone help them."

"Sure, we've already called the hospital and child services. They will be coming here to take charge of these kids."

We leave the room as Officer Terry Ray starts to lead me down the long hallway towards the stairway. As we walk toward the stairs, I see a number of the policemen and women looking in the rooms where the young kids are just lying there in really bad shape.

I ask Officer Ray, "What happened to Heriberto Quintana? He is the one who runs this place and he and his gang give the kids drugs. He also murdered some guy named Ernesto. I don't know his last name, but Quintana stabbed him right in front of me."

The officer looks at me and says, "You've had some night. I don't think you'll have to worry about Quintana anymore. It seems Quintana came into the room and began firing and he was the one who shot Chief Barese, but before he could get another shot off; your uncle used him for target practice." I think the officer wanted to try and tell me that my uncle is a hero. "He's something else, your Uncle Al."

All I could say is, "He sure is."

Officer Ray also lets me know, "You should be aware that your uncle is the one who called and told us about these parasites and to be sure we came with back up as he knew it could get violent. As a matter of fact, he was here before we arrived." I thought to myself that Uncle Al must have suspected that I wouldn't go home and that I would be in danger. Like I've told you before, I always feel safer when he is around.

As I enter the room, I see the body of Heriberto Quintana lying on the floor. His eyes are wide open. He is dead. There are police all over the place keeping order and there are other people in white coats taking care of the wounded while some of the other police officers are looking for any evidence. I look over to the couch and see the poor hooker, the young girl who had been beaten by Ernesto. She is lying face down on the couch, and she is bleeding from a wound near her neck.

"What happened to that poor girl? Is she dead?"

"I'm afraid she is. During the firefight she got up off the couch and staggered in front of Quintana and he shot her. Did you know her?"

I want to answer, but the next thing I see is Uncle Al lying on the floor. He is lying there, bleeding from a very serious wound to his shoulder, just above his heart. My body and mind begin to tremble at the site. I am standing over the guy who asked my father what his intentions were towards his sister, my mother, before they got married. It is a hilarious story and became a legendary tale in our family. Lying here is the bravest man I know, a man who embodies the essence of doing what is right and proving it every day. Here is the guy who loves me like a son and here he is dying because of me.

I fall to the floor, kneeling beside him and I start to cry. I am thinking; what would I do without him? I grab hold of his hand and grip it tightly while he is being administered to by a medic who is kneeling on the opposite side.

"Uncle Al, it's me, Chris. Can you hear me?" I need to hear his voice and have him know that I am there. The medic who is working on his wounds looks up and says, "Are you okay? Your face is badly bruised and it looks like you've got a pretty big black eye. Do you need help?"

I'm look up from staring down at my uncle, "No, no I don't. Chief Barese, my uncle, how's he doing? Is he going to be okay?'

"Chief Barese has lost a lot of blood and he's unconscious. He's been very seriously wounded and I'm trying to stem the flow of blood. He's lost a lot of blood already and there is little more I can do here. The ambulance is on its way and he'll need to be taken to the Emergency Room at Huntington Hospital where they will determine his condition and chances for survival."

Chances for survival? I couldn't fathom the meaning of those words because I can't imagine life without him. It almost didn't matter that he can't hear me because I need to tell him everything that is on my mind and in my heart.

"Uncle Al, I love you. I am so sorry that I didn't listen to you and leave this to the police. Please forgive me, please don't die, what will I do without you around? I need to know you will always be there for me. Who will I spend Christmas with? Who will yell at me for waking you up at 3 A.M.? Who will pay for our dinners every month? You can't leave me; we have so much more to do together."

There is frenzied activity all around, but all that matters to me is Uncle Al and I am helpless to do anything for him. In an instant, all the people in the room seem to freeze in time except for Uncle Al and me. I look up to one of the most glorious sights I have ever experienced.

St. Michael the Archangel is floating above me. He is surrounded by a brilliant, white light. He hovers in the space just below the ceiling. Michael the Archangel holds a sword in his right hand and he is carrying a shield on his left arm that is inscribed with the legend, "Quis Ut Deus," which is Latin for "Who is like God."

Uncle Al is still unconscious and although I am aware of all that was happening, I can't move. My whole body feels weighed down as I watch in wonder. Then we are both transported to a place in the ancient Near East. It is a sacred place, the Michaelion at Chalcedon, built by Emperor Constantine in the fourth century. Constantine had built this sanctuary to honor this as a sacred place in veneration to St. Michael, the prince of angels, and his powers heal the wounds of the faithful who come to pray.

In the Michaelion, there is a clear pool fed by a spring where Michael the Archangel hovers above the water. I watch as St. Michael dips his shield into the spring and it fills with the healing waters from the pool. It is then that my body becomes weightless and I float up until I'm there, face-to-face, with the Archangel. He motions me to hold out my hands and, when I do, he fills my cupped hands with water from his shield.

I stare down at my hands and look up at St. Michael. Words would not come, and all I could say is, "Thank you."

I float back down to where I am kneeling next to Uncle Al. I instinctively know what to do. I take the water and pour it from my hands onto his wound. When I finish, I look up to see St. Michael surrounded by the Heavenly Host of Angels and in one massive exodus, they fly towards the light.

In an instant I am back in the present kneeling alongside Uncle Al. The people in the rooms continue going about their tasks and the medic looks up at me in the state of shock and says, "What the hell? This is the strangest thing that has ever happened…"

Then something incredible takes place, Uncle Al looks up at me and says, "When I get out of the hospital, I'm gonna strangle you!"

I can't believe it—well, actually I can. I look down at Uncle Al and smile at him through tears of joy, saying, "How could you strangle your favorite nephew?"

"Favorite nephew? Leo's my favorite nephew" and he smiles back. The medic still seems to be in shock as he states what is apparent to him, "He was nearly dead just a minute ago. What the hell just happened? I've never seen anything like it."

I try to change the subject knowing he could never understand and I tell him, "Maybe it wasn't as serious as you initially thought."

Still incredulous, the medic is totally baffled when he says, "Are you kidding? The gunshot wound nearly severed his shoulder. I just can't believe it; one minute he's bleeding like a sieve, his blood pressure is dropping like a rock, he's unconscious—and the next thing he stops bleeding and now he's making jokes with you. This can't be; it's impossible."

I am relieved beyond words and I tell the medic, "Well, all I know is that you got him back and that's all I care about." But all the medic could do is to shake his head and look bewildered while he continues to bandage Uncle Al.

As all this is going on, the ambulance arrives and the EMS team starts to evaluate his condition. Once that is done, they load Uncle Al onto the stretcher, hook him up to the I.V. and wheel him out. He looks very weak, but he's alive.

I'm right beside him, holding his hand when he says, "What happened in there Chris, what happened to me?"

I tell him, "We found her Unc! We got her out! We got Tina and some other girls and boys that were being held in this rat hole. They are being cared for by the medics and child services."

"I mean what happened in there?"

"Oh, you were shot by Quintana, Heriberto Quintana. You remember, he's the scumbag that you identified from the gibberish I gave you, you know, Quintianus. He killed a low life gang member and a poor young girl who was strung out. There was a gun fight and you were able to shoot him before he killed anyone else."

"Chris, I mean what really happened? I've seen enough bloodshed to know that I was a goner and I need to know. I mean to me; what happened to me?"

"What does it matter? All that matters now is that you are getting help and they are taking you to the hospital. I am just so thankful that you are alive and you will be fine."

"Chris, I have to know the truth. I don't know what happened to heal wound as serious as mine, but it wasn't some iodine and a *'Finding Nemo'* bandage. Why do I have this nagging suspicion that you know something about all this that you're not telling me?"

I look down at Uncle Al and he is looking back up at me with those piercing brown eyes. Even though he is in a weakened state, he knows a lot about telling the truth and he knows I promised never to lie to him again. As we get closer to the ambulance I say to him, "Listen, this isn't the time or place to speak. They won't let me ride in the ambulance, so I'll follow you back to the hospital. When they allow me into your room, we can talk, how's that?"

"Okay, but remember your promise and remember I can tell when you are lying."

"I'll remember. I love you."

"I love you too!"

CHAPTER 15

I look all around the room where Heriberto killed Ernesto for my wallet and car keys. I finally find them and I run out of the building towards my car. When I get there, I find the trunk lock jimmied and my spare tire, some tools and a beach blanket are missing. I smile and think; so much for locking the car. Who cares, I am elated knowing that because of St. Michael and his miracle, Uncle Al is going to be fine, and that is all that matters to me. I start my car and I think to myself, thank God they didn't steal the engine and I drive north on Route 110 towards Huntington Hospital. It's pretty far from where Uncle Al got shot, but I was told that they have an excellent trauma unit and the doctors and nurses are very familiar with treating all sorts of serious injuries.

As the ambulance pulls into the parking lot outside the Emergency Room, the medics open the back door and rush my uncle into the care of the waiting physicians. I make sure to drive close behind the ambulance, and I arrive less than a minute later. I run up to the nurse's station in the ER and say, "Hi, I'm Chris Pella, Al Barese's nephew. I know that he just got here, but is there any news about his condition and what is being done? He was shot and it looks very serious. Is there any word from the doctor yet?" The nurse senses that I am very nervous and rambling on, so she tries to assure me that Uncle Al is in good hands and getting the best treatment possible.

"Dr. Scanlon is the attending Emergency Room physician. He and his staff have years of experience with cases of serious trauma wounds, very much like Chief Barese's. I know you are worried, but I want to assure you that your uncle is in the best of hands." She smiles a smile that can only come from years of practice and I thank her and sit down in the nearly empty waiting area. After about an hour, I hear someone call my name. It's a doctor who is looking around the waiting room, he stops when he sees me looking up with an anxious look on my battered face and black eye.

He asks, "Mr. Pella? Are you Mr. Christopher Pella?"

"I am and please, call me Chris. Do you have any news about Chief Barese? I'm his nephew, a family member, you can tell me about his condition, right?" I feel that I need to say I'm family because of what happened when Fred was admitted to the hospital and they were not permitted to release patient information to anyone but family members.

"My name is Dr. Richard Scanlon and there is something I have to tell you."

Now I'm getting nervous, "Doctor, how's my uncle is he okay? Please doctor; don't hold back I need to know if he's going to make it."

Dr. Scanlon seems to be in a state of total disbelief when he tells me, "I've been practicing for nearly 30 years, but with what happened to your uncle, and from what we can determine now, he is about the luckiest man alive."

I want to jump for joy, but I need to know, "What do you mean?"

Dr. Scanlon explains, "Well, in all my years I've never seen a wound as large and potentially life threatening begin to close up and heal so fast. His recovery is truly miraculous. The entire staff is looking at your uncle as some kind of super hero."

I get serious for moment when I let the doctor in on something. "Well, we do refer to him as 'Ball Breaker Man,' but that's just among our family and friends." I think it's important for the doctor to know this.

The doctor laughs and then says that they are performing some more tests, but it will be at least another couple of hours before I can see him. I thank the doctor and I ask him to thank his staff for their work. Dr. Scanlon walks away, and I sit back down in my chair for the long wait.

When I look up at the clock in the waiting room, I see it's 9:12A.M. I remember that Fred is in the same hospital and I want to bring him the good news about Tina. Visiting hours have started at 9 A.M.

I go to the front desk and I ask one of the senior citizen volunteers working there, "I'm here to visit Fred Klein. Can you please tell me his room?"

The woman checks the computer and says, "Well, let me see. Oh, here it is, he's in Room 497. You just take the North Elevator to the fourth floor and follow the signs." I thank her and I go up to see Fred. When I get to his room, I poke my head into the opened door and see Fred lying on the bed and he appears to be asleep. I don't want to disturb him, so I just stand outside waiting for him to wake up. As I am standing there, I must have looked like a lost soul because this nurse walks up behind me and says,

"I hope you didn't hurt that guy's fist when you smashed your face into it." She says this with the most appealing laugh I have ever heard. I turn to see a stunning young nurse standing there with a chart in her hand. She tilts her head and grins at me, "So what happened to you, Rocky? Do I need to call the doctor or the police?"

"Uh, I uh, I, what do you mean?" I stumble over my words because I have never met anyone so beautiful in my life.

"I mean why are you lurking in the hallway?"

"I uh, I'm here for Fred. I mean, I'm here to see Fred. I mean, I'm here to talk to Fred.

I'm his Fred—I mean friend."

She laughs says, "Maybe I should check the 'Wanted Posters' before I let you in to see Mr. Klein."

"Wanted Poster?"

Now she laughs again and tells me, "Just wait here. I'm going to check his vital signs and, if he's up to it, I'll let you see him, but only for a few minutes only. Understand?"

"I will…I mean, I do."

The nurse says, "You have a lot of trouble speaking, don't you?"

I reply seriously, "Not usually", and that's the truth.

Another smile and she walks into the room, closing the door. I am dumbfounded because when you consider what I've just been through,

Uncle Al and Fred both in the same hospital, and now I meet the most beautiful girl in the world; I figure I have earned the right to have a nice and peaceful nervous breakdown. As I am pondering a vacation in the psychiatric ward, the nurse opens the door to Fred's room,

"Okay Rocky, you can go in, but only for ten minutes. If you try to stay any longer or make him upset, I'm going to kick your ass, which seems to be pretty easy given the way you look."

Having regained some of my composure, I reply "My ass? Oh yes, my ass! I mean, thank you and if there is anyone who will be kicking my ass, I promise it will be you."

"Very good, now don't be too long. He needs his rest." She turns and begins to walk away when I say,

"By the way, what's your name, just in case I have to send you an invitation to kick my ass?"

She turns to me and says, "My name is Elizabeth. What's yours?"

"I'm Chris, I mean Christopher, Christopher Pella."

"Well, what is it, Chris or Christopher?"

"Everyone calls me Chris. Are you Elizabeth, Beth or Liz?"

"Everyone calls me Beth, Beth Della Russo, pleased to meet you." She holds out her hand, and I shake it.

Oh, my Lord—beautiful, smart and Italian. My mother must have something to do with this. "Well, it's a pleasure meeting you Beth Della Russo and thanks for talking good care of my friend. He's been through a lot."

She gives me a curious look and walks away.

I turn the knob on Fred's door and look inside. He is lying on the bed, eyes open with that same hopeless look I saw on his face when I went to his home. I walk into the room and stand in front of his bed, "Hey Fred, how're you doing?"

He looks up at me and doesn't answer.

I start to smile, "I've got some really good news for you."

"What news can be good except that you found Tina?"

"Well, that's it Fred, we found Tina! We found her!"

If ever there was a person that completely transformed in an instant, it's Fred. His eyes go wide and he pushes the switch that lifts his hospital bed up so he can better see me. "What?

What did you say? Mother of God, did you say you found Tina?"

"I did Fred, that's exactly what I said!"

"My beautiful baby, my love, you found my granddaughter?"

"That's right Fred! We found her!"

Now Fred starts to yell and screaming with tears running down his face. So, I join in because this kind of happiness is contagious.

Once Beth hears the commotion coming from Fred's room, she bursts open the door to the room. She looks at Fred and looks at me, and I could see that she's getting angry. "What the hell is going on? Didn't I tell you not to get him upset? Now you get hell out of here!"

Fred immediately interrupts, "No, no, this is wonderful news. This man gave me the greatest gift I could ask for."

Beth is still angry when she says to Fred, "What do you mean?"

Fred tells her, "He found my Tina! He found my granddaughter!"

Beth now looks at me, only slightly less suspicious than before, and she says, "Okay Rocky, what the hell is going on?"

As serious as I can be I tell Beth, "Listen, I was going to tell Fred all that happened to Tina. It's a pretty frightening story, and I'm not sure if Fred wants me to tell him in private, given all the sordid details, so I'll leave it up to him I he wants to hear what I have to say alone not. What do you say Fred?"

Fred looks at me and says in as somber a voice as I've heard him speak, "You found my Tina, I thank the Lord, you found her. I will need to know what happened to her and Beth can listen to what you have to tell me if she wants to. I don't want you to hold back anything Chris because if I have to help Tina, I need to know." It is a very brave statement coming from this man. He has to listen to the depravity and degradation inflicted on his granddaughter whom he loves very much. Beth has continues staring at me very hard, but her look seems to soften as I begin to tell my story.

I first turn to Beth as I need to give her background into what has happened. I tell her, "Fred is my friend and his granddaughter, Tina, was having a hard time dealing with her parents' divorce. She would rebel and stay away from home and lately she became a source of great worry to them. When Fred heard Tina went missing, he became despondent, I tried to help him so I called my uncle. He's the Chief of Detectives in Suffolk County and he set up a special team to investigate Tina disappearance."

I then go into the complete details of Tina's nightmare. I tell Fred and Tina about the drugs, the kids becoming hookers, the filth they had to live in, the pimps who brutalized them and the murder I witnessed. I also tell both Fred and Beth of my capture by the drug dealers and of my Uncle Al and his investigation. I tell them how he called the police and how he got shot killing the bastard who would have ruined Tina. I didn't mention Juliano; how could I explain this demon, this consummate evil? However, I did tell them about Heriberto Quintana, Ernesto, Manulo and Julio and how they will never bother these kids again.

For nearly half an hour Fred and Beth sit there and listening in silence. I end by telling Fred, "Tina is being taken to the hospital where she will receive the best of care. She is lucky that when these dirt bags kidnapped her, they hadn't had the time to hook her on drugs, but some of the other kids are far less fortunate."

Fred has tears in his eyes, "Chris, come over here." I go to the side of his bed and he reaches across and hugs me. It is one of the most emotional encounters of my life.

I whisper in Fred's ear, "It's over, Fred. The nightmare is over. Tina has family who loves her, and that love and support will get her through this. She needs you and you need to get better because you are her rock."

Fred is anxious and asks me, "When do you think I'll be able to see Tina?"

"I really have no idea, Fred."

I turn to Beth and ask her, "Beth, do you think that you can find this out for Fred? I know it will give him great comfort"

Beth looks at me and then turns to Fred, "I'll see what I can find out."

Fred wipes his eyes and asks, "How can I ever thank you Chris?"

I smile at my friend and say, "You can thank me by getting better for yours and for Tina's sake. Can you do that for me?"

"I can and I will." After hearing all that I said, Fred collapses back into the hospital bed, exhausted, but delighted, and falls asleep almost immediately.

Beth touches my shoulder and whispers, "Come on, Rambo. We need to leave Fred to get some rest." I smile at her and we leave the room.

Outside in the hallway, Beth speaks first, "That's some story, Christopher Pella. You really made a difference in both of their lives. I don't know if I should have been listening, but I'm glad I did. You're quite a guy."

"Hey, if you think I'm quite a guy, you got to meet my Uncle Al."

She smiles that beautiful smile, "Where is he? I have to meet him."

I tell her, "He's being given tests in the emergency room, but I'm hoping he will be in a room of his own soon."

Beth says, "Don't worry about that. We'll be sure he's well taken care of." She starts to walk away, but I don't want her to go.

"Uh, hey Beth, I need to ask you something."

She turns to me with a shit-eating grin and says, "What do you want to ask me, Rocky, or is it Rambo?"

I tell her, in my usual stammering way, "Uh, well, I want to know maybe, if you have the time, well when you have the time…" but she interrupts me:

"Yes, I will go out with you, but no fooling around on the first date, agreed?"

"Agreed!"

With that, she writes her number down and hands me the piece of paper. She turns and walks down the hall. I also turn and walk away, six feet above the floor, metaphorically speaking.

CHAPTER 16

know I should have only been thinking about Uncle Al, but thoughts of Beth keep coming across in my mind. I don't understand how I could be so taken with someone in such a short time but I am. I figure that she's beautiful, smart and funny so what would she see in a guy like me but who cares, at least she agreed to go out with me. I keep staring at the piece of paper she gave me with her phone number and I resolve to call her as soon as my face heals or as soon as I get home, whichever comes first.

I'm back in the waiting room that has become more crowded since I'd gone to see Fred. There are no more seats left so I stand by the admittance window waiting to hear some news about Uncle Al. An hour passes when I hear the phone ring in the ER admitting office. A different nurse has taken over and she looks out of the glass window and says, "Are you Chris Pella?"

I tell her I am and she hands me the phone, "Don't be too long. This is an Emergency Room, and we have emergencies here."

Before I reach for the phone I tell her, "I won't be long, I promise."

"Hello, this is Chris Pella."

"Hey, you heroic asshole, come up to room 495. Wait until you see the room I got!"

It's my uncle, and I have never been happier to hear his voice. "Please refer to me as the handsome, heroic asshole."

There's a smile in his voice, "Just get up here!"

I hand the phone back to the nurse, who looks like she is ready to put me in the corner for a time out, but I smile, hand her back the phone and thank her. I run to the North Elevator, which is now becoming my personal favorite conveyance, and I push the button for the fourth floor. The doors open onto a long hallway, but I don't need to read the signs with the room numbers again, I know exactly where the room is.

I rush down the hallway and look for Beth as I pass the nurses' station, but she isn't there, so I just go into room 495. Lying on the bed, like he's king of the hill, sits Uncle Al. In the room, there is a large hospital bed, private bath and shower, a large flat screen TV with a sound system, flowers on his nightstand, paintings hanging on the wall, two nurses trying to comfort him, two police officers standing there eyeing the nurses and there's Beth watching over all this and smiling.

I see all this and my eyes go wide. The first thing I say to all in the room, "My uncle got all this just for being shot? What is the world coming to? I can't believe that he is turning into the biggest sissy on the force. Ladies and officers, all I can do is apologize for his contemptible attitude and hedonistic tendencies. Please, don't let this get back to the Suffolk County PD before I have a chance to tell them myself. Oh, by the way, can someone come over here and rub my back? It really hurts!" The nurses laugh and say goodbye to my uncle as they leave the room.

Beth is just about to leave when I say, "Really Beth, thank you and the entire staff for taking care of my uncle, I am more grateful than you will ever know."

Beth smiles at me and says, "Well Rambo, I guess you're going to be buying me the dinner of a lifetime. What do you say?"

"Agreed!"

She turns to Uncle Al, "Listen Chief, you may be feeling better, but you had a serious wound. The doctors are only letting you stay in this ward because they expect you to rest without half the force in your room. Is that clear?"

Uncle Al smiles and says, "I'm used to giving orders, but in this case, you outrank me so I'll make an exception, and I promise to rest."

"Good." Next, Beth turns to the police officers in the room and says, "Okay guys, get out of here. If you have to stay, there's coffee in the waiting area just down the hall."

The one officer speaks for both men when he replies, "Yes, ma'am. Goodbye Chief, we were all worried and we're really glad to see you're doing better." Uncle Al thanks them both and the policemen leave the room.

Beth now gives us both fair warning, "Now it's my turn to leave, but remember Chief, you need rest, even from family, so you've got ten minutes with Chris and then I want him out of here. Capisci?"

"Si, capisco bennissimo. Now Chris, say goodbye to the nice lady."

"Goodbye, nice lady." Beth leaves the room, but as she does, I notice her back is almost as good as her front and I smile. Uncle Al seems to notice and he says, "She is very, very nice, beautiful, smart and Italian. Your mom must be pulling some strings in heaven."

I nod and smile, "Funny, I was thinking the exact same thing." I walk around the side of his bed and I sit down. "I am so sorry Unc, I know you told me to go home, and I know that I should have. Now you are here, and it's my fault. Please, forgive me."

"Hey Chrissy, don't be so maudlin. If I was dead, I'd really be pissed off, but I'm alive. The doctors can't believe it. Quite frankly, neither can I."

"What did he say? The doctor that is."

The interrogation begins, "Well, according to them, I'm a walking, living, breathing miracle. They think that I have some special healing powers that allow me to recover so quickly. Are they right, Chris?"

"No."

"What do you mean?"

"I mean that you're a great cop and a great uncle, but you don't have any special powers."

"Agreed, so what happened to me? Why am I alive when I should be dead, and what do you have to do with all of this?"

"Uncle Al, I am going to tell you a story. It's a story of a young kid who experiences something so miraculous that he had to keep it secret for more than twenty years."

"Go on. I'm listening."

I try to come up with a way of telling Uncle Al all about my secret. The last thing I want is to have him think that I am some nut who fantasizes about saints and has visions, but I fear that's exactly what he is going to think. This is going to be the most difficult conversation I'll ever have, but I need to tell him the truth, so I take a deep breath and begin.

"One day this kid gets really sick, and while he is lying in bed in complete misery, he has a vision, this vision is the first one of many, and that changes his life."

Uncle Al starts his interrogation. "What is this first vision?"

I say, "The kid meets Saints Cosmas and Damian."

Uncle Al tries to clarify what he's heard, "You mean while he's so sick, he has hallucinations of meeting Saints Cosmas and Damian?" I explain, "No, I mean he is transported back in time to the fourth century A.D."

Uncle Al, ever the skeptic doesn't jump down my throat just yet. However, he does ask me, "Who are Cosmas and Damian?"

"Cosmas and Damian where he meets these saints, twin brothers who are physicians working in someplace called Cilicia."

"This kid is able to speak with Sts. Cosmas and Damian, sees them work with the sick people at that time. This kid also sees the twin brothers perform a miracle."

"What kind of miracle?"

"They cut the leg off this black guy and put it on this white guy."

Uncle Al smiles at me and says, "I hope the black guy didn't mind." tell him, "No, he was dead."

"Chris, you know I love you, but this is crazy talk. What does this have to do with my injury?"

I plead with my uncle, "I'll get to that but please Uncle Al you need to hear this, so let me finish the story."

"Okay Chris, sorry I interrupted."

I take another deep breath and pause as I need time to figure out what I'm going to say next. After about 40 seconds I continue, "This kid is totally awestruck by what he's witnessed. At some point Sts. Cosmas and Damian then step out of the vision and speak to him; they actually step out of their bodies, face him and begin speaking."

Uncle Al asks, "What did they say?"

I answer, "They tell him that he has a purpose in life and that there are things he is expected to do."

"What kind of things?" Al seems curious.

"Oh, different things—like helping people in need, fighting evil, stuff like that." I feel weird talking this way because it trivializes the true meaning of the gift I received and the special relationships I have with the saints.

"Listen Uncle Al, I can't put into words what was said and the true meaning of all this, but this is the only way I know how."

"Okay, so this kid has a vision, meets two saints, gets instructions on his purpose in life. What happens next?"

"Well, actually, he has a number of other visions and he meets many other saints."

"Really, how many?"

"176 so far." I'm starting to question my own sanity.

"One hundred and seventy-six, huh."

I am now the focus of one of Uncle Al's penetrating stares, but I need to tell him, "Yes, but that doesn't include the ones he sees in the gathering of saints."

"Really, how many were there?"

"He couldn't say. There were too many to count; he guesses there could have been thousands."

"Okay Chris, time for a recap. Cosmas and Damian, 300 A.D., black man's leg onto a white guy, purpose in life, 175 … no, 176, fight evil, lots more at the gathering. Did I leave anything out?"

"Well, there is his prom night, and he is trying to get laid, but St. Bernardine of Siena makes him stop." I now realize I really sound like a complete idiot.

"St. Bernardine…getting laid?" Uncle Al is genuinely puzzled.

I'm getting deeper into the hole so I try to further clarify, "No, St. Bernadine isn't trying to get laid, he is. I mean the kid is."

"Chris, let's stop this nonsense and get to the truth. This is about the sorriest fairytale I've ever heard."

I have to continue, so that I can make him understand why he is still alive. "Uncle Al, in order for you to know the truth, you need to listen to me and try not to jump to any conclusions until the story is over."

"Okay sorry, I'm still listening."

I gulp and blurt out, "What I'm going to tell you next are about the hardest things I've ever had to say in my life, I am that kid."

You can read the disbelief on my uncle's face, "Oh, so now my nephew has visions of saints? How long has this been going on?"

"My first vision happened when I was fourteen."

"Who else knows about this?"

"No one, you're the first person I've ever told."

"Well, Chris, I truly feel honored." I know he is being sarcastic.

Uncle Al turns away from me and just stares out the window. I know that he needs time to process all of this, not that he believes me, but he needs time to figure out what he can do to help me. I am someone he loves like a son, with a story so crazy that he will need to confront the possibility that I have lost my mind and I need real help.

In as calm and dispassionate manner he can muster, Uncle Al tells me, "I'm sorry, Chris, this is a lot to lay down on me, and I need time to think about what you told me."

"I know, Uncle Al. Maybe I should come back later. My ten minutes are almost up anyway."

"That's a good idea. I'm a little tired and I need to get some rest. In the meantime, let's keep this to ourselves, okay?"

In as honest an answer I can give I say, "I've kept it to myself for more than twenty years, a few hours more won't kill me," I hesitate a bit, but before I leave, I tell him, "I love you."

He answers, "I love you, too…No matter what."

CHAPTER 17

When I leave the room, I don't have any particular place to go. I go across the hall to check on Fred, but when I open the door, I see he is fast asleep so I leave him in peace. I walk down the hallway and I don't see Beth at the nurses' station so I walk to the elevator and press the down button.

I get off in the lobby and I see a sign for the cafeteria. I realize that I haven't eaten in a while and I am very hungry so I make my way in there. It is just before lunch and the line is pretty short. I order a turkey and bacon wrap on a whole wheat tortilla with a side salad and unsweetened iced tea. The cashier takes my money and I find a quiet table in the corner to eat and ponder my situation.

I take a few bites of the wrap, and drink some of iced tea while I sit there alone with my thoughts. I've told Uncle Al my secret, and I know I need to convince him I'm telling the truth, but how? How can I tell him about how I found Tina? How can I tell him that he was saved by a miracle, a miracle carried out by St. Michael the Archangel? I think about Julian and I don't know if I should hold off on telling Uncle Al about him?

While I am sitting there, feeling miserable about the situation, someone stops at my table.

There is a woman standing in front of me and she asks, "Aren't you Chris Pella?"

I look up and answer, "Yes, I am. I'm sorry, but I don't seem to recall…"

"I'm Cathy Staley, Tina's mom."

I immediately stand and offer Tina's mom a seat, "Oh, Mrs. Staley. I'm sorry I didn't recognize you, please, sit down. How are you doing? Have you been to see Tina? How's she doing?"

"Please call me Cathy, I'm fine now but I was despondent since Tina went missing. I just saw Tina and though she seems to be weak, she seems in better spirits. She's still undergoing some tests and the doctors are detoxifying her now. She'll be kept in the emergency room for a while and they assure me that she will be fine physically. However, the effects of the drugs still need to be determined and they won't know that for a while."

"I'm sure she will be fine and that is wonderful news that her spirits are up. I'll be sure to stop by when she can have visitors."

Cathy pauses for a moment holding back tears as she tells me, "I can't begin to imagine what this has done to her psychologically."

I don't know how to respond and all I can think of saying is, "She will be fine, I just know it."

"Chris, I was up to see Dad, I mean Fred and he told me about what you did to find Tina. I … I…I don't know what to say, how to thank you. My baby girl in that horrid place, I shudder to think what may have happened to her if you and your uncle didn't help." Tears are rolling down her cheeks and she begins to sob.

I reach out to hold her hand to offer some small comfort. "Cathy, Tina and Fred are getting the best of care. Their love for each other, and your love for them, will get you all through this. I am just so grateful that they are okay."

Cathy responds as she wipes away her tears, "So am I…so am I."

"I know why Tina was rebelling Cathy and I know Mr. Staley loves her too. The both of you will be great comfort to both her and Fred in the weeks ahead."

Cathy tries to smile and says "Jack and I will be sure to not let our personal problems get in the way of her recovery because she will need all the support she can get. Tina is all that matters now."

I reach for Cathy's hand and hold it, "Tina's lucky to have you, Jack and Fred. If there is anything I can do, please, let me know."

"I will, and thank you from the bottom of my heart." I get up as Cathy stands. She looks me straight in the eye, gives me a hug, kisses my cheek and walks away.

Given all that has happened, all the people I've seen, make it feel like I'm on a roller coaster ride of emotions. I sit back down and lean my back against the chair. After a short while I pick up my turkey wrap to take another bite when someone else comes over and stands at my side. I look up and there is Beth holding her lunch tray. I couldn't be happier to see her right now.

Beth gives me a stern look and says, "We haven't even gone on our first date and you're cheating on me already?"

I give my patented look of smugness and tell her, "Well, I've got to keep my options open; after all, I am Rocky or Rambo, and my reputation is important."

She's quick to respond, "I guess I'll have to sit right here and make sure that no one else gets to you before I have the chance." So, she sits down opposite me and laughs.

I am determined not to let her get the upper hand, so I tell her, "I'm not so sure, what if something better comes along?"

"Well, that works both ways, buster. You know there are a lot of handsome doctors in this hospital and few of them wouldn't mind getting on my better side."

I immediately observe, "Hey, you don't have to worry, all of your sides look great to me."

Beth smiles that fabulous smile and I know that I am sunk. I love looking at her, hearing her talk and wondering what it would be like to be with her. She must sense that I'm preoccupied by something though, so she asks, "When I was standing on line, I saw you talking to that woman, who is she?"

"That's Tina's mom, Cathy. She was in to see her daughter and Fred and she recognized me."

"My God, that poor woman, she must be going through her own personal hell given all that happened to Tina."

I explain to Beth how I feel, "I truly believe that once she is able to put this horror and pain behind her, she'll be able to see a bright future for her daughter. Isn't that what every parent wants?"

Beth looks at me, but all she can say is, "Wise beyond your years."

I laugh, "I wish I was. Come to think of it, if I'm so smart, how come I'm not rich? Huh, Elizabeth Della Russo, how come I'm not rich?"

"Well, God may have different plans for you."

I must have gone pale, so Beth quickly says, "Sorry, Chris, I didn't mean you're going to die or anything like that."

I calm down, "No, no I just overreacted. For some reason, I just thought about all that happened to me today and I hope that God doesn't have plans to make me do that again."

Beth laughs and we continue to sit together, in comfort, eating our lunch and getting to know each other a little better. She then stops eating and says, "Hey Rambo, just a reminder that this doesn't count as a date, got it? I'm expecting something better than this spinach salad. Comprendere?"

"Si, io comprendere."

As Beth gets up from the table, she says to me, "Bella, Grazie per un buon pranzo."

I respond, "You're welcome and I promise the dinner will be nicer." Now I am totally captivated and my mother must be in her glory.

CHAPTER 18

I wait for a couple of hours before I go back on the North Elevator up to see Uncle Al. What am I going to say that could possibly sound sane to my uncle? I try not to think about what his reaction might be, but I guess if I were him, I'd have the same dread and worry. I walk to room 495, open the door and go inside. I see Uncle Al sitting up on the side of the bed and I rush to him,

"What are you doing? You've been seriously wounded and the doctors want you to rest. Now you have got to lie down."

He protests, "I feel fine."

I remind him, "Well, feeling fine and being fine are two different things. Come on, lay back down, here and let me help you." I put my arms around his shoulder and he leans back onto the bed.

His concern is apparent, "Chris, we will get through this together. I know you must be confused, but you have to believe these are hallucinations. They're not real. I know someone who can help us find just the right doctors…"

"Unc, it figures you would think I'm crazy and frankly I don't blame you. While I was out, I was thinking of ways to convince you that I am telling the truth. The fact is that I know what has been happening to me is totally unbelievable." I feel I have to say it, "Do you trust me?"

"Of course, I do. Chris, you're my…"

I take a deep breath, "I mean trust me enough to let me finish what I am going to tell you, if not for my sake, for Mom's."

He gives me one of those looks that say he's been taken and lets me know, "You play dirty, but yeah, I'll listen to you, not just for your mom's sake."

I breathe out a sigh of relief and continue my story, "Thanks Uncle Al, I really appreciate it. So where was I, oh yeah, the prom. I'll tell you the complete story someday, looking back, it was really funny, but for now I want to tell you about Tina, and how I found out she'd been kidnapped."

I continue to tell Uncle Al about my vision of St. Agatha outside of Book Revue. I tell him of all the sordid details and when the vision was over, all I could think of is to run in the street and call him.

"Remember when I tried to lie to you about how I knew where she was?"

"Yeah, I remember."

"Well, I knew it because I saw the room Tina was in. St. Agatha also showed me with all the degradation and depravity she had to endure in her time. I saw St. Agatha being raped. I saw her in prison being tortured, and I saw Quintianus."

"You saw Quintianus; he's a real person?"

I tell him what I know, "Yes, he lived more than 1,500 hundred years ago and when you asked me if I could remember anything, I gave you his name because that was all I really had and if it meant anything I knew you would find a connection."

I continue, "When I told you that I just went for a ride last night, I was really telling you the truth. I wasn't trying to find Tina; I just wanted to clear my head. It was either divine providence or pure dumb luck that I happened to stop in front of the house where Tina was being held captive."

Uncle Al is allowing me to go on with my outrageous story that I know he doesn't believe, but a promise is a promise so he says, "Go on."

The terrors of the night before come flooding back into my mind, but I have to get the story out so I continue to tell Uncle Al what happened. "I snuck inside the house and hid behind some boxes, but I was caught by Heriberto Quintana—about the craziest person you will ever hope to meet, except for me, of course." I lower my head and when I look up; I hope to see Al smiling and I see he is.

"What happened then?"

I point to the bruises on my face and tell him, "Well, for starters, he gives me a black eye and does this to my face," "I watched Heriberto Quintana as killed one of his guys, Ernesto, for beating up this young girl that he called his property. Quintana then tells these two other guys, Manulo and Julio, to drag me upstairs and lock me in a room with bugs, rat and lord knows what else. On my way to the room, just before they lock me in, I look over and see Tina, unconscious, lying on a filthy mattress. Unc, she is in the exact same room that St. Agatha showed me in her vision—the exact same room!"

I think to myself if I should I tell Uncle Al about Juliano? I am really in a dilemma as to whether I should tell him, but I decide not to, just yet anyway. Telling him about the Saints are one thing, a demon from hell is entirely another.

I go on with my story. "So, I stay in this rat and roach infested shit hole for a while before the scumbags come back for me. I don't know what to do, but I am sure of one thing, they are going to kill me. While I'm being held prisoner, I have another vision, this time it's St. Mary Magdalene. Uncle Al, I was there! I was at the house where she wiped the feet of Jesus with her hair and anointed them with oil. Uncle Al, I saw Jesus."

"My God, Chris" Uncle Al looks totally dumbfounded and frightened.

It took all my strength to tell him that, "I know. I know what you're thinking; I'm nuts, and I don't blame you, but I swear on all that is holy, I am telling you the truth. St, Mary's message is that Tina is innocent, she is loved and worth saving and that I am the one that needs to help her."

At this point, there is no way I can stop telling my story, so I keep talking, "I also had Tina on my mind, trying to figure a way to get us both out of there when the door opens and Heriberto and the two guys, Manulo and Julio, drag me into her bedroom. They tie my hands and throw me on the bed where they want me to rape Tina. I struggle to try and free myself but I am unable to move. Then Heriberto hears a noise downstairs and he sends Manulo and Julio to see what is going on. After a while we heard gunshots and screaming so when they don't come back, Quintana pulls out his gun and leaves the room."

I pause to take a breath and say, "I think you know what happens next because you were there, and I wasn't."

"Is that it? What about my wound? What about how it was healed? Which one of your saints did this miracle?"

I gulp, "It was St. Michael, St. Michael the Archangel."

Uncle Al looks at me in stunned amazement, "Wait, you mean the same St. Michael the Archangel that drove Lucifer into hell, that Michael the Archangel?"

"I'm afraid so."

"Chris, can I speak?"

"Sure, you can."

With all seriousness and utmost concern Uncle Al says, "Chris, we need to get you help. I love you and I want you to get the help you need to stop these visions or hallucinations or whatever you want to call them. Chris, I am sure that you believe that you can see saints and that these visions are real, but you can't be seeing saints."

"Why?"

"Because it's impossible, that's why."

"By whose standards is it impossible?"

"By everybody's standards, that's who." Uncle Al is getting agitated and I don't want to see him get upset.

I try to explain, "I don't want to upset you; I really don't. I only tell you these things because I know you need answers to why you healed so fast. Do you want me to stop telling you the story, or should I continue?"

He looks very tired when he asks, "What else is there to say?"

"Well, I can tell you how he did it. Don't you want to know?"

"At this point, sure, tell me. What harm can it do? I'll ask for the padded cell next to yours, so we can be together."

I start to break into a smile, but stop as I relive the event where I almost lost Uncle Al. "You were lying on the floor, blood pouring out of your shoulder just above your heart. I'm kneeling next to you, frightened from not knowing what I would do without you around. It is then that St.

Michael appears to me in a vision, and when I have these visions, everything and everybody around me seems to stop in time. First, you should know that St. Michael is not only a fierce defender of God and His entire domain, but he is also known for his healing powers. Oh, and by the way, he is the patron saint of police officers."

Uncle Al seems insulted when he says, "I know that."

"St. Michael takes me to this place, the Michaelion; it's a holy place, a sanctuary where there is a clear pool of water. He takes his shield…"

"He has his shield?"

"Yes."

"Does he have a sword, too?"

"Yes, he does. Can I continue?"

"Yeah, sure."

"St. Michael takes his shield and dips it into the water and fills it part of the way up. He then motions for me to cup my palms and he pours some of the water into them. I take the water and pour it onto your wound. When the vision is over, your wound was beginning to heal. I know all of this sounds so incredible and so impossible, but it's the pure and simple truth. It was a miracle Uncle Al, a full-fledged miracle and you are alive today because of it."

Uncle Al seems to have run out of arguments, "What can I say? What can I do? How can any of this be possible? Chris, just think of what you've telling me and the impossibility of it all. I … I don't know how to react to all this because I love you, and I don't know how to help you."

I see the grief on Uncle Al's face as we sit there in silence trying to find the next words to speak to each other. Then all of what is around us freezes in time and a new Sainted vision comes to me.

The doctors look at St. Camillus and tell him that the wound to his leg will never heal. As a novice in the Capuchin order, he takes the news with great sadness, for he is told he may never be professed. When he hears this, he lifts himself off the bed and vows that his fervor would not be diminished, and he promises to his savior, Jesus Christ, that he will care for the sick and dying the rest of his days.

The vision now changes and I am transported to a time and place years later. St. Camillus is walking through the streets on a mission.

The streets near the harbor of medieval Rome are filled with bodies of the dead and dying. St. Camillus sees the ship at the dock and knows what he must do. The friar roams the deck among all the poor souls where he says prayers over the dead and gives the living comfort while they wait for death. The bubonic plague is a curse, but it is not for St. Camillus to understand why. All he needs to do is to try and help in whatever way he can. The pain in his leg is getting worse, but it is his penance, his cross to bear. After all, was Jesus not made to suffer greater torments?

I see the glow, which I have come to know well. It surrounds St. Camillus as he steps out of his earthly body and presents himself to me.

He knows what I have been telling my uncle. "The truth is hard for some to accept. It was true in the time I was alive, and it is still true in your time."

I am looking for guidance and tell St. Camillus, "I'm trying to tell my uncle in the best way I know how, but to him this all seems so impossible. I can understand why he is upset, but I know it is all true, I know The Sainted are real and you are all part of my life and for that I am blessed."

He uses his own life, suffering and the lessons that he learned. "I have seen the suffering in death and I did not understand why. It is faith that needs to guide your uncle and you must try to help him understand."

"But how can I help him?"

"He has also known the pain of someone he loves dying. He was given trials where his faith was tested. When you speak of these things, he will understand."

I am totally confused, "What things? I don't know what you are talking about and I need to know. Please, help me know what to say."

None of the saints could reveal themselves to anyone but me and St. Camillus looks at me and knows of my dilemma. Uncle Al needs to try and understand that and he has to have faith that I am telling the truth, even though he can't see what I've seen.

The Sainted speaks, "Your uncle will need to reach down into his soul for a memory, an image that he has buried there, long ago."

"What image? What are you talking about?"

"The death of his father and what he was asked to do."

My eyes go wide, "Wait, what about grandpa's death? What did Uncle Al have to do? I need to know, what did he have to do?"

St. Camillus says, "He had to do what is right, and he did."

"What do you mean—He had to do what is right?"

St, Camillus hold his hand up as if to say there is no more he can do or say. I will need to figure this out for myself. With that, the vision of the saint and his surroundings slowly disappear. I find myself back in the hospital room with Uncle Al who gazing out the window, still deep in thought. I try to remember all that St. Camillus said, all that was shown me. While I am sitting there thinking, it comes to me, everything I was told comes together and somehow, I am able to discern the meaning of it all.

Uncle Al, who has been silent up to now, says, "Chris, listen to me. I will do everything in my power to…" but I cut him off and say, "How did grandpa die?"

"Don't change the subject Chris. Come on, we need to discuss this."

I persist, "Uncle Al, how did grandpa die?"

Now he sounds frustrated, "Chris, what the hell does grandpa's death have to do with what's happening to you."

"Uncle Al, how did grandpa die?"

Al seems to know that I won't give up on this, so he just says, "Stomach cancer."

I ask, "Was he in a lot of pain?"

"Yes." A faraway look comes over his face when he answers.

"Uncle Al, what are you thinking about?"

"Chris, I'm thinking about you and what may happen if you continue to have these crazy thoughts about saints and visions."

"Come on, please, tell me what you are thinking. Tell me about grandpa."

The sadness of this memory is etched on his face, but he says, "I don't remember. It was so long ago."

Uncle Al is only saying this in hopes that I will stop asking him questions, but I know that he remembers everything about my grandfather's death as if it happened only yesterday. "I think you do remember and I think it is too painful to speak about. No one would blame you, but I need to know Uncle Al, please, I need to know."

"I just can't Chris. I just can't."

I didn't realize how tough this would be for him, so I say it for him, "He was in the hospital dying and you were there every day, by his side, every day." Chief Detective Al Barese lies on the bed and says nothing.

"I know how much you loved grandpa and I can't imagine how heartbreaking this must have been for you. You had to see this man, a strong, vital man; someone who loves his family, who loves his country, who sacrificed so much to make a better life for you and all his children. You had to watch him die in one of the most painful ways that could be imagined."

A tear slowly runs down out of the corner of his eye, but he remains quiet. "After a while, the disease became so advanced, it ravaged his body to the point you couldn't even recognize him. Am I right?"

Uncle Al says to no one, "He coughed up blood. He lost so much weight. He was in so much pain that the doctor had to put him on morphine."

I thought of St. Camillus and the pain he endured and I thought of my grandfather and his pain. I could see the anguish on Uncle Al's face as he has to relive this event.

I continue to try to find the words that Uncle Al couldn't, "What could you do to help him? What is it that you could do to help end his pain? I know these thoughts must have gone through your mind as you sat at his bedside, totally helpless."

"Why are you doing this to me, Chris? Why?"

I hear his question, but I don't answer. "Grandma would come to the hospital, too, as did my mom and all his sons and daughters. How awful for you to see your family watch the man they love suffer. How awful it must have been for you all to feel powerless as you all pray for him to die and end his pain."

Uncle Al looks up at me, and for the first time in my life he looked old, but as I continue to speak, he looks away.

"When you and grandpa were alone, he spoke to you, didn't he?"

"He was so weak, so tired."

"He asked you to help him, didn't he? He asked you to help him die." Uncle Al immediately looks up at me, astonished.

I tell my Uncle Al what I know to be true, "It would have been so simple, only a turn of the morphine drip and he would have fallen into a coma. He would have died; finally free of the pain that was tormenting him."

Uncle Al looks up at me and practically whispers, "How? How could you know that? No one knows that."

I let him know what I believe was in his heart. "But you didn't do it, did you? You couldn't kill your father, even though you wanted him to rest in peace. You didn't kill him because you know it isn't your decision to make. It is God's."

Uncle Al continues to stare at me, "He's my dad, and I had to watch him suffer. He asked me for help and I wouldn't help him. I loved him so much and I refused him the last thing he asked me to do."

I try to help him realize, "Grandpa was in so much pain, so incoherent; he couldn't possibly understand what he was asking you to do. He loved you so much, and he would have never wanted you to take on such a burden."

There are tears welling up in my uncle's eyes and his voice starts to crack, "It would have been so easy—just turn the little knob. It would have been so easy."

"It would have been so easy, but it's wasn't the right thing to do. God has plans for all of us and grandpa's suffering is part of His plan. I don't profess to know God's will; all I know is that His will be done."

My uncle tries to speak of his father's death. "He lived another four days in such awful pain I can't bear to think of. He died before I had the chance to tell him I am sorry, to tell him I love him, to tell him what he meant to me, to tell him I couldn't help him die even though he was in such awful pain."

For a minute or two my uncle weeps uncontrollably. He cries a torrent of tears and his chest heaves with sobs. The pain he has carried over all these years must have been a torture for him, but he kept it to himself, hidden in the back of his mind, so no one but him would ever know.

Uncle Al begins to wipe his tears away and stares at me in total incomprehension. "How do you know all of this Chris? How could you possibly know what no one else knows?"

"I know because I was told."

Uncle Al looks me straight in the eye, "Told? You were told? By who, no one in this world knows about any of this? Who told you about Dad?"

I am now able to let him know how I know all of this. "You're right Unc, no one in this world; it was St. Camillus de Lellis who told me. He told me this, so that you would believe what I've said about my visions and about all the saints who guide me through their visions. He knows of your secret. He knows your inner anguish and the guilt you feel over not being able to help your father."

"What?"

"Yeah, Uncle Al, he also told me to tell you that you did the right thing."

"The right thing?" The tears well up in Uncle Al's eyes.

"Yes, the right thing."

Uncle Al begins to weep again covering his face with his hands. I come around I sit by his side and we embrace and I tell him what I always tell him,

"I love you."

"I love you, too."

CHAPTER 19

Both Uncle Al and I sit in an awkward silence, not knowing what to say next, but not wanting to be apart from each other. It is impossible for me to ever imagine how deep this man's pain must be? For so many years he has been carrying this burden and consumed with a secret buried so deep in his soul that he has never able to forgive himself. For more than an hour, we just sit there and say nothing to each other. Finally, Uncle Al turns to me and says, "I believe you, Chris. No one could have known what happened between me and my father. You must be telling me the truth."

"Thank you, Uncle Al. Your faith, your belief that I am telling the truth means more to me than you will ever know."

My uncle reminisces about his father as he tells me, "Grandpa, my dad, was a great man. Not the way some measure greatness today, by fame or money, but true greatness that comes from the love, kindness and strength he showed everyone who knew him; family, friends, everyone."

I know what he is talking about. "Grandpa was always proud of you and our whole family and he said it to me all the time."

"I will always regret that I never got the chance to let him know, one last time, how much I love him, how much I will miss him."

I only hope it will make him feel better when I tell him, "St. Camillus told me to make sure you know that you did the right thing."

Uncle Al looks at me and asks, "Do you think that Dad will forgive me for doing the right thing?"

I smile at him knowing, "He already has."

We both look at each other and Uncle Al says, "Thank you for saying that, Chris. You know it means so much to me just to be able to tell you what I've been hiding for years. To know that you and your St. Camillus understand helps to make me able to move on and to forgive myself."

We talk for what seems like hours. Uncle Al wants to unload this burden of guilt he has felt all these years and this time seems to be the right time. He speaks of the many things that he remembers of his father, of all the things big and small that helped to build the love they both felt for each other.

"Chris, can I tell you a little story?"

"Sure!" Uncle Al begins to tell me a story that I had not heard before and I am eager to hear what he has to say.

"I was about twelve years old and I loved to play baseball. Every chance I'd get, I would go to the field and play with my buddies. I wasn't that good, but it really didn't matter because I loved the sport and I was having fun. Well, there was a local Bronx YMCA league forming a travel team that comprised of twelve and thirteen-year-old kids. All my buddies wanted to try out, so we ran down to the field where the try-outs were taking place. The coaches put us through the drills and a practice game, to evaluate our catching, fielding, batting and running bases. It was all part of a process to see how we played and to see if we were good enough to make this elite club team."

I'm just sitting there next to his bed, listening to him speak and I'm glad because I know he needs to say what is on his mind and in his heart.

My uncle is staring down at his bedsheet and he starts to play with the edges as he speaks. "When my friends and I left the tryouts, we were all sure we had made the team and I ran home to tell my mom all about it. When I got home, I start rattling off all the excitement of the day, but my mother was cooking.

She has her back to me and all that she would say is, 'That's good, Spartaco.' What I didn't know at the time was that the coach had called her earlier and told her that I didn't make the team. All my friends had made the team, except for me, but she didn't have the heart to tell me. When Dad came home the first thing my mom did was to take him aside tell him about the call from the coach."

Uncle Al unconsciously rubbed one hand into the other as if he were actually breaking in his baseball glove as he continued the story, "I was in my room oiling my glove when dad came in and he sat down on the bed next to me. I didn't detect it at the time, but I'm sure he was very sad at having to tell me that I had not made the team.

Dad said in a serious voice, 'Spartaco, I have to talk with you.'"

"I didn't bother to notice that anything did not seem right with my father. All I could think of was to tell him about the tryouts because I was so excited. I told him, 'Hey Dad, did you hear about the tryouts for the travel team? I'll bet that they want to put me in right field, but I want to try out for second base. I think that I can…' but he stops me."

"Spartaco, I have some bad news."

"I became nervous and asked my dad what was the bad news?"

"Dad put his arms around my shoulder and tells me that I hadn't made the travel team. When I heard this, I was heartbroken; I didn't know how I was going to face my friends. I know now that it was about the hardest thing for my dad to do because he knew how much I loved to play baseball, but back then I only thought about what that meant to me."

"What happened, then?" I ask.

Uncle Al faces me as he wants the words to have special meaning as a memory of his father; my grandfather. "Well, Dad decided that he would work with me so I could become a better player, this from a man who grew up on a farm, became a tailor and never played or even held a baseball in his life. Dad would watch ballgames on TV with me just to understand how the game is played. During the season we practiced daily when he came home from work—fielding, throwing, catching, hitting. Even though he was exhausted from his work, he made it a point to be sure he was there for me. I guess there are a lot of dads who would do this for their sons, but my father did it for me, and now that I am an adult, I realize how very special our time together was."

I am amazed, "Wow, I can't ever imagine grandpa playing ball."

Uncle Al smiles, "Oh, he tried and got fairly good at it."

"What about you?" I am hoping for a fairy tale ending.

Uncle Al admits, "Well, I actually became a pretty good ball player, made the travel team after someone dropped out and I became the permanent right fielder. It was a great feeling and Dad was there, in the stands, at every one of my games. I know it sounds like a 'Father Knows Best' storyline, but it's the truth. I guess some would think it was nothing really special, but it meant everything to me."

"It's a great story about you and grandpa." All I can do is smile and be happy that my uncle shared this with me.

"Yeah, it's a good story. Chris, can I ask you about your saints?"

I knew this was coming, "Sure you can."

"Why can't I see them?"

I often thought about why I was the only person able to see The Sainted. "I only wish I knew. Sometimes it can be a great burden to be the only one who can communicate with the saints, but now that you know, I can have someone to share these visions with."

"This seems like such a special gift, I mean I love you, but no offense you'd think that some great person of faith would have been chosen. Did they ever tell you why you were chosen?"

"No offense taken, but no, they never did tell me, and I've wondered about that for years. It's true, I'm not a holy person or that I've done anything special. I'm just me. Sometimes I think that I was chosen because I am nothing special, you know, just a regular guy like anyone else, flaws and all."

Uncle Al seems fascinated by what I am telling him. "Did the saints ever tell you how or why they perform their miracles?"

"No, but here's what I think: they are moved by the Holy Spirit and their faith manifests itself in their miracles and good works."

"You said that you saw Jesus Christ in one of your visions. Did Christ say anything to you, kind of like the Saints do?"

I thought about this question and how I might answer it so it would have meaning, "No, He never spoke to me. In some ways, I am glad He didn't because I wouldn't know how to answer. He's my Lord and savior, the Son of God, what could I possibly say to Him?"

My uncle smiles and gives me his perspective and that makes the most sense to me. "I guess you're better off just speaking to Him in your prayers, this way you can talk and He can listen. By the way, do you still say prayers before you go to bed?"

I smile at Uncle Al. "Yeah, I still do. Imagine a big 'chooch' like me, praying like a little kid."

He smiles back, "I think it's nice; anyway, I've got another question. When do you get to see these saints, their visions? Do all of them speak to you?"

"I can get them, what I call The Sainted visions; at any time, in any place. When I do, I can see the saints and speak to them, it's kind of weird. When I have the visions, everything around me just stands still, like time stops for everyone, but me. So far, all of them have spoken to me, except for St. Michael. I don't know why he didn't speak to me, maybe he didn't need to, but it doesn't seem to matter, you are his miracle, his gift to me." To be able to talk to Uncle Al, to pour out my innermost thoughts and to have him listen and believe me is what I've been missing all along.

Uncle Al falls in a heap back onto his pillow and tells me, "I know I'll have a million more questions to ask, but right now I'm spent. Know what I mean?"

"Yeah, I know what you mean. I'll be leaving now, but I'll be back tomorrow, and we can continue talking."

He yawns an "Okay."

I smile and say, "Thanks for believing me."

Uncle Al smiles back and says, "You're welcome. See you tomorrow."

CHAPTER 20

By the time I get home it's 8:30 P.M., and I am exhausted. The entire event happened in less than one day, but it seems like much more time has passed. I throw myself down in my chair next to the TV and turn it on hoping to relax before I collapse, in bed, in an exhausted heap. The only thing I'm interested in watching is the evening news, so I turn to the local cable news channel. I want to see how the whole incident with Police and MS13 is being reported and how they are reporting Uncle Al's injury.

The news anchor, a woman with blond hair and a total of 64 teeth, is speaking to the camera. She is in the middle of her report and telling the viewers, "…MS-13 on Long Island suffered a major setback in their criminal enterprise with the death of their leader, Heriberto Quintana and two of his gang members. A third man was also wounded in the confrontation and is now being held in police custody. The gang allegedly forced minor girls and boys into prostitution by…"

I assume that either Manulo or Julio had been killed in the gun battle, along with Heriberto. They must have added Ernesto to the total, and that meant all are accounted for, except for Juliano, but it's unlikely he will ever be found.

The anchor continues, "A spokesman for the Suffolk County Police Department told LI Cable News that all the young girls and boys are being taken to the hospital where child services will be there to treat them for traumas the resulted from their imprisonment and drugs. The children will then be reunited with their family once the doctors and counselors complete the examinations. In a related incident, Chief of Detective's Al Barese is recovering from severe wounds he suffered in the line of duty. Chief Barese, a 36-year police veteran and hero in the Parkway Murders case, confronted the leader of MS-13, Heriberto Quintana in a fierce gun battle, Chief Barese was seriously wounded and managed to kill Quintana, but not before the gang leader had killed a prostitute caught in the line of fire."

Wow, I thought, they got the story right for a change. I make a mental note to myself, I have to remember to tell Uncle Al to get a better picture for the news networks; his photo is awful. Then I think, on second thought, maybe I'll wait until he feels better and then I could break his balls for a change. I get up from the TV and go to the kitchen to get something to eat. I return to the TV to watch some more news, but before I finish half of the sandwich I made, I fall dead asleep.

When I wake up, I see sunshine coming through the sliding glass doors that lead to the deck off my living room. I rub my eyes and check my watch and I can't believe its past 10 A.M. I had slept on my couch for more than twelve hours, so I guess I needed the rest. I walk into the bathroom and look at my face in the mirror, cringe and brush my teeth. After I shave and brush my teeth, I get into the shower to wash all the grime away and, for the next half-hour, I just let the hot water run down my body. I feel like a new man; clean, shaven, with sparkling teeth and now I am ready to tackle another day.

As I pick up my dirty clothes off the floor, a small piece of paper drops out of my shirt pocket. It is Beth's number, and I make a mental note to myself to call her to plan our first date. I also need to go to the coin shop and take care of what's needed there. Before I do any of those things, however, I need to call Uncle Al.

His phone rings, and he picks up: "Chief Barese, I mean, Hello?"

I laugh at him, "Think you're back at work, don't you?"

"Yeah, the phone's been ringing off the hook. Everyone is calling to see how I'm doing. I've been getting calls from the family and friends, and everyone from the county executive and the police commissioner to the head cook in the cafeteria. It's really nice, but right now, all I want to do is rest. The phone keeps ringing, and I have to keep saying the same things over and over again."

"Sorry Unc, I didn't mean to bother you, but I want to let you know that I can't come by until later. I've got to take care of some business at the shop, but I'll be there to see you after 3p.m., okay?"

"Sure, no problem, now I gotta ask, what about that hot looking nurse? You know the one that your mom sent you from heaven, Beth Della Russo?" I just know that he's been waiting for this opportunity to bust my chops.

Like always, I know when he's busting my chops…remember he's that superhero, 'Ball Breaker Man' so I say, "Wow, thanks for reminding me, I almost forgot about her? By the way, what does she look like?"

Uncle Al lays on a thick Italian accent and says, "Like an angel who speaks Italian. By the way, do you speak to angels, too?"

"No, not yet, but I've got my order in."

"Why don't you give her a call, big shot?" I can almost see him smiling on the other end of the phone.

I laugh and say, "I'll see you later."

"Okay…I love you."

I usually say it first, but I just answer back, "I love you, too."

After I finish breakfast, I'm ready to tackle the day ahead. I get into my car to drive south down New York Avenue to my shop in the village. I open the door to find two days' worth of mail lying on the floor. I pile the mail on my desk and sit down and go through the various envelopes; there are some orders for coins as well as other packages of things I had ordered for my business, other than that, there is really nothing important. I toss the junk mail in the trash, which is also what I wish I could do with the bills, but instead I file them so they can be paid by the end of the month.

Next, I logon to my website and see that there are quite a few orders for some of the various coins and medallions I sell, and that always makes me happy. I'm generally happy when I know I can eat and pay the mortgage. I begin to process the orders and get them ready for shipping when I think of Beth. I reach into my pocket and find the paper with her number, but it is too early to call her at home, but being the decisive man of action that I am, I decide to call her at the hospital.

The phone rings, "Hello, Huntington Hospital, how may I help you?"

"Good morning, can I speak with Nurse Elizabeth Della Russo; she works on the fourth floor."

The person at reception replies, "Let me see, ah yes, here is her extension, I'll put you through now. Have a nice day."

I say, "You, too," and my call is put through to the nurses' station. "Nurse Diane Breuer, how may I help you?"

"Good morning, may I speak with Nurse Della Russo?"

Nurse Breuer asks, "Whom shall I say is calling?"

"Would you please tell her that Chris Pella is calling?"

She practically jumps through the phone, "Wait, are you Rambo, I mean Rocky?"

"Huh?"

"Are you Rambo or Rocky?" and Nurse Breuer starts cracking up.

"Did she tell you all about me getting beaten up?" I'm sitting at my desk turning different shades of red.

Now Nurse Diane takes the time to explain, "One thing you should know, all the female nurses' around the world have a code we live by."

"What's that?"

"Anytime there's story about a new guy, you spill your guts or you're out of the sisterhood. By the way, Beth's just been elected the president of our chapter after the story she told about you." Nurse Breuer laughs out loud, but I think she starts to sense I'm feeling embarrassed, so she says, "Hang on, she's right here."

Beth picks up the phone and in a very professional manner says, "Nurse Elizabeth Della Russo, how may I help you?"

"Thank you for letting the world know about my unfortunate accident with a bad guy's fist."

Her sympathy knows no bounds and she says, "Oh, you're welcome; it brought much needed comic relief, at your expense of course, to the very stressful job we nurses perform each and every day."

I give up. "Well, glad I could be of assistance."

Now Beth can't hold it in any longer and she busts out laughing and I can hear some more laughing in the background as the nurses hold their first annual "Make Chris Pella feel like an Idiot Day."

"Sorry, Rocky…it was too good to pass up. So, how come you called, huh?" Beth pretends, but she knows exactly why I am calling and I can almost see her smiling on the other end of the phone.

"I want to ask you out for Saturday night. What do you say?"

"Wait a minute, buster. Where are you taking me? Remember your promise…"

I stop her and say, "Yeah I know, the dinner of a lifetime, so I figure that I will leave it up to you. Pick anyplace you want to go and I'll gladly take you there."

Beth ruminates as if deep in thought and says, "Mmmmmm, well, let me see, there's always Mac's or Prime, but I don't know if I feel like steak. Um, how about Piccolo's, no it's usually too crowded on Saturday nights, I know, Besito! I love Mexican food, and they make the best…"

She's speaking and I'm enjoying the fact that she picking some of the top places in town so, I say, "You're not scaring me, I just got my allowance and the money's burning a hole in my pocket."

Then her answer comes out of left field, "Well, in that case, why don't you just make me dinner?"

"What?"

Beth says, "You heard me. Why don't you just make me dinner at your place?"

"Are you kidding?"

Beth says, "I never kid about food, why don't you make me dinner?"

By this time, I smell a rat, or more likely, an Uncle Rat, "You've been speaking with my uncle, haven't you?"

Now she starts to sound indignant, "Who me? Do you think he would do something so deceitful, so devious as to interfere with what he hopes will be a budding new relationship? I take umbrage at your insinuation that he would act in such an underhanded manner. Of course, he told me! He says you are a great cook and that you have a condo overlooking the harbor, so what do you say?"

"Beth, I really want to take you someplace nice. I'm not the great cook that I'm sure Al told you I am. Come on; let's go out, anyplace you want."

Now she is getting peeved at me, so she says, "I don't want to go out to a restaurant; I want you to make me dinner! Si sente che cosa sto dicendo?"

I know when I'm beaten so I tell her, "Si, I hear what you're saying. But remember, if you don't like my cooking, you still have to go out with me again—you can't hold it against me, agreed?"

She knows when she's won and says, "Agreed! So now that's settled, I'll get your address from your uncle. Do you want Al to give me a time or do you want to tell me when I should get to your home?"

I can't believe that I've got the both of them giving me orders; "No, I'll tell you, how about 6:30 p.m. for drinks and dinner will follow."

"Sounds great Rocky, now I have to get back to work, I guess I'll see you later when you visit."

"I count the moments!"

She starts laughing and hangs up and I lean back in my chair and smile.

CHAPTER 21

After I hang up the phone, I start to think of some things I need to do for the big dinner date. First, I need to clean the house. I am actually kind of a neat freak so my condo looks pretty good but it's got to look great for Beth. Second, I need to plan a menu of what should I make for dinner? I want this to be the best dinner I've ever made. After all, making a good impression on Beth is my goal.

It's Wednesday, and I figure that I have three days to decide what to serve, shop for the ingredients, clean-up and, through it all, hope for the bruises on my battered face to heal. I spend the rest of the day doing work at the shop, figuring that I would try to get to the hospital around 5 P.M. so I can spend the evening with Uncle Al. I enter my sales into the computer, adjust my inventory and process and pack up the orders. Next, I'll go to the post office to ship all the items before I head to the hospital.

While I am driving to the hospital, I start to plan my menu. I have all the makings for cocktails—vodka gimlets are my favorite. I also need to select a good robust red, maybe Chianti and a medium dry white wine, probably Sauvignon Blanc to serve at dinner in case Beth wants either. For the dinner menu, I think that I'll start with a specialty of my mom's; an incredible recipe for scallops in cognac sauce. The next course has to be pasta; capellini with fresh tomato and basil and for the main course, a traditional veal Osso Buco with roasted potatoes. Some people like to serve Osso Buco with rice, but I prefer roasted potatoes and, as a vegetable, broccoli rabe sautéed with garlic and olive oil. I think that the menu sounds pretty good and I plan what I will need to buy at my favorite Italian specialty market, Grometti's, where I shop for all my special dinners.

All this thinking of food has made me hungry, so I stop into the local deli by the water for a quick roast beef sandwich and sweet iced tea. There is a little picnic area on the outside of the deli with tables and seating and I go to an empty bench and sit down. It is a very peaceful place, close to town that overlooks Huntington Harbor and I go there as often as I can. It's nice being able to just relax and think about all that's happened. When I finish my sandwich, I take one long look at the beautiful harbor and all the boats and I get back in my car and head for the hospital.

After I park the car and run in to see if I can spend some time with Beth and Fred before I go to see Uncle Al. When I get to the nurses' station, I don't see Beth, but Nurse Breuer is on duty and immediately guesses that I'm Rambo or Rocky as my face is a dead giveaway.

"Hey Rocky, you looking for Beth?"

"Yeah, is she around?"

"Your big date isn't until Saturday, right? So, what gives?"

"You're kidding! She told you about our date?"

"Remember the sisterhood! We get all, well almost all of the details and we won't take 'no' for an answer."

I sigh, "Is she around?"

"Sorry, she's gone for the day, but if you have a message – no matter how hot or steamy it is, you can leave it with me!" Nurse Breuer starts to crack up.

"No thanks, I'll tell her myself. By the way, how's Fred Klein doing? I'm going stop by to say hello."

"Fred's doing so much better, I hear thanks to you. He's still weak, but he's eating, walking around and taking his medication."

"That's great; I'll head over to see him now."

"Okay Rocky, see you later."

What can I do? I'm stuck with that name, so I guess I just better live with it. I head down the hall to room 496 and peek through the door.

As Fred looks up, he gives me a big smile and motions me and tells me, "Come in! Come in, Chris. I'm so glad you stopped by."

I can see Fred looks like a changed man, "Wow, Fred you're looking so much better, I'm really glad to see that."

"Thanks Chris, I'm feeling so much better. The doctor and the nurses tell me that I'm getting stronger. Hopefully I'll get out of here soon, all thanks to you."

"That's wonderful news. I am truly happy for you Fred."

Fred seems like he can't wait to tell me something, so I ask, "Fred you look like you have some other news, what is it?"

"I got some good news about Tina, too. Cathy told me that she's out of the emergency room. They've done all the tests and it looks like she will be fine, health-wise, but I'm still very concerned about her mental state."

I put my hand on his shoulder and say to him. "I know she'll be fine, Fred, as long as she has you and your family to lean on. You'll all be in my prayers."

"Thanks, Chris that means a lot."

"Well, I'm off to see my Uncle Al to get my balls broken."

Fred says, "Yeah, I stopped by his room to say hello and thank him for all he did. He shot the bastard who would have ruined my Tina and got what he deserved. I'm just so sorry and upset that Al got shot."

"I know he saw that what he did for Tina was his duty. Now he's getting great care and I'm sure he'll be fine. Now, get some rest and I'll stop by tomorrow to see you." I walk to the door and turn and say goodbye to Fred.

Next, I walk across the hall to see Uncle Al but when I open the door, I see that he is asleep. I quietly go into the room and find a chair near his bed so I can to sit down until he wakes up.

It is then that I experience a very troubling vision.

He runs into the cave hoping to stay hidden away from the demons that torment him constantly. But as he seeks cover in the darkness of the cave, he realizes that he is not alone. Looking around, he sees the glowing red eyes of demons as the beasts come from behind the rocks and out of holes in the

*ground. Their deafening shrieks force the man to hold his ears
as they crawl on the ceiling and descend on him.*

*Fearful and suffering greatly, the man reconciles to the outcome
which seems preordained. There would be no reprieve as the
devils beat him to death.*

I stand there in the darkness of the cave looking at this man and watching him die. It is heartbreaking to see him lying on the cold, rocky floor of the cave, motionless. It is then another man, maybe a servant, enters the cave and he kneels next to the motionless figure and begins weeping for the dead person. He carefully lifts and carries the body outside; as he continues to mourn the man's passing.

*The servant reaches down and lifts the lifeless form from the
cave floor. He is overcome with grief as he lays the body near
the entrance to the cave. As the servant continues to mourn, a
group of hermits finds their way to the place where the dead
man lays and they kneel in prayer for the one they know as a
holy man. In the midst of their prayer, the holy man opens his
eyes and all present are astonished that he is alive.*

*Although in great pain, he tries sitting up, but he is in such
a weakened state, he is unable to stand. He summons enough
strength to yell at the men, "Take me back! Take me back
immediately! I must face these demons! Take me back now!"*

*Afraid, the servant and the hermits do not know what to do,
but St. Anthony would have none of it. "Take me back now!"*

*That being said, they lift him and carry him back to the cave.
When they let him down, they hear the screams of the demons
and the men all run out of the cave in terror. Now that he*

is back inside the cave once more, St. Anthony can be heard shouting,

"Come forth! I am not afraid! Come forth and face the might of the God."

The demons have now transformed into vicious beasts wanting to tear the holy man apart. As the devils approach, a flash of light appears out of nowhere. It is so blindingly bright that it fills the cave. The demons become so frightened that they shriek and run to the hell from whence they came.

As St. Anthony the Abbot lies on the floor of the cave, his spirit steps out of his body and comes to my side. I am astounded by what I have witnessed and ask him what I need to try and understand, "What was that light?"

"It is the light of heaven and the mercy of God. I was in fear and thought that God had abandoned me, but He did not. He was by my side always."

"Why did you think he abandoned you?"

St. Anthony explains, "He let me suffer and I could not comprehend why."

I immediately ask, "Did you ever find out the truth?"

"I did. God was always beside me; even in my darkest hour, He is there. I had to prove my faith, show that I had no fear because of my faith, and He would abide my battle with these demons."

"Why are you showing me these things? Your visions, what do these visions all mean to me?"

St. Anthony speaks to me in such a way that I become very disturbed by his words and the possibility of their meaning. "You will be facing your own demons as I have faced mine. You will be tormented and you will know true fear as I have known. You may believe you are alone in all this, but you are not. The Lord is with you, and The Sainted will always be with you, always."

"What will I…", but St. Anthony is swallowed by the light and disappears and I am back in the hospital room with Uncle Al who's still fast asleep.

CHAPTER 22

I am back in the present, sitting by my uncle's bedside for a few minutes in silence. I need to take the time to recall the vision and try to comprehend what is going to happen now. St. Anthony cautioned me that I will be facing my own demons and I will need to be strong. My memory of demon Juliano is indelibly etched in my mind and I recall how powerless I felt when I was tied and held captive is frighteningly vivid. I remember how St. Mary Magdalene confronted Juliano, Satan in human form, and how The Sainted drove him back to the hell he came from.

I ask myself more and more of the questions that I have no answers to. What if I am alone and Satan appears? Would I be brave enough to face him? Could I survive such a struggle with the forces of hell? I know the Lord and the saints will be there for me, but I'm no St. Anthony. If I were to die, I guess I would stay dead. With all these thoughts going through my head, Uncle Al wakes up.

For a moment he looks around and seems to forget that he is in the hospital, but then he looks over to me sitting on the chair next to his bed and mumbles, "Hey Chris, do you know what time is it?"

I tell him that it's a little past 6p.m.

Uncle Al rubs his eyes, "I must have been really tired. How long have you been here?"

"Oh, I've been here only few minutes waiting for you to wake up. Actually, the peace and quiet did me some good." I don't want to tell him about my latest vision, at least not now as I need to work it out in my mind.

I ask him, "How are you feeling?"

"Oh, pretty good. I am in some pain, but I guess it would have been far worse if it wasn't for St. Michael."

"I am so grateful that you're okay."

"I know you are. Hey, have you seen Fred? Did he tell you he stopped by to see me? I was so glad that he seems to be doing much better and he tells me that Tina is recovering nicely. I couldn't be happier for him."

"Yeah, I stopped to see Fred before I came in to see you. He told me."

Uncle Al smiles with his patented shit-eating grin and asks, "Oh, by the way, how are you getting along with Beth?"

I pretend that I'm pissed off so I say to him, "What is it with you both? How come you and she are planning our date?"

"What do you mean?" He says innocently.

"You know what I mean, getting me to cook her dinner for our first date. Do you know what kind of pressure that is?"

He now pretends this is the first time he's heard of this. "I have no idea what you're talking about. I would never do such an underhanded thing to my favorite nephew, the one I love most in this world."

"Oh, all of a sudden I'm your favorite nephew. I thought Tommy was you or favorite nephew."

"How can you say such a thing? Whatever possessed you to think that Tommy is my favorite nephew?"

"Don't change the subject; let's get back to the topic at hand. Why would you collude with Beth to choreograph our first date and, of all things, have her talk me into making dinner for her?"

"This is preposterous, who told you such a wild story?"

"Beth told me."

"Beth?"

"Listen, she gave you up quicker than Saddam Hussein in that rat hole."

He knows he's beaten and reluctantly admits, "Oh well, guilty as charged."

We are now laughing out loud as Uncle Al knows that, deep down, I would really enjoy cooking for Beth, and that she would love it too.

The conversation now takes a turn toward something a more serious subject. "Hey, Unc, can I ask you a question?"

"Sure you can."

I ask him, "You've been in life and death situations; you've confronted the worst and had to deal with your own fears. What did you do to overcome those fears? How did you find the courage?"

"Chris, the first thing is that you can never overcome that kind of fear. The fear is just there and you need to face up to it. Take the instance where I came face-to-face with Quintana. He had just killed the poor kid that got in his way, and then he raised his gun and points it at me. I was beyond frightened."

I couldn't even imagine how terrifying that must have been for my uncle, but I need to find out, "What did you do? How did you get through it?"

Uncle Al is thinking, trying to find the right words to tell me, "I don't know how to explain it, but I'll try to put it into words I hope you will understand. In the situation you are in, there is only you and your fears. You reach down inside your whole being and you know there is only one way to survive: and that is to face your fears."

"Is that how you felt when you faced Quintana?"

Uncle Al confides, "Yeah, it was exactly like that. I knew that I could die, but I also knew that bastard couldn't live, not after what he'd done for most of his life. At that point there seemed to be only Quintana and me in the room and my fears seem to change into something I could use something that made me realize just what I needed to do."

"I complete his thought, "…and that was to kill that bastard before he could kill anyone

else, right?'

"Exactly, I don't know if that makes any sense to you."

"It does. It really does. Thanks."

"You're welcome. What brought all this on?"

I don't think that it's the right time to divulge anything about Juliano to my uncle, not just yet anyway. I know he is still recuperating and I don't want to stress him out any more than he already is, so I tell him, "I don't know, I guess after all that's happened, I'm doing a little introspection, trying to see what I could have done differently. I keep going over all the things I did wrong. I also keep asking myself, would I have had your guts? I have so many questions but no answers."

"Chris, believe me when I say I hope you never have to go through what you went through again. I do know one thing though, if you had to, you would have the guts to face any fear. No doubt in my mind."

"Wow, coming from the man who shot the Parkway Serial Killer and Heriberto Quintana, that's some compliment."

"Don't let it go to your head." Uncle Al smiles at me.

I smile back at him, "I won't, thanks Uncle Al."

"You're welcome. Now, what are you going to make Beth for dinner?"

I am incredulous, "What, so you can tell the world? You're the last person I would tell anyway!"

Al feigns hurt feelings, "I'm deeply hurt."

"Good. You deserve it," I say, with another big smile.

Uncle Al and I sit and for a while and just talk. I genuinely enjoy these times; it's what I used to do with my mom and dad and it always made me feel better. We talk a little more about the saints and I reveal some of my visions. I can't tell him about how St. Augustine allowed me to see visions of purgatory and hell, words would never be adequate. But I do tell him the story of my prom night with Joanie as my date and St. Bernardine as my chaperone and he starts laughing so hard that tears come rolling down his face. He can barely contain himself, only taking a breath long enough to say, "Good going Romeo…" then he convulses into hysterical laughter again.

Rocky, Rambo and now Romeo, everyone seems to be enjoying themselves at my expense. Beth, Nurse Breuer and, always, my Uncle Al, but I don't care. Just to hear him laughing and to see him smile is a wonderful thing. Finally, he calms down and says to me, "Chris that is the funniest story I've ever heard. The only sad thing is that I can never tell it to anyone."

I empathize, "Not unless you want to get locked up."

It's late and I know that visiting hours have already ended, so I say good-night to Uncle Al and promise him that I'll be back to see him tomorrow.

He has a few more words of wisdom for me before I leave, "Chris, before you go, I want you to know that you are brave. Very few people would have done what you did to save Tina.

Never doubt your courage, because if you need it, it will be there."

I smile and say, "I hope you're right."

"I know I'm right. See you tomorrow. I love you."

"Love you too."

CHAPTER 23

In spite of the fact that I have a shop and business to run, I make the time to go shopping for my dinner with Beth. My favorite specialty shop in downtown Huntington is Grometti's Fine Italian Foods. For me it's like a trip down memory lane, with all the aromas and flavors of Arthur Avenue in the Bronx. I love to look over all the homemade pastas and freshly made antipasto platters. There are the aromas of prepared Italian dishes like eggplant parmigiana, sausage with broccoli rabe over rigatoni and cheeses like Romano and Parmesan and so much more.

Vincent and Angelica Grometti are the owners and managers; they've known me and my family for years, so when I enter the store Vincent sees me and greets me with open arms, "Hey, Chris, long time no see. How's your Uncle Al? I heard all about it on the news and I'm going over to see him later."

I am so happy to tell Vincent, "Thank God, he's fine now, but you know he could have died."

Vincent says, "That's what I heard and your uncle is in our prayers."

The subject now turns serious when I tell Vincent, "Both Uncle Al and I appreciate your concern, but what the hell are you talking about, 'long time no see'? I saw you last week when I had to sell a kidney to pay for that marinated flank steak."

Ever sympathetic, Vincent tells me, "Oh, don't worry about that, you've got another kidney."

"Yeah, and I might have to sell that one to pay for what I have to buy today."

"Oh, a big order!" Vincent turns away from me and yells out to his wife in the back of the store, "Angelica, you can book that Mediterranean cruise now!" He turns back and asks, "Should I bring in extra help to load the truck or are you gonna eat it here?"

"Wise ass, just take my order and I'll pick it up on the way home."

"Heh, heh. Okay, what do you want?"

I give him my list of all I need to order and tell him that it is an especially important occasion and everything has to be perfect.

Curious as ever, Vincent asks, "Special occasion, huh, what's the special occasion?"

"I have a date with the most beautiful girl in the world, except for Angelica of course, and I want to make her the best dinner ever." I tell him about the scallop and pasta courses, then say, "I am making veal Osso Buco for the main course and I need your best veal shanks, Vincent."

While Vincent is looking down my list and writing up the order he says, "Hey, maybe I'll come over for dinner, what you say? Help you out with that girlfriend."

"You can't! I won't do that to Angelica. The minute my girlfriend sees you I know I'll lose her, after all, have you looked in the mirror lately?"

"Ah, you're right. I've been told my looks could sink – I mean, launch – a thousand ships."

We shake hands and I tell him, "I've got to get back to the shop, but I'll stop by after work. Ciao!"

"Grazie e arrivederci!"

I leave Grometti's it's a short walk back to the coin shop where I spend the rest of the day filling orders, waiting on customers and evaluating a collection that I'd just bought. I look over the contents and I note there are some common varieties of coins that are of little value, but there are some treasures and I am excited to sort through them all.

It is getting late and I want to say hi to Beth, so I call her at the hospital before I leave the shop. The last time I was at the hospital, she had already gone home and I just want to hear her voice.

"Nurses' station, Beth Della Russo speaking."

"Hi Beth, it's me, Chris. How are you doing?"

"Hey Rocky, where were you yesterday?"

"Oh, I got to the hospital late and you'd gone home."

Beth commiserates "Oh well, maybe the gods are conspiring against us?

I let her know in no uncertain terms, "They better not be, at least not until I get to make you dinner."

With a smile that I can see right through the phone, Beth says, "I'm glad you're at least buying some of the good stuff from Grometti's."

Now I can't believe my ears, "How the heck…."

Beth laughs and lets me know, "My family has known Vincent and Angelica for years; they make the best foods. I was there earlier and asked them if they knew you and I found out they did."

"That son of a…! He better not have told you what I'm making." I am getting a little pissed off.

"Don't worry, Rocky; I tried to worm it out of him, but he was tight-lipped and loyal to you. Your secret is safe."

I'm relieved so I say, "Good, by the way, do you like tripe and lamb brains."

Beth sounds very agitated when she says, "Don't even try that on me. Ask my grandmother, she'll tell you what I do to people who tell me all those animal parts are delicacies in Italy."

"Okay, okay. I promise not to serve cow guts, pigs' feet and sheep brains."

"You better not, if you value your life."

I finally find something that puts Beth on the defensive and I want to save that knowledge for a rainy day. We speak a few minutes more. She tells me that she is leaving at 5 p.m., but would see me for our big date tomorrow.

I say, "Okay, see you tomorrow?"

"See you tomorrow, ciao!"

It is just a few days after meeting Beth, but I know I am hooked, including the line and the sinker.

CHAPTER 24

Work at the shop kept me busy all day, but things have slowed down, so I close up a bit early and go to Grometti's to pick up the food I'd ordered. The place is crowded as it usually is on a Friday evening so I just take a number and wait my turn. When my number comes up, Vincent motions for me to come to the other side of the counter.

"I didn't realize your girlfriend is Beth Della Russo! She is a lovely young lady and comes from a wonderful family. You're one lucky guy!"

"I know I am! Now all I have to do is make sure I don't screw it up."

"Hey, you're a smart, good looking and come from a great family, too. Everyone likes you, but there is one problem you got."

"Oh yeah? What's that?"

"You've got no fairy godfather and godmother."

I put my hand under my chin as if I am considering the fact and I have to acknowledge, "You're absolutely right that I don't have a fairy godmother and godfather, so where do I get them?"

"Right here!" Vincent and Angelica hand me two big boxes of everything I need for my dinner and much more.

I am shocked, "What's all this?"

Vincent and Angelica smile at me, "It's a present from your fairy godparents. You take this and make Beth the best meal she ever ate. Don't come back and tell me that you screwed up, you hear?"

I look down in the boxes at all that the Grometti's have given me and I look back up at these two beautiful people that have been a special part of my life and I am overwhelmed. "I really can't accept this, but I know you won't let me pay, so all I can say is 'Sono più grato che lei sa, l'amo entrambi.'"

"Don't worry, we know you're grateful, we love you too." I hug them both and leave the store with the makings of what I hope is a dinner Beth will enjoy. I drive home and put all the wonderful food in the refrigerator. The Grometti's also include some of their fabulous miniature pastries for dessert and I am confident that this will really be the dinner of a lifetime that Beth asked for.

I get back in the car and drive to my next stop, the hospital where visiting hours end soon, so I leave my condo and jump in the car. When I get to the fourth floor, I stop by Fred's room first, but he isn't there so I go to see Uncle Al. He's looking rested and I ask him how he is doing.

"Oh, I'm fine; the doctor is going to take me down to run some more tests, but I think that it's more a precaution than anything serious. I'm not worried; I've got an angel looking out for me, and no ordinary angel, an archangel is watching over me."

I smile and say, "St. Michael certainly is, but don't piss him off, though, he can really pretty tough."

Uncle Al smiles back and while we wait for him to get the tests, we speak some more. He tells me that the Governor's office called; he is fast becoming a big celebrity. The representative of the governor had asked about his condition and whether he needs anything. "I told him that I don't need a thing, but my nephew might need a loan to pay for all the food he bought at Grometti's."

I am dumbfounded, "Why is it that everybody knows what I'm doing before I even get it done? How the hell do you know these things? Did Beth tell you?"

"No, she didn't. By the way, did you know that Vincent and I went to the same high school?" Now my uncle busts out laughing and I resign myself to the fact that my life is no longer my own. I might as well get used to it.

I throw my hands up and acknowledge that I am defeated, "That's it; I give up. By the way, I'm taking a crap at 8 p.m. so be sure to tell all the detectives under your command, okay?" He laughs even harder and I join in. When you come to think of it, it's a really small world and mine is becoming the size of a cozy Ford Festiva.

I go on to tell Uncle Al that the Grometti's made me a present of the food I'm making for Beth. "They really are the nicest people."

Uncle Al agrees, "They certainly are. So, are you ready for your big night?"

"Yeah, I'll clean the condo tonight and do what I can to prepare for the meal. I'm planning to close the shop at 12 p.m. on Saturday, and then I'll go home and finish everything else. It should be fun evening and I only hope she likes it."

"She'll love it. I think she also likes you, maybe a lot."

I practically jump out of the chair, "How do you know these things? I mean…no, I don't know what I mean."

Trying to look like he's some kind of expert on affairs of the heart, Uncle Al says, "It's very easy, for me Chris, as you are well aware, I have a special knack for identifying when people have an affinity for one another. I am also the Chief Detective for Suffolk County, State of New York. I have access to the latest technology along with the unrivaled manpower that is represented by the Suffolk County Police Force."

I am very serious when I look at Al and say, "Did Beth say something to you?"

"Yeah, she said something to me. She likes you, Chris. So don't fuck it up."

I try to tell myself, "I won't. I better not."

Two orderlies enter the room. They roll in a gurney and set it next to the bed. "Ready for your ride, Chief?"

"Yeah, just keep it under the speed limit."

Together the orderlies help Uncle Al lift himself off the bed and onto the gurney. I must have had a worried look on my face because he says to me, "Don't worry, I'll be fine. Just be sure to enjoy yourselves. Let me know all the sordid details."

With that, the orderlies push the cart into the hallway and down to wherever they do the tests. I know everything is fine, but I am worried, anyway. I go into the hallway and watch as they take Uncle Al to the elevator down for his tests.

I wish Beth was here so we could just talk, but she has already gone home and I feel kind of lonely. I do have my date with her though, and that makes me happy. I think I'll head home and get a jump on all the stuff I need to do before she comes over for dinner.

I'm actually beginning to feel like a teenager with a major crush.

CHAPTER 25

I wake up Saturday morning, I think to myself, "Well, today's the day."

When I got home the night before, I decided to clean the condo from top to bottom and began to prepare a few things so that I could be ready to cook them in time for dinner. The food that the Grometti's gave me is perfect. The capellini is freshly made, the basil is also fresh and the makings of the marinara sauce are just waiting to be combined. The veal shanks look especially good, but I know I need to allow enough time for the Osso Buco to cook and for the meat and vegetable juices to thicken.

I leave home and drive to the shop early so that I can get as much done soon as possible. I continue to evaluate the collection I had bought earlier in the week. I'm a little more than halfway through when I figure that I'd made back what I paid for the collection, which makes me feel good. As I continue to work, the phone rings, "Hello, St. Aloysius of Gonzaga Coins and Currency."

It's Uncle Al with a special greeting, "Hey Romeo, just want to call and wish you good luck on your date tonight."

"Thanks, Unc, I'll need it."

"Are you kidding? You are the best cook I know, next to grandma and your mom of course."

I am nervous and feeling totally inadequate, but I say, "I doubt it, but thanks for the compliment. I'm just spending a little more time here and then I'm heading back home to make the dinner. I'll be by to see you, but I can't stay long."

Al knows that I'm really nervous about my date with Beth when he says, "Chris, don't be silly, I'm fine. You've got to get ready so I'll see you tomorrow. Fred and I are scheduled to play a game of gin rummy, and I'll have plenty of company all day with family and visitors. Don't worry about visiting me today, just go home and do what you got to do and have a great time."

I am torn, but I appreciate his gesture, "Thanks, Uncle Al, I will, I love you."

He says, "I love you too and have a great time tonight."

I hang up and look at my watch, it's nearly noon when I finish my work so I close up the shop and get into the car. As I put my key in the ignition to start the engine, I receive another vision and I am transported to a prison cell and see a man at prayer.

As he sits in this prison, he ponders his situation and prays for guidance in what he must do before he is to be executed. The emperor has decreed that he will be beaten and stoned to death and the man had accepted his fate.

While he waits for his meal, the prisoner continues to pray. A short while passes before the jailer slides the key into the lock and opens the door. A meal of bread and water is put onto the floor of the cell, but the prisoner is more interested in the jailer than in the food.

The condemned man asks his jailer, "What is it that bothers you?"

The jailer looks at the man sitting on the ground. "Why is it that you are so interested in my troubles?"

"I am interested in all of God's children, and my Lord commands that I look to help those that I can help."

"How can you help me, you, a prisoner condemned to death?"

"My body may be captive and I may soon die, but my spirit, my soul will remain free and alive in the name of Christ."

The jailer answers in a harsh manner, "My business is my own." The jailer turns to walk out the cell door when the prisoner speaks out.

"I only seek to help, to understand what it is that troubles you. Perhaps I can be of help."

The jailer speaks in a manner that betrays bitterness and sorrow, "How can you help my blind daughter to see? How can you do this?"

With that the condemned holy man kneels in his prison cell and begins to pray. He prays so fervently that the jailer can only stare in silence at the man kneeling on the floor and says nothing at all.

When he is done, the prisoner rises and says, "Go home now, your daughter can see."

As I stand staring at the vision before me, St. Valentine's spirit rises from his body and says, "Even as we await death, we must continue to serve the Lord in whatever He commands. It is His will that the young girl sees and it is through His power that she can."

I am angry when I say to St. Valentine, "I cannot understand how you can be so generous and forgiving knowing that you will be put to death. You will be martyred at the hands of people just like your jailer."

St. Valentine answers, "It is not for me to judge these people; it is only for God to judge and He will when the final days are here."

The vision then changes. It is now the next morning when the jailer returns to the prisoner's cell. St. Valentine, in the midst of praying, stops and looks up to see his jailer standing before him. The jailer has tears in his eyes.

"Why is it you cry?"

The jailer stands in front of St. Valentine, and goes down on his knees. There are tears flowing from his eyes and down his cheeks. All the jailer can say is, "My daughter, she…she can see."

The saint smiles at the man. "It is through the power of the Lord, our God, that she has been given this gift."

"How…how did this come to be? How did your God make this happen?" The jailer is totally baffled.

"In Him all things are possible."

St. Valentine and his jailer rise and stand next to one another. The men look at each other for a long moment; the jailer then says, "It is beyond my power to help you. If I could, I would free you to go in peace, but I cannot go against the emperor's command."

The Sainted replies, "I know my fate, and it is sealed."

The jailer is now grief stricken that he is not able to help. "Can I do anything for you?"

*St. Valentine reaches into his cloak and hands his jailer a
note. The jailer takes the note and reads it aloud, "Ex tua
Valentine."*

*"Take this to your daughter and tell her that I am happy she
can see again."*

St. Valentine looks at me and smiles. "You have been told that you will
need to face the vilest of evil and have the courage to prevail. You should
also know that you will find happiness and love, and that it will sustain
you all your days."

St. Valentine then hands me a note. It is written in Latin and I read
it out loud, "Ex tua Valentine." I read it and look back up, "From your
Valentine."

"This is for you to give to anyone you choose. You must choose wisely,
for the heart needs true love so that it can keep from being broken. My
fellow saints wish this for you and we will pray you find your happiness,
your true love."

The bright light encircles St. Valentine. He smiles at me as he disappears and I smile back at him and I am very happy.

CHAPTER 26

Looking out the window of my car, I see the traffic on Main Street is getting heavy for lunch hour, so I make my way into traffic and drive home. When I get home, I set about making what I hope will be the dinner of a lifetime. I look for my mother's recipe and see she wrote that Osso Buco generally takes about two hours, not counting prep time. So, it appears that I'm in good shape for dinner at about 7:30 p.m. I also prepare the scallops, cut and season the potatoes for roasting at the same time I'm making the tomato basil sauce for the pasta. All that is left now is to roast, sauté and boil closer to the time we will sit down to dinner.

The afternoon goes by fast and at about 5 p.m. I hit the shower. I shave again as no stubble is allowed and I try to decide what to wear. I need to try and look as good as I can so I can distract from my somewhat less noticeable bruises. I look in the closet and I decide on my blue blazer, tan slacks and a white button-down shirt. I have a great pair of loafers and I consider wearing socks versus not wearing socks; I went with wearing socks. I look in the mirror and I am satisfied that my wardrobe seems to complete the traditional kind of look with which I am most comfortable.

I go back into the kitchen to make sure everything is coming along as planned and I am satisfied that it is. I set the table in my dining room, which I inherited from my mother and father and I use the plates and flatware that they only used on special occasions. Next, I arrange the table with a vase full of summer flowers and long tapering candles in the silver holders that I also inherited from my parents.

The combination of aromas from the food I'm cooking smell wonderful and everything looks great. I am ready!

The phone rings and caller ID shows that it's Beth's number. I think the worse and expect to hear, "Oh no she's breaking our date" so I answer expecting the worse.

"Hello?"

"Hi Chris, it's me, Beth."

"Hi Beth, what's up?" I am getting distraught over the prospect of her canceling our date.

"Well, I got caught up doing somethings with my mother and sister, but now I'm running a little late."

I'm totally relieved. "No problem, when do you think you'll get here?"

Beth says, "I should be there by 7 p.m. Is that okay?"

"Sure! See you then."

"Great. See you then!" and she hangs up.

Whoa, that was close. I can't believe how upset I got over the prospect of Beth cancelling our dinner. I consider that I must be in love or at least in 'like a lot' and I will use the extra time to make sure everything I've planned is perfect. When I am finished, I think there isn't much left to do, so I go onto the deck and just look out over the water. It is a beautiful summer evening, and I sit there for a while. I am looking forward to just relaxing and talking to Beth, and as I was thinking it over, the doorbell rings. I run to answer it and when I open the door, she is standing there. Her long, brunette hair falls over her shoulders and she is wearing this striking light purple color dress.

She smiles at me, "Hi, Rocky."

"Hi, Beth, wow, you look beautiful. Come on in."

She eyes me up and down, "Thanks, you look pretty sharp yourself."

"Thanks, and I'm glad to see you're right on time!" It's 7 P.M. exactly and technically she did call to change the time so….

"Hey, something smells great!"

"It's your dinner of a lifetime cooking in the kitchen. I hope you're hungry." I truly hope she is; otherwise, I'll have leftovers for a week.

Beth acknowledges, "I'm starving, but didn't you promise we would have cocktails first?"

"I sure did, I have vodka and can make us martinis or gimlets or I have wine —white or red. What is your preference?"

"Vodka gimlet…mmm, I'll have one of those on the rocks, please." I can't believe it; she likes my favorite drink.

"Great. I thought that we would sit on the deck and relax before dinner. Why don't you go through the living room out to the deck? I'll be right back with the drinks."

She says, "Okay," and I point her in the right direction.

I go into the kitchen, make the drinks and bring them out to the deck. Beth is by the railing looking out over the harbor, admiring the view and commenting on all the boats that are docked or moored. She looks so very pretty, standing there in the evening sunlight with the water in the background and I am at a loss as to what I should say next.

"Hey Beth, here's your drink. Would you like to sit down?"

She takes the glass and we both sit down on the patio furniture that I also inherited from Mom and Dad. We spend the next hour talking about our lives and families. She tells me that she was born in Huntington and she loves the town. She went to Cold Spring Harbor High School and then onto Molloy College for her nursing degree. She tells me that her father owns his own business.

"What kind of business?" I ask.

"He's in construction."

I look up in surprise, "Wait, hold on – your father owns Della Russo Construction?"

"Yes, that's him."

"That's one of the biggest construction companies on Long Island." I can't help but think that she's not only smart, beautiful and Italian now I have to add rich. Mom, what were you thinking? How could I ever hope…?

Beth seems very proud when she tells me, "He built his company to what it is and he's a great father, too. He works very hard for us and I love him very much. I also think my mom is very special, too. She spends much of her time taking care of our family plus she's president of the parish council and does charitable work raising money for a number of very worthy causes. My mom's always there for us and I'm really proud of her."

"I'll bet you are. I'm curious, what is the 'us' in your family?"

"Well, I've got a younger sister, Jamie and a younger brother, Tim. They can be real pains in the ass, but I love them always." She says this with a laugh in her voice.

Beth takes hold of the conversation and says, "Now it's your turn. This is a very nice condo, so selling coins must pay pretty well."

I laugh, "It's okay, I guess, but I still need to buy my clothes on sale. You see when my mom and dad passed away; they had a really nice three bedroom home not too far from here. They also managed to invest conservatively in whatever they could set aside. They also bought bonds and saved some money to put into CDs. My dad never really made that much money, so I guess he wanted security for the retirement that they never got to take. Anyway, the home and the money eventually came to me in the will and I was able to buy this place, open up the shop and put some money in the bank."

I hadn't thought about the legacy my parents left me in a long time and I say to Beth, "I guess I am blessed in the fact that I had the wonderful parents I had and that they gave me everything they could, even in death."

Beth looks at me and says, "Wise beyond your years."

"I'll say it again, if I'm so smart, how come I'm not rich?"

Beth looks into my eyes and maybe even my down to my soul and says, "I think you are a rich man in many ways."

We sit there and look at each other for what seems like an eternity until she says, "Hey Rocky, what about dinner, didn't I tell you I'm starving?"

"Huh…uh, I mean yeah, no problem it's all done, just a little last-minute mixing and heating."

"Need any help?"

"No, I've got it under control, how about another drink?"

Beth looks and me and says, "Hey, if I have another one of these, I'll get hammered and I might have to break our deal."

I ask her, "Our deal? What deal?"

"No fooling around on the first date, remember?"

"Oh yeah, that silly rule. I completely forgot and I was hoping you would, too. Anyway, we have wine for dinner and I promise it is of the pure and chaste variety."

Beth laughs and says with the brightest smile, "Okay, as long as it's of the pure and chaste variety,"

I'm thinking dinner will not be long in the making as I sauté the mushrooms for the scallops before I put them in the oven to bake. I add the cognac sauce and bake them for five minutes. I place a large pot filled with water for the pasta and place it on the stove to boil while Beth and I eat the scallops. When it's time to serve the pasta, I've have also sautéed the broccoli rabe and I'll heat it just before I'm ready to serve the Osso Buco. I am convinced that everything is going great and I'm somewhat anxious to hear what Beth will think of the dinner I've prepared.

I go back out to the deck and tell Beth that dinner is ready. I take her into the open dining area and hold her chair while she sits. She seems to be very pleased when she tells me, "Wow, flowers and candles…I must be pretty special."

I look over at her and say, "You are."

Beth becomes a little embarrassed and she looks away. It is an awkward moment, but I think that she needs to hear it from me. She immediately regains her composure though and says, "Thanks, but the rule is still in place."

I just say, "Damn it!" and we both laugh.

Beth and I sit down and I serve the first course and pour a glass of Sauvignon Blanc for both of us. I think the scallops are a little tough, but the cognac sauce is the perfect complement and she eats them with gusto. Beth is eating with real delight and she tells me, "These are fabulous! How did you ever make these?"

"Oh, they're really not too hard to make. It is my mother's recipe and we always had them on special occasions." After we both finish, I get up, clear the scallop plates and tell her, "The pasta is almost done, so just give me a minute."

I leave the table and go into the kitchen. I'm working at the stove, draining the capellini pasta, when I feel a pair of arms encircling my waist. I put down the sieve and turn around and come face to face with Beth. We look into each other's eyes and it is inevitable that we kiss. It is a long, passionate kiss and I feel like I have never felt before.

When we stop, she looks up at me and says, "I don't know what made me do that? We just met, but I feel like I've known you forever." Beth looks puzzled.

"All I know is that I fell for you the first time I saw you."

We kiss again and hold each other for a moment when Beth says, "Do you think it might have been the scallops in cognac sauce?" and we both crack up laughing.

Beth pulls away and says, "I want to help."

I give her a task, "Okay, take the capellini and put it into the pasta dish and add the tomato and basil sauce to it. I've already sautéed the broccoli rabe already and we can eat the pasta while it warms up."

"Okay, Rocky, by the way, I love broccoli rabe."

Beth sets about doing what needs to get done and a few minutes later, we are back at the table eating our pasta and enjoying each other's company. I open a bottle of Chianti which I think works great with the pasta course. While we eat, I learn that Beth became a nurse because a favorite aunt of hers is a nurse and her aunt loves what she does. She tells me that her family vacationed in Maine every year as she was growing up. It was at a cabin on a small lake near the town of Bridgeton and they were some of the happiest times of her life. Beth says she learned Italian from her grandmother and loves to speak it when they are together. I smile at her stories…

It's my turn and I tell her about growing up in the Bronx and how my mother gave me a love of cooking. I tell her about my dad and how hard he worked and that he always regretted never finishing high school. I tell her about my great uncle, Zio Francesco and how I'd watch him play bocce. I tell her I love what I do and, even though I'll never be rich, I can't imagine doing anything else. She smiles at my stories…

"Hey, I've got to tell you that you are batting a thousand so far. The capellini with tomato and basil is fabulous. I don't know if I can eat another drop."

"Well, you better leave some room for the main course…veal Osso Buco with roasted potatoes and broccoli rabe. I hope you like it."

Beth is happy to admit, "Like it? Osso Buco is my favorite dish in the whole world. You are an evil man, Christopher Pella. Do you know what you've done? You have ruined my diet, that what."

In all seriousness I counter, "Well, I can always throw it out."

Beth counter-counters, "Not if you value your life."

I laugh and go into the kitchen. The Osso Buco is practically falling off the bone and the sauce has thickened just a bit so it is perfect. I think about this evening for a moment and I figure out that my mother and some of the saints have to be helping me with this dinner because I've never cooked so well in my entire life. I place the veal shanks on a platter, spoon the sauce over the top and put the rest in a gravy dish. I surround the meat with the roasted potatoes and put the broccoli rabe with lemon slices in a serving dish. Everything is done and it looks perfect, well as perfect as I can make it, and I proudly march into the dining room. Beth is there like she is posing for a photo, with a knife in one hand and a fork in the other, smiling as she anxiously awaits the main course.

I place the platters between us and say, "La cena e servita!"

Beth responds, "Guarda meraviglioso, I miei complimenti al chef."

"The chef gratefully accepts your compliments and he hopes you enjoy your meal." With that, I set about serving the dish to Beth and myself. I open the bottle of Chianti and pour each of us glasses and we begin to eat our dinner. Even if I say so myself, the Osso Buco is fabulous. When Beth takes her first bite, her eyes go wide, and she looks up at me with this surprised look on her face: "This is unbelievable!"

I pump my fist and say, "YES!"

My attempt to make Beth her dinner of a lifetime turns out better than I could have hoped for and I think of my mother and how she would so be happy to see us now. After a while, Beth is completely full, but she's eaten only half of her meal is eaten I kid her and say, "I'll take that away now."

"Listen buster, if you do anything other than pack this up for me to take home, I'll give you more than a black eye."

"Promise?"

She laughs and says, "Promise."

We clear the table and load up the dishwasher. I put on the espresso and suggest we wait for a while before desert, which Beth agrees to whole-heartedly. It is getting dark, but we both want to sit out on the deck and enjoy this beautiful summer evening. There is a warm breeze and the lights from the road across the harbor reflect off the water. There an occasional boat heading for one of the marinas but at this time of night most of the boats are moored. It is very peaceful, a perfect setting for what is becoming the perfect evening.

Beth turns to me and gives me a wonderful complement, "Chris, I'll say it again, that was a fabulous dinner. I know how hard you must have planned and worked for this and I am so happy you made all this for me. Sono una ragazza fortunate."

"I'm the fortunate one. A beautiful woman, a beautiful night, great food and wine — what more can a man ask for?"

Beth looks at me seriously and says, "I told you, no fooling around on the first date!"

I just burst out laughing and she joins in. It is the perfect date. We sit on the deck for a while in comfortable silence. It's great to be able to sit with someone and just feel that you don't need to say a thing, just being together is enough.

After a while, Beth says, "This is a beautiful spot overlooking the harbor."

"It really is," I answer, "I was lucky to get it, given the location. Some of the furniture you see inside belonged to my parents and I couldn't give it up, so I brought it here."

Beth is genuine when she says, "It's nice that you think of your folks the way you do. I feel the same way."

We continue to sit, staring at the water while watching a party boat of fisherman returning from a day on the bay. Beth and I make small talk, enjoying the night and each other's companionship when I ask Beth, "Where do you live?"

"Well, my folks live in Lloyds Neck and that's where I grew up, but I now have a townhouse in Northport down in the pits. You know where I'm talking about?"

I'm really impressed, "Yeah, I do and I've driven through there. It's really beautiful; right on the water."

She seems very proud of where she lives. "Yeah, it is great. My family is into boating and I have a small boat — a 24-foot Chaparral. I love to go out on the waters off Huntington Harbor and Northport Bay. Sometimes I just cruise around and look at the homes along the shoreline. For me, it's very relaxing."

I go down the list in my mind; she's beautiful, smart, rich and Italian and she's got a boat. Mom, you're killing me here. "Wow that sounds great."

Beth lights up! "Hey, I've got a great idea. Would you like to go out on my boat one of these days? It really is a lot of fun. We can bring a picnic lunch and we can cruise the waters. What do you say?"

"Isn't that a coincidence? I've also got a boat."

"Really, what kind?"

"It's a five-inch rubber floater, lime green…I use it when I take a bath."

She doesn't seem to appreciate my sense of humor, "Very funny, what do you say?"

"Well, okay, but only if you let me bring the gas, my lunches are not nearly as good as my dinners."

"Okay, you've got a deal. You bring the lunch; I'll bring the boat."

We sit for a few more minutes and I get up and go in to get the coffee. I pour us both a double espresso and put out the platter of the miniature pastries that came along with all the food from the Grometti's.

Beth pretends she is outraged, "Oh, no!"

"What?"

"Napoleons…my personal favorites of all time; I'm going to kill Vincent when I see him." She looks angry as she reaches for the pastry, but her face takes on a whole other look when she takes her first bite.

"This is so delicious; maybe I won't kill Vincent after all." When we are done with our dessert, Beth looks at her watch.

"Well, it's way past midnight. I've got to work tomorrow, so I have to get home, but I've had a wonderful time, really." Beth and I get up from our chairs.

"So have I, it's the best time I've had on a date, ever. I only say this because I need to put pressure on you for our next date." I hold her hand as we walk to her car. I stand in front of her, pull her close and hold her. She feels soft and warm and I never want this moment to end. I kiss her, and she seems to melt in my arms. When we stop to look at each other, it seems that we both know we have found something very special.

CHAPTER 27

It's Sunday morning and I get up late and I go to a late mass. After church, I take a ride to Huntington Hospital to see my uncle and tell him about my evening with Beth and what a great time we had. Beth is on Sunday duty, but she's not around when I walk past the nurses' station. I actually had planned to stop in to see Fred, but he isn't there so I walked across the hall and into Uncle Al's room.

When I open the door, the first thing Uncle Al asks me is, "So how did the big date go, Romeo?

"Uncle Al, she is the most amazing woman I've ever met."

"Wow, sounds pretty special. So how did she like the dinner?"

I am all smiles when I tell my uncle, "I have to tell you this; it was about the best dinner I have ever made. Everything seemed to be perfect and I kept thinking that mom and the saints were watching over me to make sure I didn't screw it up."

Uncle Al appears to look very smug, "I can believe that and whose idea was it to make dinner for your girlfriend?"

I admit, "Yours, and you were right. I should only be so lucky if she was my girlfriend but I think that this couple thing is a longshot. Oh, by the way, she has a 24-foot Chaparral and she loves to go boating."

"Boy, looks like you won the jackpot."

"Yeah right, what does a guy like me have to offer a girl like her? If Mom is involved in this, she overshot the mark."

Ever sympathetic, Uncle Al says, "Hey jerk, take inventory. You're a good-looking guy, a solid citizen, you make a decent living — yeah, I know you'll never get rich, but who cares? You're even a great cook so all in all, you're not so bad. As a matter of fact, I'd go out with you."

"Wait a second, even I have standards. Oh, by the way, did you know her dad owns Della Russo Construction?"

"Wow, no kidding. Hey, didn't your dad work for Della Russo Construction at some point in time?"

It hits me, "Holy shit, I totally forgot that. I can't believe what an idiot I am."

As if I wasn't feeling insecure enough, Uncle Al says, "Well, I can believe you're an idiot. Listen pal, let things go the way they want to go and don't over think this. She likes you and that's all that matters."

"I guess you're right, but it does give a guy an inferiority complex."

"Are you kidding? You talk to saints. If anything, you are the one who stands head and shoulders above us schlubs." Uncle Al is looking remarkably good after his ordeal, and I tell him so. He smiles and says, "Well, like I told you, I have a guardian Archangel and that makes all the difference in the world."

We continue to speak for a while longer and before I am about to leave, he tells me that things are looking good, health wise and the doctors will let him know in a few days when he might be able to leave.

On hearing the good news, I am thrilled, "That's great!"

I have been checking his house every day and picking up his mail, which I have in a plastic bag. I hand it over to him, "Oh, by the way, I've been to your house, all is well and here's your mail. I included your checkbook, a pen and a bottle of aspirin; looks like you've got a lot of bills in there."

He reluctantly takes the mail, "Thanks Chris, I appreciate it. It will give me something to do after I finish cursing."

Then I have an idea. "Hey, if they let you leave soon, why don't you come and stay with me for a few weeks until you get back on your feet?

You'll have all the comforts of home, I can cook for you and I make sure you have everything you need and when you feel better, you can go back home."

"No, I couldn't impose like that."

"Of course, you can, you already do, anyway. Come on, I want to make up for almost getting you killed. What do you say big guy?"

"What about your girlfriend? Won't that put a cramp in your style?" Uncle Al has a way of butting into my life.

"No problem. I'll just lock you into your bedroom and, when she comes over, I'll tell her that you're embarrassed about your anatomically correct blowup doll collection. Come on, you know you want to come over. Come on, I'm begging you stay with me."

Uncle Al smiles and says, "You really are a good guy for wanting to do this. Sure, I'd love to come and stay with you and thanks for being a terrific nephew, well except for almost getting me killed."

"Great! I'll make sure that everything is set and ready for you."

We talk a bit more about my date and about the saints. I tell him about my vision of St. Valentine and about the note he gave me. It is written on a parchment type of material and it is written in beautiful script.

"This really happened? Can I see the note?"

"Sure," I pull the note out of my shirt pocket and show it to Uncle Al.

My uncle carefully holds the note in his hand; he looks at the back, holds the piece of parchment up to the light and examines it closely. He reads the inscription aloud, 'Ex tua Valentino'; Chris, do you know what this is? It's a relic, an actual relic given to you by Saint Valentine himself. I am in awe."

After Uncle Al says this, I realize the same thing, "You know, I never thought of it that way, but I guess it is a relic. He wrote it in Latin; I think that's because he knows Beth loves to speak Italian and well the language has its roots in Latin. I only hope that Beth and I are still together because I want to frame it and to give it to her on Valentine's Day."

Uncle Al smiles at me and says, "I couldn't think of a better gift."

"Neither can I."

We talk for a little while longer and plan what he will need when he moves into my condo. I let him know that I will go to his house and bring back all those things and not to worry about anything else.

The last command he gives me is, "…and don't forget my cookies and cream frozen yogurt. I can't wait until they let me eat that stuff again. It's like living with the Taliban here in this hospital."

I assure him, "Don't worry, if the doctors say you can eat it, I'll be sure to have it for you."

Uncle Al looks a little tired, so we say our goodbyes, but it seems that he has something else to say to me:

"Chris, you really are a great person. Beth sees that in you and she knows that you are special. Don't defeat yourself before the contest even begins. You are chosen to be a messenger of God on this earth and if God sees something special in you, then that's what counts.

Capisce?"

"Capisco e ringrazio."

"You're welcome…I love you."

"I love you, too."

CHAPTER 28

As she becomes conscious, she feels the cold, damp earth under her body. She tries to move into a sitting position, but with every movement, she finds herself becoming dizzy and disoriented. Where is she? The space all around her is dark, and the air is close and she is nearing the point of hysteria.

"Hello? Hello? Is anybody here?" No answer, no footfalls, no sound.

"Please, I need help. Somebody, please, help me."

…Still no answer, no footfalls, no sound.

After struggling for a time, she manages to get up into a sitting position; as her eyes become use to the darkness, more of her surroundings come into focus. There is cold, hard dirt and small stones on the floor of what seems to her as a prison of sorts. The walls bleed water from the jagged rocks that jut out from all sides. She thinks that she might be in a well…Yes, that's it. She fell into a well, but how, when? Nothing seems broken, but she aches all over and she is so very tired.

She knows she can't stay like this. She must get up off the ground. She has to summon the strength to walk around, even though it is dark. She has trouble seeing her own hand in front of her face, but in spite of it all she just knows she has to get up and moving. She struggles for what seems like a very long time…all the while, she is thinking she will never find the strength. But in what seems like an eternity she finally gets off the cold floor.

She must start to move but now that she tries, her legs become wobbly and she has trouble holding herself up so she leans against the rock wall of the place that has become her prison. She is only 116 pounds. How could her body feel so heavy? She grabs at the walls and walks all the way around the perimeter of the enclosure. From what she can tell, it is not so much a well, but rather a cave—no, not really a cave, more like a pit. How can this be? What is she doing in a pit? How did she get here? She can't remember and that makes it all the more frightening.

Wait, she remembers something! Margaritas! That's right, margaritas! But what about them? She loves margaritas and sometimes she has too many, but after all she is single, 24, pretty and there is always a guy willing to buy her a margarita or three.

Wait, she remembers something else. Julian! That's right, Julian! But what about Julian? He is so handsome and he dresses so nicely, very stylish… she loves the look. She is very familiar with his type. After all, she goes out with a lot of handsome, stylish men, but Julian is above them all and he likes her; he really likes her.

She walks around the pit once more and thinks that this place is looks like shit compared to…what is the name of her favorite hangout place? "Mia's Casa!" That's right, "Mia's Casa!" Now it all seems to be coming back to her, the margaritas, Julian, Mia's Casa, but where is she now? How did she get here and why is she here? These thoughts run though her head, but the more she thinks of where she is, the more frightened she becomes. She keeps thinking that she needs to keep calm, but that is not easy.

In what seems like a very long time, she finally hears a sound. The crunch of gravel under someone's shoes—then "ping," a tiny stone drops by her feet. She looks up, but it is too dark to see to the top. "Ping," another stone drops by her feet. She wonders what is happening, and as she looks up, she says, "Hello? Is anyone there?" She realizes that there really could be someone there, so she screams.

The screams are welling up from a place of fear so deep she can't stop. When she looks up, a tiny stone comes down. This time it hits her in the eye. It hurts, really hurts, so she moves back from the wall and hears a sound that she has never heard before. It is the sound of a million wings flapping and shrill cries; a cawing sound? Cawing birds? What are birds doing here?

Maybe they live here?

She tries to understand, but she can't think anymore. Her body aches, her head hurts and she just can't think anymore. As she wanders further into the madness of the moment, something brushes her hair, and she screams. Staring up into the darkness, she can't tell what it is, but it has to be one of the birds. "Whoosh"—again the sound by her head, but this time, it seems to pull on her long, blonde hair. She screams again and tries to find a corner of the pit where she can hide.

As she runs, she trips and falls and one of the birds swoop down to peck at her knee. She cries out in pain, but mostly in terror, "Leave me alone!" Another bird comes down and claws at her arms with its talons. As it flies away, she sees the ebony-colored feathers reflect what little light there is.

"Wait, I know that bird! That's a crow! But why are crows attacking me?" The answer would never come as the flying mass of black crows swoop down into the pit. They fly, each time closer and close, but this time when she screams, no sound can be heard.

First, they tear at her clothes, then at her body. Flailing arms, terrorizing screams are her only defenses against the onslaught of the crows. Her extreme pain is changing to numbness.

Panic, all-consuming fears swirl round in her mind "What is happening? Why me?"

For a moment, the crows stop and there is complete silence. The birds are perched throughout the pit, on the rocks and on the ground…waiting all about her in absolute silence. The crows look at her as she hugs herself. She feels the blood oozing out of the open wounds. Her salty tears flow and sting the cuts on her face.

She was pretty before, but she is pretty no more.

"Hello, Celine."

Who knows her name? Who cares?

"I'm down here," she screams, but her throat is so raw that it hardly is more than a whisper.

"What are you doing in this dreadful pit?" asks the concerned voice.

"I don't know…I don't remember how I got here. Please, help me! I'm bleeding."

"What happened, Celine?"

"I was attacked. I was attacked! I was attacked by crows! They are still here. They're here in the pit and I'm frightened. Please, help me."

His voice is calm and it seems to soothe her and she is finally able to speak without the hysterics.

"Can you help me? I'm hurt, and I need help. Can you help me?"

"Oh, I'm sure I can help."

The crows start to flap their wings, they shriek a shrill cry, they start to fly—first ripping her arms, then her legs and next they take out her eyes.

There is the crunch of gravel beneath his shoes as he walks up to the Celine's body. She doesn't look at all good and for this, he is very happy. The crows surrounded him, but he isn't worried. They always do what they are told. Julian continues to stare at Celine as if in a trance. He knows that there must be closure and he knows what he must do. He reaches down and lifts her once pretty, silk dress. Under her dress, her legs and thighs are smooth and untouched by the crows. He knows they would be because he told the crows not to touch her there. As he lifts her dress, he fondles her mound, but not in a way that resembles passion or lust, it is more like an examination. Her panties need to go, so he rips them off and throws them aside. Now she lays there dead, naked from the waist down and he smiles.

Slowly, painstakingly, he moves his hand into her vagina. He feels the moisture of her juices. After all, she is only dead a few minutes. Further and further his hand, wrist and lower arm makes its way up her canal and he stops. There is no strain, no feelings or emotions, no reason on Julian's face or in his mind—he is there for a singular purpose.

He stops as if he feels something. He does feel something and he grabs a hold of it. In a split second, he removes the recently conceived fetus and it dies.

Celine didn't know she was pregnant.

CHAPTER 29

It's just ten days after Al was shot that he is released from the hospital. All the doctors and nurses are still in total amazement. When asked about his miraculous recovery, he will smile and tell anyone who would listen that it is all because he started drinking beer when he turned twelve-years-old. As he leaves the hospital the entire staff lines the hallway to applaud him for his speedy recovery and his bravery. Chief Al Barese is not accustomed to all this attention, but he is thankful and he gratefully acknowledges the care and attention he received while in the hospital.

He agreed to move into my condo when I asked him to stay with me for the next two weeks and it is a great time for both of us. Uncle Al tells me a number of family stories that I had never heard before; some funny, some sad, but sitting there with him gives us time to bond. During the time he stays with me, I'm also able to make sure that he relaxes, eats right and gets better. I love to cook, so I get to make him all his favorite foods and I'm sure he gained back all the weight that he lost in the hospital. But the day comes when we both know that he is well enough to go home and we are both glad, but a bit gloomy.

"Hey Chris, looks like you will be getting your digs back. I'm going to go home tomorrow and back to work next week."

I smile and let him know, "I figure you'd be leaving when I noticed that the silverware went missing."

He laughs and says, "Well, the price of silver has never been higher; at least that's what I hear on the radio."

I mean it when I tell him, "Unc, having you here has been great and aside from the fact that you're a slob, I'd do it all again in a heartbeat."

"Thanks, Chris, you've been a terrific host and I am so fortunate to have you as a nephew. I had a wonderful time, too."

"I really am going to miss you, Uncle Al."

"Okay, enough with the slobbering. Now what about the beautiful, smart, rich, boat owning Italian girl? What was her name? Mildred? Harriet?"

I'm in on the joke so I say, "Beth."

"Yeah, that's right, Beth. So, how's that going? When are you two getting together again?"

Beth had stopped by the condo a few times to see both me and Uncle Al, but there has been no time in our schedules to make another date. Either I'm working or she's working, so we keep trying to find a time that we are both free. "Well, she came by to visit and we talk all the time, but the getting together part has taken a back-seat over the last couple of weeks, but we do have another date all set."

"Really? When?" Now Uncle Al's is curious.

"We're going out this Sunday; we are going boating on Northport Bay. I've got to admit, though, I'm a little nervous about this. I can't help but think we come from the two different worlds and I'm still feeling kind of insecure."

Uncle Al keeps reminding me, "How many times do I have to tell you this? All that stuff will work itself out and whatever happens usually happens for the best. So just sit back, relax and enjoy her company."

"Yeah, I guess you're right. I look forward to spending the day with her. Beth and I speak all the time, but we haven't gone out since our first date and I am excited to see her again, just to be alone with her, know what I mean?"

"Yeah, I do and I don't blame you. By the way, you remember my second-in-command, Dan Orello?"

"Yeah, a really nice guy as I recall. What about him?"

"After he gets off the night shift, he's gonna stop by here and drive me home tomorrow, so don't worry about driving me there."

"You sure? It's really not a problem."

"No, I'm sure. Anyway, I want to get a complete update about the department and the case load, so it will be quality time for us."

Uncle Al and I spend the rest of the evening eating, talking and watching TV. As I know it will be his last day with me, I buy him a half-gallon of cookies and cream frozen yogurt and he attacks it. When it gets late, we say our good nights and go to our bedrooms. I try to fall asleep, but sleep just won't come. It is then that I have another vision.

The day is grey and overcast. Mothers, fathers, town elders, clergy are standing on the shores of Lago Delle Grazie, Lake of Thanks—but there is nothing to be thankful for. The bodies of the children lie cold and lifeless on the shores of the lake. The wails of the assembled parents can be heard all the way to Tolentino. How could this have happened? How could their children be dead, drowned? Even though they mourn, they still question why and plead to God to bring their children back to life.

They ask over and over again: Why has God abandoned us? But there is no answer to their entreaty, no relief from their torment.

In the midst of all this sorrow, the people look to the holy man, the preacher, the worker of miracles for answers to their questions. It is then that St. Nicholas appears to the crowd, having heard the cries from his cell in the monastery.

All who know The Sainted venerate his holy ways. Is he not much loved by all in the town? Has he not worked with the poorest of his flock? Has he not been the only solace for the thieves and murderers that have been imprisoned or would be put to death by the authorities?

St. Nicholas feels the anguish of his congregation and he weeps with them. The villagers implore the holy man to work his miracle for them and for their children.

He continues to weep as he walks beside the bodies of the young children. The men and women of the village surround him, but it is only the children that matter—all else disappears from his sight. St. Nicholas carries a flower, a beautiful lily in his left hand as he stops to pray over these poor souls. He kneels down by the body of a young boy, no more than seven years old. The rest of those present at the lake kneel down as well and pray with him. The prayer seems to put St. Nicholas into a trancelike state as he places the lily on the forehead of the dead young boy.

A few moments pass, then the boy opens his eyes and looks up at the priest kneeling by his side. The boy's parents are frozen in place, not understanding the miracle, but as they realize what has happened, how they have been blessed, they rush to the son and hold him in their arms.

The miracle is repeated twice more; each time a young child is resurrected from the dead. The parents in the crowd stare in utter astonishment. Their children are returned to them, resurrected from the dead in what has to be a divine gift, a miracle, given to them by the saint living in their midst. They have no words—only wonder.

The priest, the wonder-worker, turns to the crowd and tells, "Say nothing of this, and give thanks to God not to me. I am only a vessel of clay, a poor sinner." St. Nicholas of Tolentine then turns toward the path and makes his way back to the monastery.

St. Nicholas steps out of the scene and looks into my eyes. "I cannot bear to see their suffering, and it is only through the divine mercy of Jesus Christ that I am able to dispel their sorrow. These young children will grow to know the Lord and they will hold Him close all their days."

I am joyful for the miracle that I have been allowed to witness and for the love that St. Nicholas has shown the families of these children, but I need to ask, "Why have I been shown these things? Why have I been shown this miracle?"

St. Nicholas looks up to heaven and then down to me and says, "I am showing this to you so you may know the true power of faith. Faith is what allows miracles to happen; faith and hope are all that is left for the souls in Purgatory."

The vision now changes and I am taken to a hillside outside of village of Tolentino.

The holy man is kneeling in prayer. He is weak after having fasted for more than four days. There now appears beside him, an evil figure not of this world with his face hidden from view. The demon is tormenting the holy man, and there is no relief from the suffering he endures.

St. Nicholas cannot think. He cannot even remember his prayers. The demon is holding a long, wooden stick in his hand and he is beating the saint who cannot fight back. The demon laughs and continues the fierce blows to the back, to the arms, to the neck and head.

"You are a fool; your miracles are worthless and God does not care that you suffer." The beating continues more brutally than before and the demon continues to laugh.

St. Nicholas, weak and suffering, is barely able to mutter this prayer, "Dear Mother of God, grant me peace, so that I may prepare my soul to appear before the Lord."

The demon screams at The Sainted, "There is no mercy. There is no reprieve from the pain that I will bring down on you. Your God and your Christ are gone, and you are forgotten." The fiend then brings the long stick down in one massive blow and St. Nicholas falls unconscious, his body and face swollen and bleeding from the beating he has taken.

The horror of the scene fades into the background and St. Nicholas stands before me again. "I beseeched the Blessed Mother for relief from my enemies, and she granted me that wish."

"Why does this demon, this devil, torture you?" I ask him the question, not really expecting an answer.

St, Nicholas responds, "He is prideful and he is jealous. He seeks the souls of men and women, but with each miracle I perform in the name of Christ, that corruption of souls becomes harder and harder. The demon tortures me because he knows he cannot defeat the power of Heaven."

That having been said, the scene comes into full focus; the demon is still beating the unconscious man. St. Nicholas and I are looking at this and the devil stops and raises his head. I look at St. Nicholas, but he doesn't look back. He points to the evil spirit before us. I am transfixed on the figure as he lifts the cloak from his head and slowly turns to me. I turn pale, for all I see is Juliano.

The vision of St. Nicholas and Juliano is so disturbing that I have the most fitful sleep. When I wake up the next morning, I feel sick to my stomach, so I run to the bathroom. The nausea passes. I shower, brush my teeth and shave to start another day. As I pass Uncle Al's bedroom, I see that his closet is empty and the bed made. I guess it is at that point that I realize he is really gone and I acknowledge to myself that I will miss having him around.

When I go to the kitchen, I see the breakfast table is set and on top of my plate is a note from my uncle.

Dear Chris,
Well, these two weeks flew by in a flash, and I am so grateful that you let me stay with you while I was recovering. To tell you the truth, I never really needed to recover and I think you know why.

I must say, you are the perfect host and a great cook. I went on your bathroom scale this morning, and guess what? I am back to being overweight, thanks to you! I must have consumed an extra ten pounds in fat, carbs and calories, so I can honestly say, I forgive you for getting me shot, but not for the heart attack I can expect to get in my later years.

I've been thinking about all the stories of your saints and what you have shared with them. What you have experienced is truly amazing and I can only say that you are truly blessed. The saints you are privileged to meet and the visions you are privileged to see can only be viewed as the miracle in your life, both as a great gift and a massive burden, one that I know you take very seriously.

I also sense that there is something that is troubling you and you are very worried over it. I guess you just don't want to speak about it now, but I want you to know that I am always here for you whenever you feel like talking.

Well, I hear Dan's car pulling into the driveway, so I'll close this by saying thank you.

Love,
Uncle Al

PS. I just set the table, I didn't prepare the food. You're much better at cooking than I am.

I smile and put the note down; glad for our time together and glad that he is my uncle. I wonder how he knows about my worries. I guess, after years of being a cop, you have instincts about those kinds of things. I haven't told him about the demons, but because he has a cop's intuition, he knows there is something wrong.

Someday I will be ready to share that side of the story, but not now.

CHAPTER 30

Well, Sunday is finally here and I am excited to spend the day with Beth. The weather is picture-perfect. There's bright sunshine, clear blue skies and warm breezes that all go into making this a beautiful summer day on Long Island.

I had gone to Grometti's the day before and bought all the items that I want to make for lunch. I've made sandwiches with fresh baked semolina bread, prosciutto sliced paper-thin, fresh mozzarella, roasted red peppers and romaine lettuce with a special oil and vinegar dressing. I also made a wonderful arugula salad with cherry tomatoes, sliced onions and more of the special dressing.

I pack the cooler with a bottle of delicious Cabernet Franc, along with a few of bottles of Peroni Nastro Azzurro, an Italian brewed pale lager along with a half-dozen bottles of water. For dessert, I made a fresh fruit salad with seasonal melons, cantaloupe, honeydew, watermelon, and I mix in some red and white grapes. I sneak in some napoleons so Beth can curse at me while she enjoys every bite; I'm all set.

I pack up my car and head toward her townhouse on the water. Beth lives in a gated community in Northport, which is part of the township of Huntington and just a short ride from where I live. As I turn down onto the street on the hill leading to her place, I get a glimpse of Northport Bay and all the pleasure crafts that are enjoying the water on this spectacular day. The sun glistens on the water like sparkling diamonds, and the salt air is fresh and fragrant.

There is a sign that welcomes you to her community called 'Northport Bay Townhomes' and I pull up to the gate and punch in her number and she answers, "Hello?"

"Hi Beth, its Chris."

"What do you want?" She says in a perfectly serious tone.

"Uh, I thought we had a date today."

"Wait, let me check my calendar. Hmm, I don't seem to have a Chris written in for today, but I do have a Rocky."

I smile and answer, "Oh, sorry—hi, Beth, it's me, Rocky."

She laughs though the speaker and says, "That's better. Come on in; I'm number 72 Northport Bay Court."

A buzzer sounds, and the gate opens to let me in. I drive down the private road into a beautiful residential complex of townhouses, all along the water. The homes are of a few different sizes, but they all have similar look and style. There are attractive plantings of trees and flowers throughout, a number of lovely ponds with fountains and expansive manicured lawns that make the surroundings appear like a park. I continue to drive along the main road past the clubhouse with its pool and tennis courts, there's even a small playground and, all in all, it seems like a fabulous place to live.

I pull into a parking space reserved for guests, and walk up to her door to ring the bell. Beth opens the door and for a minute I am caught speechless. She looks simply stunning. She is in white shorts that seem to add about twelve inches to her already long and flawlessly shaped legs. She is wearing a light blue blouse that clings to her body and emphasizes the contour of her waist and breasts. To complete the look, she is wearing elegant leather sandals, silver jewelry and some wonderfully fragrant perfume.

I try, but I can't hide my expression when I tell her, "Wow, you look gorgeous, if you don't mind me saying so."

She blushes a little, but bounces back and said, "I don't mind and thanks. Want to come in and see my place?"

"Sure, I've always wanted to know how the other half lives," I say this as I walk into the foyer.

Her house is beautiful, about what you'd expect in a waterfront community on Long Island. The architectural features of the three-story townhouse include vaulted ceilings, hardwood floors, a kitchen with cherry cabinets and a floor of terra cotta tile. She has a huge master bedroom and bath plus two spare bedrooms with two more baths. There's a family room with the latest in built-in audio and video. She also has the living room and dining room decorated in a combination of modern and antique furnishings. Light floods into all the rooms through large windows and sliding doors that look out onto a lagoon that leads to the bay. There is an atrium as you enter the front door, a large deck in the rear off the main floor and a patio on the ground level.

From the deck of her townhouse, you can see the private marina at the end of the lagoon. Beth tells me, "Each resident is entitled to access a slip space if you own a boat. That's where I keep my boat; the Fun-A-Bout."

"Your boat is called 'Fun-A-Bout'?"

She explains to me, "Yeah, I don't get much time off, so it's a thinly veiled reference to my favorite leisure time activity—having fun." Beth has prepared coffee and some bagels and we relax on the deck and talk about the beautiful day and her beautiful home.

"I know I'm a lucky girl and, looking around here, you probably think that I was given everything on a silver platter, but that's not the way it happened. My dad and mom always made me realize the value of accomplishing something on my own. I think that's why I work as hard as I can because I don't want people to assume that I'm a member of the lucky sperm club. I really want people to know I did a lot of it on my own, of course with some help from my family." She is very serious when she speaks, and I know it is something that is very important to her.

I nod my head in agreement, "I know what you mean. If it weren't for my family, I couldn't do what I do, but I also know that they cannot make me succeed. I need to do it on my own to truly know I've made it." Now I'm being serious.

We sit in silence for a few minutes. I am feeling a bit uncomfortable with the serious tone that the conversation has taken, so I say to Beth, "Hey, did you know that my father worked for your father?"

She seems surprised to learn this. "You're kidding! Really? I have to tell my dad. Your father's name is Anthony, right?"

"Yeah, it is. I looked up some of his old pay records and it seems that he was a foreman on a number of your dad's sites." It continues to amazes me on how small our world has become.

Beth looks at me and says, "I think that's why I feel like I've known you forever."

"Hey, the cooler has wheels so what do you say we walk down to the marina? You can show me the Queen Elizabeth, a.k.a. Fun-A-Bout."

"Sounds great, but we have to do one thing before we leave."

"What's that?"

Beth gets up from her chair and walks over to me. She puts out her hand and I take it and get up from my chair. She looks beautiful as she put her arms around my neck and looks me in the eye. I put my arm around her waist and we embrace as our lips meet in a long and passionate kiss.

When it ends, she looks at me and says, "I wanted you to hold me and I didn't want to wait any more."

I hold her close and whisper in her ear, "I'm glad you're the impatient type."

Beth smiles and she allows me to continue to hold her in my arms. The day, the place, the time all seem to be ideal and I've never felt like this before. We kiss again, and Beth says, "Okay, too much fun; let's go boating."

This is one funny girl. I laugh, "Okay, let's go!"

I grab the cooler from my car, get my sunglasses and we start walking towards the marina. There are paths through the complex and I get to see the clubhouse and some of the other townhouses. When we get to the gate of the marina, and look out over the water, I'm able to view a panorama of the bay with all the pleasure crafts. A short distance away I see a small island in the center of the bay that I'd forgotten is there.

I ask, "Hey, Beth, what's the name of that island in the middle of the bay?"

"Oh, that's Pit Island. It was named that because this entire area used to be a sand pit. Over the years the sand was mined and used to help build major roads and highways. When the sand was all mined out, some enterprising developer purchased the land and built these townhouses. He also dug out the lagoon to give every resident a waterfront home and the rest is, as they say, history."

"That's some story and some great place to live" I say, while admiring the incredible view.

We walk down the dock until we reach the slip space where I drop the cooler down and help Beth remove the canvas. After we take off the canvas, I tell Beth, "What a great-looking boat. How long have you had it?"

Beth tells me, "It's a 2008, but I bought it used and I've had it for four years. I just love it. It's not too big and not too small and I can manage it by myself. Its great size for the bay and it is perfect for when I go water-skiing with friends, but most of the times though, we just chill.

The thing is we have fun all the time; hence the name 'Fun-A-Bout.'"

No argument here, "That works for me."

Beth starts the engine and expertly maneuvers the boat out of the slip space and down the lagoon to the bay. Her plan is to cruise along the perimeter of the bay, so we can look at the beautiful waterfront homes. There are a number of other crafts on the water, but there is plenty of open water so we motor at a low speed to give us time to enjoy the day.

"Aren't those places along the water wonderful? I just love to cruise around Asheroken, Eaton's Neck, Centerport and Lloyd's Neck. I enjoy looking at the homes". Beth seems to totally relax as she puts herself in the moment and so do I.

I agree, "This is truly a beautiful place and I can see why you love it,"

"My mom and dad have a really nice view from their home in Lloyds Neck. I'll be sure to point it out if we pass it."

"Great!" Now I'm thinking her parents' home is on the water in Lloyds Neck; mom you're killing me here."

She looks on the deck and asks me, "Hey Rocky, what's in the cooler?" See what I mean, totally at ease.

"Remember? I promised to bring the gas. Well, Vincent and Angelica made sure that I wouldn't disappoint you. In the cooler I have my special prosciutto sandwiches on semolina bread, a nice crisp arugula and tomato salad and some red wine and Italian beer. I hope you like it."

"Sounds wonderful! Why don't we finish the tour and then we can anchor near Pit Island and have our lunch?"

"That works for me."

The sun and the warm breezes feel wonderful as we continue motoring around the bay. It is a very relaxing time. Beth and I don't feel the need to speak; we just feel comfortable in each other's company. When it is close to 1 P.M. we decide it's a good time to anchor and stop for lunch. Beth spots a place near Pit Island where she can anchor the boat so we would be out of the way of any traffic.

We take out the deck table, set it up in and opening in the floor provided for just that purpose. I take our lunch out of the cooler and I place a sandwich on Beth's plate along with tossed salad and the dressing and hand it to her along with a cold Peroni.

Beth's reaction to her first bite is to say, "Mmmmm, this is delicious. You have to tell me how you make the dressing."

I say, "It's really simple—white wine vinegar, canola oil, spices. I'll write it down for you when we get back."

Beth says a muffled, "Sounds great" as she takes another bite of her sandwich.

As the day goes on and the time with Beth is so perfect, it seems like a dream. The calm waters, sunshine and a beautiful woman make me feel that I am lucky just to be here. Beth and I talk through the entire lunch about many things, great and small, all the while feeling more and more comfortable with each other.

My gaze falls on Pit Island and I ask Beth, "Have you ever been to Pit Island?"

"No, the water is very shallow and there are large, jagged rocks just under the surface. Trying to get a boat close enough is a blueprint for disaster—or at least a $5,000 'fix-the-hole in the hull' bill."

I can't imagine why, but I am becoming more curious about this place. "Do you know who owns the island?"

Beth just shrugs, "I don't know. I guess it belongs to the county or the state, but since no one ever goes there it just stays the same. Why are you so interested?"

"I don't know, maybe pirate treasure. Do you know what pieces of eight and gold doubloons are going for?"

She asks the perfunctory question, "No, what are they going for?"

I ponder an answer, "Well, depending on the age, the denomination and the metal content of the coin, the value could range from…"

Beth stops me in mid-sentence, "I'm just making small talk and trying to be polite. Don't try to make me one of your coin collector buddies." Beth says this with such a beautiful smile that I don't care that she isn't interested in coins or collecting.

"Okay, you got me at my boring best. I promise never to bring up how I make a living and one of the things that make me happiest. Who cares if you don't care? I can take it. I remember when I was a little boy…"

I am speaking when Beth gets off her seat and sits right next to me. She puts her arms around my shoulder and looks me straight in the eye. "Do you want to discuss some old metal coins, or do you want to kiss me?"

It is a question that needs no answer. I reach over and hold her tight in my arms and I kiss her with a passion that is returned in kind. My feelings for Beth are becoming so strong that I have to stop in the middle of the kiss and just look at her.

"Beth Della Russo, you are the most beautiful woman I know and I can't believe that I am here with you."

"I think you're beautiful too, or should I say handsome? I love being here with you, too. It's just so weird how I feel about you; I know I've said it before, but it's like I've known you forever."

While we are speaking, the temperature drops and the air suddenly turns cold. I look up at a large, ominous grey cloud directly overhead. The cloud completely blocks the sun and the sky becomes darker. The wind starts to pick up and when I look over the bow of the boat towards Pit

Island, I see strong gusts actually bending the top of the trees that appear near their breaking point.

Beth is bewildered and says in an anxious voice tone, "I've never seen anything like it before. The only place that is dark is right over the boat and Pit Island." She points to the island, "Just look at the trees bending in the wind; you don't see that anywhere else. What could be going on here?"

"I don't know, but do you think it's safe out in this weather?" I say, worried that something might happen to Beth.

"Maybe you're right. Why don't we head back to the marina and we can sit on my deck and enjoy that so-called fabulous Cabernet Franc?" She says this in a lighthearted way, but I can sense she is worried.

I try to change the subject, "What do you mean 'so-called fabulous Cabernet Franc'? Just wait until we get back, and taste it for yourself." I tell Beth that I will hoist the anchor, and secure all the other gear on the deck and while I'm getting it done, she can start the engine.

She turns the key, but the engine won't turnover. "That's funny it always starts on the first try. I wonder what's wrong." She tries to start the engine again, but to no avail and the wind is picking up. We both then realize that the boat is being carried toward Pit Island and the jagged rocks that surround it.

Beth yells to me to lift the anchor, so I run to where it's stowed and try to open the hatch. There is an electric winch with a switch in the hatch where the anchor is stowed. I need the winch to work as the anchor has become much too heavy to be lifted by hand. I struggle to open the hatch so I can find the switch, but the hatch won't budge. Beth is still trying to start the engine, but now the anchor seems useless as it is being dragged along the bottom of the bay.

The boat keeps drifting closer and closer to the rocks and I call out to Beth, "Beth, where is the engine compartment?" She tells me that it is under the seat near the stern of the boat. I hope and pray that it's not stuck like the anchor's hatch. I get over to the stern and lift the bench seat and it opens fine. I look down into the engine and smell gas and I'm guessing that there is a leak, and in a few seconds, I see the problem. A fuel fitting has come loose from the tank and gas is spilling into the engine compartment.

"Beth, don't prime the engine anymore; the fuel fitting came loose and I need to hook it back on."

She is getting more worried by the minute, "Okay, but hurry, please! The boat is drifting and we are getting too close to the rocks."

The waves on the bay have gotten very choppy and the boat is rolling back and forth. I know Beth is frightened and so am I, but I need to get this done. I reach into the engine compartment and grab the hose and fitting and reattach it to the tank. I also find the coupling that keeps the fitting in place and I reattach that. I yell over the wind, "Try starting the engine now." On the first attempt, Beth is unable to start the engine; neither is she able on the second attempt.

"Try giving it a little more gas," I say.

The anchor on the Fun-A-Bout has continues to be useless as it drags along the bottom of the bay toward Pit Island. As the situation is becoming more desperate, the moment freezes in time and I have a vision.

Appearing on the water on the port side is a saint clothed in the brown habit of a nun and surrounded by a halo of golden light. Her hands are folded in prayer and there is a fresh, bleeding wound on her forehead. The scene suddenly changes and I am in a medieval church.

> *At the altar stands the groom. By the look of his robes, he is a wealthy man and not used to be kept waiting. The priest walks to the middle of the altar and faces the crowd that has gathered. It is then that the bride approaches from the rear of the church and marches toward her intended. She is a child, no more than twelve years old, and she is to be married.*

I stand on the side of the altar when the scene changes yet again and I am in the home of the now-adult woman.

> *Her tears will not stop as the men carry the body of her husband into their home where Rita has built a life together with Paolo. Through the prayers, patience and the kindness of his wife, Paolo Mancini has become a better person, but now he is dead.*

He was killed by Guido Chiqui who had sworn vengeance on Paolo for some real or imagined insult.

Her sons, Giovanni Antonio and Paulo Maria, stand silent as they stare at the body of their father. La Vendetta has taken his life, but his sons pledge vengeance would be theirs.

Their uncle has been poisoning the minds of his nephews, demanding vengeance for his brother's death. "You cannot let this go unanswered. Your father lies in the cold earth because of Guido Chiqui and for this he must die. Do you hear me? Die!" Their uncle now makes his nephews swear revenge.

Rita knows this would be their response, so she stands before her two sons. "Do not listen to your father's brother who would have you commit an act of murder. You must not seek revenge. It is a mortal sin and you will be punished, condemned to spend eternity in hell. You must know that it is only God who can deliver the justice you seek. I have forgiven Guido Chiqui and you must do the same."

The scene changes once more and now it is St Rita who is standing alongside the graves of her sons. St. Rita of Cascia steps out of the scene and turns to me.

"I mourn the loss of my sons, but I thank the Lord that they did not seek revenge. They did not die in sin."

I ask her, "How did your sons die?"

She answers, "They died of the bloody flux."

St. Rita, the patron saint who helps those in very anxious situations, has lived through such things that no parent should have to. I realize why she is sent to us and I beg her, "I don't know what to do. Beth and I are in great trouble. Can you please find a way to help us?"

St. Rita looks me in the eye and says, "I know you are in a desperate circumstance and I am here to show you the way." St. Rita reaches into her cloak and takes out a perfectly formed red rose. She hands the rose to me and says, "The power of God is infinite as is His mercy. When you place this red rose on the waters you will see that all will be calm." St. Rita of Cascia, a woman whose life of devotion and piety are glorified still today, slowly vanishes and I am back in the moment.

The storm keeps raging as the boat is carried closer and closer towards Pit Island and the surrounding rocks. I scream above the wind, "Beth, can you start the engine?" Just as she is trying to answer, an enormous swell comes over the side of the boat and lifts Beth right off her feet. She screams and the rose drops from my hand as I leap to save her from being washed overboard. At the exact moment she is about to go overboard, I jump to her side of the craft, managing to grab her arm. I pull her back and bring her to the relative safety of the deck before she is washed over the side and drowns.

As she is coughing up water, Beth looks up at me and says, "My God, Chris, you saved my life."

I see the rose floating in a puddle on the deck so to distract Beth, I tell her, "Try to get the boat started." She turns away from me and I lunge for the rose. I grab it and throw it off the side, onto the waves that are threatening to completely swamp the boat. In an instant the waters calm, and the dark grey cloud literally melts away.

Beth turns the key and the engine starts on the first try. She turns and at the gauges and all is running perfectly. Now Beth is totally bewildered as she looks at me for answers, "What— what happened? How in the world…?"

Beth seems to be in shock, so I have her sit down while I get everything ready to motor back to the marina. I'm able to get the hatch open and lift and stow the anchor with the winch. Then I take hold of the steering wheel and guide the Fun-A-Bout away from Pit Island and the rocks that would have wrecked the boat, possibly killing us both. As I steer the boat and set a course back to the marina, I look at Pit Island and all seems to be just like it was before. The trip back takes about fifteen minutes and by the time we get to the slip space, Beth is feeling much better.

"Hey Chris, you've done enough good deeds for one day. Let me dock her; this can get tricky."

"Wait? Who's this Chris guy? I thought I was Rocky—or at least Rambo?"

"Believe me, in my opinion, you're both right now." Beth says as she expertly brings her boat into the slip space and we tie up the Fun-A-Bout.

We get off the boat and just stand there, dripping wet. For a moment we try to gather our thoughts to come up with the right words to say to each other. When I finally speak, all I can think to say is, "Some fun, huh!" I burst out laughing. Beth joins in and soon we are both in laughing hysterically.

After a few minutes, we calm down and Beth says, "Why don't we go back to my place and have some of that fabulous Cabernet Franc?"

I will not let her initial insult to my wine go unanswered, "Oh sure, you practically drown and all of a sudden my so-called fabulous Cabernet Franc becomes my fabulous Cabernet Franc."

Beth just looks at me and smiles, "Well, after the kind of day we've had I think that as long as I get to drink a glass of Cabernet Franc, or any wine for that matter, it's always fabulous."

I look back and say, "How true."

I take her in my arms and just hold her and she holds me back.

CHAPTER 31

She embraces her mother and father, holding them tightly, for the journey to Proceno will be long and difficult. Agnes knows that she may not see them for many months and this makes her sad.

She is also leaving her beloved Montepulciano, her beloved Franciscans. Even though Agnes was born into wealth, she has been happiest in the convent with these wonderful nuns and their simple ways of life and devotion to prayer. Agnes is only fifteen, yet she has been enjoying complete peace. Now she must leave for Proceno in the county of Orvieto, to found a new convent for the Dominican Order. The journey is very tiring, but Agnes would use this time to explore the secrets of God, the Father in prayer.

It is late winter in the year 1283 when Agnes arrives at the large stone building that serves as the convent. At the entrance to the convent there is a group of priests assembled anxiously awaiting her arrival. Agnes is truly surprised by this and uncomfortable with what she feels is more importance than she deserves. "Good priests, I am honored that you would be here to greet me on my arrival."

The leader of the delegation says, "Good sister, we bring blessings, greetings and a message from His Holiness Pope Nicholas the IV."

Agnes is incredulous, "The Holy Father has a message for me? What could the His Eminence possibly want of me?"

The priest that has been chosen to relay the message speaks to the young nun speaks, "You are being called to serve your God and your church in a way that you may not have imagined."

Agnes, barely fifteen years old cannot imagine what her calling could possibly be, "In what way does His Holiness ask me to serve?"

The priest tells the young woman and all that are present, "You are to become the abbess of the monastery in Proceno."

It is Agnes who cannot believe what she is being asked to do, "I, an abbess? Surely His Holiness knows that I am only fifteen years old. I am not worthy to serve in such a position." The shock of such a request is apparent on the young girl's face.

"The pontiff has asked me to make it known that you are to receive special permission and dispensation to perform your duties as an abbess at so young an age. You are to build your community with all due haste to begin serving the Lord and His faithful."

What is she to do? She had come to know joy and peace through prayer and now this would become harder and harder for her to continue her life's journey in peace. Agnes did not know what to do or how to respond to such a request. At fifteen, she is not worthy. It would be better for the nuns, the community and the church if she refuses, but how can she refuse the Pope? All seems preordained, and knowing she must obey His Holiness, Agnes reluctantly accepts appointment as the abbess of the monastery at Proceno.

Seven days pass and all are gathered at the church to witness her election as abbess. There are the group of priests and nuns of her order present, and with them, the entire townsfolk of Proceno. Young Agnes, wearing the robes of an abbess, stands in the center of the altar awaiting her appointment and humbled by the blessings she would receive from the bishop. Once she is consecrated, Agnes rises from her kneeling position, faces the assembled crowd and says, "Let us pray to our Lord to grant me the holiness and wisdom I will need to succeed in this mission in His name."

A worshipful stillness falls over the church as the entire congregation bows their heads in prayer. It is then that a bright light encircles the interior of the church. Hundreds of small white crosses appear miraculously overhead. These crosses, light as feathers, begin to fall on the priests, nuns and all the townspeople who have assembled in the church. They look around, above and at each other in wonder. Agnes knows it is a sacred sign for she has seen other signs in her young life.

Someone in the crowd shouts, "It is a miracle! God has pronounced His blessings on the new abbess." The crosses rain down on all, and all know it is a signal from heaven; a celebration of Agnes' consecration. The consecration of a young woman, born of divine lights and ready to serve the Lord in ways she has yet to fully understand.

CHAPTER 32

My relationship with Beth is going great, we see each other as often as our schedules allow, and it is apparent that we genuinely have strong feelings for each other. Maybe we are even falling in love, and that makes me very happy and nervous at the same time. My business is also going well, especially with what I am doing on the digital side of things, and I'm looking at other opportunities to expand. All in all, life is good and getting better!

Uncle Al and I still meet on a regular basis, so when I ask him to meet me for dinner one evening, he seems very happy. It has been a few months since the dreadful events Tina had to endure and now that he is completely recovered from his injuries, he seems in great shape. I always look forward to seeing my uncle for dinner and having one of our leisurely, fun times together.

My favorite neighborhood restaurant is a place called Sal D's. Frank and Sal make great Italian food and their chicken scarpariello, on the bone of course, is the best you will ever taste. It's one of those friendly places where I always feel relaxed, and it's where I go to enjoy great food, conversation and a little too much wine. When I arrive, I tell Frank that Uncle Al will be there at 7 p.m., and as always, he makes us feel like family. First, I think I need to explain this outward show of affection that you notice throughout this book; it's mostly an Italian thing. We like to hug and kiss each other, men, women and children alike, and I really can't say exactly why all I know is that I've been doing it since I was about one hour old.

Because Frank is Italian, he gives me a hug and a strong handshake and tells me, "You know you're my best customer, so where have you been? I expect you to eat here at least three times a week."

"Three times a week, huh? How about you pay my credit card bill and I'll eat for free?" He kids me, so I kid him right back.

"Okay, no problem, now just be sure you send the bill to me and' when I get around to it, I'll send you a check. After all, what are friends for?"

I say indignantly, "Right and I'll have my perfect credit score ruined by your sloppy bookkeeping. I'm gonna continue to eat here at least twice a week and nothing you or anyone else says will stop me!"

Frank quickly responds, "Okay, Okay, no problem. Wait, at least twice a week?' Does this mean you might eat here three times a week?"

I consider this and respond, "Well, yes, I might."

"Then I'll see to it that you get my special first-class treatment! After all, I've got three kids to send to college", Frank says, with a big grin on his face.

Since when have I been given the pleasure of supporting everyone's kids so I tell him, "Hey, you're beginning to sound like Vincent Grometti. He expects me to pay for his Mediterranean cruise, and now you expect me to pay for your kids' college? What the hell is going on here?"

Kidding over, we both laugh and he takes me to my table. I had arrived at the restaurant about fifteen minutes early and have a chance to get seated before Uncle Al walks in. I'm in a good mood and when I see him come in, I wave and pull out his seat. As he walks closer to me though, I look at his face and I all I can see is a tired, troubled man. I've been down this road with Uncle Al before so I know he needs time to relax a bit before we can open up to each other.

We embrace, sit down and I order a bottle of my favorite Chianti. While we're at it, we also order dinner. I order chicken scarpariello and Uncle Al orders their amazing pork chops with vinegar peppers.

"Hey, Chris, how're you doing?"

"Good, Uncle Al, really good."

"How's the shop?"

I give him an update, "Oh, things are fine. Business seems to be getting better and I get to hear jokes from the old guys who like to come in to get away from their wives. Their wives actually make them do chores around the house. Imagine that; their wives expect these guys to do work!" I hope that he will smile at my poor attempt at humor, but Uncle Al is uncharacteristically preoccupied.

"Hey Unc, there's a naked woman behind you with a toll-free number on her chest and a sign that says, 'I want Al.'"

He suddenly looks up and says, "Uh, sorry what did you say?"

I become a little worried given what he has been through and the stress of his job. "What's up? You look like something's really bothering you; are you feeling okay?" Since I told him of my visions, Uncle Al and I would discuss police work from time to time. He usually never gives me the intimate details of the cases he is working on, but he often needs to unload on someone outside the department, and I am a favorite sounding board of his. For Uncle Al, it's a way for him to think through the crime and organize his thoughts.

Before he speaks again, he heaves a very heavy sigh and looks me in the eye. "We found another body, same mutilation, same MO, same wounds, same sex. We will need to wait to see the coroner's report, but I know beyond a doubt that the latest victim was pregnant just like the other two."

Uncle Al has mentioned only one such crime in the past, but the brutality of it was so shocking that my heart sinks to think it happened again and all I can do is ask, "When did this happen?"

"The body was found yesterday, but the body was so horribly mutilated that the coroner can only guess that the victim was dead for a few days, but he can't be completely sure so I'm waiting for the results of the autopsy." Uncle Al looks at me with genuine sadness in his eyes and, I can tell, in his heart.

The wine comes to our table personally served by Frank who makes some small talk combined with his usual good nature. When he sees that we seem to be preoccupied, however, he tells us to enjoy the wine and that the meal will be coming out soon.

Uncle Al seems to be talking to himself when he says, "Why are these women being killed in such a particularly ugly way?"

"What do you think, Unc?"

Al looks around to be sure no one is listening to our conversion. "This is just between us, so what I am telling you won't leave this table, right?"

"Right," I say.

"At this point we don't know very much, but it looks like we have a serial killer on our hands—three pregnant women, three bodies brutally mutilated in the same way. We have no motives, and the killer has left no actionable clues as far as we have determined at this time.

Plus, I'm afraid that if the media starts digging into this, it will cause panic and make our work even tougher."

"Whoa, I am so sorry." I don't know what else to say.

Uncle Al confides to me, "With regard to the three women we found, they were murdered and their bodies were left in some kind of deep opening. One woman was found in a deep gully, another woman was found in a deep, dry well and the last victim was found at the bottom of a deep pit. Toxicology screenings show that the first two victims were drugged. But here's the weirdest, most disturbing element of all; on close examination the coroner can tell by the shape and the number of wounds, that a flock of large birds, he believes crows, had ripped apart the women's bodies and gouged out their eyes."

"Crows? Did you say Crows?"

"Yes! The coroner says he thinks its crows". He says this in a loud voice, but he realizes his mistake so he looks around to be sure no one is listening and he whispers to me, "Can you believe it? Crows!"

I couldn't imagine crows attacking someone in that way and I ask, "Did the attack happen after the women were killed?"

"According to the coroner, the first two women were alive at the time they were attacked by the crows. I don't know for sure yet, but I'd bet money that the third victim was also alive when she was attacked by crows or whatever. I can even begin to fathom the terror they experienced." Uncle Al says this with a very heavy heart.

I would never betray a trust so when Uncle Al unloads the horrors of these murders on me, all I can do is remain seated in stunned silence. When I finally do speak, I ask him, "How can this be? Do you think the killer trained these crows? I mean like trained them to kill? It all seems impossible to me." I try to reason these horrors; what kind of person could do something like this? And crows…why crows? How could this happen? It seems to me that it is an act of pure evil and I think of my saints and the type of evil they have confronted through the centuries. I also think of Juliano and that frightens me even more.

Uncle Al is thoroughly perplexed. If the victims were all attacked and killed by crows, he can't even guess how or why. If there is someone behind the killings, he has no clues to follow up on. He looks around to see if anyone is listening, "Chris, I know that I shouldn't put this you, but can you ask for help? You know from your … compatriots up there." He then tilts his head up and lifts his eyes to heaven.

Sometimes my uncle has problems calling the saints, saints. It isn't because he doesn't believe, but if he acknowledges that I am talking to saints, he is sure both our sanities could come into question. "Unc, it really doesn't work like that. I get the visions when they come, and they can come at any time, I have no control over them."

I can detect a quiet desperation in his voice as he pleads, "I know I shouldn't ask, Chris, but I am almost certain that this will happen again and very soon. If you could just see the bodies of these murdered women and speak with their families…I mean…you'd understand what we must do anything we can so this doesn't happen again."

"I know, Uncle Al, but I don't have a way to summon The Sainted. They come to me when they want to come and they can summon their visions at any time. It's their decision, not mine." We stop talking when the waiter, a good guy named Rich, comes to our table and places the food in front of us and refills our wine glasses. Rich asks if we need anything else. We thank him and tell him everything is fine and he leaves.

Uncle Al's sadness is magnified by his sigh when he says, "I guess you're right, but I feel so powerless. These women are being murdered and there are no clues, no evidence, nothing I can follow up on. It's like there is an evil spirit that just comes and goes as it pleases."

My face turns ghostly pale and Uncle Al seems to snap out of his funk and he says, "Chris, my lord, you just turned white as a sheet. Are you okay?"

"Uncle Al, I have to tell you something, but I don't know if you'll believe me. You've taken my word about my visions, but there is something else I need to tell you. It's something I couldn't say to you before because I need you to believe me about the saints first but maybe now's the right time."

Uncle Al looks at me bewildered and says, "What do you need to tell me that is so bad that it made you turn pale?"

I admit to him, "I think you may have suspected something was bothering me, you even hinted at it in your letter when you left my home to get back to your house."

Uncle Al says "I knew it. Chris, you can tell me anything, I am always here to listen and help if I can."

"I know you are Unc. I've told you I've seen the holiest of visions, but you should know I've also seen the purest of evil. I've seen the Satan himself."

"What?!" Now Al says this so loud the people at the next table turn to see if anything is wrong. He says he sorry to the couple sitting there and he turns back and faces me, "Chris, what did you say?"

I know that Uncle Al is taken aback by what I am telling him, so I reiterate, "I've seen Satan himself. Well, at least I think he's the Satan or at least one of hell's legion. He is a demon so vile, so vicious that…"

I take a moment to stop to gather my thoughts and I continue, "Let me put it this way, he was there in the house when I was looking for Tina. He was in control of the men that were getting kids hooked on drugs and turning them into child prostitutes. It was he who wanted me to rape Tina."

"Chris, I understand this is the worst of men. A vile human being, but…"

"No, Uncle Al, he isn't human. He is a demon sent from hell to corrupt, to create havoc, even to kill. He knows about me and he knows about my visions—no one knew these things, not even you at the time."

"Chris, I can see why you would think this, but how can you be so sure?"

I then begin telling my story of St. Mary Magdalene and of how we were transported to the crypt after the Resurrection. I told Al that the demon became frantic at merely being in the place where Christ's body had been interred. I told Uncle Al about how the demon transformed into such a hideous figure that I couldn't even look at his face.

"His first name is Juliano, but I don't know his last name or even if he has a last name. I guess when you're from hell, it doesn't matter what your real name is." I look down at my plate of food and realize that I hadn't eaten any of my food. I look across at Al's plate and it also hasn't been touched. Looking back up at my uncle, I say, "I've thought about this a lot. It seems to me that you can't consider the consummate good as embodied in The Sainted without having the ultimate evil like Satan on the forces of hell. It's the consummate good versus the ultimate evil, kind of like the flip sides of a coin."

Uncle Al looks at me with those penetrating eyes and says, "Chris, I believe you. I guess if you can have visions where you talk to saints, it's not out of the realm of possibility that you can speak with demons or even to Satan himself."

I thought about this and I try to explain, "This is different Uncle Al., this Juliano, whether demon or Satan, can be seen by anyone and he can speak with anyone. The Sainted only seem to appear and speak with me and only me."

"You say it was at the drug house where you first saw this Juliano character. What did he look like? How old was he? How did he dress? You say his name is Juliano, did he speak with an accent?" Uncle Al, being a cop, always asks such questions and the questions keep coming as I try to answer.

"He is a very handsome man, elegant and polished looking; you know the type. He looks about my age, maybe a little older or even a little younger, I don't know for sure. He dresses very well in expensive suits; the kind I can't afford, even on sale."

"Okay, anything else?"

"Well, he doesn't speak with an accent, but he does speak in that very refined manner, kind of like an English gentleman, but without the British accent. Know what I mean?"

"Yeah, I do." I can tell that he is thinking like a cop who is in the midst of an investigation.

"You know Uncle Al, when you say that you thought it was some evil spirit doing these horrendous murders, I immediately thought of Juliano."

Uncle Al instantly asks, no he demands to know, "I can see, but why do you think he committed these murders?"

I try to calm him down, "Oh, I don't mean to say he is the killer, but he certainly seems evil enough to me. It's just that these murders are so vile, so wicked, that I can see it might be the work of the devil."

At that moment Rich comes back to the table and looks down and sees our two plates are still full of food. "Is there anything wrong with your dinner, gentlemen?" Rich is clearly upset we haven't devoured out meals.

I tell him, "No Rich, everything is fine, but when Al and I get to talking, we sometimes lose track of time. Do you think you can take these back to Frank and ask him reheat them for us?"

Rich smiles and says, "Sure, no problem." He takes the plates and goes back to the kitchen. As Rich walks away, Al is watching him to be sure he is out of earshot. When he knows we can't be overheard, Al says to me,

"It's probably, at best, a long shot, but I'm going to run that name through our criminal data base to see what comes up." I'm glad that Al is trying to do something, even though I suspect it will be futile. I say, "I expect you're right and nothing will come up, but it seems like it's worth a try."

"Hey Chris, getting back to what we were talking about, can you please ask your friends to help us out here? I hate putting you on the spot, but it seems that's all I have left. These poor women are being killed—no, not killed, they are being mutilated beyond recognition, no forensic evidence, no leads, no nothing and we are powerless to do anything about it."

He is dead serious, and I don't have the heart to tell him again that I can't control when or where the saints appear to me. I tell him that I would try, but not to hold out much hope if I don't get the kind of help he's looking for.

We continue to discuss this when Rich comes back to the table with our food. He places the plates in front of us and declares, "Frank told me to tell you that you better finish this before it gets cold again or he's coming out to kick your asses. I think he meant that in the nicest possible way."

I look up at Rich and then look over to Uncle Al and we both crack up. Al pronounces, "Sure, I'll bet he feels real brave with a ladle in his hand."

Well, as it turns out we are both very hungry, so we dig into our meals with genuine gusto. My chicken is excellent, as usual and it is served with linguine in the same sauce as the scarpariello. Al's pork chops are tremendous with just the right amount of heat from the cherry peppers. He also had pasta on the side in a garlic-lovers marinara.

For five minutes, we eat like condemned men devouring our last meal, and the next time we come up for air, Al mutters to his plate and looks up at me,

"I can't get over how much I love this food. How's yours?"

"Great, this is my favorite dish, but I have to say the pork chops are my second favorite."

We continue eating and talking about different things…anything but the murders. Then Uncle Al springs a surprise on me. He tells me he's met a woman who he seems to like very much. Her name is Eileen Silverman and she's a schoolteacher in Huntington. Uncle Al has a big smile when he speaks about her "Yeah, she teaches eleventh grade math at Huntington High School and is a widow. Her husband died five years ago in an automobile accident, and she is just starting to get back to having a social life. I think she's very pretty. She has a wonderful smile and great sense of humor."

I'm curious, "How did you meet her?"

"You're not going to believe this, but I actually met her at a supermarket. Can you believe that? Right next to the pre-cooked barbecued chicken! She lives alone and she was buying dinner for the evening, just like me. We talked and talked and I guess we each needed some company, so I asked her if she would like to have dinner. I then took her over to that new diner that opened up on Main Street and we had a great time."

"Wow! You're kidding! My uncle, the pickup artist, is meeting strange women in the supermarket." I pretend I'm making fun of him, but I am really very happy. He is such a great guy and it would be a good thing for him to meet someone.

He tells me about their dinner together and she sounds like a really good woman, and I'm curious, "Does she have any children?"

"Eileen told me that she has a daughter and a son, but they're both out of the house and living on their own. Her daughter works as a pediatric nurse practitioner and her son is software design engineer."

"Wow, they sound really smart. Have you met them yet?"

"Nah, it's really too soon."

I like hearing him talk about anything but the murders. "What did you tell her about yourself?"

"I told her I'm a cop, and I think that's the only reason she agreed to go out with me to the diner. That was our first date, but I asked her out for dinner next Saturday and she agreed. I am looking forward to it. Speaking of dates how's Beth?"

"Well, if my time with Beth got any better, I'd think I died and went to heaven. She's a great person in so many ways, and she doesn't take any shit from me."

Al smiles and tells me, "That's good, keeps you on your toes. Are you two getting serious?"

"Yeah, well I'm getting serious, and I guess she feels the same way, but I keep thinking that I could never offer her the kind of life that she has now."

Uncle Al has a way of getting to the bottom line. "Cut the bullshit, it seems to me that if you love each other, all that other stuff will work out. Oh, by the way, you aren't exactly destitute you know."

"Yeah, well, I may not be destitute, but you should see her parents' home in Lloyd Harbor. They've got more bathrooms than I've got cans of San Marzano tomatoes and I've got a lot of cans, by the way, they're on sale, the 28 oz. cans are only $1.99 with a minimum $25.00 purchase, so I stocked up…"

"Shut up and listen to me, Julia Childs. Does she keep bringing up her money to you? Does she flaunt her family's wealth in front of you?

Does she expect you to buy her expensive dinners or expensive anything for that matter? Does she look down on what you do or how you live? If you answered yes to any of these questions, you're right; she's a shallow, self-absorbed, money-hungry bitch. If the answer is no, then you need to give this whole two different worlds thing a rest."

I guess my uncle is right, but I still can't get it out of my mind. I think that this is the reason that I haven't let the relationship get really serious. Uncle Al sees that I'm quietly thinking about what he said, so he turns the conversation back to the demon Juliano. "This guy, or should I say devil, Juliano, did he tell you anything else that we can use to get insights into the situation?"

I try and think of anything that might help, "Not really, but his right-hand guy, Heriberto…you know, the guy who shot you."

"Yeah, I seem to remember something about being shot."

"Well, Heriberto ranted something about bringing the forces of hell down on me. I took it as his tirade against the world, but now that I look back it seems that it could mean he knows the true nature of Juliano. I don't know, all that has happened just so weird that I don't know what to think."

"Anything else you can think of?"

"Juliano told me that I have never had to face the ultimate evil, and that he will show me its true meaning. After that episode, I had a few visions, and the message in each one was that when I face the vilest of evils, I need to be strong in my faith and have the courage to stand against whatever evil I would be facing."

Uncle Al asks me, "Is that the reason you questioned me about facing your fears?"

I admit, "Yeah, and I keep questioning whether I would be brave when the time comes to man up. It's easy to hope that I will be brave in facing that kind of horror, but I don't know if I can."

"Chris, you can never really know how you would react to the kind terror you may have to confront, but you should know that you are not alone. You are chosen by God for a reason and that reason will become apparent to you at the time of your greatest challenge, a time when all you hold dearest is questioned."

When all I hold dearest is questioned…Uncle Al's words ring like a warning bell in my head and it makes me very frightened.

CHAPTER 33

I'm usually not the type that gets depressed, but when I get home after my dinner with Uncle Al, I'm really down.

I am exhausted, but all I can do is pace up and down the floor of my condo trying to think things through. I think of the horror that awaits me and the evil I will have to confront. I think about my own faith, and my own dread, as I keep asking myself, would I have the courage to face evil on my own? Fear is such a crippling illness; yes, it is an illness. I only hope that I can have the ability to cure myself when the time comes.

I want to call Beth just to hear her voice, but it's late and I know she has an early shift at the hospital. I consider that even though I am wide awake, I still need to rest, so I go to my bedroom and turn on the TV. I switch to the news channel knowing that I will get bored and fall asleep, but exactly the opposite happens. I hear the anchor lead off with this, "We have breaking news! It has just been reported to the LI Cable News Center that the horribly disfigured body of woman has been found. Sources report that upon examination of the victim at the crimes scene, the investigators think it likely that the young woman, possibly in her twenty's, may have been pregnant."

When I hear this, all I can think of is Uncle Al and the uproar that the leak of this murder to the media will cause. The news anchor continues, "Our sources also tell us that the woman— whose name will not be released until her family has been notified—was so badly mutilated that she is unrecognizable and that forensics would need to use fingerprints and dental records to identify her."

Thoughts of the dinner with my uncle make me painfully aware of how he wants to keep this under wraps until the police have solid information on the killer. Now it seems the whole world knows. I can't imagine how the details of the murder could have gotten out? Who could possibly have told the media? I'm still listening when I nearly fall off the bed, "Sources also said that this is not the only incident where a young woman was murdered and her body mutilated. It seems that there were two prior murders committed in the same brutal way and the police have been keeping this under wraps. Speculation is that there is a serial killer on the loose, and the police department is trying to determine who it could be. We will continue to bring you updates on this breaking news story as we get them…"

I have to speak to Uncle Al, so I lower the volume on my set and pick up the phone to make the call.

"Hello," Uncle Al answers the phone in a totally disheartened voice.

"Hi Uncle Al, I guess you turned on the news."

"I did. Chris, this is the thing I've worried about most and it's happened, blasted over the news, so every nut in the world will try to claim responsibility. I am at my wits end. What can I do to catch this bastard? How will this nightmare end?" Uncle Al is not talking to me; he is just talking.

"Can you guess who might have told this to the press?"

"I can't imagine that anyone on my team, or in the whole department for that matter, would ever leak this out. I'm calling a meeting first thing in the morning and I'll try to get to the bottom of this, but I'd stake my life that it isn't one of my team." I stay silent because I don't know what to say to him.

"Chris, you still there?"

"Yeah, I'm still here, but I just don't know what to say to you. I wish I could help; I really do."

Uncle Al asks me again, this time pleading, "Chris, you can help by getting your saints involved. Ask them to help you like they did with

Tina. Please, we have to catch this scumbag, so he can't murder anyone, anymore."

The last thing my uncle wants to hear is all the reasons why I don't have the power to summon the saints to help, but he needs to have some hope, so I say, "I will try, I really will, I promise." There is little more I can do, but I want to give him some solace.

"Thanks, Chris. Listen, I have another call coming in, so I have to get off, but please call me if you have any visions and let me know what they tell you, please."

"I will, Uncle Al, I promise I'll call if I have any visions, any at all. Just take care of yourself. I love you."

"I will and I love you, too."

He hangs up the phone. I sit up on the bed, more depressed than before. I keep thinking of the words, "…when all you hold dearest is questioned." My family, my friends and Beth are all I hold dear. I can't let go of the feeling that they can be in real danger and that Juliano could somehow be involved. Thoughts keep swirling around in my head. I say my prayers before I turn in like I always do, and then I look at the ceiling until sleep finally takes over and I'm out for the night.

The next day I awake still troubled, but it is a sunny day in early autumn and my mood seems to change. I start to make breakfast, but before I do, I stop and pick up the phone and call Beth.

"Hi Beth, its Chris, how are you?"

"Hi, I'm great. Had a few emergencies earlier, but things are down to a dull roar. How come you're calling? Is everything okay?"

"Everything is fine, I just want to speak with you, and tell you that I miss you."

The line goes quiet for a moment until Beth whispers, "I'm glad you did, and I miss you, too."

I can't lie to Beth, "Actually Beth, something is wrong…very wrong."

I hear the concern in her voice, "What! What's wrong? Are you okay? Tell me, Chris, what's wrong?" I don't want her to worry; maybe I shouldn't have said anything, but I guess it's too late now.

"I had dinner with Uncle Al last night and…"

But Beth interrupts, "Is he alright? Oh my God, he didn't get hurt on the job, did he?

Chris, please tell me what happened."

"No, Beth, Uncle Al is fine. Well, he's in good health, anyway. He is in the midst of an investigation and it's tearing him apart."

"Can you tell me about it?"

"I guess I can. It's been all over cable news and online. I haven't looked at the news sites or seen the papers this morning, but I'll bet it's in there, too."

The line goes silent for a few seconds and then Beth gasps, "Oh my God! I just picked up the paper, Chris. It's on the front page; they say it could be a serial killer. My God Chris, those poor women."

"I know it's truly a horror story, and it's been eating Al alive."

She asks me, "Does he have any leads or suspects?"

I made a promise to Uncle Al that I would never talk about any of the things that we discuss relating to an ongoing investigation, but so much has already been leaked to the press that I know I would still be able to keep the promise. "Listen Beth, do you think we can meet for lunch? I'd really like to see you and we can talk. I'll tell you what I know, which is just about the same stuff that's in the news."

"Sure, I have lunch scheduled at noon. Does that work for you?"

"That's great, Beth. I'll meet you in the hospital cafeteria at noon."

"See you then." She hangs up the phone and I start my day.

CHAPTER 34

The mood at the Suffolk County Police Headquarters is grave as the team of detectives gathers in Chief Barese's office. The Chief is visibly upset as he faces his team to discuss the latest developments.

"This is a bad situation that has just gotten much worse. Since the story came out, we've had over fifty calls from the usual group of nut jobs, all confessing to be the serial killer. We need to check them all out, but you know as well as I that the leads are all dead ends. What this will do is to cut down the manpower we have, and that's going to make our job much harder. I feel bad having to ask this, but I need to know, did any of you mention this case to anyone, anyone at all? Family…friends…anyone?"

Dan Orello is the first to answer, "Chief, you've known us all for years. We've been through a lot together, and I can say this on my life; no one in this room told anyone about these murders."

Chief Barese runs his fingers through his hair and just sighs, "I know, I know, Dan. I'm sorry for even asking the question; it's just that this is tying me up in knots. These innocent women, innocent pregnant women, have been killed in such a vicious manner, and I feel powerless in trying to find the killer, or killers."

Det. Christina Shannon speaks next, "I was thinking about these women, too. They are all young women and all were pregnant, but I can see this causing fear and panic among all women of any age. What makes me most disheartened is that we can't even get a solid lead and that scares me."

Det. Avery Michaels cuts in, "Me, too. When I saw those photos of the women torn apart by crows and their fetuses on the ground beside then, my heart broke. What kind of person, or persons, would do such a depraved and evil thing? Using crows, or whatever kind of birds they are, to rip apart flesh like that, and then some maniac ripping the fetus from the womb like that…" Avery can't find the words, so she becomes quiet.

The group sits silent for a few minutes, and then it is Det. Christian Oliver, who speaks up, "Chief, I don't know about the rest of you, but I'm not used to feeling powerless. We have to do something. We have to have some kind of plan to catch this bastard and stop these killings. I think we need to follow up on anything that could be connected to the case; anything, no matter how remote."

"I agree there are no—wait…" The chief stops mid-sentence, "I want you to check out this name in our data base; Juliano. It is probably nothing and will lead to nowhere, but let's try anyway."

Det. Shannon springs to life and asks, "Juliano? Who is this guy, Juliano? Does he have a last name? Do you think he has any connection to this case?"

Uncle Al is beginning to have second thoughts about sending his team on a wild goose chase, but it seems to awaken his team from their very somber mood. "I really can't say who Juliano is or even if he has a connection to the case. I don't have a last name, but he's supposedly very good looking, well dressed, with posh manners. I'd like to know if there is anyone named Juliano in our files, or if he, or a person like him, has been connected to any other crimes at all, including murder."

Det. Dan Orello is always looking to explore all the angles, all the possibilities. "Okay, Chief we'll get on it. Anything else that you think we can work on?"

"Not right now, but I would like to know who leaked this thing to the press, so keep your eyes and ears open for anyone who could be the guilty party. Got it?"

They all respond, "Got it chief."

The detectives start walking toward the door when the Uncle Al stops them, "Wait a minute. There is one more thing. I want to you interview all those young girls and boys that were being pimped out of that drug house on the South Shore. Ask them if they ever heard of this Juliano. You might also want to talk to that scumbag we caught at the house; he might know Juliano."

Det. Michaels asks, "Chief, do you really think this guy may have been involved in both incidents?"

"This is a lead that came up when I spoke with my nephew Chris the other night. He seems to remember overhearing some of the kids saying that name. He didn't say anything about it at the time because he was worried about me. I really don't know if this guy Juliano has anything to do with the serial murders, Avery, it's just a hunch, but I've learned to play hunches, so let me know what you find."

"We will, Chief" and they all leave the office anxious to get started on the first lead they've gotten in their investigation.

Chief Al Barese suddenly feels better—not because he feels any closer to catching the killer. He just feels better because he and his team are doing something—no matter how far offtrack it may be.

They are doing something, and sometimes, doing something is better than doing nothing.

CHAPTER 35

I feel a little better after speaking with Beth, but I am still very troubled. Once I eat breakfast, I drive to the shop to catch up on the mail and process the online orders that have piled up over the last few days. I'm doing my work, but my thoughts always return back to the evil that I could be facing. I also keep thinking about Uncle Al, and his problems, and my hope for justice for the murdered women. Justice so they may rest in peace, and justice to help their families find closure.

It is then that the shop disappears and I am in a tower high above the city of London.

The executioner is waiting for the man he must behead. The King has commanded his execution, and it will be carried out. How could someone so high, so respected have fallen to so low a state? He has lost everything, his position, his estate, his prestige and now he will lose his life. He could have obeyed his sovereign lord and compromised his beliefs to a small degree. What harm could it have done? He is a wise and learned man, and he could have found the words to help conciliate his faith and his king. He would then be restored to his former position.

How could he be so foolish? How could he sacrifice his own life? After all, he has a family.

The blade is honed very sharp indeed. It will be a clean cut about the neck, momentary pain, and it would be over. This is a man who had the ear of the king, a man who is revered for his brilliance and integrity, and now this is a man who is the subject of scorn and ridicule.

Why has it come to this?

The executioner looks up as the door to the top of the tower opens. In walks the man whose grace, dignity and strength are more apparent than ever before. As he walks into the room smiling at the men who are there, he turns to the executioner and declares, "Be swift of the axe for I have not a moment to waste."

He continues to smile as he remembers what he has written as a margin note in his Book of Hours: "Give me your grace, good Lord, to set the world at naught…to have my mind well united to You; to not depend on the changing opinions of others so that I may think joyfully of the things of God, and tenderly implore His help. So that I may lean on God's strength and make an effort to love Him. So as to thank Him ceaselessly for his benefits; so as to redeem the time I have wasted …"

As the man readies himself for the fate which he is destined, he makes the sign of the cross and walks towards his executioner. His hands are not bound as he lays his own head on the wooden block. When the axe falls, the head of St. Thomas More comes to rest in the basket below.

I watch in silent sorrow for the man and, as happens many times before, the saint steps out of the vision and appears in front of me. I look at him, and he seems to know what I need to ask. I am becoming very agitated by what I have witnessed and I am looking for questions that need answers. "Why was this done? Where is the justice? You lost everything—why aren't you angry?"

St. Thomas More looks at me with a penetrating stare, "Have you learned so little from my brothers and sisters? I did what I must do. You must first learn to love the Lord, and never compromise the truth. If I would have compromised my faith, and all that is sacred, it would mean that I had no faith at all."

I am trying to find words to reply, but they aren't coming. I just look at him dejectedly.

St. Thomas More continues, "You ask, 'Where is the justice?' At the end of days, the answer will be, in the Lord's hands. Until then, it is for man to dispense their forms of justice, and how justice is dispensed will determine man's fate."

I look at the saint with sadness, "Will there be justice for the murdered women?"

St. Thomas says this, "That is for you to decide."

The vision changes; I am transported to a place unknown to me. It is dark, spacious and the walls are dripping wet with water seeping through crevices in the rocks that surround me. I don't know where I am or why I'm there, but I begin to hear the sound of traffic noise, the sounds of cars and trucks speeding by. Judging from the noise, I am near a highway or some major road. I also hear bulldozers along with the rattle of jackhammers and I try to look up, but all I can see is blackness.

I start to walk around this dark space when I see some movement on the ground in a far corner. I can't make out who or what it is, so I slowly walk in the direction of the movement. As I do, I hear what sounds like the flapping of wings, the flapping of many wings. I turn away from the moving thing on the ground then look up again. This time there is more than darkness. On the ledges above are tiny shining eyes staring down at the same movement that I have been walking towards. In an instant something crosses my field of vision and flies straight through me. At first, I don't comprehend, but then I realize I am not actually in this place, I am a spirit only witnessing what is now happening. As I turn my gaze to the huddled mass on the floor, I begin to realize that it is a person. The person seems to be struggling to get up, and as I move closer, I see a woman who looks to be in her twenties, and she does not seem well.

"Are you okay?" I say before remembering that she can't hear me.

When she gets to her feet, she looks around, not comprehending her situation or even where she is. In a low, slurring voice, she holds her head in her hand and utters to no one, "Oh, my head. What happened?" She is off-balance, leaning on the wall, until she feels able to start walking to explore the darkness.

"Where the hell am I?" Her voice is getting stronger. As panic begins to set in, she shouts as loud as she can, "Hello? Hello? Can anybody hear me?" There is only silence in response.

Then she yells "Ouch, what the…" and looks up.

As she did, a large black bird drops from the ledge above and jabs its beak into the frightened woman. She screams, and from that moment on her screams do not stop.

I then recognize what is happening, but it is too late for the woman. Thousands of crows swoop down in a torrent of shrieking black menace. They tear at her body, rip at her arms and then they take out her eyes.

I shout at the dreadfulness of it all, and in a moment, I am gone from the scene. I find myself surrounded by darkness again, and then a light illuminates the darkness as St. Thomas again appears before me.

I yell at The Sainted, "How could you allow this to happen? That poor girl, how could you allow this to happen?" I scream this to him, finding myself near hysteria.

"It is not for us to be in command of evil in whatever form it takes. It is the essence of evil that has allowed this to happen. Do you not remember St. Agatha, St. Rita and St. Fabius? Why did God allow their suffering, their martyrdom? Free will…it allows for good and it allows for evil."

I cannot fathom the reasons for St. Thomas More to reveal all this to me, "Why am I shown this horror?"

St. Thomas More stands before me in the bright glow of his heavenly halo and tells me, "To deliver justice" and with those final words, he disappears. The next moment, I am back in my shop, still in a state of shock. When I realize that the vision is over, I grab the phone and quickly dial Suffolk PD and I'm put through to Uncle Al's office.

"Chief Al Barese here."

I can barely get the words out, "Uncle Al, there's been another murder."

"What!"

"There's been another murder, Uncle Al and I was there. I witnessed this poor woman being torn apart."

"Wait, Chris, slow down a little. Tell me what happened."

I try to slow down my rapid breathing to be able to tell Uncle Al of my experience. "I was in the shop thinking about all that you are dealing with, and I had another vision."

"You did? Who was the saint in your vision?"

I say, "St. Thomas More."

"St. Thomas More? You mean the lawyer, the philosopher, that St. Thomas More?"

"Yes. I witnessed his execution in the Tower of London," I tell my uncle as I try to catch my breath.

"Calm down, Chris—what did he say to you?"

"I asked him about the women who were murdered and I asked about justice for their deaths and he told me that it is for me to decide whether they get justice or not."

"What did he mean by that, Chris? He can't possibly expect you to bring this lunatic demon to justice."

I don't know how to respond to this because I have been told what is expected of me. Saints. Cosmas and Damian had told me of my purpose in life and what is expected of me. I thought that I knew the answer, but now I am questioning it all.

Uncle Al understands my silence, but he needs to ask me, "You said there was another murder; tell me what you saw."

I want to be able to tell Uncle Al as much of the details as possible. "I was in a cave or pit or whatever. I saw the helpless woman being torn apart by crows. Thousands of crows, Uncle Al, and it seemed like they knew what they were doing. They knew she was helpless and they were there to tear her apart."

"Chris, listen to me. Do you have any idea where this cave or pit is any idea whatsoever?"

I think about my time in the cave and remember the sounds that I'd heard. I tell him that I think it is in a place near a highway or some large main road, and there are the sounds of cars speeding by.

"Anything else?" Uncle Al is getting anxious.

"I also heard the sounds of some construction going on. You know, bulldozers, jackhammers that type of stuff. That's really all I was aware of."

"What about the cave or pit itself; is it small or large? What else can you tell me, think Chris, is there anything else you remember?"

"I really can't say if it was large or small. It was very dark and the woman was huddled on one of the sides of the cave. Uncle Al, if you could have seen how they attacked her, how they…" My voice trails off as I think of the terror she must have felt.

"Okay, Chris, it's okay. Did St. Thomas More tell you anything else about the murdered women, anything that could be useful?

I am almost apologizing, "No, nothing."

Uncle Al usually has good instincts, but I know that he is totally puzzled by all of this. "Okay, Chris. Can you come down to the office? I want to go over all this and I think that it would be better to do it with you in person."

If Uncle Al thinks that it would be better for me to go, then I will go. "Sure, I'll get over as soon as I can."

"Thanks Chris, see you in a little while" and he hangs up the phone.

As I begin to put things away at the shop, I remember that I told Beth I would meet her for lunch so I call the hospital.

The phone rings and she answers, "Nurses' station, Beth Della Russo speaking."

"Hi Beth, it's me, Chris."

"Oh hi, how are you doing? How's Al?"

"Well, I just got off the phone with him and he'd like me to come to his office. I think he needs to bounce things off someone outside the department and he asked me to stop by."

"You know, Chris, I can't stop thinking about those poor women. I read the paper and heard some of the reports on the radio and TV. It sounds so senselessly violent that it's hard to imagine who might have done this."

"I know, Beth; I feel the same way," I say this knowing that there is another dead woman ripped apart by crows and someone or something so evil that it defies description. After a short lull in the conversation, I say, "Listen, Beth, I know I promised you lunch, but Al sounds really down. I think he'd like me there now but I need to break our lunch date"

Beth sighs and says, "Sure, no problem, well, I guess I'll see you sometime." She sounds as disappointed as I am.

I get an idea, "Hey wait a minute Beth, how about dinner tonight? I'd really like to see you and we can have more time together. Are you free?"

Beth immediately perks up. "I was hoping you'd ask. Sure, I'm free, what time do you want to meet and where?"

"Can I give you a call later at home? I don't know how long I'll be with Al, but as soon as I know I will give you a time to meet. We can meet at the Santa Rosa Café; how does that work for you?"

"Sounds good, see you there." She stops for a second and then she whispers, "I miss you and can't wait to see you."

"Me too, I…I'll see you later." I want to say, "I love you," but the words just don't come out.

CHAPTER 36

Its forty minutes before I arrive at the Suffolk County Police Headquarters. I go through security to the front desk and ask for Chief Detective Al Barese, but I notice him coming down the hallway and rounding the corner when he sees me.

Uncle Al tells the man at the desk that I'm with him and says to me, "Hey Chris, thanks for coming. Let's go to my office." He walks me down the hallway to his office, however before he opens the door, he says, "Listen Chris, I need to keep my team focused on this case so I'm going to come up with something that explains the whole Juliano thing, so just go along. Okay?"

"Sure Uncle Al, whatever you say."

When he opens the door there is his team sitting on chairs surrounding a small conference table in his office. He introduces me, "Chris, I'd like you to meet my team. I think you know Det. Orello."

"Sure, hi Dan, good to see you again."

"Same here, Chris, good to see you, too."

Next, he introduces me to the two women on the team: "This is Detective Michaels, and this is Detective Shannon."

"Wow Chief, you didn't tell us he's so cute!" They say this just before they start to laugh.

"Okay you two, cut it out." Their laughter turns into a smile as my face turns red.

"…and this is Detective Christian Oliver. Now that you've been introduced to the group, I want to tell you what we've been talking about." Uncle Al explains this as I sit down in one of the chairs set around the table. "Chris, my team knows that you are responsible for rescuing Tina Staley and exposing those pieces of shit that ran that drug and prostitution ring. I've also told them about our conversations and some of the things you remembered after you were questioned."

All of a sudden, I become nervous. I can't imagine that he told them anything about my visions, but what else do these people know? So, I hold my breath and wait for him to continue as my uncle looks me straight in the eye, as if to say, just keep your mouth shut.

"I also told them about the guy named, Juliano, that you overheard being mentioned by a kid that was in the house. You said that you thought it was just the name of some john, but we've been doing some digging around in our database and the team has come up with a few things."

I immediately sit up straight in my seat and ask, "Things, what things?"

"Chis before we go on, I don't think that I need to remind you that everything we discuss here is in complete confidence."

"Of course."

"Well, I'll let each one of my team members tell you what they've found, starting with Detective Michaels."

She speaks to the group, "Thanks, Chief. Well, we came up with some very interesting items. First, we got a hit on a guy with the name Juliano who is somehow connected with a string of suicides last year in California. There is no real connection between the victims, but they all committed suicide in the same way; they slit their own throats. In one of the suicide notes, a young woman mentions the name Juliano, and it appears he is of the same general description that Chris gave the chief. We checked to see if the Orange County police have any leads, but it seems that this Juliano just vanished into thin air."

The group sits in silence as Det. Michaels continues, "Next, we get another hit on the database, not on the name Juliano, but on a Julian—again, no last name, but the same general description you gave us. This time it's related to a series of brutal murders committed by the serial killer, Sam Stellment. Sam pretty much didn't care who he killed, so we have men, women and child victims, and in each case, he cut out their hearts while they were still alive. He was judged to be criminally insane, and he is now locked up in some Illinois institution, and should be there for life. Stellment told investigators that he did it because he was asked to by Julian."

You can almost feel the tension in the room mount as she continues. "The last incident of a crime connected with the name Juliano is, and here's the interesting part, the deaths of eight young prostitutes from an Atlanta area in a crack house. It seems that this Juliano was involved in some way with a drug ring that pimped out these kids by getting them hooked on heroin and crack cocaine. Sound familiar?"

We all start to look at each other as she continues, "What happens next is that one of the fathers of some poor kid that was dragged into this mess comes looking for her. Well, he finds her alright, but when he confronts the scumbags that are operating out of the house, they overwhelm him and tie him up, sound familiar, Chris? Before they look to kill him, they go around to all the kids that are in the house at the time and murders them all. They do this because they think that the police are onto them, and they need to get rid of any and all the potential witnesses. They then planned to leave town and get as far away as possible. Now here's the weird part…"

I think to myself, "Did she say 'weird part?' How could this get any weirder?

"The killers now come to get the father, but he has managed to get free of the ropes that are tied behind his back and gets hold of a baseball bat he finds in the corner of the room. When the killers get to the room, the father smashes the bat into the face of one of the guys, immediately jamming his nose through his brain. When the other guys see this, they grab for their knives and guns, but Dad is ready. He gets another one in the balls, I mean testicles, and the bad guy falls to the floor and out for the count. Gunshots are now being fired and everyone is scrambling for cover. The next thing, batman takes aim at one of the two men left standing, and he clips him on the side of his head, crushing his skull. I mean like brains and all are on the floor. So, the last guy standing sees what's happened and he takes the gun and starts to fire widely, but the dad is one step ahead and he clobbers the last one, but not before he gets shot dead himself."

I can't believe this story, so I say, "How the hell did they get all the details of this horror show?"

"Glad you asked. When the police arrive, they see the carnage and they are tearing the place for any survivors and who do they find? The guy who got busted in the balls—I mean testicles…"

Uncle Al interrupts, "It's okay you can say balls."

Det. Avery Michaels smiles and says, "…in the balls and he is scared shitless so he starts to spill his guts. He told the cops everything about how the gang went about killing the kids. He told them everything about the dad with the bat, and that's when this guy says that his gang who is headed by…want to guess?"

Uncle Al is getting a little peeved, "Just tell us."

"Juliano."

I am sitting there in stunned silence. I can't imagine having to deal with what police deal with every day, but as I hear of the bloodshed and the butchery, I have to be glad it's not me who's on the frontlines of this.

Uncle Al asks her, "Avery, do you have anything else?"

"No, not yet Chief, but if he is involved in any other mass killings, he hid them pretty well. I'll keep checking with other districts around the country and let you know if there are any other reports that mention Julian or Juliano."

"Thanks. Det. Shannon, it's your turn."

"Well, Chief, Det. Orello and I interviewed the kids from the drug house. Most are still in pretty bad shape given the trauma and the drugs, but I did get some very interesting information from some of them." Det. Christina Shannon then takes a very dramatic pause before she continues, but maybe this isn't such a good idea because Uncle Al is getting impatient, "Well, are you going to tell us or what?"

Everyone could see the chief is getting peeved. "Sorry, Chief. Of the twelve young girls and young boys we interviewed, there are three who acknowledge that they have seen Juliano. There may have been more, who knows, but some are either so scared or so screwed up that we feel their information could be suspect. The first kid we interview is Destiny Pride—that's her real name. Destiny Pride is a local kid who is only fifteen-year-old, but has been on the streets for more than a year. She tells us that Heriberto raped her every day for weeks at a time and she was also forced to have sex with the others in the gang and she was beaten if she refused. We asked her if she ever heard of the name Juliano, and she became very nervous."

I ask the question, but I think I know the answer, "Did Destiny tell you why she became nervous when you mentioned Juliano's name?"

"Well, as she explains it, Juliano is a very, very creepy character. So creepy that hardly anyone would even look him in the eye. Destiny says he talked funny like, and I quote, 'Some of those news guys on TV.' She also says that every time he is around, something bad would happen. I ask her to tell me what happened that's bad and she tells me that one of the girls accidentally spilled soda on his fancy shoes and the next day she disappeared. Another time, one of the boys was fooling around with a cigarette lighter he found. He said it belonged to Juliano and the next day the boy was found dead. There were other incidents, but she says that all the girls are so frightened of him that they just kept quiet."

As the picture of Juliano emerges, I can see that all the detectives are conjuring up descriptions like "psychopath" or "sociopath" or some other psychological term to describe a serial killer of historic proportions. I know differently and I think Uncle Al thinks the same as I do.

Det. Shannon continues her report. "The next young girl we interview is Aisha Thompson. She is from out of town and was taken to this drug house by members of MS-13 who supply a lot of these kids from all over. She is only sixteen, but she has been a prostitute for almost three years. She says that her parents are both drug addicts and she grew up on the streets. Aisha met Juliano at the house and she thought that he was nice at first. He gave her candy and cigarettes and she likes that he is so good-looking and has such fancy clothes. She says that one night he came into her room to lie down beside her in the bed. Aisha thought that he wanted to have sex, but he just laid there. She turned over to try to touch him and, when she did, her hand got burned badly, I saw the scars."

Det. Oliver asks, "What happened to Juliano after the kid got her hand burned?"

"She said that as she was crying from the pain, he got up out of bed and walked to a dark corner of her room and disappeared. She might have been high or in shock at the time, so we need to presume that he just walked out of her room, but who knows."

Uncle Al looks very tired at this point and he asks, "Anything else, Christina?"

"No, Chief, nothing else, but I'd love to get my hands on this Juliano or Julian. These are just kids."

The chief answers for everyone when he says, "I know you would and so would we all."

He turns to the next detective for his report. "Anyway, your turn Christian have at it."

"Well, gang; it seems to me that I won the lottery when I got to interview Manulo. He is a low-level hood who took his orders from Ernesto Vasquez, a higher-level hood who reported to Heriberto Quintana, the top-level hood at the LI chapter of MS-13. I spent more than two hours questioning this bastard to see what he knows about Juliano, and I've got to tell you, this guy is six fries short of a happy meal. It is beyond strange that Manulo won't even say the name, Juliano, all he refers to him as is 'el Diablo', 'the Devil', for the uninitiated."

When Det. Oliver says this, Uncle Al and I just look at each other as he continues to give his report to the team, "Anyway, Manulo tells me that Juliano would come by the house every few days and, when he does, something terrible would happen, pretty much what Christina heard from the kids."

I am getting real nervous hearing all these horrific things, but it is kind of like a train wreck; you don't want to look, but you can't turn away. I ask him, "Did he let you know some of the 'terrible' things that happened?"

Det. Oliver looks at me and says, "He sure did, it seems that this guy Juliano doesn't only target kids for torture or death, he reserves some of that for the crew. A little story…there was this soldier in the gang, a low-level thug who was used as kind of an enforcer. His name is Oscar Rivera and he was about a tough as they come, and about as insane as you can be without getting locked up. Heriberto used him to keep the girls and boys in line, to keep the neighborhood in line and to take care of problems when they come up. In his case, a problem meant to kill someone who needs killing. As Manulo tells it, Rivera comes into the house one day and he seems either drunk or high on something and he starts to beat up one of the hookers, practically kills her, for no reason. Quintana tries to stops him, but even he is scared of Rivera, especially a high "I don't give a shit" Rivera. When it's over, Oscar collapses into a stupor and Manulo and Julio drag him into a bedroom to sleep it off." You can feel the tension as we all sit listening to this, trying to guess what's going to happen.

"As I later learn, it seems that Rivera had a penchant for beating up people of all sizes and shapes. It had been costing the drug enterprise undue loss of revenues and an undue amount of scrutiny by the authorities so to speak. Well, as luck would have it, in walks Juliano who sees the hooker, and questions Manulo about what happened. Manulo tells him the whole story and, when he is done, Juliano asks him where Oscar is. Manulo points to the bedroom door and Juliano thanks him and goes into the room. Well, a few minutes go by and Manulo can't fight his curiosity, so he goes to the door and tries to listen in, but he can't hear a thing. So next he figures he'd open the door a crack to peek in. When he does, the door swings wide open and Manulo is face to face with Juliano. Juliano grabs Manulo by the throat, lifts him two feet in the air, you heard right, two feet and with one hand throws him across the room. This must be one strong dude if you can believe Manulo. Anyway, Manulo lands on his ass and when he looks up, he sees Oscar Rivera hanging in midair, nothing holding him up, just his body floating in midair and he's literally cut down the middle like a pig in a slaughterhouse. Now get this, while Rivera is hanging in midair, he starts to cry and tries to speak to Manulo, but his jaw is cut in half, so he can't. Juliano now walks over to Manulo and while he is standing over him, the body of Rivera spontaneously combusts—it turns into a ball of fire."

Det. Oliver stops for a moment to look around the room, trying to gauge everyone's reaction to what they are being told. He sees that each person is somewhere between shock and disbelief, so he continues, "Manulo freaks out and starts screaming, but Juliano simply turns to him and says, in Spanish mind you, 'Si alguna vez espires una palabra de esto a nadie, podrá disfrutar de la misma suerte que tu amigo Oscar. ¿Entiendes lo que estoy diciendo?' Manulo refused to say it to me in English, but I got a translation of what Juliano said and this is, 'If you ever breathe a word of this to anyone, you will enjoy the same fate as your friend Oscar. Do you understand what I am saying?'"

Virtually at the same time, Avery and Christina say, "Holy shit!"

Christian agrees, "Holy shit is right. Manulo said that he was so frightened that he covered his eyes and when he opened them again, Juliano is gone. There's no trace of Oscar anywhere in the room, not even ashes, nothing."

Chief Al Barese questions Christian, "You don't believe any of this bullshit, do you?"

"Well, Chief, I don't say I do and I don't say I don't, but all I know is that Manulo believes it."

There is a collective sigh around the room as each of the detectives try to comprehend all that has been told to them about Juliano. At last, Dan breaks the silence: "I don't know about anyone else here, but I think we must immediately be suspect of a lot of what we've been told. We are dealing with mentally unstable individuals, drug addicts and career criminals most of whom are beyond redemption. We have to assume that most of it, or at least some of it, is bullshit."

Det. Shannon chimes in, "Maybe, but one thing they all have in common is Juliano or Julian, and that's a fact."

Dan rubs his neck and admits, "You right about that, but what do we do now?"

Det. Oliver says, "It should be brought to everyone's attention that there is already an APB out for Juliano in relation to the mass suicide in California, plus we'll add the incidents at the drug house to the list. I think we should leave Manulo's account off for now. What do you say, Chief?"

Uncle Al looks back at his team and answers, "I think that's a good idea. We need to get as many eyes on this as possible. I think we can all see that this guy, Juliano or Julian, or whatever the fuck his name is, has been involved in some very grisly murders. I also think, and I may be way off base here, but I also think that Julian or Juliano could be a person of interest in the murders of the women that are currently under investigation."

Det. Shannon is the first to answer: "You could be right chief. It seems like a possibility and, quite frankly, it's the only lead we've got." As the entire group is discussing the possible options, the door to Al's office opens and in walks a uniformed police officer.

"Sorry to interrupt Chief, but I've got some bad news, uniformed officers found the body of another victim. The woman was found in pretty much in the same condition as the others, torn apart by crows or birds, eyes gouged out and a bloody fetus next to the body."

Uncle Al looks miserable as he asks, "Where did they find her?"

"They found her in a large pit in the path of some road construction off Exit 61 on the LIE. The road workers were doing a survey when they came upon the hole, the men climbed down to investigate and that's when they found the body."

Det. Orello laments, "Well, that just adds more fuel to light a very hot fire under our asses and get this solved." He turns to the uniformed officer and asks, "Was anything else found?"

"Well, the investigators are still combing the scene for clues, but there is a footprint of a man's shoe found near the body. We should be able to get a plaster cast of it and we will try to determine the size and brand."

Uncle Al interrupts the officer, saying, "Listen…" the chief now squints to read the name on the badge, "Listen, Officer James. I want you to tell the police at the crime scene that they are to close it off. No one enters unless I approve it. Do you understand?"

"Yes, Chief."

"Thanks. You can leave."

"Yes, Chief." The police officer turns and leaves the room.

The entire team seems to fall into a depressed state when they hear another knock on the door. Another young police officer enters the room and asks to speak to Detective Oliver. Christian identifies himself and asks the uniformed cop what he wants.

"Well, Detective, I was told that you interrogated a prisoner Manulo Estaquino yesterday and I thought you should know." This can't be good news, but we all hold our breaths.

"Know what?" Det. Oliver asks.

"Manulo Estaquino was found dead in his cell. He hung himself in an apparent suicide."

CHAPTER 37

All who are gathered in the chief's office just sit there, shell shocked, after hearing the news about the poor, mutilated woman that was just found. The team is doubly depressed because Manulo is dead and he could have given the team an even more detailed description of Juliano. I feel guilty that I can't admit to having seen him; in the end though, it all seems useless to me anyway. This is a demon who could transform into anything or anyone he wants to, so what is the point? The police are chasing a phantom, a soulless, heartless beast from the depths of hell and there seems little they can do to stop the slaughter of innocent women.

Chief Barese is the first to break the silence: "Dan and Avery, I want you to go to the scene of the latest murder and be sure that nothing gets left out or missed. Report back to me as soon as you can, got it?"

"Yeah chief, we got it." And they both leave the room.

"Christian, go down to the prison cell and see what you can find, a note scribbled on the wall, some kind of clue, anything."

"Will do, Chief," and he leaves the room.

"Christina, update that APB on Julian to include the things we discussed, except the details about Oscar Rivera's presumed death and be sure it goes out immediately."

"I'm on it, Chief," and she leaves the room.

Now it's just Uncle Al and me alone to go over what we know and what we can do. I feel that I need to state the obvious to Uncle Al, but I say it anyway, "You know that the APB will be useless; Juliano or Julian is a demon and can change to whatever he wants to be. That poor kid Aisha and creep Manulo were telling the truth about what they saw. You know that, don't you?"

Uncle Al sighs, "I know, I know." He is sinking into a deeper state of melancholy.

"Unc, at this point you've got to figure that Juliano could have been involved in these murders, but how can we possibly stop him?"

"Listen Chris, this is why I am asking for help from the saints. I figure the best way to fight hell is to get help from heaven. You've got to reach out to them again…beg them…plead with them for any way to stop this evil." Uncle Al says this with such a heavy heart that I have to get up and put my arm around his shoulder.

"You know I will try and if the saints appear, I will ask them to help. I promise, but did you forget what I was told?"

Now Uncle Al becomes animated, and he wants to make sure that I get the message. "No, I didn't, Chris, but this whole "delivering justice" is way out of line. You are not equipped to battle drug dealers, let alone a demon from hell. St. Thomas More told you that delivering justice for these women is up to you, but how are you supposed to deliver this justice? Huh, how? Are you going to fight him with fists or guns or knives? Here's a thought; maybe you can put him under citizen's arrest and prosecute him under the U.S. Criminal Justice System like they want to do with those terrorists. Chris, the last thing you should do is to try and help the situation by putting yourself in the middle of this mess."

I want him to know that I'm not looking to be a hero, so I say to him, "I know and, believe me, the last thing I want to do is to put myself in the middle of all this, but if it is meant to be my fate or destiny or whatever, then I have no control over what happens?"

"Chris, you can control it by calling me and letting us handle it. I love you; you are my sister's only son, I promised her that I would take care of you and I take my promise very seriously."

"I know you do, and I love you for all you have done for me." I tell this to him because I think he needs to hear it and I also want to get off this subject. As we continue to talk, my uncle keeps reminding me that I could get killed trying to stop this evil, and that I have a responsibility to let law enforcement handle bringing justice to the victims.

I ask him in all seriousness, "How can the police department hope to bring a demon to justice?"

He thinks for a while and he responds, "Maybe you just confront this demon with goodness, unwavering faith; maybe it's that which trumps evil? I don't know, but I do know that this has to stop and it will if I have anything to say about it."

You may have gathered while reading this book that Uncle Al is a man of principle and, when he says something, he truly means it. I look at my uncle, hoping for another miracle in our lives. "Maybe you're right, maybe we can use good to trump evil." I also think of St. Mary Magdalene, how this devil became furious when confronted with the goodness of prayer.

We continue our discussion of the investigation when the phone rings and Uncle Al picks it up, "Chief Barese here", there is a slight pause as Uncle Al says, "Hi Dan, what's up?" He listens to Det. Orello and then says, "Hold on a second." He cups his hand over the receiver and says, "Listen Chris, this is going to take a while, so if you want to leave, go ahead. I'll call you later and let you know what's happening. In the meantime, please, don't take any chances. If something comes up, just call and let me handle it. Okay?"

"Sure, Uncle Al, I'll speak to you later. Thanks, and I love you."

He smiles back at me, "I know you do and I love you, too."

I walk out of his office and down the hallway to my car. It is about 5:30 p.m. and I think of Beth. We have plans for dinner and I am looking forward to seeing her again. Her shift ends at 3 P.M. so I call her at home, but no one answers. I get in my car and start to drive home. About halfway to Huntington my cell phone rings and I'm able to connect through my car's Bluetooth.

"Hello"

"Hi Chris, it's me."

"Hi Beth, I just tried to call you, but no one answered."

"Sorry, I was on the other line and I couldn't get off in time to answer your call. How's your uncle?" Beth is genuinely concerned.

"He's okay, but this case is really a mess and it's so strange that it defies all logic. I know I promised to tell you what I know, but some of what I've been told is so tragic and horrific that I can't even bring myself to repeat it."

"Chris, I understand, believe me, I do. I just want to be able to see you. We can talk or not talk about it, it's up to you."

"Thanks for understanding, Beth. I'm calling because I want to know if we are still on for dinner."

"We sure are."

"I can meet you at Santa Rosa's Café at about 6:30, if that works for you? We can relax a bit; I think I could use a margarita."

"That would be great; I could use a margarita, too."

"Terrific! See you then."

"Actually, Chris, I'll need to be a little late. I have the guy coming over to look at my boat.

He's going to service it and wrap it for winter storage. Can we meet a little later, say 7:30?"

"You mentioned something about that so there's no problem; that works for me. I'll see you then."

"Chris, before you hang up, I want to tell you something."

Beth sounds like she has something important to say, so I ask, "What is it? Are you okay?"

The voice on the other end of the phone goes quiet and I ask, "Beth are you still there? Hello?"

"Hi Chris, I'm still here, I just want to tell you something, but it can wait until we meet for dinner."

"Is everything okay, Beth? Are you sure you don't want to tell me now?" I start to get a little concerned.

All of a sudden, she seems to perk up and tells me, "Don't worry, Rocky; everything is fine. I'll see you at Santa Rosa's Café at 7:30!"

"Great, I'll see you then."

I get to my condo thirty minutes later and that gives me enough time to shower, shave and relax a bit before I meet Beth for dinner. The days are already getting shorter and, and by six o'clock, it is nearly dark. I remain very troubled by what I heard in Uncle Al's office and I resolve not to speak to her about any of it. At the same time, I am happy that'll see her at dinner. My feelings for her are already very strong, but I still question myself as to why I can't tell her that I love her.

Before I get into the shower, I call the café and make a reservation. I shower and it feels good letting the hot water run over my body; it relaxes and reinvigorates my whole being. I put on some khaki pants, a long sleeve polo shirt and a new dark brown leather coat that I had bought at an end of the last season.

The drive to Santa Rosa's Café is only fifteen minutes and I get there early. I'm seated at a table and the waitress brings me water and some tortilla chips and salsa to munch on while I wait. I think about ordering a margarita before Beth arrives, but I decide to wait, so I order an ice tea instead.

It is late and I am getting hungry and I gobble down the chips and salsa. When I look at my watch, I see the time is 7:24p.m.; Beth should be arriving soon. I keep thinking about what she wants to tell me. We haven't been intimate yet and it really doesn't seem to bother either of us, but I am sure it's something we both have thought about. Maybe she wants to become lovers? Maybe she wants to take our relationship to another level? Maybe she wants to tell me that she loves me?

We've told each other that we love one another often, but there is always something that gets in the way of any sort of commitment. I think about all the possibilities and then I think about what my answer would be. Why can't I bring myself to tell her what I know I feel in my heart—a simple, uncomplicated "I love you?"

CHAPTER 38

The night winds turn the temperatures lower as the cold air passes over the grounds surrounding the townhouses.

Beth is waiting. She is anxious, lost in her thoughts. There are so many things that need to be said, but that would have to wait until the time is right. She looks out over the bay at the lights on the other side, to the left and to the right, but always the looming darkness in the middle; Pit Island.

The cheeriness of the fire burning in her fireplace should warm more than the body, it should warm the spirit, but the flames throw off surprisingly little in the way of warmth. Beth considers this strange, but it doesn't seem to matter.

What is this feeling of expectation? Was it her imagination? What is this yearning, this feeling, this passion?

The doorbell rings. It is not unexpected, but it still startles her. Beth wants to answer immediately, but there is something that holds her back at first. The excitement starts to mount as the doorbell rings again. This time she cannot resist. She has been waiting for this time to be here.

"Who's there?" she asks, but it seems she already knows.

"Mr. Apollyon," he answers.

"Mr. Apollyon?" she questions the odd name, but she opens the door to let him in anyway.

"My word, don't you look lovely this evening. I hope I haven't intruded on your plans." "Not at all, won't you come in, Mr. Apollyon?" She smiles, she likes this man.

"Thank you, and please, call me Julian."

CHAPTER 39

I look at my wristwatch again, check it against the time on my smart phone and they both read the same, 7:56 P.M. and I consider that it's not like Beth to be late. I think about her lateness and rationalize that it is taking more time than she expected for the man readying her boat for winter storage. I tell myself that I will give her until 8:00 p.m. and then I'll call to see how things are going.

I have already ordered a margarita on the rocks because I need some fortification for a conversation that may happen, never happen or happen only in my mind. It's now 7:58 P.M. when the door to the restaurant opens. I look up but I'm disappointed that it isn't Beth. So, I continue to wait until my self-imposed deadline comes around.

At 7:59 P.M., I think what the heck, its close enough for government work, and I call her home phone, but I only hear her prerecorded message; "Hi, this is Beth and I'm not available, but just leave a message after the tone and I will call you back as soon as I can. Have a wonderful day…"

Nice message I think, so after the first beep, I say, "Hi Beth, it's me, Chris. I'm at Santa Rosa's and I'm one margarita ahead of you, so I'm wondering where you are…", but before I can complete my message, a familiar voice comes on the phone.

"Hello, Christopher, it has been a while since we last spoke. I hope you are doing well. It is I, Julian, or Juliano, if you prefer."

My mind freezes and I find myself unable to speak.

"Christopher, are you still there? It is rather rude for you to not acknowledge my greeting; after all, it is only common courtesy. Hello Christopher? Come now, I know you are there."

"I'm here." It is all I am able to say.

"Ah, that's much better. Are you enjoying your drink? I hope you are because I expect that you will need to buttress yourself for what I fear will be a very long evening."

"Where is Beth? What the hell are you doing at her house?" I find myself yelling into the phone and the patrons of the restaurant begin to look over at my table.

"Ah yes, Beth! She is quite a woman, isn't she? I find her most charming, an eager ingénue—more than a nurse, don't you think? As luck would have it, she will be playing the role of a lifetime and I expect to be her costar. I imagine we will become quite close and it is rather exciting for me—quite exciting!"

"Listen, you piece of shit from hell, if you harm even one hair on her head, I'll…" but Julian doesn't let me finish.

"What will you do Christopher? Your saints will abandon you; did you know that? They will set you aside like so many old magazines."

I grow angrier by the minute. "You lie, they are more powerful than you can ever imagine."

Julian chuckles a bit: "You mean that pathetic attempt to intimidate me at the cave? Mary Magdalene was a whore in life, and she will always be a whore and Anthony, that pathetic abbot, whom I had beaten nearly to death, he felt my wrath. Do you think that they, or any of The Sainted, can ever defeat me or my minions? If you do, I fear that you will be sorely disappointed."

"What about St. Michael the Archangel. I seem to remember that he kicked your ass and sent you to the depths of hell. What about him?" I have this overwhelming need to defend The Sainted.

Julian is taunting me. "Ah, Christopher, I have learned so much more since then and I've had far more practice capturing the souls of mankind than you could ever imagine. Ah Mankind! Their weaknesses, their lusts, their excesses and their plethora of sins, oh the list goes on. The souls of men, now let's be sure to have gender equality in this equation, and women are fodder for my cannon. They are easy prey because the freedom of evil is easier to accept than the constraints of good. I do hope I am using the proper grammar and context." Julian laughs out loud over the phone.

I become very frightened for Beth, fearful for all the women Julian will continue to murder and, for the first time, doubtful about my saints and questioning my own purpose in all of this. I am overwhelmed with a feeling of total helplessness and unable to think about anything that I can do against Satan himself?

"Oh Christopher, I do hope you are still there?"

"I'm here."

"I know what you are thinking, you want to know what you should do, and well I'll tell you! We should try to meet as soon as possible. I recall that you and I have discussed having ultimate evil confront consummate good and, unfortunately, it appears that you are the only advocate for the good side of things. Tsk, tsk that is such as shame. This will be a daunting task for someone, how shall I put it, of your limited ability. What say you?"

I don't know how to respond.

"Christopher, oh Christopher, do I detect some reticence on your part? Tick tock, tick tock, time marches on and you will need to confront your own fears, your own weaknesses and, yes, even your own faith."

My only response is to say, "Where?"

"Oh, come now, Christopher, take a guess."

"Fuck you, I don't feel like playing your games, where?"

"My, my, aren't we a bit testy. Pit Island, of course. I believe you know where it is. You and Beth had that wonderful day on the water, remember? You may want to bring something warm and dry as it can get a little wet at times, which I'm sure you can attest to."

The realization then hits me as I blurt out in stunned amazement, "It was you who caused that storm and it was you who almost got us killed."

"Of course, it was me. I love it when you struggle, but alas, I let you live to fight another day."

"Wait scumbag, have you forgotten about St. Rita? It was her intervention, her miracle that saved us. Your power may be great, but her power comes from God."

"Believe what you will Christopher, but I fear that when you are in most need of God, He will be as absent as He was when those women died. Comprendere?" He speaks this mocking the Italian that Beth and I like to speak.

Julian continues toying with me and I know it, but I need to buy some time to try and figure out what I can do.

"I want to speak with Beth," I demand.

"I'm afraid that's impossible."

"Why? Where is she? I want to speak with her now." I am starting to realize that I have no power at all and Julian is looking to make Beth his next victim.

"I'm afraid she's in an area with very poor cellular reception. Pit Island has little in the way of cutting-edge technologies, amenities or guest services, so to speak, but I assure you that she will be in fine spirits the next time you see her."

I know Julian is enjoying every minute of this conversation. While I am speaking, I put a $20 bill on the table and leave the restaurant. "I won't come until I speak with Beth." I say this, all the while knowing that I will go no matter what.

"Oh, you'll come, Christopher, you'll come. There are two irresistible reasons: one is Beth and the other is to face your fears. This conversation has become too sophistic and I am going to end our discussion now."

"Don't you hang…" but Julian, the demon Satan from hell, hangs up the phone before I can finish. I try calling again, but the line goes dead.

I rush out the door and stand on the sidewalk outside the restaurant thinking about my next move. I run to my car and head for Beth's townhouse, trying not to think the worst but knowing the worst can happen. It is close to 9 P.M. when I reach the gates leading to the complex and then I realize that I have no code to open them. Just as I prepare to dial her phone, the gates open.

"Son of a bitch…" I know it has to be Julian so I enter through the gate and drive towards Beth's townhouse.

My mind is going in all directions while trying to contemplate what I to do next. I remember that I didn't call Uncle Al and I grab my phone to dial his office. When the desk sergeant answers, he tells me that the chief is out at a crime scene, so I hang up and dial his mobile phone.

"Hi Chris, what's up?"

"Uncle Al, he's got Beth, Julian has Beth."

Al yells into his phone, "What! How do you know?"

I am breathless as I am telling my uncle about the call with Julian. "Uncle Al, I called Beth's home when she was late for our date. While I was waiting at the restaurant, I tried to phone her, but Julian…" and then the line goes dead. I try to call him back, but the connection is completely gone. I drive my car down the road that winds through the complex until I reach her townhouse.

I pull into her driveway, jump out of the car and run towards the atrium entrance. The front door is slightly open and all the lights are on. I push the door open wider to get a better view inside, but there is no one I can see on the first level. I slowly walk into the kitchen from the foyer and then into the great room, but there is still no one there. The remnants of logs are still smoldering in the fireplace, but they don't seem to throw off any heat. I continue to search for Beth, going from room to room on the ground level and on the second floor, but I find no one home.

I walk back down to the main floor; I remember that I haven't looked in the garage. The garage is off the kitchen and as I open the door, I become more cautious. I slowly open it to avoid any surprises and I turn on the lights. I take a look around and all I see is Beth's car on one side and her bike, water skis and some storage boxes piled on the other.

I decide to walk into the space to see what I can find and as soon as I do, I see a note taped to the garage door. The note is written on a material that I have never seen or felt before and it feels very strange when. I pick it up to read what it says and as I stand there, I read the note aloud to myself;

My Dear Boy,

I am thrilled that you could make it. As you can see, Beth and I are gone and await your arrival. Beth is in good health and good spirits and I know that she is anxious to see you, too.

Pit Island will be a bit difficult to get to and since we are already using the Fun-A-Bout (don't you just love the name!), I have taken the liberty of reserving a small watercraft for your convenience. You will find the conveyance tied to a cleat in Beth's slip space.

By the way, your uncle will be of no use to you. I hope that my discussions with the media didn't cause too many problems? At any rate, I'm afraid you are all alone in this quest of good versus evil and, I assure you, evil will win.

Oh, Christopher, I think it's only fair to warn you that if you have any reservations about coming to our little soirée, I will have no alternative but to assure that Beth enjoys the same fate as Celine and the rest of the poor unfortunates.

At any rate, we eagerly await your arrival.
Bon Voyage!

When I finish reading the letter, it bursts into flames, and as it drops to the floor, it totally disappears; ashes and all.

I run to my car and drive to the marina. The road is dark, but the marina is lit with a few lights and I'm able to see a small inflatable in Beth's slip space. The boat has a 15 H.P. outboard motor and is tied to the cleat as I was told. Before I leave, I try to call Uncle Al again, but the line is still dead.

I reconcile myself to the fact that there is little else I can do but take the boat to Pit Island. I get onboard, untie the line and I pull the cord to the outboard motor, starting it up immediately. I guide the boat out of the space and head toward the darkness in the middle of the Bay that is Pit Island.

CHAPTER 40

"Chris! Damn it, Chris! Answer me! Damn it!"

Chief Detective Al Barese is practically screaming into his phone, but there is no answer on the other end of this line. What little he's heard from Chris on the call made him very afraid for his nephew's safety. As few members of his team are still at the latest crime scene and he turns to Det. Dan Orello.

"Something's very wrong, Dan."

"What? What is it, Chief?" Now Dan is getting concerned.

"I just got a call from Chris. He said something about his girlfriend Beth is being held by Julian."

"What? You're serious?"

"I am serious. I told Chris that if there is even a sign of any trouble, he needs to call me, immediately, but before I could get any details, the line went dead." Al Barese seems more frightened than Dan has ever seen before.

"Chief, calm down. Did he say where he was?"

"No, not exactly, but he told me he called Beth's home when she was late for their date. The last word I heard Chris say was 'Julian' and that's when the line went dead. You got to figure that's where he's headed."

"Just hang on Chief, I'm going to call the local precinct and ask them to send some officers to her house. Do you have the address?"

"No, but she lives in Northport, those townhouses by the water, have them look up her number. Her name is Beth, no wait, Elizabeth Della Russo; she's brunette and very pretty. I think she's 29 or 30 years old, 5'6" or 7", 115 to 120 lbs. Beth's a nurse and she works at Huntington Hospital. She drives a 2016 Ford Escape and she owns a boat called the "Fun-A-Bout" that she keeps at the marina in her complex. Dan, she's Chris' girlfriend, but she was also my nurse when I was in the hospital and I want to get this scumbag before he does anything to her. Got it?"

Dan is writing all this down before he calls the Northport Police Department and tells Al, "I've got it, Chief."

Dan makes the call and relays the information and when he's finished, he says, "We're just about done here and Avery can tie up any loose ends. Do you want to go over to Northport to see if we can find anything?" Dan is becoming as anxious as Al, and he wants to be there when they get Julian.

"Are you kidding? Let's get moving now!" Chief Barese and Det. Dan Orello climb the ladder that leads out of the pit and they run to the Chief's car. With sirens blaring, they speed off west on the LIE towards Northport.

CHAPTER 41

The cold wind churns the bay waters choppy as the small boat pushes through the waves. The rain splashes against my face, my clothes are completely soaked and I am very cold. The distant darkness that is Pit Island now looms larger as I get closer and closer. My only focus now is getting to the island without killing myself, but I have no idea about what I will do when I get there.

When I see that I am about halfway to the island, it starts to rain even more heavily than before; a cold and constant wind-driven downpour that has made things much worse than before. I continue to be pelted by large drops of rain and I think to myself, "It just figures this would happen…" but then I surmise that this must be Julian's way of welcoming me to my nightmare; his hell.

When I am less than fifty yards from what appears to be the shore-line, I hear a creaking sound and I'm close enough to make out the hull of a boat that's jutting out of the water. I can't make out for certain what exactly it is, but I fear it can only be the wreckage of the Fun-A-Bout. With only the hull of the boat sticking out of the water, I can't be positive; however, in my mind, I know it can't imagine that it could be anything else. Given the rough waters and the small outboard motor, it's impossible to get there any faster than my small inflatable can take me. All the while

I am heading toward that island, I try to close my mind to the possibility that something will happen to Beth.

I cut back on the throttle and cautiously maneuver the craft toward the wreckage, fully aware of the rocks that are very close to the surface of the water. The boat has a very low draft, so I'm able to move closer without having the deck of the inflatable ripped apart by the jagged rocks below. When I get about twenty feet away, I see a huge hole in the hull of the sunken boat and it appears to be abandoned. Still, I need to see for myself to be sure, so I further reduce the speed to a crawl to try and take a closer look.

A few minutes later, I'm close enough to know that it is Beth's boat by its size, color and markings. I manage to grab a line and toss it over one of the railings on what had been the Fun-A-Bout. I tie up the small craft, so I can pull myself closer to the wreck to see if there are any other clues as to where Julian and Beth might be. That's when I first see the message. The message is burned into the side of the boat and it reads, "Abandon all hope, ye who enter here. Love, Julian!" When I finish reading, the message explodes into flames and evaporates into thin air.

The shallow water and rocks below make it virtually impossible to motor on any further, but I am close enough to the shore that I untie the inflatable from the railing and paddle in nearer to the shoreline. When I think I'm close enough, I jump out into the freezing cold water. As soon as my feet hit bottom, I can see that I am standing in about three feet of water. I am still holding onto the line, and with great difficulty I attempt drag the inflatable toward the shore and onto Pit Island.

The rain continues to come down harder and the wind is picking up. I am soaking wet and the cold wind penetrates my clothes that stick to my skin. When Beth and I were out on her boat, I seem to remember that the island appears to be about seventy yards long and about forty yards wide. There's no light from the moon and I can barely make out some very large boulders and tall trees on the island, but not much else. As I slog through the water, I look around to try and get my bearings hoping to see where I might find some kind of shelter from the terrible conditions. I am unable to see ahead as I make my way through the water and I need to move cautiously over the rocks at the water's edge so I won't stumble or slip and I finally get up the embankment.

Once I make my way to the top of the embankment, I try to walk when I can, and crawl when I have to. There are no paths, only rocks, bushes and trees, but there are no signs of where Julian might be holding Beth captive. As I cautiously move towards what I think is the center of the island, I stop to rest by a huge boulder and that's when I see something that looks like it has been chiseled into the side of the stone.

I look closer to see what it reads, and I see it's another message from Julian, "Christopher, you're getting cold," and as soon as I read the chiseled message, the entire etching burst into flames and vanishes.

I expected this of Julian, playing games and taunting me. I look around hoping to see something that will point the way, but there is only heavy rain and a cold wind. I start to head back in the direction that I came from when I fall over a tree stump. As I grab onto a low hanging branch to get my balance, I see something carved into the tree. I read a message that says, "You're getting warm, good lad!" and as before, the carved message bursts into flames and disappears.

I lift myself up off the ground and look around again. There seems to be no real direction I can go in as everything looks the same, especially when seem through heavy rain and winds. I start to think that knowing Julian's efforts to taunt me he is making it very difficult and confusing. I think to myself out loud, "Pit Island? Pit Island, Pit…" then I realize there must be an entrance to a hidden pit around somewhere and that what I need to find.

With renewed purpose, I continue to walk in the same general direction that I have been going when I come upon what looks like a piece of material torn off of a woman's yellow slick raincoat. I pick it up off the ground and look at another message written, in magic marker, on the back: "Oh Christopher, you are getting hot!" I throw the torn piece of coat to the side, but before it hits the ground it bursts into flames, no remnants, no ashes, no message. I'm sick and tired of these games and I become more determined than ever to find Beth, to confront this demon from hell, to just get this over. While I continue to struggle to keep my footing, I reexamine my own doubts about the saints. I need to try and understand that, after all I have been shown, after all the saints have taught me, how can they abandon me now? I ask that question of myself over and over, and the answer always comes back the same, they won't desert me, not in my hour of greatest need.

The wind and rain are now so strong that they nearly lift me off the ground. I manage to walk another thirty feet when I see what appears to be a sign. The rain is coming down too hard for me to read it from where I'm standing, so I push against the wind to get a closer look. When I am standing next to the sign, I grab a hold of the side of it to help keep from being blown away and to read the message:

Warning Trespassers
Oh, not you Christopher.
Well, I must say I am proud of you.
You are sizzling hot,
Welcome! Dear Boy! Welcome!

I immediately back away from the sign and look around to see where Julian could be. My mind is running wild as I don't know what to expect next. Julian is Satan and has command over demonic forces in a way that I will never understand, let alone defend myself against.

In my panicked state, I try to take a step backwards, but at that exact moment the ground beneath me gives way and I fall into an abyss. I tumble a long way down the side of the hole and crash onto the ground below. I bang my head during the fall, and I am fading in and out of consciousness when I hear, "Welcome, Christopher! Welcome! We are so happy to see you, dear boy! You are a sight for sore eyes! Welcome!"

CHAPTER 42

Chief Barese is at the wheel of his car as it careens down the expressway at over 95 miles per hour. The sirens blasting and the cars in the center lane shift to the left or right to give his police car the right of way. The chief is yelling at every driver that is in his way, "Get out of my way!"

Dan's white-knuckled hands are gripping the dashboard and he shouts, "Chief, you got to slow it down! You will get us killed and that won't help Chris or Beth." Al knows Dan is right, so he slows down to a moderate 80 miles per hour.

The chief is consumed by thoughts of his nephew and Beth and the danger they are in. It is at least ten minutes before Al says his first words, "Dan, this has to end. No woman is safe and now Chris and Beth are in grave danger while this bastard is out there. I intend to see that he is brought to justice if it's the last thing I ever do." Uncle Al suspects what Chris knows to be true; Julian is a demon, perhaps Satan himself, and there is little chance he will be brought to justice. Al knows what is also important to him and that's to see Chris and Beth are safe; he is very worried when he says aloud, "They have to be safe."

Dan assures the chief, "Don't worry chief, we'll get this guy. It seems that he's made his first mistake."

The chief looks over at his partner and asks, "What's that, Dan?"

"I know this guy is like a ghost, Chief, but this is our first solid lead ever. As a matter of fact, Chris is the first person who's not an addict or thug or serial killer that has even spoken to the man."

"I guess you're right, but we still need to get him or I'm afraid that Chris and Beth could be his next victims."

The detectives continue west on the LIE until Uncle Al gets off exit 53 and heads for the Sunken Meadow Parkway. It is after 11P.M. and there is little traffic on the road as it winds toward the last exit for Route 25A. As the car speeds west on the road towards Northport, a voice comes through the car's two-way radio:

"Unit 9 to Unit 1, come in, Unit 1."

Chief Barese answers, "This is Unit 1, Chief Barese here."

"Chief, this is Officer Jim McGowan out of Northport PD. We are at the home of Ms.

Della Russo."

"Well, what did you find?"

Officer McGowan answers, "When we arrived, the front door was open and the lights were on. My partner and I did a thorough search of the residence and there is no one here."

Det. Orello jumps into the discussion, "This is Detective Orello; are there any signs of a struggle, anything out of place that you could tell?"

"Nothing that we can see, everything seems to be in place. Ms. Della Russo's car is still in the garage and we are just about to go to the marina to see if her boat is still in its slip."

Uncle Al says to the officer, "We are on our way and we will meet you at the marina. What's the number of the slip space?"

"It's number eight, Chief."

"Okay, see you in about five minutes."

CHAPTER 43

My entire body aches after landing on the hard dirt floor. I had the wind knocked out of me when I landed on the floor and now, I'm gasping for air because I can't find enough breath to even speak. I am lying on the ground, dazed and confused about my surroundings, but slowly my mind becomes a bit clearer. I carefully check my arms and legs and nothing seems to be broken, but when I try to get up off the ground, I only fall back down in a heap. Finally, when I am able focus, I see that I'm in a huge underground cavern. There is the main open area where there are a number of large jagged rocks and boulders scattered about. Surrounding the area are many foreboding dark corners and crevices. Being in the main open area I feel very vulnerable and I know that I can't continue to lay there. After a few minutes I am finally able to lift myself up into a sitting position and that is when the figure of Julian appears from behind a large boulder. As he approaches me, I can see the evil on his face that I have seen before.

He is standing above me looking down as he taunts me, "I do love dramatic entrances, don't you Christopher? I believe they set the tone for all that is to come and there is much more to come. Don't you agree?"

I know I can speak, but I don't want to give him the satisfaction. "Come now, Christopher, you can at least be civil."

I finally found my voice, "Fuck you, you piece of shit!"

"My, my Christopher, there is no need for you to use such profanity. After all sure you realize I am considered to be among the first of the Sainted, aren't I?" He seems to sneer at the word "sainted."

I then scream at him, "You are nothing like The Sainted, you are a murdering piece of shit from the depths of hell!"

"Now, now, what did I say? Let's be civil. What say you?" Julian's pomposity is palpable when he says, "You are most welcome here. I would have had something specially prepared for you, but as you can see, there is little in the way of cheer in this place." He then looks at me with mock distress and in a condescending way he says, "Oh my, Christopher, now I can see why you are so testy. You are soaking wet and still a little foggy from your grand entrance; here, let me help you." As he merely mentions my condition, my clothes become completely dry, my mind is clear and the pain is gone.

With renewed strength, I am able to lift myself off the floor. I touch my clothes, my arms and my face and find that my clothing is completely dry, I feel no pain and I am bewildered when I ask, "What the hell? What did you do to me?"

"Christopher, I can see you were in very sorry shape and, as you can see, I am in perfect shape. We cannot have these kinds of imbalances between us; dry versus wet, up versus down, cold versus hot, love versus hate and of course, good versus evil. As this test of wills is ordained, I intend to assure that in our contest of faiths, evil has equal billing with good—maybe even have the starring role. What say you?" Julian offers this with the utmost sincerity.

Of course, he expects no answer from me, but he asks again, "What say you, Christopher?"

"I say go fuck yourself. Where's Beth?"

"Oh, Beth, well she's in make-up right now. Beth will be appearing for the first, and most likely, the last time ever in the starring role of this passion play. Isn't that exciting! And the best part, I am her leading man! Imagine that, a leading man in a passion play! Mom would be so proud!"

"Fuck you, let's cut this bullshit and get it over with." I am very angry and I figure that at this point I have little else to lose.

Julian smiles, "Oh my, Christopher, you are in a hurry to die and endure everlasting torment, aren't you? Well, you are my special guest and I will be sure to accommodate your wish. Ah, but there is so much more to see before the conclusion of this drama of good versus evil."

"I don't want to see anything you have to show me."

"Oh, Christopher..."

I interrupt him: "Stop calling me Christopher, fuck face."

Julian looks at me and his face turns into that of the demon I had seen in Christ's tomb. I become very frightened and I stumble back towards the wall of the cave. Julian, the demon, grows to more than twice his size and his eyes turn flaming red as he screams a hideous shriek, "I will call you whatever I choose!"

Then in a flash, he is back to being Julian and he speaks to me again, "Dear boy, you do not want to make me angry. I do dreadful things when I'm angry, so please, forgive my momentary lapse. Now that it's settled, I will continue to call you Christopher, is that acceptable?"

I just look at him and say nothing.

"Good. Isn't that nice—friendly enemies, you and I!"

"I will never be a friend to a murderous fiend like you."

"That is probably true; however, I do have a special evening planned for you and there will be guests and all. I am so very excited."

"Where's Beth?"

"All in good time, Christopher, all in good time."

Then, in a split second, the floor of the pit is transformed into what looks like the set of a late-night TV talk show. There is a desk with a throne like seat, a sofa on one side and there are bright lights that shine in all directions over the stage. Along with the lights, the sound of a drum roll can be heard along wild screams and applause that emanate from the dark corners. The applause continues unabated as Julian appears in a white tuxedo as he stands under an eerie red spotlight. He looks at me like I am the audience, and I hear an announcer that sounds exactly like that guy who introduces the wrestling matches at the arena. His booming voice enthusiastically proclaims, "Ladies and gentlemen, welcome! Welcome to the premier of "What the Hell!" We have a fabulous line up for you tonight, but before we begin, let's give a rousing welcome to the originator and star of 'What the Hell', here's the one, the only, JULIAN!!!"

The invisible crowd is now in a complete frenzy, yelling and hooting, screaming and laughing at what they hope will be a show of all shows. Julian is basking in the limelight and relishing the applause as he keeps saying, "Thank you! Thank you!" while pretending he is calming down the crowd saying, "Please ladies and gentlemen, I am truly overwhelmed by this much deserved show of devotion!" and the audience can be heard laughing at Julian's attempt at humor. Finally, Julian is able to hush the audience until all that can be heard is a low murmur. He then looks me straight in the eye and with hellish delight; Julian starts to speak in a slow, deliberate way until he reaches a nerve- shattering crescendo.

"Christopher, and all of the audience in our studio tonight, I am so very excited about the very special treat I have instore for you! Introducing dead from the depths of Hell itself, our first guests have been waiting in the wings and are now ready for their time in the spotlight! Murder, perversion, mayhem, drugs, child prostitution and a list of sins, too numerous to name, makes them the perfect first guests to appear on our premier. I could go on and on about these boys, but we'll let them speak for themselves. Ladies and gentlemen, please put your hands together for the trio that has worked so hard to give evil more meaning than ever before. Ladies and gentlemen, I give you ERNESTO VASQUEZ, MANULO ESTAQUINO and JULIO ALMENDE!"

The invisible audience goes absolutely wild. There is cheering, yelling, whistling, screaming with peals of laughter and thunderous applause. Julian is in his glory, absorbed in the out-of-control reaction of his minions. I am frightened by what could possibly be coming next, but it doesn't take long for me to find out. From the large boulder to left of the talk show set, where Julian is sitting, appears something out of a nightmare. The three men, or rather remnants of men, are attached to each other in such a way that they look like they're playing some degenerate game of Twister. Their bodies are covered with gaping wounds and cysts that ooze blood and puss. Ernesto, Manulo and Julio are screaming for mercy, screaming for forgiveness, screaming for release from their torment. Julian seems oblivious to their entreaties as he continues to bask in the applause of the phantom spectators.

Finally, Julian turns to them, "I know you three have so much to say, but we have a special surprise for you, our guests!" A hush comes over the audience as they wait to hear what the special surprise is.

Julian slyly smiles and looks around at the invisible audience and he pauses for effect. He relishes the time that he stays silent allowing the excitement to build. Then he finally says, "For all of you in the studio tonight, I want you to give a very warm, or should I say very hot welcome to the merciless angel and the all-fire demon, Aftemelouchos or as you may know him, TEMELUCHUS!"

I slowly turn towards the boulder where I first saw the three spirits of the evil men from the drug house. As I do, the figure of Temeluchus emerges as a demon of enormous proportions from behind the huge rock. The demon carries a fork of fire in one hand and, in his other hand he carries an iron rod with three hooks dangling from heavy chains. Ernesto, Manulo and Julio are now staring at Temeluchus in abject fear and, through flaming eyes shining bright; he is glaring back at them.

The audience is going completely wild. They sound like they are out of control excited and Julian senses that this is the moment he must act. His minions are waiting for what is to come and he is determined not disappoint them. "Ladies and gentlemen, would you like to hear from our three guests?"

Immediately, there is a roar from the unseen crowd, "YES!"

Ernesto screams, "Forgive me, please, forgive me. It was all Heriberto's fault! You must forgive…" and then Julio jumps in: "I am innocent! I didn't do nothing! I was just there; please, I didn't…" Manulo is now the last to join in as he pleads, "You must believe me. I was only following orders from Heriberto. I am not guilty of nothing. You must believe me." Now all three tortured souls are screaming over each other so loudly that you can't understand what they are saying, but you know what they want.

Temeluchus stands in front of the trio, continuing to glare down at them as they scream for forgiveness. It is then that I hear a frighteningly hideous bellow from this hellish demon that seems to come from the depths of his being. "BE QUIET! YOU HAVE DAMNED YOUR SOULS!"

The three damned souls cower as the demon stares down at them with eyes blazing. At first, they are too afraid to speak, but Julio summons up enough courage to make an appeal for him and the entire group. He looks up at Temeluchus: "Please, please have mercy on us. We have done many evil things, but we now know that we have sinned against God. Please, forgive us. We did not…"

Temeluchus roars a shriek and the unholy trio as well as the audience, all go quiet. "He who has not had mercy, neither will God have mercy on him. I am His chief of torment and it is foretold that the souls be delivered into my hands and they must be taken down into hell. Let me take them into the lower prison, let them be cast into torments and be left there until the great day of judgment."

It seems that Ernesto, Manulo and Julio have come to a new realization of the horror that they will face for eternity. They continue to beg for mercy as they to try to explain their vile and evil crimes against so many innocent and guilty alike. All the while, the three damned are crying, cursing and screaming; it is such a pitiful sight, but the audience is taking great delight in their suffering.

The three continue, "Please, you must listen; you must forgive us.

Ernesto pleads, "We will repent. We will atone …"

But Temeluchus will hear no more from any of these men who have damned their own souls. He screams at them, "Your pleas for forgiveness come too late and fall on deaf ears. You are condemned to suffer an eternity of torment and I am here to make it so!"

A sneer appears on the demon's face and with that, Temeluchus takes his fork of fire and in three short strokes opens the entrails of each of the men. Their guts spill onto the floor of the cavern. Those that were once alive frantically try to pick up their own entrails and stuff them back into their bodies, but it is a lost cause. Then, the three turn back to look up and cower at the giant demon standing before them. Temeluchus then takes his iron rod and with one mammoth stroke he jams each of the hooks into the heads of Ernesto, Manulo and Julio. The demon lifts the men off the floor of the cave, shrieks a savage cry and in a burst of flames, they all disappear.

It is a mind-numbing and horrific scene and I feel like I am about to go into shock. The sheer magnitude of what I've witnessed leaves me with feelings of fear and dread and beyond that, a creeping sense of hopelessness.

There is complete silence from the invisible audience. Julian seems delighted waves good-bye to Temeluchus saying, "Fair thee well dear fiend, I mean, dear friend!" Next, he turns to me, "Ah, Christopher! Wasn't that magnificent?" Now he turns to face all the dark corners of the cave, "Ladies and gentlemen, wasn't Temeluchus wonderful!"

A thunderous roar of approval comes from the imaginary crowd. Julian continues, "And what about the trio of evil? I mean I'm asking, were they fabulous or were they fabulous? What say you all?!"

There is now another gigantic roar of approval from the shadowy minions. With his arms held high in the air, Julian is now acknowledging the screaming, whistling and deafening applause. He is clearly reveling in it all. I sense what is happening as Julian allows this horror to continue. He wants to terrorize me and he's enjoying the prospect of my denying The Sainted—denying my faith before I die because I will have abandoned all hope as God will have abandoned me. I might not be in hell, but then again, I am as close as you can get. I'm thinking now would be a good time for a sign, another vision, but I know I'm alone. Julian gets up from his chair on the talk show set, and walks closer to the phantom audience and closer to me.

There is a low murmur coming from the crowd as the devil looks around at his indiscernible adoring fans. A big smile crosses Julian face and he proclaims, "Thank you, thank you all so very much! Drum roll, please! Ladies and gentleman, our next guest needs no introduction. He grew up on the mean streets of El Salvador, he became an entrepreneur at a very early age, and he's enjoyed much success in the drug, murder, robbery and child prostitution arena." The crowd's excitement now is starting to increase and the air seems thick with anticipation of what is to come.

Julian is now becoming even more animated. "Many of you may not know this, but I, your ever dutiful host, have had a close working relationship with this man in the past and there are numerous stories I can tell you, but let's not wait another moment!" The crowd claps in unison, and they are starting to chant, "HERIBERTO … HERIBERTO … HERIBERTO!"

Julian shouts to be heard above the crowd, "Now for the first time on any stage anywhere on this or any ethereal plain; heavenly, unearthly or otherwise; Ladies and gentlemen, please give and rousing and hellish welcome to HERIBERTO QUINTANA, and his ever-faithful sidekick GLASYA-LABOLAS!"

In an instance there erupts another massive outburst of applause and cheers from the phantom viewers. After I hear Julian's announcement, I frantically look around trying to see where the condemned soul will appear, when out from behind the rock next to the stage comes what I fear is Heriberto Quintana, but he isn't alone.

Quintana floats onto Julian's mock studio set three feet off the ground and sitting on his back and shoulders is a hideous demon with a long, sharp knife. Glasya-Labolas is using the knife to peel the skin off of Heriberto's body. The evil spirit appears in the shape of a vicious dog but with the wings of the mythological Griffin. He is baring long sharp teeth and he has hands instead of paws for slicing Heriberto's flesh with his knife.

I recoil in horror at witnessing what is happening to Heriberto. As the gang leader sees me sitting on the floor of the cave. His eyes are pleading with me as he tries to scream, but he can't scream; he has no mouth. The fiend, Glasya-Labolas, is slicing large chunks of skin off his back, sides, stomach and even his face. Once the demon cuts off skin, more grows back immediately. I can see that Heriberto is in horrendous pain, all the while he is staring at me in wide-eyed terror.

Julian waves his arms, welcoming his guests "Come Heriberto, come! Sit down. We are thrilled that you were able to make it to the premier of 'What the Hell'. I am sure there are so many things that the audience would love to know about you so before the show, we asked these lovely folks in our studio to write down questions." Julian, holding up a stack of index cards, says, "I have a stack of them right here in my hands and I'll bet the audience can't wait to hear the answers. What do you say members of the audience?" The unseen audience screams a collective, "YES…YES…YES!!!" All the while Julian continues to take special delight at the horror of this situation.

Heriberto floats over to the set where Julian is sitting. There is a chair and a sofa next to Julian, but Heriberto does not sit down; he merely floats above it. Glasya-Labolas, however, does sit down and he continues to cut the skin, this time down Heriberto's legs.

Julian is playing with the group of index card questions in his hand, and he starts to read from one of them, "Heriberto, the first question is from Milt Lessenton who hails from the Halls of Montezuma and asks, "Why the hell are you are in Hell?" Julian looks questioningly at the card and he turns to his guest and asks again, "That's a good question, why the hell are you are in hell?"

Heriberto is in unbearable pain as he looks at Julian and tries to bellow, but there are only his screams of silence. Julian looks back at the audience and says, "I think that our guest is a bit shy, but I have inside information that I will share it with you. Heriberto is here because he was very naughty—very, very naughty. He saw to it that a number of people did not get to see their next birthday. But I have special treat; if anyone in the audience can guess how many people Heriberto has murdered, he or she will win this brand new Veg-O-Matic! It slices, it dices, it crinkle cuts, it juliennes and it washes easily with plain soap and water and when your done it stores easily in a cabinet or draw and its completely portable so you can even take it with you when you travel!"

The invisible audience goes crazy yelling out numbers: 7, 56, 2, 12, 8, 63 and all the while, Julian in enjoying the audience participation immensely. Finally Julian signals that he wants quiet and the voices go still as he speaks, "Are those all the answers? Anymore? Well, ladies and gentlemen, I am sorry to say you are all wrong." There are groans from the unseen fiends, and here is the correct answer, "Heriberto Quintana has killed an incredible eleven people; yes, you heard right—eleven people and, as if that were not enough, he ordered the murder of seven more! I also have it on good authority that Heriberto did most of these murders with a very sharp knife AND it is Glasya-Labolas who was Heriberto's inspiration!"

Now the groans of disappointment change to wild cheers and applause as I sit watching as this horror continues to unfold.

The invisible audience finally quiets down and Julian continues, "The next question is Hermione Loglin of Dodsonville, Iran who asks, 'What does Glasya-Labolas do with all the skin he's peeling off Heriberto?' That's a very good question, Hermione." Julian then turns to Glasya-Labolas and asks, "What do you do with all that skin?"

Glasya-Labolas shoots a quick look at Julian, but the demon does not answer. He is far too busy peeling the tattoos off of Quintana and waiting for them to grow back, so he can peel them off again. Julian guesses that Glasya-Labolas is too busy to answer so he says, "Well, it seems that I will have to intercede again. I happen to know, from the same good authority, that his skin is used for any number of things. As a matter of fact, I use it for my personal stationary." Julian looks at me with blazing eyes and a revolting smile.

"Stationary?" I say to myself. The garage, the note—oh, my God; it was the note from Julian on Quintana's skin that I picked up and read. I look back up at Julian while I unconsciously wipe my hands to try and rid them of the filth. He sees this, and he knows that I know and that makes him smile.

I turn back to find that Glasya-Labolas' total demeanor has changed and he appears very angry. The devil starts to shriek and rant at Heriberto. With each shriek Heriberto's terror only grows, but he cannot move. He is powerless to act. Glasya-Labolas then stops ranting and howling and raises his blade, but this time, he doesn't bother to peel the skin on Heriberto; he just drives the long knife into Heriberto's body. Again and again, the demon thrusts the blade into Quintana and with each thrust, Heriberto writhes in all-embracing agony. He wants to die, but he knows he can't die: he can only feel unbearable pain. He cannot scream; he has no mouth. The whole time the audience is silent and Julian is looking on, grinning with utter delight and amusement.

All at once, Glasya-Labolas stops driving his knife into Heriberto and in an instant, the beast swings the long knife and cuts the head off of Heriberto and it falls onto the floor. I try to turn away in revulsion, but something makes me look back at the gruesome scene and when I do, I see Heriberto's head on the floor—his eyes are wide open with the same terror and pleading, as before, for an end to his torture.

I'm staring at the demon fiend as he picks up the severed head in one hand and places it back on Quintana's body. I detect an almost imperceptible smile that comes across Glasya-Labolas as he continues to stare at the object of his torment and, with one deafening howl, the both of them burst into flames and are gone. At first there is deathly silence, but then the entire phantom crowd roars with riotous approval.

Now Julian is back, in his best host mode, as he walks in front of the audience and back to center stage. "Ladies and gentlemen, was that not the most amazing feet of hellishness you've been privileged to have seen?" I hear another riotous roar of approval, and I close my eyes to try to escape from this horror, if for only a moment. I use this time to say a silent prayer; a prayer I hope will be answered by the Sainted.

The peace is very short lived as Julian says in a singsong voice, "Christopher, oh Christopher."

"What the fuck do you want?" I am angry and afraid at the same time, but that is the only thing I can say.

"I sincerely hope you are enjoying our show. I must admit it is a bit impromptu, given Manulo's recent, shall we say, departure. There was no time for rehearsal, no time for practicing our lines, but it was spectacular in spite of it all, don't you think?"

"Fuck you…"

"No, Christopher, it is you who will be, as you put it, fucked. Your prayers will go unanswered. God and your precious Sainted have all abandoned you, and you will have to face evil all by your lonesome."

I lift myself off the dirt floor and stand there dispirited. I have seen the true nature of evil, the true nature of hellish malevolence, and for the first time, I see the possibility of evil triumphing over good. I fall on my knees in despair waiting for some sign, but recognizing that it may not come. I now consider the possibility that I will need to face this encounter on my own.

"Ah, I see you are finally coming to terms with the inevitable. But don't fret, you still have time to come around to my way of thinking. Our show is only starting and there is so much more to see."

Julian looks up at his unseen minions and spreading his arms wide, he says in a loud voice, "My dear friends are you ready for more?" The crowd responds in an earsplitting unison, "YES!"

"Are you ready for more surprises, more intrigue and more evil?" and the crowd responds with another resounding "YES!"

"Well, get ready for our next guest!" Julian continues to revel in the adoration of the crowd. There is a broad, openmouthed smile on his face as he is encouraging the riotous applause. "Ladies and gentlemen, please welcome someone who needs no introduction! The gracious, accomplished and beautiful woman who has stolen the heart of our honored visitor, Christopher Pella!"

I immediately look up in a complete and utter state of panic as Julian announces, "BETH DELLA RUSSO!"

CHAPTER 44

The rain is coming down very hard and the wind continues to be strong as the chief's car speeds through the open gate Northport Bay Townhomes' complex. He drives toward the marina at the end of the main road. In the distance, Dan and Al can make out the lights from the patrol cars that are already at the scene. He turns into the same area where the residents' cars are parked and he pulls into an open space near the marina entrance. Both men scan the area until Uncle Al spots his nephew's car.

"Dan, that's Chris' car by the marina gate."

Dan looks over to the chief and says, "Let me go take a look to see if he left any clues behind."

While Chief Detective Barese is concentrating on the area surrounding the marina, he's approached by one of the uniformed officers: "Hi, Chief. I'm Officer Jim McGowan; we spoke over the two-way a few minutes ago."

"Yeah, what have you got to tell me?" Chief Barese is all business now.

Officer McGowan tell Chief Barese, "Well, after your call, we did a second thorough search of the townhouse, the parking lot and marina itself and we came up empty. It's dark and we may have missed some things, so we'll be sure to cordon off the area and come back in the morning for another search."

"Right, what else?"

"We went down to the marina to Ms. Della Russo's slip space number eight and it's empty. We also looked at all the other crafts in the rest of the slips, but there is no boat with the name Fun-A-Bout. My partner, Officer Barker and I, decided to stay here at the lot and wait for your orders."

"Okay, I want one of you to go back to the house and make sure that it's secure. Monitor any activity; calls, neighbors, anything and get back to me immediately. Got it?"

"Got it, Chief. Oh, by the way, there is something strange."

The chief answer with uncharacteristic impatience, "Well, you gonna keep me guessing? What was it?"

"Well, Chief, when I was down at the slip space, I seem to have heard the sound of an outboard engine somewhere out on the bay. It seemed strange given this weather. I couldn't see what type of boat it is or where it was going, but it sounded like it was headed for Pit Island, but I can't be sure."

The chief has calmed down a bit and tell the policeman, "Thanks Officer McGowan. I just want you to know that one of the missing people is my nephew, Chris Pella and I'm very worried. Sorry, I didn't mean to snap at you, thanks for your good work."

"No problem chief, I totally understand. I'll head back to the townhouse and keep my eye out for anything that looks strange."

Al smiles at the cop and says, "Everything seems to look strange tonight. Just stay safe, that's all I want."

"I will." Officer McGowan leaves and goes back to Beth's home.

Al looks around and sees Dan still by Chris's car and he walks over. "Dan, did you find anything?"

"No, there's nothing here, all's pretty much like it should be. Let's go down to the marina and check out the slip space."

"We can, but I don't think it will do us much good. The uniforms were down there and did a search of all the slips and they said there is no sign of the Fun-A-Bout. Officer McGowan did say something that could be useful, though. He said that while he was down on the dock, he heard the sound of an outboard engine somewhere out on the Bay. He couldn't tell what kind of boat, but he thought it could be headed for Pit Island."

"You're kidding, a boat out in this weather? Seems strange, don't it?" Dan and Al turn toward the bay, but all they see is darkness.

"Yeah, it is strange, that's why I think we need to check it out. Call the Harbor Patrol, and tell them to get out here pronto. We'll meet them down on the dock."

"Will do" Dan runs towards the chief's car to make the call.

Uncle Al turns to the darkness and tries to make out any form, but it is useless. He fears for Chris, he fears for Beth and he fears that more people will die tonight.

CHAPTER 45

My heart is pounding so hard that it feels like it will burst through my chest. I am looking in every direction waiting to see Beth. I don't have to wait long because from the opposite end of where the others made their entrance comes Beth.

She looks amazingly beautiful as she seems to glide across the hard earth floor of the pit. Beth is wearing a loose fitting, long flowing, dazzling white gown up to her neck. She is radiant with her long, dark hair falling across her shoulders. I am still on my knees, but looking up, as I watch Beth walk towards me. She stops in front of me, bends over, puts her hand on my cheek and smiles. I don't know how to respond, but I ask her, "Beth, are you alright? My God, what happened? What did Julian do to you? Beth, please say something."

Beth doesn't answer me; she just continues to smile. She looks over her shoulder at Julian and turns toward the stage and begins to walk toward him.

I try to reach out and stop Beth from going to Julian but I am frozen in place. I scream, "Beth! Stay away from him; he is Satan come to life! He's killed all those women and he will kill you. He must have you under some kind of spell; Beth, stop before he kills you!" I am finding myself becoming hysterical.

Beth is about halfway toward the stage when she turns back to face me. Her smile is even brighter and she says, "Don't be so sure, Chris." She turns back and continues to walk toward Julian.

I still can't move, but I am able to calm down a bit. I'm more confused than ever; what's happened to Beth, why is she acting like this? The only thing I can think of is that Julian must have some kind of demonic hold over her. I am anxious, searching for some idea, some way to get us both out of this horror show. If there is ever a time for my saints to appear it's now, but it's still clear to me that I am alone. Still on my knees, I put my hands together and begin to pray, "Oh Lord of all, I pray that You and all of The Sainted will hear me. I pray that you will show mercy on us and lead us from this darkness into the light of your goodness." When I finish my short prayer, I look up and I see Julian and Beth on the stage. They are standing next to each other and they are both smiling,

Julian speaks first, "Christopher, what must I do to convince you that there is no reprieve for you from God or your precious Sainted? My dear boy you should also know, there is no mercy of God. To quote an old phrase, 'God is dead,' especially for you."

Beth now asks, "Julian, please let me speak to him." She looks at me with loving in her eyes and longing in her heart. "Rocky, I have learned so much since I have been here. You need to understand that all you believe in, all you hope and pray for is gone. It was never there because God and The Sainted have turned away from you; they have turned away from all of us long ago."

I can't believe what I'm hearing, she knows about the Sainted. She knows my secret and Julian has told her. I look up at her in shock and I am speechless. How can this be? How can Beth be saying these things?

I want her to stop saying things that go against everything we believe in, but she will not stop. "Yes, Julian has told me about your visions, but you need to understand that it has all been a hoax, a game that God plays with Julian. It's all a sham to get you to believe, but what are you to believe? Are you to believe in them, The Sainted? The Sainted are charlatans; they allow you to believe in some obscure notion of faith, but when you really need them, they are nowhere to be found. They toy with us, they lead us on, they show us the light of God and when we are in the hour of our greatest need, they turn on the darkness."

Julian stands to the side of Beth and is content to let her do the talking. Beth does not appear to be under any kind of spell and she seems lucid, and in complete control. I try to comprehend what is happening, to find the logic to explain it all, but my mind is spinning from the realization that everything I know, everything I have had faith in and everything I feel for Beth and about Beth is false.

"How can you say these things, Beth?"

"I can say these things because I now know the truth. I know what you call evil is the only truth. If it was not for evil, there would be no God. The truth behind what Julian represents cannot be denied. Men and women are inherently evil. They look to commit sin and they have an insatiable appetite for what they consider bad. Then again is this really bad? Isn't what we have been told is evil more like the freedom of choice? Oh, I know people do bad things, and they get punished; remember Heriberto?"

"You can't possibly believe that, Beth? You can't possibly buy into what this beast represents? This twisted logic that says if you like it, its fine; you are too smart for that." I say this, but there is no conviction in my voice and none in my heart.

"What is the true nature of evil, Rocky? Is it Heriberto killing someone or is it Julian punishing him? Come on Rocky; tell me is this what true evil is? I think you know the answer and it's not what you have been taught all these years in Catholic school. That has been the big lie, the fable created by mullahs, monks, priests and rabbis to keep us all in fear and under their control." Beth is confident in what she what she believes, even cocky with her twisted logic and I am beyond knowing what to do.

I try to find my voice and tell Beth, "It seems to me that both Heriberto and Julian are guilty. Both are meant to be condemned to eternal damnation and what I have seen today just makes it clear what the monks, rabbis and priests have taught is true. There is evil and there is punishment and there are rewards reserved for those who love God and…"

Julian now interrupts, "Oh Christopher, don't be so naïve. There is no reward because there is no mercy of God—only incentives, shall we say, for His select few. Ah, but there is punishment because there is me!"

"What about those poor women you killed? What punishment did they deserve? What was the purpose of their deaths?" I find myself screaming at Julian who just stands there and smiles.

"Well, to tell you the truth, the reasons can be found in the age-old battle between heaven and hell, Christopher. It is God who commands that numbers of souls be the final arbiter of who wins and who loses in this eternal conflict. It is God who makes me seek the souls of men and women of course, because the one who gets the greatest number wins! Unfortunately, and I admit it, I am not infallible. When you make an omelet, you need to break some eggs, don't you agree?"

"Are you kidding? You killed those women and their babies because of some kind of game you are playing?" I am incredulous.

"Ah Christopher; the women and the babies, yes, the babies—two souls for the price of one. Alas, when I'm angry, I do dreadful things. You must admit, though, God also allows dreadful things to happen, does He not?" Julian is baiting the exchange, and he smiles as he waits for my reaction.

I am speechless.

Julian senses that I have no response, so he says, "Death is inevitable. If God did not want us to die, He would have made us eternal, but alas, He does not care, and He is content to allow evil to flourish under the guise of free will. A little secret, Christopher—there is no free will. Mankind has evolved, now there is only good and evil and, over the ages, more and more turn away from God towards me. Quite frankly, God is getting worried. It seems preordained that one of us will triumph and guess who that one is?" Julian paces by the stage while he let his words sink in.

Beth reaches out and puts her hand on Julian's shoulder and asks, "Julian, may I speak to Chris?"

"Of course, you can, my dear, but I fear you will need to do a lot to convince this young man of his misplaced faith in a misplaced faith…very droll, if I do say so myself!" Julian continues to smile.

Beth comes and stands in front of me, takes my hand and I rise to my feet. "Chris, do you remember the last time we spoke?"

"Yes, I remember."

"Do you remember that I wanted to tell you something?"

"Yes."

"Do you want to know what I was going to tell you?" There is a genuine desire in her voice and brightness in her eyes.

"I don't really care," I lie.

"I was going to tell you that I want you and me to become what I've wanted for so long. I want you and me to become lovers. I wanted to tell you that I love you, and that you are all I've ever wanted." I stand there thunderstruck, but before I can find the words to respond, Beth lets her gown drop to the floor and she stands before me completely naked. She looks flawless, the most beautifully perfect woman I have ever seen, and I feel the fear and hatred in me turn to excitement as I gaze at her magnificent naked body.

"Chris, am I all you have imagined? I am here for you; I am yours for eternity." Beth reaches over and puts her arms around my shoulder. Making love to Beth is something I have only imagined, but now I am holding her in my arms. She is all I've ever imagined, and she looks at me longingly, lovingly. As she comes closer and closer, I feel her body press against mine and the warmth of her touch is like a potion that makes my desire for her stronger than ever before.

"Chris, touch me. Please, kiss me. Make me feel you inside me." And with that, our lips meet, and I am transported to a place of unimaginable pleasures.

CHAPTER 46

Al and Dan walk down to the dock and wait for the Harbor Patrol to arrive. They had gone to the chief's car for rain gear, but the gear is little help as the rain continues to come down heavy and the wind is blowing fiercely. Chief Barese is getting both nervous and wet. "How long did they say it will take for them to get here?" Dan responds, "Not long. The harbormaster was at home in bed when they called, but he lives right near the harbor. He said that he and his crew will be here in about twenty to thirty minutes." Al seems to be grateful for the news and thankful that help would be here soon.

At the far end of the dock is a small cabin with an ice machine and a place to stow gear for the boaters who lease the slip space. The two men enter the cabin and stare out the window overlooking the dark waters. Al tries to focus, but his thoughts are on Chris and Beth and what danger they may be in. He also thinks of Julian and what terrors the demon has planned for them.

Waiting is always the worst part of a cop's job, and both Dan and Al have done their fair share of waiting. They want to have another cup of hot coffee, but they've run out of coffee. They've now stop speaking to each other as they have run out of things to say, so Al and Dan just stand there, in silence, waiting for the Harbor Patrol boat to arrive. As it happens, they don't have much longer to wait, for in the distance appears lights from a fast-moving boat that is heading for the marina.

"Dan, why don't you call Officer McGowan? Let him know that we're going with the Harbor Patrol to check to see if we can find Chris and Beth, and to see if we can find her boat. He and his partner should also keep us posted if anything happens on his end."

"Will do" and Dan makes the call.

Once they see the Harbor Patrol boat getting close to the marina, Al and Dan leave the cover of the shed and walk down the ramp to meet the boat. When Al sees the craft, he sighs. It is mostly an open deck with a small protected area that could barely shelter a dog from getting wet, but it did have two powerful 250 HP Mercury engines so at least they can continue to get wet, fast.

One of the Harbor Patrol crew jumps onto the dock as the boat pulls in. He grabs the line and ties it to a cleat to keep the craft as stable as the strong wind will allow. The harbormaster is the first to introduce himself, yelling above the howling wind, "Hi, I'm Ron Cunningham, Harbormaster."

Al introduces himself, "Hi, I'm Suffolk County Chief of Detectives, Al Barese and this is my second in command, Detective Dan Orello."

"Pleased to meet you both, can you give us some details about this search we are going conducting?"

Al tells the harbor master, "Well, there are two missing persons; one is my nephew, Chris Pella and the other is his girlfriend, Beth Della Russo and…"

Ron Cunningham interrupts, "Is she any relation to Paul Della Russo who owns the construction company?"

"Yeah, that's his daughter."

"Well, for years he and his family have been great supporters of what we do. They have contributed to our programs; you know boating safety and training, fundraising and all, so whatever you need, we'll be sure to get it for you."

Al and Dan look at each other and welcome the assistance. "Thanks Ron and we are very grateful, but you should know that they both may have been kidnapped. Have you been following the story about a serial killer mutilating women?"

Ron says, "Yeah, I have."

"Well, we have it on good authority that this serial killer may have identified Beth as his next victim and Chris is out there trying to find her right now."

"Enough said. Let's get onboard. By the way, where are we headed?" Al and Dan say, "Pit Island" at the same time.

"Wait a minute, did you say Pit Island?"

Al and Dan say, "Yeah" at the same time again.

The harbormaster looks really worried: "Do you guys know anything about Pit Island? If you do, you'd know what a dangerous place it is, especially if you're on a boat and even more dangerous in weather like this. There is no way we can get close enough with this craft to be able to let you get off onshore."

"Listen, Ron, we don't care. Just get us close enough and we'll take that inflatable you have on the rear of your boat and motor in ourselves. Just stay close enough in case we get into trouble."

"Chief, I really don't think this is a good idea. Maybe we should get the Coast Guard to help us out."

Al makes it clear that he wants to go now. He tells Ron, "It will take too long, by the time the Coast Guard is able to get here, both Beth and Chris could be dead and the killer could get away. Just take us close to Pit Island, and in the meantime, you can call the Coast Guard if you want. Okay?"

"Okay, Chief, but I still don't think this is a good idea." With that, Ron Cunningham and his crew begin to prepare to get underway.

Al and Dan get onboard and try to get out of the way so the men can do their jobs. The crew has some extra rain gear onboard and Al and Dan each grab one and put it on over what they are already wearing. It seems to help a little bit, but the men are reconciled to the fact that they are getting soaked, whether they like it or not.

The engines come to life and the boat eases its way out of the slip space and into the darkness of the bay toward Pit Island.

CHAPTER 47

The cave evaporates and becomes a place where light meets liquid and melts into one another. There are sounds, but unlike any sounds I have ever heard before. Beth and I are alone, floating in the liquid light.

I never imagined I could feel like this. Beth holds me in her arms, and I feel the passion she wants me to feel. Her lips are full and moist and she puts all inhibitions aside as she presses her soft, supple body against mine. Slowly her hands find the buttons on my jacket. She stops kissing me and looks into my eyes, as she does my coat slips off into nothingness. I take her in my arms again and I hold her tightly with my hands exploring all of her curves, all of her.

Beth slips her hand under my shirt, and she runs her long nails lightly across my chest. I feel myself quiver as my body tightens at the delight of her touch. She stops kissing me, but as she gazes into my eyes, she tears open my shirt and begins to caress my nipples with her tongue. I have never felt anything like this, ever. All I can think is that I want to possess her, to make love to her, to make her mine.

I stop her and begin to kiss her lips while working my way to her neck, shoulders and her breasts. I gently touch her perfectly formed, rounded breasts and begin to suck on her nipples. I am in a rapturous state, experiencing a sensation that I have never felt before.

Beth is breathing heavily as she moves her body back and forth against me. All I want to do is to make love to her, be inside her, feel her softness and watch her as she has an orgasm.

"Chris!" she says panting, "Chris, put your cock inside me! I want to feel you inside me! Please!" Beth is pleading and groping for the belt on my pants with one hand and stroking me with the other.

My feelings are so intense that I want them to last forever, but there is so much I need to say. "Beth, I love you, but I have to know."

Beth stops kissing me and looks up as she answers, "I love you, too! I love you so much."

I look into her eyes and try to see through her soul when I ask, "Where are we Beth? Why are we here? I need to understand."

She smiles and says, "We are in the perfect state of ecstasy. We are here because we love each other and we will be together forever."

I try to allow the passion subside because I need to comprehend, to hear Beth tell me what this is all about. "What has Julian got to do with all this? You can't possibly believe all of what you said to me."

Beth continues to kiss me as she answers, "Julian does not matter. Chris, all I believe in is you and me. We need each other and we need to be together, in love, forever. That is all that matters; that's all there is." She whispers this to me as we are wrapped in each other's arms. Our desire continues to mount as we embrace and explore one another's bodies.

I don't want to, but I pull back for a moment, "No, Beth, please hear me out. Just you and me, that can't possibly be all there is. What about growing old—children, family, friends, home? What about helping people and providing comfort to those in need? There is so much more to life."

Beth takes a step back and I get to see her in all her stunning nakedness as she says, "Chris, I am your family now…I am your best friend. How about helping me and giving me comfort? Chris, my love, I am your life and you are mine."

Beth's words snap me back to reality, a reality I don't want to face. I am trying to find a way to let her know how I feel. I do love her, but my entire life can't be a mistake. There has to be more. "Beth, life cannot only be about the two of us; it has to include so many others. It has to include

God, His Son, the forces of Heaven and the Sainted. I have seen miracles; I have seen the joys and heartache of loving beyond oneself."

Beth looks at me; she looks at my face, searching to see some sign that I'm questioning my beliefs. I look back at her as she practically begs me to listen. "Chris, what you have seen is false. It is God and His Sainted playing games with your soul. God would do anything to get His own way—including coercion, lying, temptations and even miracles to get what He wants. Chris, God is not here for you and He is not here for me. God has abandoned us, given up on us, and He will ultimately concede in the game He plays with Julian. That is the future of humanity, and that is why there are only us."

"Beth, that's just not true and you know it. God has never abandoned any of us. He is always there to give us His blessings and mercy. What He doesn't do is tell us what to do; we have to figure that out for ourselves. That is our decision, the choice between good and evil— that is free will."

Beth raises her voice, "Chris, there is no free will. There is only what we want in life; there is only what we desire because, in the end, there is only you and me."

I am now staring at Beth; she has become a total stranger to me. The passion I felt before vanishes, and I am looking at someone I thought I knew, but now I come to the realization that I know nothing about her at all. Beth steps back. She is now fully clothed and her gown mysteriously reappears. She is no longer the loving beauty that she was moments ago. Her eyes now tell the story of the hate she feels for me and this becomes more apparent with every passing moment.

The blissful state that we were in begins to transform. As her hatred grows, so does the darkness and when I try to reach out to Beth, there is an explosive force that sends me reeling backwards. When I come to my senses, I am back on the floor of the pit looking up at a smiling Julian and an angry Beth.

CHAPTER 48

When the patrol boat comes close to Pit Island, the harbormaster switches on a bright spotlight mounted to the bow of the boat. Ron Cunningham slows the boat down considerably, as he is familiar with the currents and the dangers that hide just beneath the surface of the bay waters.

We are about seventy yards from the shore of the island when the harbormaster cuts his engines and gives the order to anchor the craft. Turning to Al and Dan, Ron says, "This is about as close as we should go. It's still pretty far, but with this rain and wind we could find ourselves in very serious trouble."

Al says, "We understand. Dan and I will use the inflatable to get to the shore of Pit Island and start our search. You can call the Coast Guard whenever you want. As a matter of fact, I think it is a good idea just in case…" Chief Barese's voice trails off. Everyone on the boat seems to know that he is preparing himself for the possibility that Beth and Chris could be dead, and the Coast Guard may need to help look for their bodies.

"Okay, we will." The harbormaster turns to one of the crew and tells him to give Al one of the two-way radios. "Here, take this with you, this way we can keep in contact. When the Coast Guard arrives, they will have the ability to get to you and help with your search."

Al replies, "Thanks for all your help. By the way, how big is Pit Island?"

Ron thought and said, "Roughly 80 yards long and about 50 yards wide. It's not very big, but in this weather, it'll seem a lot larger."

"Thanks, Ron."

Dan is all set and says, "Ready to go, Chief?"

"Ready as I'll ever be." The men climb aboard the inflatable that has already been lowered into the water. The small outboard motor starts after three tries, the lines are untied and thrown to Dan, and the tiny boat slowly makes its way towards Pit Island. The short journey is treacherous as the boat is buffeted by the strong wind and rain along with swells of two feet or more. The light from the patrol boat helps at first, but the further away they get, the dimmer the light, and after a while, it is no help at all.

While Dan navigates the small craft, Al seems to spot something, "I think I see the hull of a boat jutting out of the water, near rocks along the shoreline—over there, see? Can you try and get closer?"

"Yeah, I see what you're talking about." Dan slowly maneuvers the boat until they are practically next to the sunken craft. The men try to see if they can find the name of the boat, but there is none they could see, but they are able to see a registration number along the side near the bow.

Al uses the two-way to call and ask if the harbormaster can help identify the owner, "Ron, this is Chief Barese. Can you hear me? Over."

"Yes, Chief. I hear you, over."

"We found a partially sunken craft, but can't identify her by the name. We did find a registration number; can you get us any information? Over."

"What's the number? Over." Al reads him the numbers of the registration and Ron tells him it would take a few minutes, but that he would get right back to him as soon as he has the information.

The rain and wind continue to pound both Al and Dan. At this point, they are close enough to Pit Island that they both decided that waiting is not an option. They are about ten feet from shore and they tie the Harbor Patrol inflatable to the sunken vessel. Al is the first to jump in and he finds that he's in waist deep in water and he is able to get a foothold. Al struggles his way onto shore with Dan immediately behind him. When they both are able to get beyond the rocks along the shore, they see another small inflatable.

Al yells to Dan, "This looks like it might be the boat Chris could have taken to Pit Island."

Dan yells above the wind, "I think you're right; we should check our weapons. This could get ugly!"

Al knows that given the nature of the evil that Chris and Beth are confronting, a gun, no matter how large the caliber would be of little use. Still, he can't disclose this to Dan, so he just agrees, "Okay, I'll check mine."

After their weapons are checked, they try to get a fix on where they will begin the search. They walk toward the center of the island and head for the east end. It is a very small area to cover, but with the rain and wind, it will take far longer than they expect to work their way across. As they make their way inland, Dan notices that there is something sticking out of the ground. He can't make it out, so he taps the chief on his shoulder, "Take a look over there. What do you think it is?"

"I don't know." Al tries to see what it is, but the rain obscures it. "Let's walk over and see." As they get closer, they can make out that it is a sign. Al reads the words aloud:

"Warning Trespassers"

CHAPTER 49

After I've shaken off my initial disorientation I get up off the floor. The talk show set is gone, the audience quiet. Julian and Beth are just watching me, waiting to hear what I will say. They both realize that I was able to fight off the temptation and with it my doubts about God, Jesus and The Sainted.

Julian speaks first, "Ah, Christopher, how sad. Look at what you have given up, the pleasures of the flesh, of eternal joy, of life without end. Now you will be relegated to being another witless soul who will spend eternity knowing that God and The Sainted were not here for you, much to your regret, I'm sure. You will now come to realize that I am the only one left standing in judgement."

I am coming to the realization of my fate, but I am resolute in my faith, no matter what happens. "You can do with me what you want, but I will never deny my faith."

Julian begins to pace back and forth, but never stops looking at me. "How noble of you, Christopher, I am very impressed. You think that your pitiful death will have some meaning in the vastness of heaven or hell. Let me assure you that your death will have no significance whatsoever because no one cares, least of all God and The Sainted."

As Julian's words begin to sink in, I hear noises coming from all the dark corners of the pit. They are unfamiliar sounds, sounds that I have never heard before and they send chills through my very being down to the depths of my soul. The terror of my situation becomes all too clear as I look into the dark corners of this forsaken hole in the ground and see what looks like thousands of menacing eyes, shining brightly.

Up to this point, Beth has remained quiet, but she leaves Julian's side to stand in front of me. "Why? Why did you reject me? What could you possibly gain? I was willing to give you all that I am, my whole being." Her voice cracks and I see a tear in her eye.

"Beth, it does not have to be like this. Don't let Julian's lies dictate how you will spend eternity. We can be together always, even in death. We can live in the light and in the mercy of God."

Beth's look hardens, and she turns away from me and back to Julian. "He sees nothing."

Beth's gown falls to the floor, and she is standing naked in front of Julian. He smiles as he looks at her nude form and reaches for her. She goes to him willingly, and they embrace as I watch in total disbelief. "Beth, NO! Don't do this, he's a demon. He will…" but I stop in mid-sentence as the hideous shrieks and snarls from the corner of the cave grow louder.

I look around and, at first, I see nothing, but then I do.

From every dark corner of the hollow, the legions come out from hiding. Demons as dreadful as Temeluchus and Glasya-Labolas, but in such numbers that I stand frozen in abject terror. Julian smiles, "Ah Christopher, I have asked my minions to entertain you while Beth and I enjoy some pleasures of the carnal variety. Every now and then, I enjoy diversions of this type. It helps to keep me grounded."

I am only two feet from the wall behind me, but I back up anyway. The demon creatures are coming at me from all sides and I am in a hopeless circumstance, facing my own death. I scream at Julian and Beth, "I am not afraid. I am not alone."

"Oh, dear boy, I'm afraid you are alone." As Julian says this, I hear another noise and look up. It is the flapping wings of thousands of crows circling above my head.

CHAPTER 50

Dan looks over the sign that is posted, "Al, it's just a warning sign."

Al yells above the wind, "I know, but maybe Chris came past this way looking for Beth. If she is with Julian and…" but he is cut off by the voice on his two-way radio.

"This is Ron Cunningham. Come in, Chief, this is Ron Cunningham. Over."

"Ron, this is Chief Barese."

"Chief, we looked up the registration number you gave us and it is for the boat, the 'Fun-A-Bout', registered to Elizabeth Della Russo."

When Dan and Al hear the news, they look at each other. They secretly know it had to be Beth's boat, but they were hoping they were wrong. Al answers the harbormaster, "Thanks Ron, we suspected as much."

Ron tells Al and Dan, "Some other news—we called the Coast Guard, and they are on their way."

"That's good. We can use the help."

"I'm sure you can, Chief, oh and I called Beth's parents as soon as I found out. They are on their way here; I know that they are worried sick."

Al asks the harbormaster, "Ron, I've got a question. We found a sign warning trespassers about coming here, but there is no indication who put up the sign. Who owns the island and who takes responsibility for it?"

"Chief, I've been on that island a number of times and explored it all over and I've never seen a sign. I don't know who the island belongs to, or who is responsible for it, I always assumed it belonged to the county or the state."

Al also thought as much, but wonders, "I guess that's a good assumption, but why would anyone put up a sign like this in the middle of the island where no one could see it." Al is just thinking out loud,

Harbormaster Cunningham answers him, "I don't know who would have put that sign up without telling us."

Chief Barese assures Ron, "No worries. I was just wondering. We are continuing our search so let us know if anything else happens, over."

"We will and good luck—over and out."

Dan and Al look back at the sign and speculate its origins while considering what they should do next. They had originally planned to start at the east end of the island, but finding the sign seems to create more questions than answers.

Al speaks first, "This killer has committed the murders of these women in pits, right?" "Yeah," Dan answers.

"And this is called Pit Island, right?"

Dan immediately sees the possible connection. "Yeah, it is."

Now Al becomes animated, "And what might you find on Pit Island?"

"A pit!" Dan yells.

"Now let's see if we can find an entrance to this pit", and they both begin looking.

CHAPTER 51

As the demon legions come toward me, I am terrified, but I know what is to come and I am reconciled to my fate.

I drop to my knees and begin praying, but as I do, the minions stop their movement towards me. I look up, and the beasts frantically begin to move to either side of the pit in order to make a path for someone or something. The ground begins to shake as the demons cower, trying to hide from what they fear.

I have no idea what to expect and Julian knows this when I hear him say, "Christopher, I would like you to meet Asmodeus. He has special plans regarding your death that he would like to share with you."

I look down the path that has been created by the demons on both sides and I see Asmodeus for the first time. Asmodeus is enormous, more than thirty feet tall and nearly as wide. Asmodeus is an enormously strong and powerful fiend that emerges from the darkness in all his hideous glory. The beast has three heads; the right is one of a bull, the center like that of a grotesque looking man and the left is the head of a demon ram. Asmodeus sits upon a dragon that could only have come from the depths of hell. The dragon has the tail of a serpent and, from his mouth, it is breathing flames. The minions continue to scramble to get out of the way, trembling in absolute fear of this evil spirit.

Julian wants to prolong my agony. "Oh, Christopher, you will never be able to guess this little-known fact about Asmodeus. Asmodeus governs seventy-two of my demon legions. I believe you see some of them here in this pit. They are of the lower-grade demon spirit variety, but under Asmodeus' guidance and effective leadership, they can prove quite effective in assuring that the task at hand gets done."

Asmodeus stands about twenty feet away from me as he looks down. Perhaps I am in shock, or perhaps I have nothing to lose, but I summon the courage to say to Julian, "Is that all you got?"

Julian laughs at my poor attempt at bravado. "No, no Christopher. It is not all I've got, but I assure you, it's all I'll need as you will soon find out."

Asmodeus looks to the ceiling way above where he stands and he lets out a hideous cry as flames burst from the dragon's mouth into the air above. Nearly paralyzed with fear, I stare at this creature from hell, accepting the reality that I am about to die. I close my eyes in prayer waiting for the end when I hear a shrill cawing from the crows above.

I open my eyes to look above and see thousands of small white crosses falling gently from nowhere at all. The crows begin to take flight, circling above in mass confusion and fear. As the crosses touch the crows, the birds literally melt into a dark putrid slime that falls to the floor of the pit below and evaporate into nothingness.

The demons now shriek at what is happening to the crows and this causes even more panic among them. No matter how hard Julian's minions try, there is no escape. The miracle of the crosses spells their doom and the crows seem to know it. At first Asmodeus and his legions appear bewildered at what is emerging above their heads. Slowly, they realize what is happening and as they do, their merciless hostility turns to overwhelming terror.

Asmodeus looks down from the ceiling and stares at me. The hatred in his eyes express that he will take vengeance for this blasphemy on Julian and him. The creature's three heads all turn to me as the dragon from hell that Asmodeus rides takes a cautious step forward. My back is already against the rock wall—there is nowhere for me to go—it seems that only a miracle can save me now.

Asmodeus holds out an empty hand and lance magically appears. The monster raises the lance taking aim at my chest, while he looks at me with a smile that chills me to the bone. While taking pleasure a taunting me, he fails to recognize that the crosses are gliding past the crows and onto his legion. The evil fiends look up in terror and begin to run around riotously, trying to find cover in the hollows of the pit, but it is too late. Impossibly loud screams and screeches fill the air in the pit as the crosses touch the demon hoard. With each cross comes unbearable agony and pain and, in a matter of moments, the beasts are reduced to slime and the muck that begins to disappear almost immediately.

Asmodeus now sees his fate and he cannot escape it. He looks up to see dozens of small crosses land on him and the devil dragon. Both Asmodeus and the dragon try to scream as his body and all three heads begin to melt into rotting ooze before they can. Then, in one massive explosion, Asmodeus and the dragon vanish into nothing.

The cave is empty of all except for Julian and Beth. They stand next to each other, untouched by the crosses, but dreading their fate. The crosses that destroyed the demonic crows and fiendish beasts lay all around the pair in a perfect circle. I move away from the wall and walk towards where Beth and Julian are standing.

As I stand before them, I can see only fear and contempt as Julian spits out the words, "You think that your cursed Sainted can stop me? I am eternal; I am legion! I will triumph over the God of Heaven and the souls of mankind will be mine!"

I ignore Julian and turn to Beth. "How could you believe him? How could you doubt your own life, your own faith? You chose darkness over light, evil over good. You've condemned yourself." I am grief-stricken.

But Beth says nothing, and just stares at me.

I need to know. "Beth, say something!"

Julian is standing behind her and he puts his arms around her waist. His hands caress her body as he starts to stroke her breasts. She closes her eyes as he lets his hands find their way all over her.

I scream, "Stop it!"

Julian laughs and he continues as Beth begins to writhe against him experiencing the utmost pleasure.

I need to stop it, to try and save Beth from the demon that controls her completely, but before I get to them, a bright light begins to fill the pit. The radiance finds its way into every corner. Where there once was darkness, now there is only light. I stare into the light, and in the center appear the form of what I have seen before and know to be The Sainted. It is the vision of St. Agnes and she now stands before me.

She does not speak at first, but turns and faces Julian and Beth. They stop their sexual act and look up at her defiantly in spite of their failure to tempt my faith and the will of God.

"What do you hope to do here, woman? God will never defeat me, for I am the reason He exists! I am the true power," Julian screams at St. Agnes who just stands there staring at who she knows to be Satan.

"Silence, you cursed demon!" St. Agnes holds up her hand and Julian stops speaking. He tries to seem unfazed by the saint standing before him, but there is genuine fear in him and she knows it.

"You have turned away from God. Your pride has made you believe that you are like God, that you command the heavens like God, that you hold sway over men, but even with your lies, temptations and legion, you will never defeat the Lord our God. He is always, He is forever and He is the way to eternal life and everlasting peace through His Son."

St. Agnes then turns to look at me and says, "We must always trust that our Heavenly Father will hear our prayers, and give us whatever is for our own good."

"Please, forgive me," I say, "I thought that God and The Sainted abandoned me. I let temptation blind me to what I know to be true."

St. Agnes smiles at me. "It is free will that causes your doubt, but it is free will, a choice of good over evil, which brought you back. God and the saints are always by your side and you should take solace in that. You were willing to make the ultimate sacrifice for your faith and, it is for this, you are forgiven."

Julian and Beth scream in rage at St. Agnes and me, but they would not leave the circle for fear of the crosses that surrounded them. Having nowhere to go, they let me see their true nature. It is Julian who changes first, turning into the horrible demon beast I have seen before. His fury grows and he roars a screech that shakes the interior of the pit.

I am prepared for Julian, but I am not prepared for what Beth would turn into. The skin on her body turns into what looks like scales of a reptile, but they are golden in color. Her hands grow to three times their size, with long tapering nails as sharp as knives. Beth's beautiful brunette hair falls out in clumps while protrusions resembling horns grow from her head. It is the change in her face, however, that I hadn't expected. Her eyes become large black circles; her mouth grows wide with protruding fangs and the rest of her teeth become pointed.

She is no longer my Beth—she is a demon Beth. I just stare at her with an overwhelming sense of sadness.

St. Agnes speaks to the devils trapped in the circle of crosses. "You have tried and you have failed. There is no mercy for you, for you would give none back. God has condemned you to the lake of fire that is your hellish domain and that is where you are to go."

The demons, Julian and Beth, begin screaming and shouting curses and insults, but they are only words. Their threats are sapped of any power by the Heavenly Hosts who have battled them for ages. I hear a rumbling from above and, when I look up, a cloud forms amidst the sound of rolling thunder. I look back at the devils in the circle and see true terror on their faces. A moment later a bolt of lightning cuts through the cloud and strikes the demons Julian and Beth. They explode into pieces and disappear. I look at the place where Julian and Beth were, and they are gone; all the crosses are gone and only St. Agnes and I are left.

I don't know what to say or what to do. I tell St. Agnes that I loved Beth; I want her to know that Beth meant everything to me. I cannot believe that she denied her faith and now that Beth is gone, and I know I will mourn her loss for as long as I live. I am in a state of total despondency and I don't know how to deal with it all. God and His Sainted have saved me, but for what? Am I to live lifetime of loneliness, of yearning for a love that I'd found, but now have lost? I am alive, but I feel empty inside.

"I know you believe in the goodness and mercy of the Lord, but you are in pain." St. Agnes looks at me tenderly, knowing the anguish I am feeling.

"I do believe, but sometimes it's impossible to understand why God allows things to happen in the way He does."

"Christopher, it is you who said you may not know God's will, but you know His will be done…a time for every purpose under heaven."

St. Agnes smiles at me as something miraculous appears in the center of the pit.

CHAPTER 52

Dan and Al have been searching frantically for an opening that will lead them into the pit when the wind and rain suddenly stop. A full moon appears in a clear night sky and the men just look at each other in utter puzzlement and Dan speaks first, "How do you figure the rain and wind just stopped like that?"

"Who cares? This will give us the break we need to find the entrance. Let's keep looking."

The men decide that each would take half of the island and do a thorough search for an opening they hope will lead them to Beth and Chris in time to save their lives. They create an imaginary grid of the area and begin looking around every rock and under every bush. This goes on for about ten minutes before they hear the sound of a boat fast approaching the area.

"It must be the Coast Guard." Al picks up his radio and calls the Harbormaster. "Ron, this is Al, over."

"Hi Chief, I guess you heard the Coast Guard coming toward us."

"Yeah, we did. We'll go near to the shoreline and wait for help."

"That's a good idea, Chief, over and out."

The Coast Guard anchors near the patrol boat. In what seems like a matter of minutes, a group of men on board lower a small craft into the water, climb into it and begin making their way to Pit Island. The small craft approaches and Al and Dan can see that there are four men on board. They maneuver the craft expertly through the rocks and shallows and onto the shore.

As the men disembark, one shouts, "Are you Chief Barese?"

"Yeah, I am."

"Chief, I'm Captain Warren Talbot" and he holds out his hand. The men shake hands and climb up the rocks to higher ground.

"Captain Talbot, this is Detective Dan Orello. I have to say we are really glad to see you."

"Glad to help. Ron, I mean, Harbormaster Cunningham, gave us most of the details behind the search, but is there anything else you want to add?"

"I suppose you know that we suspect a serial killer has kidnapped Beth Della Russo and taken her here. Her boyfriend, my nephew, Chris Pella, went after her. We believe they both are on the island, given that an inflatable we believe was used by Chris located by the shore and the wreckage of Beth's boat can also be seen nearby."

Capt. Talbot is taking note of what he is told, "Got it, anything else?"

Dan says, "We were beginning to search the whole island when we heard your boat coming. The chief and I believe there is an entrance to a pit somewhere hidden and we hope that will lead us to where Chris and Beth are."

"Well, it's a small island and we've got the manpower. Thank God it stopped raining, that should make it a little easier."

Al says, "One more thing, we found a 'Warning Trespassers' sign with nothing else written on it. Do you know who owns the island, Captain?"

"No, not really, I guess it belongs to the state or county, but I don't know for sure. I can always check."

"Thanks, Captain, that's not a bad idea, but in the meantime, let's get to work."

Al, Dan and the Coast Guard Captain and crew make their way toward the sign. The men spread out over a large area to begin their methodical search of every square foot. They look around each rock, bush and tree to check to see if there is some opening to an underground cave or pit.

For about half an hour they all continue to search until one of the petty officers' yells, "I think I found something."

Al is the first to run to see what the seamen has found. Sure enough, not ten feet away from the warning sign, there is a small opening hidden behind a large rock with tall shrubs growing all around. The opening is small, but could fit a man. Al takes out a flashlight and shines it down the narrow hole, but the light doesn't penetrate the darkness, and it's too deep to see anything.

Dan says, "We've got to go down that hole, Chief, how about us getting a rope and harness?"

"Good idea, Dan, Captain, do you have any ropes and harnesses we can use to lower ourselves down this hole?"

"We sure do. I'll send one of the crew back to the boat to get us what we need." The captain orders one of the crew to go back to the inflatable while Al and Dan stand near the opening.

Dan doesn't want to acknowledge what could be a possibility, but he knows the chief would want to hear any eventuality, even if it is bad news, "Al, you know that it's possible that Beth and Chris, well, you know, they could be…" His voice trails off.

"I know, I know. It is a possibility, but I don't want to think about it until I have to. At any rate, we need to get this resolved one way or another." Chief Al Barese turns toward the hole in the ground and peers into the darkness. He shivers a bit and hopes it's only from the cold.

CHAPTER 53

A growing luminescence fills the pit with a wonderful brightness and in the center of it all something or someone begins to emerge.

St. Agnes kneels in reverence and anticipation of what she knows is coming. I look down at her and do the same thing. As I drop down on my knees, an image begins to materialize. As I am on my knees, it becomes clearer and I start to comprehend the overwhelming significance of the vision.

The Blessed Mother, holding the infant Jesus, appears before us.

St. Agnes seems to be in a state of complete and utter ecstasy that totally consumes her spirit. The vision is so overpowering to me that as I am kneeling, motionless and speechless, I am able to take in all that I am privileged to see. The Holy Mother Mary comes and stands before St. Agnes. She knows of The Sainteds' love and devotion to all that is good and holy and the mother of Christ smiles at her.

The Blessed Virgin Mary's voice fills the air as she says to St. Agnes, "You have done much through your miracles, prayers and kindnesses. You have suffered in the name of my Son and for this you are blessed for eternity."

St. Agnes has tears in her eyes, "Dearest Blessed Mother Mary, mother of Jesus, Son of God, I am not worthy of your praise."

Mother Mary replies, "You are more than worthy to be among The Sainted." The Blessed Mother opens the palm of her hand to reveal a golden cross. She takes the cross and places it around the neck of the speechless St. Agnes.

I feel like I am the last person who should be there experiencing this wonder.

The Blessed Mother continues smiling and says to St. Agnes, "The love of God and His love for all mankind knows no bounds; you have given everything in His name." The Holy Mother Mary takes the infant Jesus and hands Him to St. Agnes.

The saint is overwhelmed the gesture, she cannot comprehend the honor she is being given. St. Agnes gazes lovingly at the infant, and she looks up at the His Mother as she places baby Jesus her arms. I have never seen such pure joy and happiness on a face like I see on that of St. Agnes. She gently hugs the baby and touches His soft cheek as He smiles.

The Holy Mother then turns to me and tells me, "Your trials have been most difficult, but you have shown your courage through faith in the Lord. You were told you would deliver justice and, through your faith, justice is done." The Blessed Virgin Mary then raises her head and looks toward the rear of the cave. She lifts her arm and points in that direction.

I look behind me to see four apparitions beginning to solidify. They are the forms of four women and, as they become clearer, I see both puzzlement and underlying sadness on their faces. I turn to the Blessed Mother, trying to find a reason, an answer to who these women are and then I realize what I am witnessing. I turn immediately to St. Agnes, who is still entirely absorbed with the infant Jesus. She has tears of joy in her eyes that stream down her face as she looks up at Mother Mary. Reluctantly, St. Agnes gives the baby Jesus back to His mother and then The Sainted turns to face the four women.

As she turns toward the women, I see St. Agnes holding in her arms four infants—the four innocent victims of Julian's evil madness. The four women each stare over at the babies in St. Agnes' arms, and their sadness is transformed to complete joy. They slowly walk towards their babies; instinctively knowing which one is theirs, and they each take the infants from the saint to hold them close in their arms. Each of the women then looks up at St. Agnes and the Virgin Mary holding her Son. The mothers are in such a state of absolute happiness, holding their babies and crying tears of joy. The women look at the vision of the Blessed Mother, wanting to express their elation, but can only say, "Thank you" and with that, the women depart into the lights of heaven.

The Blessed Mother speaks to me, "Justice is done. It is the will of our Lord that the innocent live in His light and blessings for eternity." In an instant, the vision of the Holy Mother and the infant Jesus become golden glow as they are welcomed back through the gates of Paradise. St. Agnes and I watch as they disappear and leave us alone in the pit. She looks at me and says, "There is one more message I must give you before I leave."

"What it is?" I ask her.

"For Satan, it is all important that evil triumph. All that seems real, all the temptations, all the promises are illusions meant to prey on weaknesses in order to destroy one's soul."

"I know that now."

"What you do not yet understand is the power of good over evil, the power of truth over lies."

I am puzzled, "Why are you telling me this? I don't comprehend…" Before I finished speaking, I hear sounds and words coming from a corner of the pit.

"Ugh, my head, where am I?"

My eyes widen, and I look at St. Agnes. She smiles as the glow from her halo gets brighter and she declares, "May the blessings of the Lord our God be with you and yours all your days" and she is gone.

I am frozen in place, but now suddenly I jolt back to reality. With the heavenly light gone, the cave is now nearly in complete darkness. I feel my way around the rock wall and boulders that cover the floor of the pit as I attempt to make it over to the spot where I think the sounds are coming from.

A voice echoes, "My head…Where am I?"

It is a voice that I know, so I scream, "BETH, BETH! Is that you? Where are you, Beth?"

Beth hears my voice and shouts, "CHRIS! I'm over here, Chris! Please, help me! Chris! Please, help me!"

I am overjoyed Beth is not the demon in the cave, she never was. Julian had tried to make me lose my faith in her and in The Sainted, but it was just another one of his lies. "I'm coming, Beth, just stay where you are, and keep speaking to me. I'll follow the sound of your voice."

"Chris, please hurry. This man, Julian, came to my house; he said he was there to work on my boat, but that's the last thing I remember. My head is killing me; it's like I've been drugged."

I am getting close and I want her to keep talking. "Did that bastard do anything to you? Are you hurt in any way? Are you all, right? Please, tell me!"

"I think I'm okay, Chris. My head is killing me, and I'm a little bruised, but I can't seem to get on my feet."

"Just stay where you are, Beth. Just stay there, I'll find you." Her voice seems to be getting louder and I know I'm getting closer.

Beth is getting anxious. "Please hurry, Chris; I'm frightened. Julian could still be here." "I'm almost there Beth—just hang on." I want to get her mind off the horror of the place and what she has gone through, so I ask her, "What did you want to tell me when we last spoke on the phone?"

Beth goes silent and finally stammers, "I…I wanted to tell you something."

"What is it, Beth? You can tell me."

"I…I wanted to tell…"

I am feeling my way around the cave trying to find the path that will lead me to Beth. I keep talking, "What? What did you want to tell me, Beth?"

She then blurts it out. "I wanted to tell you that I love you." She says it as if she has to get it out before she loses her courage.

My heart jumps, and I yell to her, "Beth Della Russo, I am so much in love with you that if I don't get to hold you soon, I think I'll…" But I stop speaking as I come around the side of a huge boulder and see Beth lying on the ground.

I get down on my knees and lift Beth into my arms. She is still very weak and a bit disoriented, but she holds me as tight as she can. For a few minutes we just hold each other; then I say, "I love you, just in case you didn't hear me before."

"I heard you, and I'm not going to let you forget it," Beth says, with a smile that makes me smile right back.

Then Beth becomes frightened and looks up at me, "Where is Julian? Do you think he's here? My God, Chris; he's a maniac! What can we do? Is he still here?"

I want to keep her calm, so I tell her that Julian must have escaped when he heard me coming down the entrance to the pit. I assure her that she is safe and that when she could walk, we would climb out of the pit and try to get help.

Now Beth just stares into my eyes. "You saved my life again."

I look into Beth's beautiful face and say, "Well, I think you're worth it" and I smile at her.

We sit for a few more minutes until we hear sounds and voices on the other side of the cave. By this time Beth is able to stand on her feet, but she is still a little wobbly. I sit her back down on the ground when I hear a familiar voice and I know its Uncle Al to the rescue.

"Chris! Beth! Where are you? Are you okay? Chris, Beth—please answer me!"

I shout back, "We're over here!"

I hear a lot of talking—it seems that Uncle Al brought a whole bunch of people with him. I have never been happier to hear his voice and I know that the nightmare is over. I sit back on the ground next to Beth and just hold her hand. I tell her, "Well, looks like we've been rescued. Uncle Al seems to have brought the troops, and they can get us out of here."

"Chris, how did you find me? How did you know I was here?"

"It's a long story and I will tell you over a bottle of my extra special Cabernet Franc."

Beth looks at me, "You came for me; you risked your life for me. How can I ever thank you?"

I hold her tight and say, "Well, telling me you love me is a good start."

"That's true, but, seeing that we are way beyond our first date, what do you say we fool around, a lot?"

I smile, look down and then move back to hold her in my arms and say, "Agreed!"

EPILOGUE

Uncle Al, Dan and the Coast Guard come to our rescue managing to get us out of the pit. Beth is too disoriented to make it out of the pit on her own, so the Coast Guard assisted in getting her out with by rigging a stretcher and pulley. We all boarded onto the Harbor Patrol boat for the trip back to the marina.

The heavy rain and fierce winds have ended and a beautiful starlit night helps guide us all back. The boat motors steadily through the waters of the bay towards the marina while Beth and I huddle together on a seat looking back at Pit Island as it getting smaller and smaller in the distance. We silently gaze at the outline of the dark and forbidding island trying to understand what we have just gone through. The terror we just experienced slowly diminishes the further away we get, but we know it will never truly vanish. The monotonous hum of the boats engines is most welcome as Beth and I just sit, exhausted by the entire horror we've experienced. I am hypnotized by the humming engines as I look over the bay to the small rocky island when suddenly I notice the trees swaying and what appears like movement of the boulders in the water. I immediately stand up and call this to the attention of Harbormaster Cunningham, Uncle Al and all else on board to look and see what is happening.

Beth questions me, "Chris, what's wrong? What is it?"

I am staring at the island and I tell her, "I don't know, but there seems to be a lot of movement going on around Pit Island."

Ron Cunningham slows the boat and everyone on board turns and looks towards Pit Island to see what is going on. At first, we all hear a number of cracking sounds and then we see a large fissure splitting straight down the middle of the island. I continue to stare in disbelief as Beth keeps asking, "What's going on, Chris?"

"I really don't know, but it seems like the island is coming apart." I turn to the Harbormaster and ask him and he seems dumbfounded by it all and admits, "I don't know either; I've never seen anything like it in my life."

Uncle Al and I are both bewildered by what is happening. But we look at each other, silently becoming aware that this is the work of the unseen forces, the forces summoned by Julian.

The cracking sounds grow louder and all of us onboard the patrol boat can see the trees and bushes on the island splitting apart. There is another, even louder, cracking sound as we now see a great divide in the island forming and getting larger and larger by the second. The cracking sound now becomes a thunder-like rumble and the island shakes as if there is an earthquake.

The boat is far enough away so that we can see the entire event happening. In an instant, the island caves in on itself and disappears under the waters of the bay. Everyone just stares and the stark realization of where there once was a small island, now there is nothing.

Ron speaks first. "I've never seen anything like that in my life. What could possibly have caused Pit Island to come apart and sink?"

No one wants to answer because no one can even take a guess. Ron contacts the Coast Guard vessel and the captain and crew are just as puzzled. Captain Talbot says he will conduct an investigation and report back to the harbormaster, but I suspect that nothing of Julian, the demon horde or the incident will ever be found.

As we head back to the marina, there is a large crowd of people anxiously waiting on the pier. Standing in the very front of the crowd are Beth's parents with her brother and sister waving at Beth. Beth jumps off the boat and runs into their arms. There are tears of joy and heartfelt hugs, all in all, a happy homecoming. We are so grateful to be safe and happy to be with those that we know and love and slowly the group starts to walk back to Beth's townhouse. Uncle Al and I are following in the rear of the crowd of people walking down the path towards Beth's home.

Uncle Al turns to me and says, "You know they won't find anything when they investigate the underwater ruins of Pit Island."

"Yeah, I know that and I am really glad that you know that too."

While we continue to walk towards Beth's home I can't put a finger on it, but have a very uneasy feeling. I don't know what made me do it, but I look to the side and detect a movement near the tree line that surrounds the grounds where Beth lives. I then hear the cry of some animal and notice some movement. I can't imagine what is happening is hidden by the woods that would make such a noise and I stop to see if I can determine what it might be. It is really too dark to see so I just stand there looking.

Uncle Al, who is walking right next to me, asks, "What's wrong Chris? How come you stopped?"

I continue to look at the wooded area and tell him, "Oh, I don't really know; I think I heard a sound, kind of like a cry. I thought I saw something move, a deer or something large; probably just my imagination."

Uncle Al puts his arm around my shoulder, "Well, come on, let's get back to Beth's house and just try to relax a little. What do you say?"

I smile at Uncle Al, "Sounds good to me."

When I turn to face the crowd in front, I see Beth leave the arms of her parents and runs back to me. She looks up and kisses my cheek, and we walk away with the rest of the group.

ST AGNES OF MONTEPULCIANO

Saint Agnes of Montepulciano was born into a noble family in the village of Gracciano, Italy, in about the year 1268. A miracle occurred at her birth to demonstrate that she was very special soul. At her birth it was recalled that burning torches appeared to encircle where she and her mother rested. A heavenly luminescence appeared and came through the windows of the entire de Signe home.

Agnes was no more than four years old when she began seeking solitude where she could pray privately for many hours to Jesus, whom she already worshipped and loved. At the age of nine Saint Agnes told her parents that she desired to enter the Dominican monastery at nearby Montepulciano. Both parents initially opposed Agnes' wish, so she prayed that God might change their opinion on her vocation. It was a short time after that her parents relented and she entered the convent and began living under the rule of Saint Augustine. The sisters in the convent where she lived soon recognized that Agnes appeared more like an angelic spirit than a human being. As young as Agnes was, she lived an austere life, sleeping on the ground with a stone for a pillow, and fasted on bread and water.

To test Agnes' holiness and commitment to her prayer life, the sisters gave her difficult duties to perform in the convent. They were greatly edified to see that Agnes regularly completed her duties without complaint, as she continued with her regimen of prayer and regular acts of charity. In fact, it was about this time that Agnes could be observed absorbed in prayer while seemingly unaware that she was suspended nearly two feet above the ground. It has also been reported that violets, lilies or roses would be found growing up through the stones where Saint Agnes had just prayed.

Several of the residents of the town of Procena built a monastery for their daughters, and naturally desired that Saint Agnes should come with some of the sisters and that she would become the prioress of the new convent. Agnes was only 15 years old at the time, and in a gesture of humility, she felt that she was unworthy of such an honor. Initially she protested that she could not accept such a high position but it was Pope Nicholas IV who commanded her to consent the office, so she agreed to become the superior of the sisters there.

There are many miracles recorded at this time involving St Agnes of Montepulciano. She frequently multiplied loaves of bread to feed those in need as Christ did as recorded in scripture. St. Agnes had also apparently reached such a level of sanctity that invalids and those afflicted with different types of mental illness would be restored to health just by being brought into her presence.

In a vision, the Blessed Virgin Mary appeared to Saint Agnes and told her that she would one day found a large monastery based on faith in the Most High and undivided Trinity. She did in fact establish such a convent under the Dominican rule, as she had been instructed by an angel in about the year 1300. Hoping to lure Agnes back to their town, the citizens of Montepulciano built a new convent hoping to lure Agnes back to them. Agnes was humbled by this gesture and she governed there until her death in 1317.

Agnes was known to have experienced several visions during her life. On the night of the Feast of the Assumption, the Blessed Virgin placed the Infant Jesus in her arms. Mother Mary encouraged Agnes to continue suffering for the love of Christ. She had been sick practically all her life and the Mother of Jesus left with St Agnes of Montepulciano a small cross to comfort and strengthen her in her own suffering. This little cross is still shown with great solemnity to pilgrims, especially during the month of May. Mary likewise vouchsafed Agnes a vision of Christ's suffering, which lasted three days.

To comfort Agnes, Mary appeared to her on the feast of the Purification while she was at Holy Mass. Mary told her this was the hour she had taken the Child Jesus to offer Him in the Temple. Our Lady smiled sweetly, and gave Agnes her Babe, her child Jesus Christ, to hold and caress. Saint Agnes was also known to have received Holy Communion from an angel.

She experienced repeated levitations, as noted above, and performed miracles for the faithful of the region. Shortly before her death, Saint Agnes was sent to bathe in springs that were thought to have curative powers. The waters did nothing to help Agnes, though a new spring emerged close by which did indeed have curative power. It was given the name "The Water of Saint Agnes." While there, the saint prayed over a child who had recently drowned, bringing the child back to life.

St Agnes of Montepulciano then went back to the monastery, where she died on April 20th, 1317, at the age of only 43. Her body was found to be incorrupt, and a mysterious, sweet-smelling liquid was observed to stream from both her hands and feet. When Saint Catherine of Siena went to pray before Saint Agnes' incorrupt body, the deceased saint lifted her foot for Saint Catherine to kiss. She also revealed to Saint Catherine that they would both enjoy the same amount of glory in heaven.

St Agnes of Montepulciano was solemnly canonized by Pope Benedict XIII in 1726. Her feast day is April 20th.

Reprinted from: http://www.roman-catholic-saints.com/st-agnes-of-montepulciano.html from The Woman in Orbit and other sources.

ACKNOWLEDGEMENTS

Unlike angels, most saints were, in life, real people like you and me. They have felt the same human emotions we all feel, gone through the same turmoil we go through, some have been embarrassed by the same things we are embarrassed by and some even learned to live and love in the same way we do.

While writing this book, I was able to reflect on my own Catholic grade school and high school religious instructions. In those teachings, I learned about some of the saints and their truly remarkable lives. It is amazing how a few of their names, life experiences and stories came back to me while researching information for this book. What is also instructive is to acknowledge how much more I have forgotten or never bothered to learn.

If you take the time, there are so many lessons about life, love, joy, learning, suffering and death in stories of the saints. Most of these accounts of the saints are real, taken from what has been recorded at their time and during the years that followed. Some are witnessed and some are drawn from legend and over time their personal histories provide guidance to many who are looking for inspiration, solace and reaffirmation of their faith.

I would encourage all who are interested to read about the lives of these truly remarkable people. With that said, I want to acknowledge and thank the following for their kindness, assistance, inspiration, visions and their miracles:

St. Agatha of Sicily
St Agnes of Montepulciano
St. Aloysius of Gonzaga
St. Anthony the Abbot
St. Augustine of Hippo
St. Barbara
St. Bernardine of Siena
St. Camillus de Lellis
Sts. Cosmas and Damian
St. Fabius
St. Francis of Assisi
St. Jude
St. Mary Magdalene
St. Michael the Archangel
St. Monica
St. Nicholas of Tolentino
St. Rita of Cascia
St. Thomas More
St. Valentine
Catholic Online (www.www.catholic.org)
Saints.SPQN.org
Wikipedia
Dan Tetrault, DT Creative, for his superior design and creativity

Excerpt from
The Sainted Trilogy
Book Two "Revelations"

His screams shake the very foundations of hell itself.

Even the torture and torments of the souls of the damned cannot quell the rage and hatred he feels. He should be exalted above all, but he has been condemned and it shall be this way for eternity. He tries to take comfort in the knowledge that God holds no power in his domain, but he has to concede that it is God whose judgment imprisons him here.

It is happening to him now…when the fury becomes uncontrollable his entire figure grows and grows in magnitude. He is now the size of what the pitiful minions call a mountain. He looks down in anger and smashes his limbs into the swarm of evil spirits and the condemned souls cowering below. The hoards scream in terror begging for mercy but he is merciless…you would think they would know this by now.

He now screams again, "I AM LUCIFER! I AM ETERNAL!"

God has condemned him to this fate. "He sent Michael to vanquish me. Michael, my brother angel, how could this be?" God has condemned a full third of the heavenly host of angels to the lake of fire for eternity. The demon recalls how he could not understand what has happened, after all, is he not like God Himself? He remembers that he would not beg for forgiveness, after all, there is nothing to forgive. It was long ago, in the beginning of times and he vows that he would seek vengeance. He would make it his eternal mission to destroy the souls of the pitiful creatures that God has placed on earth. Lucifer's sneers become full faced and clear as he thinks of how easy it is to take advantage of the free will God has given these creatures. He knows what temptations best suit men; pride, envy, lust, depravity, heresy, hatred and so much more. There are many weapons in his arsenal and Lucifer will use them all.

He knows the minds and hearts of men are weak and many can easily be led to temptation. These temptations lead to transgressions and those transgressions lead to corruption and it is corruption that leads to a sinful existence and the fall from grace. Many have found this out too late and all the damned in the hellish realm he rules are a testament to the weakness of men and the fate of their souls.

He would have his revenge against God, revenge against His Son and revenge against the cursed Sainted, especially his brother Michael. Yes, he would have his revenge. His rage continues to grow as he thinks of the encounter with the man and woman in the pit. He thinks to himself, how could he have not seen how powerfully they protect Christopher? How could he not have seen the power of the cursed Sainted, and how their meddlesome interference would deny him the one soul he now vows to possess? How could he have not seen the strength of the forces of good? He has failed to be victorious in his battle against God, His Son, the Heavenly Host and the Sainted, but there must be a way to see that victory could be his...but how?

The demon Lucifer continues to ponder these questions, but he is so enraged that it blinds him to any answers he may find. He hates that God has condemned him to this fate, he hates humanity and now he must wreak havoc on the earth so the souls of so many pitifully weak humans will be his. It is the only way to overcome the goodness of God and redress this greatest of injustices done to him.

This is his dream, his one overwhelming desire, but how will it be made manifest? It is then that a thought comes to him and it is the first time in a long time the Lucifer smiles. God may have the Sainted, but he has something far more powerful.

From the burning lakes of fire and the molten pits that surround Satan hellish realm they come...he merely thinks it and they assemble. He commands the princes of hell, the first hierarch of demons to appear before him, and they always do exactly what he commands. Satan looks over the unholy Seraphim at his feet and he begins to feel better. He has been cheated of his rightful place in time without end. A cruel twist of fate has forced him to make many errors and miscalculations, but that is in the past and that will change. Now the way is clear, now all his longings, all the desires he could only have hoped for will become manifest. These dark angels will assure that redemption will be his, that the forces that align against him will fail, and ultimately the souls of men will, at long last, suffer at his hand.

One by one the hellish demon masters assemble in front of him, loyal soldiers before their leader waiting to follow his command. Lucifer gazes at the devilish legion that stands at hand and as he looks at each one, it gives him pause to delight.

First there is the ever-constant Beelzebub who, with him, was among the first three angels to fall from grace. Beelzebub is able to tempt men with pride and that would be a great asset in the battle to come. Pride; Lucifer knows the sin of pride, but it is not the time to dwell on this, he will have his revenge and his so-called sin of pride will become his redemption, his victory over God Himself!

Standing next to Beelzebub there is Leviathan, an unholy prince of the Seraphim as well, who can tempt even the strongest souls into heresy. His special skills will be needed for the confrontation with the bastard faithful. For the first time those dedicated to the Son of Man will know doubt, they will know fear and they will know the true power of evil. Men and women will suddenly realize they are doomed and they will turn their backs on Heaven and curse their beliefs. They will come to this realization as they kneel to worship the supreme master of Hell itself, albeit too late. As these pitiful creatures confront the inevitable, then Leviathan will be triumphant and this will help assure his ultimate victory.

Lucifer's gaze moves toward Asmodeus, the third prince, with his burning desire to tempt men into depravity. Ever devoted Asmodeus; he would have prevailed in the battle of the pit if it were not for that bitch, Agnes. Satan assures Asmodeus that he will have his chance at retribution for the humiliation he has endured. The dragon Asmodeus sits upon breathes flames as all three heads on the demon Asmodeus roar in anticipation and bow in appreciation.

This time it will be different, this time victory will be his and it will be Lucifer they will fear.

Standing behind the first three is Pesado, the keeper of chaos. It will be Pesado that shows humans the true meaning of fear. This will occur as all goodness and honor are corrupted. It will come to pass when every one of these creatures abandons all loyalties in the vain attempt to protect themselves. Following behind Pesado is Berith, a prince of the Cherubim, who tempts men to commit homicide. Murder has always held a special place in the hearts of men and Berith will have a special role given the chaos that is to follow.

To the left of Berith there is Astaroth, the prince of Thrones, who tempts men to be lazy. Lucifer's smile becomes wider as he thinks that Astaroth has the easiest of tasks. When vigilance withers, laziness becomes the powerful force that takes over the mindset of men and women. Lucifer has great understanding of laziness and he knows it is the easiest way to lead humanity to sinfulness.

Next to Astaroth stands Verrine, another of the prince of Thrones, whose special skill tempts men to impatience. Lucifer knows that impatience can lead to so much more. Lucifer's smile continues to grow as he stares and sees Gressil, the third prince of Thrones. Gressil, who tempts men with impurity, has already captured so many of the souls that now litter the very foundation of hell itself.

Finally, there is the ever-dependable Sonneillon, the fourth prince of Thrones. He tempts men to hate and he is a particular favorite of Lucifer. He recalls how Beelzebub and Sonneillon inspired the temptation of Judas Iscariot to betray the cursed Son of God and seal His fate on the cross. Even now the screams and torment of Judas ring in terror as his punishment is meted out in each and every measure of time immemorial.

How many souls have Sonneillon and the others sent to him? There are too many to count, especially in the last 100 years! Lucifer and Sonneillon take special pleasure in tormenting and afflicting horrendous pain and suffering on the vilest of men including the likes of Stalin, Mao, Pol Pot and new arrivals like Osama bin Laden. The demons take special delight and their enjoyment is boundless, especially when inflicting the cruelest of punishments for the likes of mass killers such as Hitler. Lucifer and his demons look forward, with relish, to the torture they are inflicting on Hitler and so many more souls that are damned for eternity.

Lucifer yells "Sieg Heil!", and he bursts into laughter.

Nine in all! These are his princes, his weapons to strike at mankind and reap revenge on the self-righteous bastard Sainted of holiness. He is ready to reveal his plan, but he needs to have his first hierarchy prepare for the inevitable battle and with that he speaks,

"It is time. The forces of heaven must not prevail, and it is through you they will fail and the souls of mankind will be doomed and they will be mine.

Go and assemble the 66 rulers and the 666 legions of 6,666 demons each and let them be ready to receive my command."

The dark angels look up at Lucifer and as he looks upon their hideousness, he knows they are ready. If the battle is to be won these demons and their hoards are all that he will need. The epic confrontation between good and evil is inevitable. Dark versus light, hell versus heaven and the ultimately victory of evil over good is the plan he devises, and it will be the path to his glorious victory. These devils, demons of the first order would, at last, overwhelm the forces of heaven and then there will be nothing to stop the horror that mankind will confront.

This would be his reward, his dream come true and the reason he exists. Lucifer, once ensconced over the souls of the damned, would derive such immense pleasure from the anguish and horror he would inflict that he will finally know true pleasure for the first time in his eternal rule.

From the time he had been cast into the lake of fire, Satan has tried many times to incite God and His faithful to conflict, but it has never come to pass. He knows his strength and that of the demon hoard. He knows his plan is perfect, but he also knows it will not be easy. The heavenly host has powers too, and they will not be readily brought to battle.

The plan is all-encompassing, but there will need to be a catalyst for the impending conflict. The means to an end and it will all begin with a messenger, a conduit, and he will prepare the way. It will all start with the greatest of blasphemies, and end with the victory of Hell itself. Satan would then have his revenge and this time the Sainted and their visions will not be able to save Christopher Pella and all of humanity.

AUTHOR MICHAEL MEDICO

Michael Medico was born and grew up in New York City. He attended Power Memorial Academy High School and, on graduation, Mike joined the US Navy and served stateside during the Vietnam War. After being honorably discharged from the service, Michael attended Pace University and graduated with a degree in Marketing and Advertising.

Michael started his career in advertising and worked at various agencies until in 1980 when he founded and ran an agency specializing in direct response marketing for 35 years. Over the years he has written numerous articles published in various trade journals and has been a featured participant on industry panel discussions and workshops.

In 2013 he retired to become a full-time author with "Evil Awaits" being his first novel and Book One in The Sainted Trilogy. He has also written the political satire, "Absolutely,

Positively, Genuine, Real Fake News" as well a number of short stories.

Michael and his wife Joan have sons, Anthony and Richard, daughters-in-law, Shannon and Christina and six grandchildren. He and Joan spend time between their homes in Northport, NY and Hallandale Beach, FL.